Books By Rick Bentsen

<u>The Blademaster Chronicles</u>
The Blademaster
Willowdale

<u>The Chronicles of Xarin</u>
The Crucible

<u>The Adventures of Hamster Man and Bunny Woman</u>
**The Case of the Curious Cats

<u>Gamma Strike</u>
* Dawn of a New Age
** The Dawning of a New Age

* Released through iUniverse
** Forthcoming

Willowdale

By Rick Bentsen

Steel Drake Press
Taunton

Willowdale
Book 2: The Blademaster Chronicles

For information, contact the author at
rickbentsen@rickbentsen.com

www.rickbentsen.com
www.facebook.com/RickBentsenAuthor

ISBN: 0692402934
ISBN-13: 978-0692402931

Praise for The Blademaster

"Up until I'd read "The Blademaster" by Rick Bentsen, the closest thing I'd come to reading or seeing a story in this genre was "The Lord Of The Rings" that I saw at the theater several years ago because my husband wanted to see it.

I wanted to read "The Blademaster" because Rick and I have been cyber friends since around 2000 and I wanted to support him and his new book.

So, kind of to my own surprise, when I started reading the saga of Alana Steeldrake (First Blademaster to be named in over 300 years) and Colwyn Starseeker (Protector to Alana Steeldrake and heir to the title of First Lord of the Valendale Territory) I found myself really enjoying it!

The story flows with just enough descriptions that keep the story moving and on course.

All the characters, even the secondary ones, are really well developed. I felt like I knew all the characters in the book, even the bad guys, by the time I'd finished it.

I'm impressed with Rick's writing ability. I'm amazed at his imagination. I'm intrigued with the names of places, characters, and phrases he came up with and how they perfectly fit the tone of the story. And I appreciated the underlying moral code of love and honor that he threaded throughout the story.

And I can totally see this story becoming a movie!"

--Pat Ballard, author (Abigail's Revenge, Wanted One Groom, and others... The Queen of Rubenesque Romances...)

Willowdale

Foreward

March 6, 2015

I've been in something of a strange mood of late. I finished editing this book last week, you see. We're about a month away from it being in your hands.

I always feel a little empty when I finish a book.

Don't get me wrong. I am happy it's done. I'm happy that it will be in your hands very soon.

But finishing a book takes a lot out of a writer. We spend so much time with the characters that they become our family. Well... Our second family at any rate. We eat with them. We watch TV with them. Hell, we even sleep with them. (Not literally, of course!) And then, like our children, we send them off on their own.

Willowdale was tougher for me than others have been. I don't really know why. Much like *The Blademaster*, I laughed. I cried. (And yes, I do think it's better than Cats... And I love Cats.) This one was a little harder to let go of, though.

Those of you that have read *The Blademaster* (And if you haven't, you probably should before you read this one...) are familiar with the characters by now. Alana and Colwyn are still in love. (Yay!) William is heading towards his destiny. (Ooooo!) Cobalt is working towards his redemption. (I'm really rooting for him!) And Meryn is still causing trouble. (Gasp! A halfling causing trouble! Who would have thought it?!)

But now we're really starting to get into the motivations of different characters. Alana is starting to understand a little better why Taelin and Laeyra decided it was time for the Blademasters to return to Calthea. Colwyn is preparing himself for the inevitable confrontation with his father about being the Protector to a Blademaster, which is something that Colwyn knows his father is not going to react well to. And the whole of Calthea is slowly marching towards the darkness.

What a long way we've come since I had the first nugget of an idea for *The Blademaster*...

Willowdale

If I had left Alana and Colwyn's story where it ended in *The Blademaster*, I am sure many of my readers would have found themselves satisfied with the ending. Yes, there would have been unanswered questions, (some of which will be answered in the book you now hold in your hands.) but successfully defeating Drakkhous and going back home to Ravendale allowed me to give my readers closure.

I, on the other hand, would have gone insane to not tell the rest of the story.

And so, you now hold in your hands a first from Rick Bentsen.

The sequel to a book.

Never happened before. I know there are a lot of my readers that are quite perturbed with me that I have not written a sequel to *Dawn of a New Age* and that the promised second book of *The Chronicles of Xarin* is sitting on my computer half finished. I promise that I will get to both. And somewhat soon.

For now, though, please continue to enjoy Alana and Colwyn's story.

I am certainly enjoying telling it.

Dia duit,
Rick Bentsen

Acknowledgements

I can hear it now. "Oh, goodness me, the author is about to blather on and on about who did what to help him... Do we really have to read this?" First of all, I love the word blather and I now firmly promise to use the word far more often.

Second, no, you don't have to read this. But I would be remiss if I did not include my thanks. So, yes. Feel free to skip this section, but I shall now blather (told you I would use the word more often) on about Team Rick Bentsen and all they've done.

First of all, thanks to God for the gifts that make the writing possible. A little bit of imagination goes a long way, it would seem.

To my parents, who have been arranging many in person appearances for me to sign and sell my books. It has been a very interesting journey over the past several months, but I have enjoyed every bit of it.

To my brother without whom I would likely never have been introduced to Dungeons and Dragons. Without which.... No Blademaster.

To my continuity expert and editor, Joanna, for everything she does. As I sad in *The Blademaster*, Joanna knows the characters as well, if not better, than I do. It makes it easier to hand these books off to her when I know she will take good care of them.

To my readers, because without you, there would be no point to doing this. I love each and every one of you.

Finally to Alana and Colwyn. You came into my life like a whirlwind and have made the past several years very interesting. You two are very special to me. Thank you for letting me tell your story to the world.

Willowdale

.

For the woman who taught me the true meaning of the Second Law of the Blades.

Willowdale

Rick Bentsen

Willowdale

The second book in
The Blademaster Chronicles

Willowdale

Chapters

The Prophecy of the Coming of the Age of Darkness
As prophecied by Bahalla Maranal, the Dream Weaver
31 Years after the Great Purge

In the waning days of the Age of Light, one who wears the white shall fall to the rites of the Dark One. Only the true power of the Child of Light can save her soul.

When the One born of the Light goes to the twice dead city, she shall fall to the darkness, as one of her own shall betray her. Only the slim blade of the Second Law of the Blades can save her.

When the twice dead city falls empty a third time, the storm clouds will gather, and sabres will rattle in their scabbards. The blight of war shall be upon the land, and only the One born of the Light can lead the charge against the darkness.

On the wings of war comes the Age of Darkness.

What came before...

In *The Blademaster*...

n the town of Ravendale in the Southern Dales of Calthea, a warrior woman, Alana Steeldrake, who knows nothing of her parentage awoke one morning. The man she loved, Colwyn Starseeker came to find her that morning to bring her to see the High Priest of Taelin.

When they got to the Temple of Taelin, they were sent on a quest to discover what happened to a priestess in Tornith, a city in the northern part of the continent of Calthea. Tornith is a dark city dedicated to the Dark God, Thraal.

On their way to Tornith, Alana, Colwyn, and their companions, William Stonehands (a mage), Meryn Swiftfoot (a halfling), and Balaam Otakis (the High Priest of Taelin) journeyed to the city of Valendale to consult the sage, Isaiah Talon.

They found the city completely deserted, save for some warriors of Thraal who were there to try to catch them. After defeating the warriors, Alana consulted the sage who directed her to the Elven Woods, where she would finally learn her destiny.

In the Elven Woods, the companions were given directions to a hidden temple at the heart of the forest. In the Temple of the Blades, Alana learned that she is the first Blademaster in 300 years. After hearing all that is entailed with her new position and that she must marry someone she truly loves, Alana and Colwyn agreed to get married. Colwyn underwent the Test of the Blades and succeeded, thereby earning the right to marry Alana.

After the wedding, the companions started north towards Tornith. Along the way, they found a new companion, a dragon named Cobalthaxillius.

Once they crossed the border from the Southern Dales into Dracomyr, the companions came to the Stonegate

Mountains where they were taken prisoner by goblins. The goblins began to take the companions to Tornith in cages. Partway there, the companions escaped and made their way the rest of the way to Tornith.

In Tornith, Alana tried to infiltrate the ziggurat of Thraal, but was captured. She was told she would be sacrificed to Thraal.

When the time came for the sacrifice, she was bound to the altar on the top of the ziggurat. Before she could be sacrificed, Balaam threw himself over her body, forcing the ceremonial dagger to kill him instead of her.

Alana got free and killed the High Priest of Thraal.

Balaam was sent to Limbo, where he freed the people that had been sent there by the High Priest of Thraal when he sacrificed them. Also freed was the Dark God himself.

The companions buried Balaam's body at sea and then returned to Ravendale, knowing that their next adventure would come soon...

And so begins the next part of The Blademaster Chronicles....

Willowdale.

Prologue
The Nightstalker

The high Priest of Thraal scowled as he stormed through the ziggurat of Thraal in Tornith. It had been four days since the chosen warrior of that accursed god Taelin had killed his predecessor in the position of High Priest to Thraal. Adouon Darkholme was still angry about it. He had not particularly liked the lich. No one at the ziggurat of Thraal actually liked the lich. But the idea that someone could just waltz in and behead the High Priest was disturbing to him, especially since he held the position of High Priest now.

The fact that the Dark God had been freed from his prison did little to mitigate Adouon's anger. He wanted revenge on the Blademaster, and he intended to get it. One way or the other. He wanted to destroy her.

"I will have her head on my wall for a trophy," he vowed to himself. "She will pay for what she has done to you, Lord Drakkhous. I swear it will be so."

He swept down the stairs towards the High Priest's sanctuary. He had been the High Priest for four days, and had been named so by no less than the Dark God, Thraal himself. But he was having a hard time believing that the sanctuary was his to use. He was making very good use of it. Adouon was determined that no one would be able to do to him what Alana Steeldrake had done to Drakkhous. The lich had been very sloppy. He had underestimated the Blademaster and her companions. Adouon would not make the same mistake.

For the past three nights, Adouon had been working with his god about how best to dispose of the Blademaster. The Dark God had shown Adouon a plan of attack over the course of their work. This night, Adouon would learn the last of what he needed to know. It would be the beginning of the end for the Blademaster. Adouon reveled in that thought. It would be a glorious death. He could not wait for the execution of the Blademaster. It would be perfect. The Blademaster would not survive the encounter. And she would suffer intensely for what she had done. As would her companions.

Even though Thraal had already given him most of the instructions for creating this new weapon, Adouon still did not know what to expect. It would be as much of a surprise for him as it would be for the Blademaster. He savored the unknown and knew that it would be good. Anything that Lord Thraal had imbued with power sufficient to kill a Blademaster in her prime had to be a good thing.

He entered the sanctuary alone. He had been instructed that no one was to hear the plans that Thraal had in mind for the Blademaster. It was not for anyone else to know what was to happen until the time was right. An evil grin spread across his face as he thought of the Blademaster lying in a pool of her own blood. It was something that he could not wait to see.

He knelt down before the small altar in the sanctuary and closed his eyes. The censer on the altar was full of burning incense, aromatic smoke wafting up to fill the room. He pulled the sleeves of his robes up to just past his elbows, and he pulled the dagger from his belt. There was one component left that needed to be added to the incense in order for Adouon's prayer of supplication to be heard. As he had the past three nights, he poked his arm lightly with the dagger, drawing off a single drop of his own blood on the tip of the dagger. He took the blood and added it to the burning incense. The smoke rising from the censer turned from a murky grey to a dusky red as the blood combined with the incense. This change in the smoke told him that all was ready for his supplication to be heard.

"Lord Thraal, hear my prayers," Adouon spoke softly, his voice low and deep in the silence of the sanctuary. "All has been prepared as you have directed. I await only the final instructions for this task. I ask that you come to me now and show me what I must do to rid Calthea of the Blademaster."

There was a silent whoosh in the air and all the candles in the sanctuary blew out all at once. The only light left was the soft glow emanating from the censer, bathing the room in an eerie red light. The soft red glow was barely enough to light the shadows around the altar. The first time that this had happened, it had caught Adouon off guard. It was the fourth night, and it had happened the same way each night, so he was used to it at this point. He also knew it meant that his Lord Thraal was about to appear in the sanctuary with him. It was exciting, although he had once found the prospect terrifying. But the fear had given way over the past four nights as he had realized just how much he was in Lord Thraal's favor. He knew that the previous three nights would not have been possible without Lord Thraal's favor being upon him. He knew that successfully ridding Calthea of the Blademaster would cause that favor to grow.

"You have done well, my High Priest," Thraal's deep, resonant voice sounded through the empty sanctuary. The Dark God made his presence felt to the High Priest. When Thraal lifted the darkness, Adouon could see the shapeless form on the other side of the altar, a tear of the very air floating in midair showing as blackness upon blackness. Although he had been freed from the prison that Taelin had kept him in four days before, Thraal still had not regained enough power to create a physical body for himself. It was something that would take some time. "I am well pleased with your work."

"Thank you, my lord," Adouon smiled and bowed to his god. "It is my pleasure to serve you."

"It is time for us to begin the final preparations for our revenge," Thraal continued. "I have gone over all of the incantations with you. You know what you need to do. Tonight will be your final instructions. Tonight you will learn about the person that you will need to use as a base for this weapon. The person must be selected very carefully or all will be for naught. There are very few of my followers currently in Tornith who exhibit the proper qualifications to become the instrument of our revenge. I will leave it to you to discover who among my faithful will be the one to become my chosen weapon. I believe that, when I give you the requirements, you will think of someone very quickly. I have someone in mind. I have no doubt that you will think of this person. I believe that she will be perfect for our purposes."

"What are the requirements, Lord Thraal?" the High Priest asked eagerly. Adouon pulled a roster of the followers of Thraal that were in Tornith. "What must I know to select the right person for this assignment?"

"To begin with, just as the accursed Blademasters are, my champion must be a woman," Thraal began. "Taelin and Laeyra, curse their eyes, are right in saying that women end up making better champions than men. I do not know the reasons why, only that it seems to be the truth. Maybe it is because women are not so easy to distract once they have their mind set on a goal. The reasons why matter not. It needs to be a woman who becomes my champion."

Adouon opened the roster of the followers of Thraal in Tornith and picked up a fresh quill and ink. He crossed off the name of every man on the list, leaving just the women, which cut the list of potential followers of Thraal by over half. It was still a large number though. He hoped that the rest of Thraal's requirements for this champion would narrow it down some more.

"What is the next requirement, my lord?" Adouon asked softly. He looked over the names still on the list. "There are still too many for me to be certain I will have the right one."

"She must be human and she must be of the warrior class, not the priests or the mages," Thraal continued, his form writhing in excitement as he passed on the instructions. "This is very important. Only a human can effectively track and fight another human, and as a warrior, she could use any kind of weapon. Doing otherwise would leave this instrument of our revenge at a distinct disadvantage. If we are to be successful, we must not give the Blademaster any sort of advantage."

"I understand," Adouon nodded as he crossed off more names the roster of Thraal's followers. "That certainly makes sense, my Lord. But that still leaves over a hundred of our followers. Surely there is another requirement? There are still far too many that fit the requirements for me to effectively choose one.'

"She must be one of the elite warriors who were made from the gentlest girls that were recruited. This will make her far more of a formidable weapon," Thraal continued with glee. "She must be absolutely ruthless and unswervingly dedicated to our purpose. She will have but one duty and she must be left to fulfill that duty as she sees fit. She must possess great focus and determination. Of paramount importance, though, she must have a great deal of hate in her heart. That hate will be the basis for her abilities. Only hate can counter love."

Adouon kept crossing names off his roster as he thought about what Thraal had said. First he eliminated all the women who were not elite warriors. That left about thirty women. He took those names and wrote them down in order of how ruthless they were. When he looked at the name at the top of the list, a sadistic smile slowly spread across his face. Without a doubt, she had to be the woman that Thraal had been thinking of. As he thought about it some more, he realized that she could have been the only choice for this assignment. Any of the other elite warriors would be good choices if she failed. He did not think that any of the others would be needed, though. He was supremely confident in the abilities of his top choice.

"Kera Rayden," Adouon announced quietly. He looked back at Thraal. "She is the only choice that I can see, my Lord Thraal. If she can not kill the Blademaster, I do not believe any of the other elite warriors could."

"It is agreed then," Thraal laughed. "Kera Rayden will become the first Nightstalker. You will perform the ceremony this very evening, Adouon. After the ceremony is complete, you will send her to the city of Willowdale. That is where she will attack and kill the Blademaster. See to it at once."

"It will be done just as you say, Lord Thraal,' Adouon bowed. "This night will see the beginning of our revenge upon the Blademaster."

"I know that it will be done," Thraal boomed out an evil piercing laugh. "We will speak again after she has been sent to Willowdale."

Thraal's form started to fade from view. Adouon stopped watching. He was already contemplating the ceremony. It was a ceremony that had to go just right or the Nightstarlker would not be created. Worse, Kera Rayden could die. That would be a waste of a good warrior. But the most important reason he could not fail was that it was a personal vendetta for him. What the Blademaster had done to Drakkhous had to be avenged. If not for the lich, then for Adouon himself. He still did not believe that someone had been able to simply remove the lich's head, and he was not about to sit and let that same thing happen to him. He believed that following Lord Thraal's directions for this ceremony, he would prevent that from happening to him. He wished that he could be there to witness the death of the Blademaster. It would make his revenge all the sweeter, but it was enough for him to know that, once the ceremony was complete and Kera Rayden was bound up in the power that Lord Thraal would gift upon her, the Blademaster's days would be numbered.

Adouon stood and stretched. It was time to find Kera Rayden to begin the ceremony. There was no time like the present. Adouon wanted to get started right away, because the ceremony did not have to be performed at any specific hour, according to Lord Thraal's instructions. Besides, the sooner they conducted the ceremony, the sooner the Nightstalker could start on her assignment to kill the Blademaster. He wanted to see the Blademaster quivering in fear and worry as soon as possible. He knew that Kera would see to that.

As soon as he left the sanctuary, he went looking for Mariska, the woman he had made his assistant. He had been impressed with the way Mariska had handled herself when the Blademaster and her companions had been at the ziggurat of Thraal. Well, he had really been impressed with her long before that. He had been keeping an eye on her since the day she had appeared at the doorstep of the ziggurat four years before demanding to become an acolyte to Thraal. The woman had been prone to flights of fancy, but she had also been a devoted acolyte and had served her Lord Thraal well. It had not been Mariska's fault that the Blademaster had escaped the binding spell that she had cast on her. The Blademaster's halfling companion had used the shadows as only a thief could and surprised Mariska by stabbing the woman in the back. It was just one more thing that the High Priest wanted revenge on the Blademaster and her companions for. Adouon had been able to heal Mariska, but the near loss of her burned at him. The fire inside of him that longed for revenge against the Blademaster and her companions burned hot. He had come to realize that he loved Mariska. He had not let her know how he felt. After the healing, she had started to look at him in a different way. It was as if she knew his feelings for her without having been told. It was as if those feelings he had for her had been transferred to her during the link that was required for healing her. He thought about what he little he knew of how healing spells worked and realized that his feelings for her probably had been transferred through that link.

Adouon did not understand why he still felt that it was necessary for him to hide the fact that he loved Mariska. The lich had known, of course, but he had not given Adouon any trouble over it. Nor could he. Drakkhous had done all that he had as part of a deal with Thraal to return his true love back to the world of Calthea. Thraal did not seem to care if he loved Mariska, and Adouon knew that Thraal had to know his feelings about the priestess. It is difficult to hide one's true feelings from his god. Adouon knew that, so long as he did not allow his feelings for the priestess to interfere with his ability to do the Dark God's work, Thraal would not have a problem with his loving Meriska. So why did he feel it necessary to hide his feelings? One day, he would have the answer to that question. Until that day, he would keep his feelings for Mariska to himself.

He found her near the door leading to the stairwell up to the Great Fire and the sacrificial altar. Neither of them had been back near the Great Fire since the night the Blademaster was to be sacrificed. It wasn't for any specific reason that neither of them had gone up there in the four days since the attempted sacrifice. Adouon did not want to relive the memories from that night. He knew that going up there would bring all of those memories back. But the ceremony to create the Nightstalker had to take place up on the altar by the Great Fire. He was prepared to block out any unpleasant memories that were bound to come during the ceremony. He hoped that Mariska was prepared for that as well.

"Mariska," he said softly as he came up to her. "I need you to go find Kera Rayden as quickly as you can. I want you to bring her here to me. You will accompany us up to the Great Fire and assist me with a ceremony."

"I will be back with her presently, my Lord Adouon," Mariska smiled at him. She started to run off, but turned back to the High Priest. She ran her fingers through her hair. "What kind of ceremony is it?"

"Lord Thraal has given us the means to take our revenge on the Blademaster and her companions," Adouon grinned evilly. "Tonight we shall embark on our mission to kill the Blademaster. We will have bloody retribution for what she has done to us."

"I would be honored to help you with this worthy goal, my Lord Adouon," Mariska smiled. "The Blademaster must die for what she did to Lord Drakkhous. But know this. The halfling is mine to kill after what she did to me. I will bathe in her blood."

"I would not even dream of getting between you and the halfling, Mariska," Adouon laughed. He clapped her on the shoulder. "Now, go and find Kera Rayden. The sooner you bring her here to me, the sooner we can be on our way to avenging ourselves on the Blademaster and her companions."

The High Priest watched her go. There was a smile of satisfaction on the young priestess's face. He could understand why she felt so satisfied, as he felt much the same way. He knew that it would not be long before the new Nightstalker was created and sent on her way. It would be good to have the Blademaster sent to walk with Taelin and Laeyra. As far as Adouon was concerned, it could not happen fast enough. He knew that the Nightstalker would not fail. He longed to loose the Nightstalker on the world to do what she was going to do. He would love to be going with her, but he knew that she would prefer to work alone. That was just another reason she was the right choice to be the Nightstalker. She would not be distracted by any companions. Nor would be distracted by love interests, for she loved no one.

The one thing that most piqued his curiosity about what was about to happen was how Kera Rayden would react to her new abilities and status in her god's eyes. He wasn't so much concerned about her reaction. He knew that she would accept it without question. It was not in her nature to do otherwise.

As he climbed the stairs to the Great Fire, Adouon thought about what he knew about Kera Rayden. She'd just turned thirteen when she was brought to the ziggurat of Thraal. She had been the gentlest of girls. Adouon remembered how she had feared everything when she first arrived. Her fear excited him, filling him with a sort of heady intoxication. He watched with pleasure as that fear was used to break her of her foolish desire to follow Taelin. Her goal in life to that point was to become a priestess of Taelin. And she might well have been a good priestess for

Taelin. Fate, however, had interfered with those plans. It had taken over four years for Adouon to turn her away from Taelin, but he had finally succeeded. She had been broken. Adouon believed that, because of how long it had taken to break her, Kera Rayden would have a special purpose in her service to Thraal.

Once she had been broken, Kera Rayden had served Thraal without question or hesitation. It amused Adouon to think about how, had she not been broken and made to serve Thraal, young Kera Rayden might have gone to fight alongside the Blademaster instead of now being sent to kill her. Fate was a funny thing sometimes. Adouon had no doubt that becoming the Nightstalker was Kera Rayden's destiny. He had once seen her take on four knights from the Southern Dales that had been sent to kill the lich Drakkhous. Not only did she kill all four of the knights, but in the brutality of her assault, she had continued hacking the four knights to pieces long after they had been killed. Adouon had admired her brutality and had vowed then to keep an eye on her.

And he had. He had watched her blossom into an elite warrior, one beyond anything that the followers of Taelin could muster. She was a killer through and through, and a brutal one at that. She had been assigned the most difficult missions that the High Priest could find, and she had successfully completed them all. Her new abilities would make no difference in her service to Thraal. Adouon figured she would enjoy the extra power she was about to be granted by Thraal. He did not think he would need to worry about her. She would flourish in her duties as the Nightstalker.

He reached the top of the stairs and stepped out onto the top of the ziggurat. The heat from the Great Fire washed over him as he walked over to the sacrificial altar. He had not yet conducted a sacrifice for Thraal. He knew that one day he would sacrifice someone on this very altar, just as he had watched dozens of sacrifices conducted by Drakkhous. He did not think that he would enjoy the sacrifices the same way that Drakkhous had, but the lich had been depraved in ways that Adouon could never hope to be. He ran his fingers along the stone of the altar, feeling the warmth of the Great Fire. The Great Fire had never, in all the time that this ziggurat had stood in Tornith, been allowed to go out. It was imbued with a special magic that allowed it to burn without fuel. Adouon did not understand the magic involved that allowed such a thing to happen, but he did not need to. This was one of those times when understanding was not required, only obedience. He was determined that the Great Fire would not go out on his watch as High Priest of Thraal.

He'd left the door to the roof of the ziggurat open. He did not think that it would be long before Mariska would join him on the roof with Kera Rayden. He figured it would not take long for the priestess to find Kera. Mariska had ways of finding people quickly. Adouon had trusted on that ability when he tasked Mariska to find the woman who would become the first Nightstalker. He would wait patiently, although patience was not his strong suit. He just wanted this ceremony to be over so that the Blademaster would be on her way to the spirit world.

It was not long before his excellent hearing caught the sound of two sets of foot falls coming up the stairs. He did not turn, because he knew who it would be. No one else had any business coming up the stairs to the roof of the ziggurat. Unless a sacrifice had been called, none of the followers of Thraal came up to the Great Fire. He moved over to the other side of the altar. He made sure that all the preparations for the ceremony were in order. When he was satisfied that they were, he nodded to himself in silent satisfaction. Soon the foot falls stopped, and he looked up at the door to the ziggurat. When he saw Mariska and Kera in the doorway, he motioned them forward. They came and stood on the opposite side of the altar as he was.

"Priestess Mariska said that you desired to speak with me, my lord?" Kera asked softly. She was a very soft spoken woman, which had always rather surprised Adouon considering the ferocity with which the woman did everything else.

Adouon looked Kera Rayden over, nodding in satisfaction to himself. She was wearing her normal black leather armor. The armor shirt went all the way down to her wrists and came up all the way to her neck. Her hands were sheathed in black leather gloves, the back of the gloves armored heavily so that when she hit someone it would do as much damage as if she had hit them with a blunt weapon such as a club. The leather pants extended all the way down to her boots. Her boots came up almost to her knees and were heavily armored. The only part of her body not covered in armor was her head. She had long dark hair tied back in one long braid. Piercing blue eyes stared back at the High Priest as he looked her over. She stared back at him defiantly, as if daring him to attack her. He had no intention of doing so. She was as beautiful as she was deadly. She had no weapons on her at the moment, but the High Priest knew she did not need any weapons to kill.

"Yes, Kera, I do," Adouon smiled broadly. He motioned towards the altar. "You are here to help me with a small but important ceremony for Lord Thraal. I believe you will like the results of the ceremony as well."

"I have no desire for ceremony, Lord Adouon," Kera scoffed. "I am a woman of action."

"I know you are, Kera," Adouon nodded. "And I have action for you after the ceremony has been completed."

"Oh?" Kera raised one delicate eyebrow. "Who do you want me to kill?"

"The Blademaster," Adouon's smile grew wide and menacing. "When the ceremony is complete, you will be far more powerful than you are now. You will be the Blademaster's match. I expect that you will be able to kill her after Lord Thraal imbues you with the power he shall grant you this night."

"What do you want me to do, my lord?" Kera asked. Her voice betrayed how intrigued she was at the thought of having so much power.

"Lie on the altar," Adouon commanded. When she flinched, Adouon laughed. "No, you are not to be sacrificed, Kera."

"I would hope not," Kera grunted as she lay down on the altar. "It would be hard for me to kill the Blademaster if

I were dead myself. Just get on with it, my lord, so I can be on my way to glorious battle with the bitch."

"Yes, it will be a glorious battle, indeed," Adouon murmured. He picked up the idol of Thraal that he had previously laid out on the altar. "You will once more do Lord Thraal proud."

Adouon closed his eyes and said a silent prayer to Thraal as he slowly circled the altar. He stopped on the opposite side of the altar than he had started on and looked down at Kera. She had closed her eyes, not sure she wanted to see what was about to happen to her.

"Lord Thraal, you have commanded this woman to become your champion," Adouon began softly. "I demand, then, that you come and fill this woman with the power that you have promised to gift her. Take her hate and amplify it. Give her the power necessary to do what must be done. Allow her the power to rid the world of the hated Blademaster and her companions. I ask this as you have commanded me."

"It will be done,' Thraal's voice floated out from the Great Fire. "Kera Rayden, from now on, you shall be known as the first Nightstalker. You will stalk the Blademaster through the shadows of the world. The shadows shall be your weapons. You will do me honor by ridding Calthea of the Blademaster and her companions. So mote it be."

A shard of pure light burst off from the Great Fire and arced into Kera Rayden's body. The woman opened her eyes wide and light shot from her pupils off into the night. She screamed in pain and pleasure and arched her back. After a few minutes, the light faded, and Kera settled down onto the altar once more. She closed her eyes again and, slowly, her breathing returned to normal.

Finally she opened her eyes and settled her gaze on Adouon. There was a power in that gaze. And a deep hatred he had never seen in her eyes before. He knew that the power transfer had been successful.

Kera Rayden was no more.

The Nightstalker had been born.

"I am ready, Lord Adouon," Kera said softly. "I am ready to kill the Blademaster for Lord Thraal.'

"Then follow me to the portal. I will send you to Willowdale," Adouon nodded.

The Nightstalker stood from the altar and nodded. She swept down the stairs leading into the ziggurat to her quarters, where she picked up her weapons. When she met Adouon and Mariska down by the portal chamber, she was fully armed. With all of her weaponry, she looked to be an even more formidable woman than she had when she left the altar. She moved with an easy catlike grace, and every move was made with a definite purpose.

"The Dark God chooses his Nightstalkers well," Mariska said wryly. "The Blademaster will have a hard time with this one."

"That is the plan, Mariska," Adouon laughed. "Are you ready, my dear Kera?"

"I am ready, Lord Adouon," the Nightstalker nodded. "Send me though the portal."

Adouon led the way into the portal chamber. The portal was in the center of the room, a dark and swirling rip in space. Adouon stepped over to it and waved his hand in front of it.

"Willowdale," he said softly.

The darkness swirled faster in response to his soft command, and the image of a city floated in the swirling darkness. The image in the portal swirled in the darkness, eventually revealing itself to be a dark alley near the center of the city of Willowdale. Kera did not hesitate. She stepped through the portal and was gone in an instant.

"It is done," Adouon smiled. "The Blademaster will die by her hand very soon."

Part 1
A New Journey

Chapter 1
Reunion

is life was torture, plain and simple.

Every day for a hundred years, Darius Redwind had been forced to do the bidding of the Dark God, Thraal. It was an unholy deal that had put him in the service of Thraal in the first place, but it made no difference. Nor did it make any difference to him that this unholy deal would return his Lilliana to him. Had he not entered into this deal with Thraal, he would have been reunited with her in death a century before.

It irked Darius that by agreeing to this unholy alliance, it prolonged the time until his reunion with Lilliana.

But there was nothing he could do about it. His soul was enslaved by the deal. It was what gave the lich, Drakkhous, life. There was only one way he could be released from the deal with Thraal, and that would be for the lich to be killed. He did not think it possible for someone to kill the lich, for Drakkhous was very strong indeed. While he longed for that day when he would be free, he also feared it. He believed that his Lord Taelin would deny him the honor of walking with him in death. It was an honor that was reserved for the most devout of Lord Taelin's followers. He felt that betraying Lord Taelin by accepting Thraal's deal was one way to very quickly fall out of favor with Lord Taelin.

He could only pray that Taelin's light and wisdom would allow Lord Taelin to forgive him for this grievous sin.

With each sacrifice that Drakkhous made, he felt his soul drifting further and further away from being able to walk with Taelin when he was finally released. But the sacrifice of Merinda Delwyn made him believe that he was truly beyond redemption. It had been the first time the lich had sacrificed a priestess of Taelin, and he could feel how much more the lich had enjoyed the sacrifice than any other. But the sacrifice had sickened Darius. He could only watch in horror as the lich carried out the sacrifice. When the Dark God had spoken after the sacrifice, it had shaken him to the core. But the words that were spoken were even more unnerving than hearing the Dark God speak for the first time since Darius had accepted his deal. For the rest of his time in this world and the next, he would never forget the Dark God's words.

The woman's eyes opened to show two flaming red coals. She opened her mouth and spoke, but the voice was not the same as before. This voice was much deeper and masculine. So deep, in fact, that it vibrated the very bones of the priests standing atop the ziggurat.

"Those who do not wish to burn in the Great Fire must leave now," the voice said. "Only High Priest Drakkhous may remain."

The priests took no time at all to follow the voice's command. They all went flying down the steps of the ziggurat, leaving only the lich to stand atop the ziggurat.

Drakkhous fell to his knees in obedience and respect. "My Lord Thraal. I am your humble servant. What may I do for you, Your Greatness?" the lich rasped.

"Arise, my friend," the Dark God said softly. "You have, as usual, done well."

"Thank you, my Lord," the lich said as he stood. "Now, what is your command?"

"The accursed Taelin has found a way to bring the Blademasters back," Thraal explained. "Even now, one walks the world. I do not yet know her identity, but you are to find her and sacrifice her to me. Only then may I walk the world again."

"It shall be done as you say, Lord Thraal," the lich bowed.

"Good," Thraal smiled. "I leave you to your work. Do not fail me, lich. You know the consequences for failure."

The red glow faded from the woman's eyes and she fell into the Great Fire, but Drakkhous did not notice. Darius, however, watched in horror as the body of the priestess fell into the Great Fire

Darius did not want to be responsible for Thraal returning to Calthea. And he feared what would happen to the world should the Dark God be allowed to return. But the fact that a Blademaster once more walked the world gave Darius hope that there might be a way to be free of this deal with Thraal. Surely, he hoped, a Blademaster could kill a lich. Even one who did not know the full strength of her powers would be a force to be reckoned with, would she not? He knew from the tales of old that a Blademaster who was fully committed to the Law of the Blades and accompanied by her Protector was something that very little could stand against. Not even, he fervently hoped, a lich. So as far as Darius was concerned, there was indeed hope for release.

When he saw the Blademaster in person for the first time, he knew she would kill the lich and free him from his service to Thraal. He need only wait and watch, something he had been doing for over a century. Another few days of waiting would make no difference to him.

When Drakkhous told Alana about Lilliana and about his reasons for doing what he was doing, Darius felt sick. He knew the Blademaster would use information such as that against him. Although the lich was in control and would be the one the Blademaster would use that information against, Darius could not bear to have his love used as a weapon. It tore at his heart. He knew that, even though it would be used to hurt the lich, having his love for Lilliana used as a weapon like that would wound him to his very core. It was not something he was looking forward to.

But he knew that it had to happen if he were to be released. And he very much wanted to be freed from his service to the Dark God. He regretted every moment that he was in service to Thraal. He felt that his betrayal of his Lord Taelin became less and less forgivable with each passing day. It distressed him to think that, for he had been close to being named High Priest of Taelin when it happened. He had been young for the position. That youth and temperament was likely a large part of the reason he got himself into this situation to begin with. While he was in service to Taelin, his commitment to the Lightbringer had been second to none. That was the reason the deal he had accepted from Thraal had disturbed him so much. The deal had been that, in return for Thraal's bringing Lilliana back to the world of the living, Darius would allow his soul to become the source of power for the lich Drakkhous. He had not been told what the lich's goals would be, but he had known from the first that those goals would not allow him to continue to serve Lord Taelin. When he found out that the lich was going to work towards freeing Thraal from his prison, he knew he was doomed. For in order for the lich to succeed in freeing the Dark God, Darius would have to have a part in it. He knew that his Lord Taelin would not appreciate one of his own priests helping to free Thraal.

The night that Alana Steeldrake was to be sacrificed to Thraal, Darius prayed to Taelin for deliverance from his service to Thraal. He hoped that the Blademaster would find a way to kill the lich, and, as a result, set him free. He neither knew nor cared what would happen to his soul were he to be freed, but he hoped to find out that evening.

As the lich prepared for the sacrifice, Darius prepared his soul for his release. He did not doubt that the Blademaster would kill the lich. A Blademaster, he knew, was a combination of Taelin's wisdom and Laeyra's luck. It was a combination that the Lord of Chaos had not yet been able to match.

Darius watched in horror through the lich's eyes as Drakkhous disrobed and mounted the altar for the sacrifice. He looked down at Alana and looked directly into her eyes. Darius saw the fiery determination that marked a true Blademaster. And he knew that his time of freedom was almost upon him.

What happened when the lich started the sacrifice happened so fast, Darius almost didn't catch it. He saw Alana close her eyes. He heard a battle cry and then he saw the High Priest of Taelin come diving across Alana's body as Drakkhous brought the dagger down in a killing stroke. Darius applauded silently, for he knew that it was the opening that the Blademaster needed to kill the lich. Drakkhous was knocked off balance, freeing Alana to get her swords.

Before the lich knew it, she had both of her swords crossed at his throat.

As he continued to look around, Darius noticed that the priestess Mariska was lying in a pool of her own blood. Adouon was kneeling next to her, his hands on her chest. He had a look of intense concentration on his face, and his eyes were closed. He was mumbling a whispered prayer to Thraal, and Darius knew that he was trying to heal her. He realized that the halfling companion of Alana's must have appeared out of nowhere and stabbed Mariska. That had to be what had caused the binding spell to fail. He knew the Blademaster had been bound up in a binding spell. It was the only way the priests of Thraal would have been able to keep such a woman as the Blademaster incapacitated long enough for her to be bound to the altar.

He watched the Blademaster as she looked over at William and Colwyn. William had just cast a dispel magic spell on Colwyn to release him from the binding spell he was under, and the two men were racing over to the altar. Meryn was joining them as they arrived.

"Nice timing, Little Bit," Wiliam smiled as he mussed the halfling's hair.

"Good job, Meryn,' Colwyn smiled. "Good job indeed. For once, I am quite glad you're around."

Alana nodded and smiled at the halfling before turning back to the lich.

"I told you what would happen to you if I got free of the binding spell," she said quietly. "I truly hope that your Lilliana is far more forgiving a woman than I am."

With a great grunt, Alana yanked the two swords apart, slicing the lich's head from his body. Darius felt the swords bite through the lich's flesh as if it was his own. He sighed happily as his soul slipped into nothingness. He was free at last.

When he awoke, Darius found an old man sitting there watching him. Darius frowned deeply. There could be no doubt as to who the old man was.

"What...?" he croaked. "What are you doing here, my Lord?"

"Watching you, Darius," Taelin smiled broadly. "You're rather a fascinating case. I know why you did what you did. The question I have for you is do you have any regrets over your actions?"

"Only every day for a century," Darius groaned. He closed his eyes, not wanting to look his god in the face. He was ashamed of his betrayal, and he didn't want to see the shame reflected in Taelin's eyes.

"Then your sins have been forgiven you, Darius," Taelin nodded. He reached over and touched the priest lightly on the chin. "You will walk with me."

"My lord, I haven't earned the right to walk with you," Darius protested softly. He opened his eyes, and tears rolled down his cheeks. "Why would you allow me such an honor after betraying you as I did?"

"You have much to learn still, my child," Taelin chuckled. "Perhaps you will understand in time. For now, I wish for you to accompany me to the Temple of the White. There is someone who will be there soon that I would like you to speak with."

"Very well," Darius nodded. He stood up slowly and walked over to Taelin.

The god took his former priest by the hand and they walked off through the city of Tornith. No one gave them any notice as they walked by.

When they arrived at the Taelin's temple, they were not even questioned, simply shown to a small room. Taelin sat in a comfortable chair by the fire and smiled at Darius.

"I want you to wait outside until you are called for, Darius," the god instructed. "You will find others waiting to speak to my Blademaster as well. Talk to them. I believe you will find some of your answers with them."

Darius nodded and left the room. Outside, two other souls waited, those of Balaam Otakis and Merinda Delwyn. Darius sighed deeply when he saw them and turned away in shame.

"Don't turn away, Darius," Merinda smiled. Her smile was bright and inviting. She walked over to him and pulled him towards herself and Balaam. "Things happen as they do for a reason."

"What reason could there have been to betray my lord Taelin?" Darius asked in a strangled whisper.

"Perhaps in time you will understand that," Merinda shrugged. "For that we don't have the answers."

"Then what answers do you have?" Darius asked bitterly. "Lord Taelin said that you would have answers for me."

"The only answers we can give you are the ones that are already inside you," Balaam said softly. "The answers of forgiveness."

"Forgiveness?" Darius frowned. "I don't understand."

"You will," Merinda smiled. "Seek the answers in yourself. The truth of these answers is within your training. For now, though, we must go. The Blademaster awaits us."

Darius watched them go, sighing to himself. Seeking the answers inside himself would be great if he knew what questions he was seeking the answers to. But he did not know the questions to ask. All he knew was that he was hurting. A lot. And he wished he knew how to not hurt. Nothing that Balaam and Merinda had said helped. At least not immediately. He hoped that in time their wisdom would make some sense.

He listened as Taelin talked with Alana. Balaam and Merinda had been in there for a few minutes, and he could hear them talking as well. He couldn't make their words out clearly, but he knew it was a good conversation for them. After a few minutes, they came out again. Balaam smiled at him. Merinda placed her hand on his shoulder and gave him a smile as well.

"This should help bring you some closure, Darius," she said quietly. "Alana is a remarkable woman."

"Yes, I know," Darius nodded, a slight smile playing across his face. It was the first time he'd smiled, even slightly in a long time. "Only a remarkable woman could have killed Drakkhous and set me free. It was quite something to watch."

"You saw what happened?" Balaam asked, amazement in his voice.

"Balaam, I saw everything that happened over the entire century that I was enslaved to the lich," Darius said quietly. "So many of the things I saw, I wish I could forget."

"I don't know that I'll ever understand what you have seen," Balaam nodded. "But I know that you are free from it now. Good journey, my friend. I will see you on the walk. We both will."

Darius nodded and turned his attention back to the door. He had almost missed his cue to enter, but he heard it, because Taelin had spoken loudly enough to make sure he would hear it.

"There is one more person who wishes to speak with you before he goes to walk with me," Taelin's voice boomed through the door. Darius slowly walked into the room and glanced nervously at Alana before going over to Taelin and bowing to him. He turned back to Alana and smiled sadly. The Blademaster looked at him curiously, and he had the oddest sensation that she already knew who he was.

"My name is Darius Redwind," Darius breathed as he bowed to her. "I am the man who became the lich Drakkhous. I wanted to thank you for freeing me from the lich's body. I don't know if my Lilliana will forgive me or not, but at least I no longer am in service to Thraal. Lord Taelin has granted me his forgiveness and will allow me to walk with him. Thank you, Blademaster, for making it possible."

"You're welcome, Darius," she smiled. "May the luck of Laeyra guide you in your quest for forgiveness with Lilliana."

Darius looked at Alana, a curious expression on his face. There had been no animosity in her voice, and he wondered about that. How could she have no animosity towards the man who had been responsible for Thraal coming back to the world? And even more, he had almost sacrificed her to Thraal as well.

"Thank you, Blademaster," Darius bowed again. "I must go to her now."

"Good journey, Darius," Alana said to his back as he turned to leave.

"To you as well, Blademaster," Darius said softly. "You truly are worthy of the title of Blademaster. Lord Taelin chooses his Blademasters well."

With that, he bowed once more to Taelin and walked out of the room. He felt Alana's eyes on him every step of the way. When he was out of the room, he leaned against the wall and closed his eyes. He was beginning to understand a bit more, although he still questioned the validity of the answers he was finding. There was a part of him that wondered if he was imagining the answers. It was not long before the god left the room and rejoined Darius.

"What have you learned?" Taelin asked softly as they began to walk through the halls of the Temple.

"That life is more complicated than it would seem," Darius forced a smile. "I don't believe there are any easy answers, but I think I might finally know what the questions are."

"And that, my child, is a good start," Taelin laughed.

Darius and Taelin walked to a set of stairs that went down to the crypts below the Temple of the White. It was the one place that Darius had never dared to go in any of the temples dedicated to Taelin. He had managed to get out of any duties that involved going into the crypts. He feared what would be in the crypts. And that fear kept him from going there. But now, he had no choice, because Taelin was in control. Had Darius not strayed, Taelin would have been for all of his life.

"I've never been in the crypts before," Darius said softly, fear in his voice. "And I am afraid."

"There is a first time for everything, Darius," Taelin smiled slightly. "And there is nothing to fear in the crypts. All that is down there is the bones of priests and priestesses dedicated to me. But it is only through the crypts that you can begin the walk with me."

"Then I guess I have no choice but to conquer my fear," Darius sighed. "I've never been good at that. My fears have often gotten the best of me."

"Your fear has served you well, Darius," the Lightbringer shrugged. He stepped forward and pushed the door to the crypts open. "Until now, that is."

As they stepped into the white marble crypt, Darius shuddered slightly in fear. He knew that nothing could harm him at that point, because he was already dead, but the fear remained. The fear of the crypts was so ingrained that it had gone all the way down to the deepest reaches of his soul, and so, even though he was dead, his soul remembered the fear and felt it. But when he looked around at the marble walls and sarcophagi for the first time, he realized that there was nothing to fear.

Until he saw the portal of light at the other end of the room.

"What's that?" he asked Taelin softly, indicating the portal.

"That?" Taelin raised an eyebrow. "That, my child is the way to my celestial home. Only those who have departed the world of Calthea can even see it. You must go through it if you are to walk with me. And if you are to be reunited with Lilliana."

"I do not think she will want to see me," Darius said quietly, turning away from his god so that Taelin would not see him cry. "After what I did..." He trailed off.

"We will soon see," Taelin said gently. "She knows that you are coming. I told her that this would be the night you would be joining me in the walk. I expect she waits for you on the other side of the portal as we speak."

"Do I really have to go?" Darius asked, looking over at Taelin. "after all that has happened, I don't think I'm ready to see her."

"If I leave you to your own devices, you will never be ready to see her," Taelin prodded. "Yes, you have to go. It is many years past the time when you should have joined the walk. You cannot put it off any longer."

"But what if she hates me for what I have done?" Darius asked. "I do not think I could bear her hating me."

"She has had a century to get over her anger, Darius," Taelin shrugged. "And my beloved Laeyra, whom Lilliana served, has helped her with that. Trust me once more as you once trusted me, Darius, and you will be fine."

"I have never stopped trusting you, my lord," Darius nodded. "But I'm so confused."

"As it should be considering all that has happened to you." The God of Wisdom pushed Darius forward towards the portal of light once more. "But come, now. There can be no more waiting. It is time. You must face what is to come. I will not allow you to put it off any longer."

"Very well," Darius sighed. He shuffled forward reluctantly.

As soon as he touched the portal, he was pulled through. What he saw on the other side was nothing short of breathtaking.

Taelin's Celestial Palace filled the view in front of him.

To say that the Celestial Palace was imposing would an understatement. The palace was enormous. It was an immense castle made of light and crystal. Vast towers marked the corners of the palace, which was formed in an octagonal shape. Each of the towers had a crenelated parapet. The outer walls of the castle were made of shards of crystal woven together to appear as if each wall was made of a single shard. Arrow slits were cut into the outer walls. Over the top of the outer walls, Darius could see the top of the castle proper. The top of the castle featured a crenelated wall rounded at the corners with towers of varying heights at each corner. Windows lined the towers.

Standing in the open drawbridge to the palace were two women, one of which Darius recognized immediately. Cascades of red hair fell on pale white shoulders. She was wearing the pale blue dress that marked her as a priestess of Laeyra. Her features were chiseled from marble, and her pale blue eyes, which matched the color of the dress, watched him. He knew this woman all right... there would be no mistaking the woman he loved more than his own life.

This was Lilliana, and there was no way to put this confrontation off any longer.

While he had never seen her before, he knew instinctively that the woman beside Lilliana could only be the goddess Laeyra.

Darius looked over at Taelin and sighed. Taelin motioned for him to go forward towards the two women. Darius tried to force himself to stay put, but Lilliana was drawing him towards her with her smile.

"Darius, my love," she said quietly, a smile playing on her lips. "I have missed you."

"I've missed you too, Lilliana," Darius cried. "I'm so sorry. I should never have done what I did."

"I know you are sorry, my beloved," Lilliana's smile grew. Her smile shone radiantly at him and only served to make her even more beautiful to him. "I forgave you a long time ago. I know you only did so out of love for me. How can I not forgive you for that?"

"But..." Darius trailed off.

"Come, my love. It is finally time for us to be together. Come walk with me," Lilliana smiled at him. She held her hands out to him.

"I will... be right there," Darius stuttered. He turned to Taelin. "My lord, I do not understand. How can she forgive me after all that I have done?"

"You have been gone from my service for too long, my child," Taelin laughed. "Surely you must remember the Second Law of the Blades?"

"No, I don't," Darius furrowed his brow in confusion. "What is the Second Law of the Blades?"

"You have fought against a Blademaster and seen it in action," Taelin shook his head. He placed his hand on Darius's shoulder. "I will tell it to you now, but know you now that this was the lesson you were to have learned from Balaam and Merinda. This is the Second Law of the Blades. True love breeds true forgiveness. Nothing is more powerful than the ability to forgive the one you love. And nothing brings you closer than the forgiveness of your own misdeeds."

Darius looked at Taelin for a long moment before turning away. He closed his eyes and hung his head in shame, tears running down his face.

"I have been a fool," Darius whispered.

"You understand now, yes?" Taelin raised an eyebrow.

"I understand now," Darius nodded in confirmation.

He turned back to Lilliana and stepped forward into her arms. He put his head on her shoulder and began to cry softly.

Chapter II
Midnight Meeting

The man ran down a dark and dirty street. It was really more of an alleyway than a street, but he didn't care. He was in a hurry, because the Resistance was meeting and he had to be there. He knew what had to be done for the people to be free, and he was willing to be the one to do it. But it involved him making it to the meeting without the Zeraphim knowing. He could not allow the Zeraphim to stop the Resistance from doing what they needed to. If the people were to survive, they would need to be able to act freely. That meant getting the Blademaster involved. And he knew where the Blademaster was.

It had been raining off and on for the past two days, so the alleyway was muddy and trash was piled up in the corners. It didn't matter to him, though. He would have slogged through several feet of water if it meant freedom from the Zeraphim. He did not want his people to spend another minute under the control of the Zeraphim. He knew that the Resistance had to succeed in freeing the people.

And he knew that he now held the key to their victory.

He knew that the Resistance was all that was keeping the people of Willowdale from breaking. He also knew that they could not hope to free themselves. The Blademaster would need to come and free them. All he wanted was to go home. And home meant Valendale. He missed his inn. He missed seeing people coming in and out as they went through the town. But he had not seen his inn in several months. He wished he could visit it, even if it were just for a moment. Ever since the Zeraphim had come through Valendale and rounded all the residents up, though, none of them had seen their homes. Most of them hadn't even seen their loved ones since that fateful day. He hadn't seen his wife in three whole months. Nor did he even have a clue where she and his daughter had been taken. He hoped and prayed every day to Taelin that they were safe. Somewhere along the line, he had stopped wondering about where they were and started simply hoping that they were safe.

There was a door at the end of the alleyway he was hurrying down that led into the back room of a training hall. It was one of several different places that the cell of the Resistance that Marcus belonged to used on a rotating basis as their base. They had to be careful and switch their meeting locations to different parts of the city, lest the Zeraphim catch wind of what they were up to. That would be the worst thing that could happen, for if the Zeraphim were to show up at a meeting, it would be disastrous for everyone there. Arrests and executions would be the beginning. The Zeraphim would want to make an example of any members of the Resistance that they might find.

Their executions would be public and messy.

Even the spectacle of a public and messy execution would be better than living the lives of slaves. The former innkeeper didn't know why the Zeraphim had decided to take the people of Valendale as slaves like they had. Nor did anyone else. It didn't matter. All that mattered was that they were slaves and they needed to find a way to break the chains that the Zeraphim held them by.

When he got to the door, he looked around carefully, but saw no sign of Zeraphim soldiers. Sighing with relief, he knocked on the door softly. Four knocks all evenly spaced. They had developed the knock code as the only way to know that he was definitely a member of the Resistance.

"Who is it?" a timid female voice called from the other side of the door.

"Marcus Whelan," he whispered back. "I have come as I was asked to."

"Hurry up," the woman said as she opened the door. "It's not good to be standing out there."

"Thank you, Marta," he smiled sadly. He embraced the young woman who had served as a barmaid at his inn. "Are the others here already?"

"Yes, they are waiting for you," Marta nodded. She returned the innkeeper's embrace warmly. "Have you come with a solution to our problem? We're all hoping that you do."

"Yes, I have a solution," Marcus nodded. "And it's one that the Zeraphim will never expect. I just hope that it's not too late to put it into action."

"Well, hopefully the rest of the Resistance will see the wisdom of your plan then," the young woman smiled weakly. "I just want to go home."

"So do I, Marta," Marcus chuckled. "So do we all."

Marcus followed the young woman down the corridor towards the meeting room. He hoped that the Blademaster would be willing to help them. Surely she could free them from the oppression of the Zeraphim. Nothing could be worse than continued slavery under the thumb of the Zeraphim. None of them could bear to stay under that oppression any longer. He knew he had to make the rest of the Resistance see the wisdom of his plan. If he could, then he would volunteer to go get the Blademaster. He knew that it would be a long and difficult journey. He knew that it could be the most dangerous journey of his life. But he also knew that if they did not take this chance, then no one from Valendale would ever see their home again. He could not bear the thought of failing in his journey and being responsible for the people of Valendale never being able to go home again. Marcus knew that the only way they could secure her help would be for someone to go tell the Blademaster what was happening. If the old stories about the holy warriors were true, then the Blademaster that currently walked the world would react the same way as the Blademasters of old would have and come to Willowdale to free them from their oppression. Marcus was counting on that. It was a lot to pin his hopes on, but he felt it was their only choice.

While he was hopeful that the Blademaster would help them, he did not know what one woman could do against a city full of the Zeraphim soldiers. The Zeraphim would not let the people of Valendale go so easily. He had no idea what the Blademaster could do when she got here. He did not know if he could even convince her to come. That was the other part of his plan that he did not yet have the answer to. What could he say to the Blademaster that would convince her to come to Willowdale and release them from this bondage? He had to find a way to convince her, but he was not a man of words. So he did not know what he would say to her. He had not even left on his journey to find her and bring her back and he was already having doubts about his success. But he also knew that no amount of nerves would prevent him from approaching the Blademaster about helping the citizens of Valendale. He had no choice.

He remembered the Blademaster. She and her companions often stayed at the White Horse Inn when they were in Valendale. Of course none of them had known that she was the Blademaster. He had suspected that she was far more than she had appeared. Even so, he had been surprised when the sage had told her what she was. Isaiah had visited the former innkeeper a week before. He had told him that Alana Steeldrake was a Blademaster. When Isaiah had told him that, Marcus knew that he had to find her and bring her to Willowdale. If he could convince her to come, he knew it would make all the difference to the people of Valendale. He would have two to three weeks to figure out what to say to her. It would take that long to get from Willowdale to Ravendale. And he would take all the time he needed during that trip to figure out what to say to the Blademaster to convince her to come back with him. He hoped that she had companions that would be helpful to her in ridding the town of the Zeraphim. He remembered from the stories of the Blademasters of old that the Blademaster had her Protector that journeyed with her. Not much was actually said about the Protectors in the stories, but he assumed that the Protector would also be good with a sword. He hoped that her Protector was a powerful fighter, because he knew that it would take all the fighters that could be mustered to drive the Zeraphim off.

Not for the first time, Marcus wondered about where the Zeraphim had come from. He had heard rumors of a place called Zhentaril Keep far to the northwest, but he knew nothing about it. He thought it sounded like a place that the Zeraphim might have come from because they had fairly similar sounding names. But even though he wondered about where the Zeraphim had come from, in the end it did not matter. He just wanted them to go back there.

He had been lost in his thoughts during the walk down the corridor, and he did not realize that they had arrived at the meeting room. He walked in and took his seat, still deep in his thoughts. It was when the leader of this cell of the Resistance, a burly man who had been a blacksmith in Valendale, cleared his throat that Marcus finally broke out of his thoughts.

"Welcome, Marcus," the blacksmith said. His voice was surprisingly soft and gentle considering his size. Because of who he was and how he looked, Carl's gentle nature had always surprised the innkeeper.

"Thank you, Carl," Marcus said softly. "I'm sorry I was late. I had a couple of Zeraphim soldiers notice me leave the house. I had to make sure I was not followed."

"I understand," the blacksmith nodded. "That was wise. Have you given any thought to our situation? You said you would try to come up with a solution when we talked last week."

"I have," Marcus smiled. It was a real smile, for he really believed that this solution would work. "The sage Isaiah visited me last week."

"The sage Isaiah?" Carl raised an eyebrow. "I had wondered what had happened to him. He was not taken with everyone else when the people of Valendale were taken to this gods forsaken place, was he?"

"No, he was not," Marcus confirmed. He stood and crossed the room to stand by the blacksmith. "But the sage told me something that gives me hope that there is a way for us to throw off the yoke of our oppression."

"Any hope is good," a man called from the back of the room. "What did the sage say?"

"A Blademaster once more walks the world," Marcus said simply.

It was such a simple statement, but it had the desired effect. Everyone started talking at once about the Blademasters. Excitement quickly built amongst the members of the Resistance about the thought of a Blademaster coming in and freeing them from the Zeraphim. Even the blacksmith, who had the task of keeping the meetings of this resistance cell under the rules of order, was momentarily taken aback. After a few moments, he raised his hands to silence the crowd and the noise died down quickly.

"The sage is sure of this?" the blacksmith asked.

"Quite sure. He has seen her himself," Marcus said. "And so have we. The Blademaster has visited our city of Valendale many times on her way to do missions for the White Temple. She did not know what she was when she visited us, but I have been made aware of her identity. I know where she is, and I can find her. If I can go to talk to her, I am certain that I can bring her here. She can rid the city of the Zeraphim and set us free to return to Valendale. I, for one, would rather go back to my inn and go back to my life."

"As would we all," the blacksmith nodded. "Are you sure that you can convince her to help us?"

"I have no choice but to try, Carl," Marcus shrugged. He looked at each member of the Resistance that was gathered there in turn. He saw hope dawning in the eyes of each person. Those eyes had all been dead to hope for so long. Seeing new hope in the eyes of his friends strengthened his resolve. "The longer we delay in getting her help, the longer we are forced to be slaves to the Zeraphim. I can't take much more of this. I know no one else can either. The hardest part will be getting out of Willowdale. Once I can do that, it will take fifteen to twenty days for me to get to Ravendale. It will take that much time to return with the Blademaster. I will succeed though."

"Then you should leave this very night," Carl clenched his fist in determination. "We will all keep praying to Taelin for you. To Taelin and Laeyra both. We need a little of Taelin's wisdom and light and a lot of Laeyra's luck."

"I agree," Marcus nodded. "I will prepare some provisions and leave this very evening."

"Good journey to you, Marcus," the blacksmith smiled. "We will eagerly await your return."

Marcus clasped the blacksmith's hand firmly, two friends united against a common foe. They both started at the sound of swords clashing in the front room of the training hall. Shouts were heard. Everyone there knew that the Zeraphim had found this cell of the Resistance out. The blacksmith wordlessly shoved Marcus towards the back door. The former innkeeper nodded and rushed through the door, just in time. Just after the door closed behind him, Marcus heard the front door to the meeting room burst open and Zeraphim soldiers burst into the room.

"This is an illegal gathering," he heard one of the Zeraphim soldiers shout. "You are all under arrest for treason against the Zeraphim. You will be judged and executed in the morning."

"No, we will not," Carl shouted back at the Zeraphim. "We have had enough of your oppression. The time of the Zeraphim is at an end."

He did not hear the sword being plunged through Carl's heart, but he knew that the Zeraphim soldier had just killed his friend. The thought ripped at the innkeeper's heart.   He heard Marta scream and tears started to fall down his cheeks.

Marcus knew that his friends had just sacrificed themselves so that Marcus could get away, and he did not want their sacrifice to be for nothing. He hurried down the corridor and slipped back out into the night.   He ran back to his house and made his preparations.

He would not see the city of Willowdale again until he had the Blademaster with him.

Chapter III
The Stranger at the Lucky Minotaur

wen was singing. If you could call what she was doing singing. She was horribly off key.

Alana and Colwyn were lounging at their usual table near the fire in the tap room of the Lucky Minotaur. It had been two weeks since they had returned from their mission to Tornith. They had taken time to relax, and they were glad for the opportunity to have that time. The mission in Tornith had been rough on all of them. And they knew that it would not be too much longer before they were off on another adventure. Colwyn was surprised that they had had two whole weeks to relax and heal up without something coming to ruin their relaxation.

It was starting to make him nervous.

They had not seen the halfling in two days, and William was off gathering spell components. Colwyn enjoyed the time alone with Alana with the other two gone, but he knew that when William went off on his own to find spell components, it was a sure sign that the companions were about to head off on an adventure. William had always had a sense of when trouble was about to come calling on them.

But trouble did not look like it was about to walk through the door right away. So, Colwyn and Alana were simply enjoying Gwen's off key singing. It was just a pleasant way to spend the evening. Somehow, Colwyn had managed to goad Gwen into singing with the bard. Alana didn't know what he had done to convince the girl, and she didn't want to. All she knew was that she was very much enjoying watching Gwen have fun. There was no doubt in either of their minds that Gwen was having fun. After the ugliness in Tornith, it lifted her heart to see someone having fun. Allowing people to love life was, in essence, why the Blademaster was doing what she did. And so long as she remained the innocent she was, Alana would always protect Gwen. She knew Colwyn felt the same way about the young barmaid.

The ballad that Gwen was singing was an old song written about the Blademasters of old. The song was an odd combination of sad and joyful. Gwen sang with passion, even if she did not sing it well. Nor did she sing it exactly as it should have been sung. Alana listened with rapt fascination. The songs written about the old Blademasters had taken on an entirely different meaning for her ever since she had taken on the mantle of the Blademaster.

Songs and stories about the Blademasters of old had always fascinated Alana. It never occurred to her that she might one day become a part of the story when she had heard the songs as a child. The ballad that Gwen was singing was called the Canticle of the Blademaster, and that one had always been Alana's favorite. The song told the story of the first Blademaster and the first Protector. The song had a whole new meaning to Alana, now that she had spoken to Raven Windrider and Richard Kale in the Temple of the Blades. The words of the Canticle of the Blademaster had, once upon a time, made Alana cry with the beauty of how it wove together the love story of Raven Windrider and

Richard Kale. It had always made her long for that kind of pure love in her own life.

Now, though, the words of the song filled her with a measure of pride as well as a feeling of pure and unbridled joy. She knew that she had beaten the odds by finding her own love story. She also knew that hundreds of years in the future, there would be a little girl that would let her imagination roam as she listened to songs and stories written about the love story that Alana shared with Colwyn.

She looked over at Colwyn and smiled at him. She knew that he had many of the same thoughts going through his mind while listening to the song. She reached over and gently took his hand in hers.

"This song has a whole new meaning for us, doesn't it, Alana?" Colwyn said softly without looking over at her. "Our lives are never going to be the same after all that we have gone through."

"I wouldn't have it any other way, Col," Alana's smile grew broader. "This is true love. You think this happens every day?"

"I don't suppose it does at that," Colwyn chuckled. "It has always been my belief that I am very lucky to have you in my life."

"Why don't we leave it at we're both lucky, my love?" Alana laughed as she squeezed his hand. She took a sip of her kava juice and leaned back in her chair. "Lady Laeyra has certainly smiled on us."

"That is for sure," Colwyn's laughter echoed hers. "Who knew that the Goddess of Luck would end up taking such a fancy to us?"

"Well, the old saying is that a Blademaster is a child of Lord Taelin and Lady Laeyra," Alana shrugged and took another sip of her kava juice. "If that's the case, then it should come as no surprise that Lady Laeyra would take an interest in me. And by extension, you."

Colwyn had nothing to say to that so he took a sip of his tea and listened to Gwen's singing some more. When the young barmaid suddenly stopped singing, Colwyn and Alana both came instantly alert. They knew that something had happened. When Colwyn looked at Gwen, he saw that all the color had drained from her face. He turned to look at what had captured her attention.

There was a commotion at the door to the tap room. Colwyn couldn't see what was causing the commotion from where he was sitting. Despite the fact that they had been relaxing for the previous two weeks, both Alana and Colwyn took no time in reacting to what appeared to be someone needing their help.

Colwyn was the first to his feet. He dashed across the half full tap room, gently pushing people aside in his haste to get to the door. Alana was not far behind him. As they neared the door, they could tell that someone was lying face down across the threshold to the tap room. Whoever it was, the man was in very bad shape. Alana waved to Albert to come and help them. The old innkeeper wasted no time in getting over to where they were kneeling next to the clearly injured man.

They could not tell much about the man while he was lying face down. Alana gently rolled the man over, trying as best as she could not to hurt him. She gasped when she saw who it was.

Despite the fact that blood from myriad cuts crusted his face, Alana recognized the man immediately. Seeing who the man was shocked her to her core.

"Colwyn, it's Marcus Whelan from the White Horse Inn in Valendale," she said softly, her voice carrying despite her low tones. "What in the name of Lord Taelin happened to him?"

"Unhh," Marcus groaned. He rasped his dry tongue over his lips before continuing weakly. "Alana Steeldrake. Must.... Find..."

With that, the innkeeper from the White Horse Inn mercifully passed out. Albert knelt down next to Alana and shook his head.

"I'll get a room ready for him," the old innkeeper said gruffly. "Colwyn, can you carry him up the stairs?"

"Of course, Albert," Colwyn nodded as he shifted so that he could more easily pick up the injured man.

"Gently, my boy," Albert admonished. He placed his hand on Colwyn's shoulder to get the younger man to look at him. "Gently. Take him up to room 8. I will make sure he doesn't want for anything while he is here."

Colwyn gently picked Marcus up and carried him up the stairs. Alana and Albert followed close behind. When they got up to the room, Colwyn gently laid Marcus down on the bed.

Marcus groaned again as he tossed in the bed.

"Must find the Blademaster," he said in his sleep.

"I wonder what that's about," Alana said softly, drawing a look from Colwyn.

Whatever it was that Marcus needed them for, they knew it would be some time before they found out what it was.

But Colwyn knew now that William was once again right about when to go hunt for spell components.

Trouble had indeed arrived.

Willowdale

Chapter IV
The Plea for Help

nce she and Colwyn had gotten Marcus settled in his room, Alana ordered some food to be brought up for the innkeeper to eat. Albert had been only too happy to help his counterpart from the White Horse Inn. It was a matter of professional courtesy for Albert, and he explained to Alana that the room and the food for Marcus would be on the house. Alana had balked at that saying that Albert should be paid for his services. Albert had just shrugged and said that he wouldn't feel comfortable charging Marcus anything. He went on to explain that innkeepers would not charge for food and lodging for a fellow innkeeper. Especially not an innkeeper in distress like Marcus was. It was just like any other profession, really. You did not overcharge someone in the same business when they used your services. Taelin forbid that you need their services if you overcharge them, because they will make you pay through the nose were that to happen. It was not a situation that any innkeeper would feel comfortable with. And so it was just easier to not charge Marcus for whatever services that he used while recovering at the Lucky Minotaur. Besides. Although he told Alana never to tell Marcus, he genuinely liked the innkeeper from the White Horse Inn. But he had a reputation for being a crotchety old man, so he told Alana that he would deny it if anyone said anything about his liking Marcus.

Marcus slept for several hours after they got him into the bed. He slept very soundly. It was clear to Alana that whatever had happened to the man had already taken a toll on him even before he set off for Ravendale. Although she had no idea how long it had taken him, Alana knew that the journey to Ravendale had not helped the man's condition. While Marcus slept, Colwyn tended to his wounds as best he could. He was no priest, though, and the best he could do was to put a salve on the wounds and bandage them. They would have to call for a priest from the temple of Terra at some point, but Colwyn assured Alana that none of the wounds were immediately life threatening, so calling for a priest could wait until after Marcus had rested and eaten. There would be time enough to heal his body when that was done. Colwyn had a feeling that healing the man's body would be by far a much easier task than the real healing that would need to be done.

Healing the man's emotional pain and mental suffering would be the far more difficult task. It could even be beyond the capabilities of the priests of Terra to do. He hoped that he was wrong about that though.

"You know, when we found Valendale empty except for the sage while we were on our way to the Temple of the Blades last month, I knew that we were going to have to find out what happened to the people," Colwyn sighed softly as he looked at the man sleeping on the bed. He turned to face Alana. "I had just been thinking about that earlier today too. I was going to talk to you about it tonight. I suspect that we are about to find out what happened to those people. I also think that what we learn is going to send us off on another whirlwind adventure that will cause us to once more risk our lives in order to save people's lives."

"I know," Alana nodded as she watched Marcus sleep. The man was obviously having nightmares, tossing and turning in his sleep. Her heart was breaking just watching him. Whatever Marcus had been through must have been terrible. Only something that was truly terrible could give a man nightmares like that. "Look at him, Colwyn. Whatever happened to cause Marcus that much pain has to be dealt with. This is what I was named the Blademaster for. So yes, we're heading into another adventure. There is really no other choice."

"I know," the ranger sighed again. "I suppose that all we can do at this point is to wait until he wakes up and tells us what happened. But you are right. Whatever caused this has to be dealt with."

"We never did talk about what happened in Valendale, Colwyn," Alana said softly, her eyes still on the sleeping innkeeper. "I was distracted running after the followers of Thraal that tried to kill me, so I don't know what you found at the White Horse Inn. I know that whatever you found out disturbed you though. You talk in your sleep, and you keep talking about missing people."

"I do not talk in my sleep, do I?" Colwyn furrowed his brow. When Alana chuckled and nodded, Colwyn shook his head and let out a third long sigh. The appearance of the innkeeper from the White Horse Inn had shaken Colwyn a little bit. While he was concerned about what had happened to the people of Valendale, he did not expect the situation would show up on his doorstep like this. As he had just told Alana, though, he had been planning on talking to Alana about looking into what had happened to the citizens of Valendale that night. The guest book from the White Horse Inn, and what it meant, had been nagging at him for weeks. He had been trying to relax while healing up from the injuries that he had sustained in Tornith. He could only relax so much when there were people in trouble. "It has been bothering me for a while, Alana. We need to find out what happened to him and to the rest of the people of Valendale. Before we were attacked by the followers of Thraal at the White Horse Inn, I looked at the guest book. No one had checked into the inn for almost three months before that."

"Three months?" Alana gasped. She turned to look at Colwyn. "Why haven't we been looking into this during the last two weeks instead of just sitting here in Ravendale?"

"Because we haven't been in any shape to do anything for the people of Valendale, Alana," Colwyn frowned in distaste. He hated that it was the truth. "As much as I would have liked to have done something about the people of Valendale before now, the battle with the followers of Thraal back at the ziggurat of Thraal in Tornith took a heavy toll on all of us. There would have been no point in trying to help the people of Valendale until we had a chance to heal up a bit. Such recklessness could have meant all of our deaths, Alana."

"I suppose you're right," Alana heaved a heavy sigh of her own. She looked back at Marcus "What do we do about him now, Colwyn? Whatever happened to him and the others had to have been terrible. What do you think happened to them?"

"I'm not even going to try to hazard a guess, Alana," Colwyn sighed. He reached over and squeezed her hand while looking at the innkeeper's sleeping form. He shrugged, wishing he had answers to her questions. "But you're right. Whatever happened was something pretty bad."

"I guess you're right. There's really nothing we can do until he wakes up and tells us what happened," Alana nodded. She squeezed his hand in return, seeking comfort in his touch. "Just the same, I think we should keep a watch on him tonight. Just in case."

"Just in case... what?" Colwyn furrowed his brow, not catching her train of thought. His frown deepened as he thought he should have known what she meant.

"Just in case whoever did this to him comes back to try to finish the job," Alana explained. "If he dies, then he can't tell us what happened to himself or the others, now can he?"

"You make a good point," Colwyn nodded. He shook his head, clearly upset with himself for not making that connection to Alana's suggestion himself. "All right, we'll keep a watch on him tonight."

Alana nodded and smiled her appreciation at Colwyn for going along with her suggestion. It wasn't so much that she wanted to have her way as much as it simply made sense to keep a watch on Marcus. It was as she had said. Marcus would not be able to tell them what had happened to the people of Valendale if he were to die. Colwyn knew that Alana wanted to hear what had happened to those people. Almost as much as he did. More than that, though, he wanted to go charging in to their rescue. He could tell by the way she was acting that Alana did too.

It was more than just being annoyed at what had happened to Marcus. It was true that they both genuinely liked Marcus and his family. They always stayed at the White Horse Inn when they were in Valendale. They knew that Marcus would treat them right, and he was a likeable enough fellow. But there was more to Colwyn's anger than just what had happened to the innkeeper. While he called Ravendale his home, and he would until the time came for him to succeed his father as the First Lord of Arvendale, he and Alana had spent many good days in Valendale. It was a beautiful little town, and the people were very friendly. The memory of seeing the city so empty had been haunting him ever since he had seen it. He wasn't surprised to hear Alana say that he had been talking in his sleep because he had been having nightmares about the empty streets of Valendale. And although he tried to deny it, he knew that he talked in his sleep every time that he had nightmares.

All he had been able to think was that all of the citizens of Valendale, save for the sage Isaiah, had been killed somehow. The fact that Marcus was there in Ravendale lifted his spirits just as much as it disturbed him. It was good to know that the citizens had not all been killed off, but the vision of the empty streets of Valendale still haunted him. He had to find out what had happened to the rest of the people of Valendale. If they had not been killed, then what had happened to them? Where were they? And, most importantly in Colwyn's mind, what could they do to help Valendale's people? He knew that, no matter what had happened, he and Alana would go to help them. He was in tune enough with her that he believed that Alana had already come to the same decision, but if she had not yet, he knew he would have to do whatever it took to make sure she did. He did not think that it would be necessary though. He knew that she was just as distressed about the empty streets of Valendale as he had been.

He and Alana sat there in the room, watching over Marcus all night long. They took turns napping and watching him throughout the night. They were extremely vigilant in their watch, but they need not have worried. Albert would never allow harm to find any of his guests. And so it was, when Marcus woke in the early hours of the following morning, it was after he had had a very peaceful night's sleep. Alana and Colwyn, however, were not so well rested, but they were used to not getting a full night's sleep. Between taking their turns at watch and the time that they spent between watches talking about the day's events and planning the next day's journey, they averaged about four hours sleep when they were out on a journey. It was just enough to keep them fresh, but they always wished they could get a little more sleep at night. Such was the life of professional adventurers.

When Marcus awoke, he was a little disoriented. He woke with a start, his body bolting upright in the bed. His eyes darted about the room, taking in every detail before settling on Alana. When he saw her there sitting and watching him quietly, he calmed down quickly. For the first time in months, Marcus had the feeling of safety. Now, all he had to do was to convince the Blademaster to help the people of Valendale so that all of the people of Valendale would be able to have that feeling of safety as well.

"Blademaster," he nodded his head in her direction. "Thank you for caring for me last night. But it is of the utmost importance that I must ask for your help. I believe that only you and your companions can help us."

"Eat something, Marcus," Alana smiled, offering him the tray of food that Albert had brought up for him. "We will discuss what has happened to the people of Valendale after you have had a chance to freshen up from your journey and get some nourishment."

"But, Blademaster, it is important that you understand just how much the people of Valendale need your help," the innkeeper protested. "My own comfort is secondary to the importance of making you see how much you are needed."

"Please don't misunderstand us," Colwyn smiled at the innkeeper. "We know how important what you have to tell us is, Marcus. We have been to Valendale recently, and we know that something terrible has happened there. But the few minutes that it will take for you to eat something will not, in the grand scheme of things, make that much of a difference. After you finish eating, you can tell us all about what happened to the people of Valendale."

Marcus nodded gratefully, and then he tore into the food on the tray Alana had offered to him. He was relieved, not only because he knew that the Blademaster intended to hear him out, but also because she and her Protector were compassionate enough to not force him tell his story on an empty stomach. It was always nice to know that the people you were about to beg for help were compassionate. It made Marcus feel like he had a real chance of success in his quest to get the Blademaster to help his people.

Colwyn and Alana moved off to the other side of the room, waiting patiently for him to finish eating. They talked quietly to themselves, and Marcus could not make out what they were saying. He did not care that much about what they were saying. He had come to the realization that he was very hungry, and he intended to eat everything that was on the tray in front of him. If the Blademaster and her Protector were going to be nice enough to let him eat before having him tell his story, then he was going to take full advantage of that kindness and make sure he ate his fill. Besides, all the food on the tray looked delicious.

Albert had provided Marcus a feast on the tray, wanting to make sure that the other innkeeper would have his fill. Several different varieties of eggs and meats were arranged on one plate along with a generous serving of Albert's special spiced potatoes. Albert had also included a small loaf of his pumpkin bread baked fresh the previous evening. It was something that Albert only made for special people, and the importance of the gesture was not lost on Marcus. He was genuinely touched. Albert had also included a slice of his famous chocolate pie. Marcus had heard it called the best chocolate pie in all the Southern Dales, but he had not had the opportunity to try it before then. Albert had included a note with the meal, wishing Marcus a speedy recovery from his injuries. Marcus could understand why Alana and Colwyn liked to spend their time at the Lucky Minotaur when they were in Ravendale. He knew that, were he in their position, he would want to spend time around caring people too. He felt that his own inn could benefit from a new touch of gentleness, love and caring, and he vowed to see to that when he finally got to return to his inn.

He ate slowly, enjoying everything that he had been given to eat. It irked him to admit it, but the food at the Lucky Minotaur was better than the food at his own White Horse Inn. He sighed in contentment as he ate for the food was excellent. The potatoes were especially good, spiced just enough so that the flavor danced across his tongue. And, after tasting the chocolate pie, he knew that he had, indeed, just had a slice of the best chocolate pie in the Southern Dales. The rave reviews he had heard about the pie were not exaggerated.

When Marcus had had his fill, he pushed the tray away and sighed softly. He refilled his mug from the pitcher of kava juice that had been with the tray of food. After taking a sip, he looked at Alana.

"I suppose you want to know all about what happened to me now, Blademaster," the innkeeper said softly. When she nodded, he shrugged once and took a sip from his mug. "It is a very long and sad story."

"We have time, and we want to hear the story, Marcus," Alana smiled sadly. She and Colwyn drew up seats by the bed and sat down. "We want to help, but we need to know what happened to you so that we can."

"You said that you have been to Valendale, so you know that the city is now empty," the innkeeper started. He sighed deeply and Colwyn nodded for him to continue. He took a sip of his kava juice and nodded. "It all started about four months ago. The day this all started was a quiet and peaceful day. I remember that I was sitting on that rocking chair on the front porch of my inn... you know the one I'm talking about?" When Colwyn and Alana both nodded that they knew what he was talking about, he continued. "Anyway, I was sitting on that rocking chair when these strangers came riding up to the inn. They told me that they would be staying at my inn for the duration of their visit and that I was to provide them their room and food free of charge for however long they stayed. I refused at first. But they told me they would kill my wife and daughter if I didn't comply. So I agreed. I do not doubt that they would have killed them had I not."

"Who were these men?" Colwyn asked, his brow furrowed in a look of intense concentration. "Had you ever seen them in Valendale before?"

"I had never seen them before, nor had anyone else in Valendale, no," Marcus coughed. He took a sip of the kava juice to wet his throat before continuing. "We did not find out for a few days who they were or what they wanted. But we all knew that it was going to be trouble. We all did our best to stay out of their way in the hopes that, by doing so, we would be able to keep them from harming us. It was a futile hope at best, but it was certainly worth a try."

"I take it that they did not leave you alone," Colwyn grimaced. He took a sip from his own mug, although his was filled with ale, not kava juice. He set the mug down and looked at Marcus. "What happened next?"

"Three days after the strangers showed up at my inn, the entire population of Valendale was summoned to the town hall," Marcus rasped. He took another drink of his kava juice. His voice was only a little steadier for the sip. "We were told that anyone who did not go to the town hall for the meeting would be killed. Everyone from the town showed up, even the sage Isaiah. No one was happy about it, but we were afraid of what would happen to us if we did not. So we obeyed. It was then that we found out who it was that was invading us and what it was that they wanted from us. I say invaders because that is, in essence what they were. There were enough of them that it may as well have been an invasion."

"So, who were they?" Alana asked. She was leaning forward in her chair, and she was hanging onto every word that the innkeeper had to say. Marcus had not seen her blink so far during the telling of his story. At the very least, he could tell that she was keenly interested in the story. "And just what was it that they wanted with the people of Valendale, Marcus? I mean Valendale is a peaceful city. I just can't imagine anyone having so much of an issue with anyone from Valendale to cause all of this pain and suffering for the rest of the citizens."

"They called themselves the Zeraphim, and they said that they were from Zhentaril Keep on the border of the Southern Dales and Dracomyr," Marcus said finally after several moments of hesitation. Even this far away from Willowdale, he still had a hard time saying the name of the Zeraphim for fear of them appearing. But he was not ready for the look of confusion on Colwyn's face when he mentioned the Zeraphim.

"I have heard of the Zeraphm," Colwyn said quietly, a look of quiet confusion on his face. "It is said that they are a law unto themselves, not answering to the governments of the surrounding lands and not claiming any form of allegiance to either the Southern Dales or Dracomyr. This is the first that I have heard of their doing anything outside of their keep, though, and it is certainly the first time I have ever heard of them besieging a city."

"They have done far more than simply besiege the city, Sir Colwyn," Marcus said softly, tears running down his cheeks. "They have enslaved us. That is what they told us at the meeting at the town hall. They told us that we had been chosen by their god to serve them. We were to accompany them voluntarily to Willowdale where we would be forced to live a life of labor in service to them. They told us that resistance was not an option for us. We would comply or we would die, and another city would be given the honor of serving them in Willowdale. We did not want to go, and we told them so. They told us to go back to our houses and to reconsider our decision. They suggested that we should really think about the consequences of our decision before we decided to defy them."

"What did they do to make the people of Valendale reconsider their decision to not go?" Colwyn asked, even though he knew he did not want to know the answer to that question. While he had never heard of the Zeraphim acting like this, he had a pretty good idea of what the Zeraphim had done. Hearing that he was right would only upset him more. But he did need to know all of the facts. He clenched and unclenched his fits as he added, "Please tell me that they did not do what I think they did."

"They came in the middle of the night while we were all fast asleep. I found out later on that the sleep had been magically induced. They came to each of our houses and took all of our children," Marcus whispered. His face showed to Alana and Colwyn just how much this memory still hurt him. Colwyn could not understand the pain the man was feeling since he did not have children. But he knew full well that he would be haunted by it if he had gone through what Marcus and the others had had to go through. "They brought us back together inside the town hall the next morning and they asked us if we had reconsidered our decision to not go with them to Willowdale. The First Lord of Valendale told them in no uncertain terms that we would not be slaves to anyone and that we would not go to Willowdale to be slaves to the Zeraphim. They brought the daughter of the First Lord out in front of the assembled citizens of Valendale, and they told us that they would give us an example of what happened to people who resisted them. It was a very convincing example. Without hesitation, they slit the poor girl's throat right then and there in front of the assembled citizens of Valendale."

Alana gasped and Colwyn paled. The ranger reached over and grabbed a hold of her hand, trying to comfort her as much as he could in light of such a ghastly pronouncement.

"How could anyone be so cruel?" she demanded in a hoarse voice. "To kill a child in cold blood in such a brutal way? And in front of her father?"

"All they wanted was our obedience. Killing our children if we resisted was a way to guarantee that they would get it," Marcus shrugged. He shuddered and took a sip of his kava juice before continuing. "Of course, the First Lord was devastated by the loss of his only daughter. He had lost his wife the year before to the wasting sickness and had nothing left to live for. He threw himself at the Zeraphim solider that had killed his daughter in anger and despair. I don't know if he thought he actually had a chance to hurt the man, but he had never been trained to fight. He was easily cut down. With the First Lord and his daughter dead, the other citizens of the town became dispirited. We all nodded that we would go with them to Willowdale. We did not feel as if we had any choice in the matter. The Zeraphim had seen to that."

"That's horrible," Alana cried. She wiped tears from her eyes. There was one thing she could not handle. That was an atrocity committed against a child. "Surely not everyone went to go with the Zeraphim to Willowdale. I mean, we know that the sage Isaiah was still in Valendale when we were there. Surely, other citizens must have been able to find a way to flee from the Zeraphim. Maybe some got free from them later?" Alana was hopeful, even though she had a sinking feeling that she knew that no one was able to get free.

"Isaiah was the only one who was able to escape the clutches of the Zeraphim," Marcus grunted, not happy to give the Blademaster that answer. "After the First Lord was killed and we all agreed to go with them to Willowdale, the sage stood up and told the Zeraphim that, in no uncertain terms, that he would not be going to Willowdale with them, as he had work to do for his lord Taelin. He told them that they could kill any number of children in an effort to change his mind, but they would not be able to. He said the work he had to do for Taelin was too important. I can only assume that the work he was referring to had something to do with you. After he made that pronouncement, he sent a great ball of fire towards the Zeraphim. The ball of fire incinerated the Zeraphim soldiers that were in the town hall at that time. It is too bad that not all the Zeraphim soldiers in Valendale were in the town hall at that time or we might not have gone to Willowdale and I would be warm and happy in my own inn. But there's no use trying to live on what might have beens."

"No, we can't live on might have beens," Alana nodded sadly. "What happened next? How did the Zeraphim react to what the sage did?"

"They did not react well to it at all," Marcus shrugged. He took another sip of the juice and continued. "The men that the sage had killed were a small number compared to the number of soldiers the Zeraphim had brought with them to Valendale. They wanted to make sure that they had enough men to accomplish the job, so they had brought hundreds of soldiers with them. Only the officers and men of rank were important enough to stay at my inn. The rest of the soldiers camped outside of the city limits. Despite the number of soldiers they had brought, the Zeraphim did not take kindly to Isaiah killing off twenty or thirty of their number. They took half of the soldiers that they had brought and stormed the sage's house. Of the four hundred soldiers that had gone to capture the sage, only about forty five returned from the attempt. It was then that the Zeraphim considered the sage a lost cause. I do not know what he did to all of those soldiers, but we all consider him a hero for it. We are all glad that he was able to stay free, but at the same time, we envy him his freedom. Life under the rule of the Zeraphim has not been an easy life. No, not an easy life at all."

"After all of that, they just let him go?" Colwyn raised an eyebrow. When Marcus nodded, he shook his head. "All right, so what happened after those soldiers were killed by the sage? I'm sure they didn't take that very well. Did they retaliate against the citizens of Valendale?"

"Oh, yes. They did," Marcus turned away, not wanting the Blademaster to see the tears running down his cheeks. "They took the women and the children and they separated them from the men. Then they herded us all into caravans and drove us off to Willowdale. The journey lasted about three weeks. We were never allowed out of the cages that we had been put into, nor were we allowed to see our loved ones. The cages were cramped and we were crammed into them. We were all sore and had bruises and welts all over by the end of the journey. The journey was, as hard as it was, greatly preferable to the destination."

"What was life like in Willowdale?" Alana asked, although she wasn't sure that she wanted to know the answer to the question. It was one that she had to ask in order to make sure that she knew everything she needed to in order to formulate a plan to help the people of Valendale.

"It has been pure torture," Marcus sighed deeply, still unable to look the Blademaster in the eyes. "I have not seen my wife or daughter since before we left Valendale. They use our wives and children as bargaining chips, or, to put it a bit more accurately, as hostages. They tell us that they will kill our wives and our children if we do not do what they tell us to do. We know that they have not killed our wives and children, because we get to hear their screams from time to time. We do not know what they are doing to them, and we are not allowed to see them at all. I miss Jenny and Lisa. It is extremely hard on me, to be perfectly honest. On all of us."

"I can only imagine," Colwyn said softly. His hand once more found Alana's. "I know that if I were prevented from seeing Alana in a similar situation, it would simply drive me crazy. We will get them back for you, Marcus. I promise you."

"Then you will come to Willowdale and help us?" Marcus asked, his face brightening somewhat as he turned to face the Blademaster. "You would do that for us? Thank you, Blademaster. Thank you so much."

"Yes, we will come and free the people of Valendale," Alana nodded and she smiled sadly. "But then, you had to know that we would. There is one thing I want to know that I don't. It's not something that I need to know in order to help you and your people. But I want to know. How did you know that I am the Blademaster? How did you know where you could find me? I did not even learn who and what I was until after all of you were taken to Willowdale You could not have known what I was or where to look for me without help."

"About three and a half weeks ago, I was in the room that I am forced to live in when I am in Willowdale," the innkeeper began. "The candles all went out and there was a rustling as something came in through the window. A soft voice that anyone from Valendale would know well told me about you and where I could find you. It was the sage, Isaiah. I knew that the sage would not steer me wrong, so I listened very carefully to what he told me about you. At the next meeting of my Resistance cell, I told them all of what the sage told me. We all agreed to seek out your help. We knew it would be the only way we could be free from the life of torture under the thumb of the Zeraphim. It was agreed that it would be me that would go since I was the one that the sage had appeared to. Just as we were in agreement, the Zeraphim crashed the Resistance meeting. I got out of there just in time, but everyone else who was still in the Resistance meeting was put to death. That is the way that the Zeraphim deal with people who defy them. I fear for my wife and my daughter. I fear for them greatly. I have not been there in three weeks, and I am afraid that the Zeraphim have killed Jenny and Lisa as punishment for my disappearance."

"We will free them for you," Colwyn vowed sounding a bit more certain than he felt. He still had a great many questions about this situation, and there were things that bothered him about the innkeeper's story, but now was not the time for those concerns to be known. Now was the time for comforting the innkeeper. He looked over at Alana. "Isn't that right, my love?"

"Right," Alana nodded, sensing what Colwyn was trying to do. She reached over and placed her hand on Marcus's shoulder. "We will leave just as soon as the others are ready to go, probably first thing in the morning. We will take the dragon to get there, so it will take us far less time to travel to Willowdale than it took for you to get here. You will stay here and recover from your injuries. We will bring your family here and reunite them with you just as soon as we can free them. You have my word on it, Marcus."

"Thank you, Blademaster," the innkeeper smiled at her. It was the first genuine smile that she had seen on him since he had first arrived in Ravendale. She knew that, no matter what it took, she had to do her best to keep that vow or else he would never be able to smile again. "The people of Valendale will never forget what you are going to do for them."

There was a knock on the door, and Albert made his way into the room, carrying another tray full of food. He smiled at Marcus as he set the tray down. When he gathered up the empty tray, Albert smiled in appreciation of how the injured man had eaten everything that had been sent up for him. He was happy that Marcus had, apparently, enjoyed the meal thoroughly. Although he would not admit as much to Alana, it did the old innkeeper's heart proud to know that he was able to help Marcus even this little bit.

"I see that you have cleaned your plate," Albert chuckled softly. "I brought more up for you just in case."

"Thank you, Master Albert," Marcus smiled. "But I am afraid that I might not be able to do the second tray of food justice right now. Dare I say that the food is better than even the food at my own inn?"

"The next time I am in Valendale, you will have to cook for me so that I know that you are not making an idle compliment to me," Albert laughed. But his laughter faded quickly though, and he turned to Alana and Colwyn. "There is a man that is sitting down in my tap room. He said that he is looking for the two of you. He said that he needs to speak with the two of you about your journey to Willowdale. He says his name is Isaiah. Do you wish to speak with him or should I send him away?"

Alana and Colwyn looked at each other. Alana knew that the sage appearing like this was no coincidence. The fact that he was here right after Marcus had told her the story of what happened in Valendale upset her. She frowned over at Albert and finally nodded.

"Tell him that we will be down momentarily to talk to him," Alana said quietly.

"Very well," Albert nodded. He took the empty tray and headed out of the room

"Now, what do you suppose that this is all about?" Colwyn asked, his eyebrows knitted in confusion and frustration. "It surely can't be a coincidence that he's here right now. What do you suppose he wants, Alana?"

"I don't know," Alana shrugged as she stood and made her way to the door. "But it is a good bet that the sage is bringing us more trouble. It seems like the sage always brings trouble."

With that, she stormed out of the room, the ranger in her wake.

Willowdale

Chapter V
Isaiah Consulted

Lana stormed into the tap room from upstairs, Colwyn following in her wake. They saw the sage, acting as if he did not have a care in the world, tucking into a full meal prepared by Albert and Gwen. He had his eyes closed and was chewing thoughtfully on a piece of potato. His eyes snapped open, though, when he heard them arrive in the tap room.

"It is often too long between visits to Ravendale. I tend to forget how good Albert's cooking is during the long stretches of time when I haven't been to the Lucky Minotaur," Isaiah said softly as he motioned for the two of them to come over to the table he was at. "Have you ever had his chocolate pies?"

"I don't believe you," Alana seethed, her green eyes blazing in unrestrained fury. "We just listened to a friend on what could be his deathbed tell us what happened in Valendale, and we find you here tucking into a full meal like nothing happened."

"I am all too aware of what has happened in Valendale, Blademaster," Isaiah's eyes flashed with a powerful anger of his own. "I do not need to be lectured by you about it. I am here to give you the information that you need in order to succeed in saving the people of Valendale."

"I don't want the help of a coward," Alana sneered. She turned to go. "Finish your meal. It's hard earned. Then go. And don't come back."

"Stay," Isaiah commanded. Alana stopped and turned to look at him with a raised eyebrow. She wasn't sure why she stayed, nor why she heard him out. What he had done was beyond her comprehension. "I will not sit here and be condescended to. You don't know what it was like for the people of Valendale."

"And yet you chose to run away rather than to stay and try to help them, sage," Alana shot back through clenched teeth. Her hands clenched into fists by her side, the knuckles turning white. "I was right in calling you a coward. You chose to save your own sorry hide rather than risk it to save those people."

"I had a sacred trust placed upon me. Lord Taelin bade me guide you to your destiny," Isaiah said quietly. A single tear rolled down his cheek. "You have no idea how much it broke my heart to choose that duty over the lives of the people of Valendale."

"Spare me," Alana crossed her arms. She was one wrong answer away from bolting. "There must have been a way to fulfill your duty to Lord Taelin and still be able to save the citizens of Valendale. You chose to take the easy road."

"Oh, child, I took the hardest road of all. But you will believe what you will," Isaiah shrugged. He took a last bite of potato and leaned back in his chair. "I am here to help you now to save them. I can and will give you the guidance you need through prophecy to help them. But know this. That is all I can do. I am forbidden to act directly with my magic to help them."

"Forbidden by whom?" Alana asked softly. She turned away and started to head to the door. She had heard enough.

"Forbidden by Lord Torval, one of the gods of magic," Isaiah said quietly. There was a note of frustration in his voice. It was enough to bring Alana up short. "It is the price of the magic of a sage. We are not allowed to influence events. We can only watch them and give what little help we are allowed to give to the people who can affect a change in situations. It will be the same with your friend William if he chooses to take up the mantle of a sage." He turned away from her. "As it is, I did influence events too much in Valendale. There will be a price for me to pay for my attempt to influence events. It will be a steep price indeed."

"If you are forbidden to act directly, then tell me what I need to know to save the people of Valendale," Alana turned back and fixed her glare on the sage. "Make up for your act of cowardice now."

"I can only help you so much, Blademaster," the sage sighed softly. "I am afraid that this is the only help I can provide to you at the moment. There are two bits of prophecy that I have uncovered that I believe you must hear. I do not know how or even if they will help you as you attempt to rescue the people of Valendale, but I give you these two prophecies in the hope that they will in some way help you."

"I don't like prophecies, sage," Alana growled and started towards the door once more. "They're nothing more than riddles that cause more trouble than they're worth."

"And you are correct about that, Blademaster," Isaiah bowed slightly. "Normally, I would not even bother to share these prophecies with you for that exact reason. The only reason that I am telling these to you now is that they apply to you directly. The first applies to your mission to Willowdale. The other is a warning of things to come."

"Very well, give me your prophecies," Alana turned back to face him one final time. She rolled her eyes at the melodramatic manner of the sage. But she was prepared to listen.

"The prophecy that applies to your mission to Willowdale," the sage intoned in a deep voice. "When the one born of the light goes to the twice dead city, she shall fall to the darkness as one of her own will betray her. Only the slim blade of the Second Law of the Blades will save her."

"I doubt one of mine will betray me, sage," Alana looked over at Colwyn quickly and then turned back to Isaiah. "I trust them implicitly."

"Nevertheless, it is true that you will be betrayed," Isaiah shrugged noncommittally. "I have told you the prophecy true. Your choosing to ignore the truth as I have provided it to you will not change that from coming to pass."

"So you say," Alana looked away. There was a pained look on her face as she contemplated the possibility of betrayal. "I've heard about enough from you, sage."

"I've one more prophecy that you must hear, Blademaster," the sage admonished. His tone snapped her gaze back to him. "Hear me and heed me for this too shall come to pass. When the twice dead city falls empty a third time, the storm clouds will gather and sabres will rattle in their scabbards. The blight of war shall be upon the land and only the one born of the light can lead the charge against the darkness."

"War," Alana said quietly, closing her eyes. She knew that war would be hard on the whole world. It would shake all of Calthea to its very core. "Is the war avoidable?"

"No," Isaiah shook his head sadly. "No matter how much I might wish it otherwise, events have taken place that make this prophecy impossible to avoid. I am sorry, Blademaster. The world of Calthea is headed into a war. And you must lead the forces of light if we are to have a chance."

The Blademaster looked at her husband and saw that the pain she felt was mirrored on his face. She knew that he was thinking about the sage's first prophecy, but it was the second one that Alana felt more pain over. She knew that they would all long for an ending to the war.

"Get out," Alana said quietly after a few moments. "I will do what must be done, rest assured of that, sage." She turned away from him and started to storm to the door. She stopped at the door and held onto the door's frame.

"But do not ever come to me again. You can be of no further help to me."

"I am sorry that you feel that way, Blademaster. I have only tried to help you," Isaiah bowed. He stood and started for the door himself. "I am sorry that my help is unwelcome. Should you change your mind, you can find me at my home in Valendale."

"We won't need your help, sage," Alana said quietly as she looked over her shoulder at him. "All you bring is trouble. You bring no help."

With that, Alana stormed out of the tap room, Colwyn at her heels. Once they were out of earshot of the sage, Alana whirled to face Colwyn. She fought to control the anger she was feeling. Anger would help none of them.

"Go find the mage and the halfling," she told him in a voice barely above a whisper. "We need to prepare for a journey. We'll be leaving tomorrow."

"I'm sure William will be here on his own before I even start to look for him. He has that way about him," Colwyn nodded once. "But I'll go find the halfling."

"You wanted to see me, Alana?" William asked as he came up to the door of the Lucky Minotaur. As Colwyn had suggested, William had appeared as if he knew that Alana had asked for him already. "Are we going somewhere?"

"We're leaving on a journey in the morning, William," Alana placed her hand on his arm. "Get your gear ready. We'll be leaving after breakfast. I'm not about to go on this journey without one of Albert's goodbye breakfasts."

"I'll let Albert know we're leaving in the morning on my way to get some sleep then," William nodded. "See you in the morning, Alana."

"I'll go find the halfling and meet you at the house, Alana," Colwyn smiled at her. As they always did, his smile calmed her and centered her in the armor that was his love for her. She knew not what she would do without that love. He leaned in and kissed her. "Don't kill the sage while I'm gone?"

"Tempting," Alana laughed. "Sorely tempting, but I won't kill the sage."

Willowdale

She watched the man she loved walk away from the Lucky Minotaur and chuckled softly to herself as she turned and headed away from the inn herself heading to the house that Colwyn had built for the two of them.

When she arrived at their house, there was an acolyte of Taelin waiting for her. Alana passed by the young woman, pretending that the acolyte was not even there, and walked into the house. She pulled off her boots and set them next to the door. The acolyte followed her inside the house but said nothing, seemingly knowing that Alana would not talk to her until she was ready.

Alana thought the acolyte showed far more promise than the High Priestess of Taelin did.

Alana poured herself a glass of kava juice and sat down at the round dinner table that Colwyn had made for them. She looked at the acolyte and motioned for her to sit. The acolyte tentatively sat in the chair across from Alana. The acolyte looked to be a little uncomfortable to be in the Blademaster's house.

"What can I do for you, Acolyte...?" Alana asked softly, trying very hard to not scare the poor acolyte any more than she already had.

"I am Acolyte Deera Jana, Blademaster," the acolyte said, her voice quavering. "I have come with an important message from the High Priestess of Taelin, who bids you come speak with her. She has a mission for you and your companions. She wishes for you to come speak with her immediately. It is a matter of some urgency."

"I cannot," Alana said simply. "Tell your mistress that we will be by to see her by and by, but we will not be accepting any mission from the Temple of the White at this time."

"My lady, the High Priestess will not be pleased to hear these words," the acolyte gasped. The color drained from the young woman's face. "She told me not to come back without you."

"I have just had a very disturbing encounter with the sage Isaiah Talon," Alana stood, her voice rising slightly. Her fists clenched at her sides. She took two deep breaths and closed her eyes. When she opened them again, she released the tension in her fists and locked her fiery gaze on the acolyte. When Alana spoke, she spoke with the ringing voice of authority that she seldom used, but knew was an innate part of her abilities as a Blademaster. "Return to the High Priestess of Taelin, Acolyte Deera Jana. Remind her that Lord Taelin and Lady Laeyra created the Blademaster to serve all of the people of Calthea, not just the High Priestess of Taelin. She is to provide to my Protector and I the assistance that I require of her, not the other way around. If she has a problem with what I have said, she can come see me herself. Otherwise, my Protector and I will be by to see her in the morning to discuss what we need from the Temple of the White."

"I will tell her your words, Blademaster," the acolyte bowed and hurried out of the house.

She almost bumped into Colwyn coming into the house. Colwyn, ever the gentleman, stepped aside so that the young acolyte could leave.

"What was that about?" Colwyn raised an eyebrow, clear amusement on his face. He dropped the two large bags of provisions he had brought in by the door and took her in his arms.

"The High Priestess of Taelin has requested our presence," Alana leaned into his chest. "I politely declined. I am afraid that this has just been one of those days."

"You used the voice didn't you?" Colwyn stroked her hair gently and lovingly. "That's the only way I could see that acolyte being as scared as she was."

"She wouldn't leave," Alana shrugged in his arms. "Did you find the halfling? Is she settled in so that she won't cause any trouble between now and when we leave in the morning?"

"Yes, I got her settled in. She'll meet us in the tap room for breakfast in the morning," Colwyn continued stroking her hair. She tightened her arms around him in response to his touch. "William will check on her tonight to keep her out of trouble. On my way out, I ran into Albert. He gave me these sacks of provisions to start us off. He'll have the rest ready in the morning. He'll also have our usual breakfast."

"Of course," Alana laughed. It was good to laugh. She knew, though, that there were going to be little to laugh about in the coming weeks. The moment passed quickly and her tone turned serious. "We need to go to the Temple of the White first thing in the morning, Colwyn. We need to have a new priest assigned to us. And I suspect that Miss High Priestess Naomi Mastairs is going to give us trouble."

"When does she not?" Colwyn asked with a little groan. "She dislikes both of us. She believes that the day you became a Blademaster was a dark one. The less said about what she thinks of me, the better."

The two of them laughed and settled down to have something to eat. It would be an early night for both of them. Alana intended to be well rested before going to battle with the High Priestess of Taelin. It was a battle that neither of them was all that eager to take on.

Chapter VI
The Long Journey

Zana knew she could no longer put off this confrontation. It was one that neither she nor Colwyn had been looking forward to. She had asked Colwyn to meet her at the Temple of the White after checking on William and Meryn, and he had made it to the Temple before she had. It was necessary for them to secure a priest to travel with them. While Colwyn had not gotten along with Balaam during their journey together, he felt more comfortable knowing that there was a priest along to heal the party. This new High Priestess of Taelin, though, was difficult to deal with. Neither of them liked nor trusted Naomi Mastairs. They did not understand how she could have become Taelin's High Priestess. They would have preferred anyone else in the position.

Colwyn was waiting for her when she finally got to the Temple of the White. He was dressed as if he was expecting trouble, wearing the clothes he would normally wear for a journey. He was wearing his elven chain mail that the High

Priestess of the Blades had given him right before their wedding. He had a forest green shirt and breeches pulled over the mail, and he had a forest green hood pulled up over his head. The bastard sword his father had given him was in its scabbard on his back. His bow was slung over his shoulder, and his special quiver hung on his belt so he could pull arrows out easily.

He was dressed for battle.

The significance of the outfit he wore for the confrontation with Naomi Mastairs was not lost on Alana and she smiled broadly. She, too, had dressed for the occasion in her Blademaster armor with her twin longswords strapped to her back. It was a new configuration for her swords. During their down time, she had been experimenting with new ways to wear her longswords, and she found she liked having them crossed against her back. She found them easier and quicker to draw this way. Her long auburn hair had been tied back with a black velvet band Colwyn had given her a year before. She had always loved how it felt to have that velvet in her hair.

"Clearly, we were thinking the same thing," Colwyn smiled when he saw her. "This will indeed be a battle."

"It is always a battle with that woman," Alana smiled back. "She will rue the day when she thought she could control me."

"Lord Taelin has trouble controlling you. Why should this woman think it would be easy?" Colwyn laughed heartily. "Not that I would have it any other way, mind you!"

"Shall we go slay the dragon, my love?" Alana said, a twinkle in her eye.

Colwyn kissed her gently on the cheek. He went up and pulled the door open for her. He motioned for Alana to lead the way into the temple. Alana smiled at his gallantry and strode purposefully before Colwyn into the Temple of the White. Before he entered the temple, Colwyn pulled his hood back off his head in an offer of respect to the god whose temple they were entering.

Acolytes and priests ran around the great hall of the temple. No one afforded the two of them more than a passing glance. It appeared that it was a busy morning at the temple. The two looked at each other and Colwyn could see the amusement dancing in the Blademaster's eyes, and he had an inkling of what she was about to do even before she turned back to the hustle and bustle in the great hall.

"I am the Blademaster, Alana Steeldrake," her voice boomed with the authority of her office. As Colwyn had expected it would, all motion in the great hall stopped. Everyone in the room turned to look at her. She waited until she was sure she had every single person's attention before she continued. "I have come on urgent business of our Lord Taelin. I would speak to High Priestess Naomi Mastairs immediately."

Colwyn held himself in check, but he almost broke into applause at her little speech. He knew that when her words were relayed to the High Priestess, the woman would be angered. The dislike they had for Naomi Mastairs was mutual. After meeting this new High Priestess for the first time, Alana had asked Taelin how Naomi could have risen to the position. Taelin had just shrugged with a little smile and said something about keeping the Blademaster humble. Colwyn was starting to understand what Taelin had meant.

"Yes, Blademaster Alana," one of the priests bowed low. "I will go get the High Priestess immediately."

The priest almost fell over himself in his haste to exit the great hall. Alana chuckled at the sight. Colwyn was not quite so amused as she was.

"I think it's possible that you might have overdone it slightly, Alana," Colwyn said softly.

"You can't overdo something like that," Alana shrugged. She crossed her arms as she watched where the priest had left the hall. "Especially not considering what Marcus told us. You can only show strength. Besides, that was fun."

"I don't think Naomi will think it was fun," Colwyn snorted.

"I have to show strength and determination in my dealings with her," Alana scowled deeply. She let her distaste for the woman show. "She'll walk all over us if I don't."

"She thinks she owns you because she's Lord Taelin's High Priestess, you know," Colwyn pointed out. He turned to look at her. "She's not going to like your attitude."

"She can kiss my right big toe for all I care. I'm sure she'll be angry, but she will assign a new priest to us," Alana turned and fixed her glare on her husband. "I'm not going to Willowdale without one."

High Priestess Naomi Mastairs was not a happy person. When she was named to the post of High Priestess after Balaam Otakis was killed, she wasn't aware that she would have to deal with so many strong willed personalities. Worst of all, though, was that incredibly irreverent woman that Taelin had made a Blademaster along with the noble fool that was her Protector. She would have rathered just about anyone named to the position of Blademaster other than Alana Steeldrake.

What made her angrier than anything else about the Blademaster was that Alana would not submit to her will. Naomi felt that, as the High Priestess of Taelin, she should be able to keep the Blademaster under her control. This Blademaster, though, was strong willed and did things her own way. It angered Naomi greatly. The day before, she had sent a missive to the Blademaster summoning her for an assignment. The messenger had come back with a message that Alana had refused to come to the temple. There was no explanation, just a flat denial. All that the acolyte would say was that the Blademaster had demanded the acolyte to inform Naomi that she would be to the temple "by and by" to discuss something she required from the Temple of the White.

Naomi had no intention of giving the blasted woman anything she wanted.

Naomi draped herself in her robes of office and knelt before the small altar in her private sanctuary. She lit a candle on either side of the altar and closed her eyes.

"Lord Taelin, please hear my prayer," she said softly. "I come to you in supplication to ask you to for some measure of control over your Blademaster. She is far too strong willed and not compliant to your will. She refuses to undertake missions for the Temple of the White, believing she knows best as to what she should be doing."

"Maybe she does," a strong masculine voice called from behind Naomi. "Maybe, just maybe, it's you that doesn't understand what it is the Blademasters are for. I know full well that this Blademaster is following a course of her own making. You have missed the entire point all these years, my High Priestess. Maybe, you should spend some time studying the Law of the Blades before you chastise my Blademaster for fulfilling her purpose."

"My Lord Taelin," Naomi bowed low before her god. "You honor me with your presence."

"And you dishonor me with your service, Naomi Mastairs," the Lightbringer said angrily. "You dare try to force my Blademaster to turn away from her rightful mission for your own purposes? You disgrace your rank and my name. I should remove you from the High Priesthood now. But I won't. I will give you one further chance to serve me. If you continue to displease me, you will find yourself put out from the Temple of the White."

"But, Lord Taelin..." she began, pleading with her god.

"The Blademaster is here with her Protector," Taelin advised her. "A young priest is on his way here to bring you to them now. You will go to them. You will provide them with exactly what they ask for. And then you will spend time in solitude in your sanctuary studying the Law of the Blades until you understand. Yes?"

"It shall be as you say, my Lord Taelin," Naomi bowed low.

"See that it is," Taelin nodded. "I will be watching you. Do not displease me again, and do not go against me when it comes to Alana Steeldrake again."

The Lightbringer did not wait to see how his High Priestess would react. He simply faded into a puff of smoke, disappearing completely. Naomi had no doubt that he was still watching however. She knew that he always would be.

She fell to her knees at the altar and wept bitterly. Once more, the Blademaster had caused her disgrace. She vowed that she would one day have the final word as to how the Blademasters were to be used. She did not know how it would happen, but she looked forward to the day.

Naomi was still on her knees weeping when someone knocked on her door. She assumed that it was the young priest that Lord Taelin said would be coming. After taking a moment to compose herself and wipe the tears from her eyes, Naomi smoothed out her robes and stood.

"Enter," she demanded. She turned towards the door as the young priest entered. "What do you want?"

"Forgive my intrusion, High Priestess," the young man bowed low in front of her. "I was sent to get you. The Blademaster and her Protector are here. They are demanding to speak with you."

"Tell them I will be there in a moment," Naomi closed her eyes. "Do not let them be alone anywhere in the Temple while they wait for me."

"But, High Priestess..." the priest began.

"Do not question my orders," the High Priestess thundered, interrupting the young man. "The Blademaster and her Protector are not to be left alone anywhere in the Temple of the White."

"It will be as you say," the priest bowed low. He stood and left the sanctuary in a hurry.

Naomi sighed deeply as she readied herself for the coming confrontation. She knew that it would be unpleasant dealing with this arrogant woman. She was determined that it would be unpleasant for the Blademaster as well.

They were still standing where the priest had left them when he returned to the great hall. Alana and Colwyn were quietly talking about something, although the priest could not make out what they were discussing from where he had entered the hall. He did not wish to intrude on them, so he stopped not far from the doorway and waited for the Blademaster to notice him. Unlike the High Priestess, he had a great deal of respect for the Blademaster. He knew that Alana and Colwyn had a higher purpose than simple missions for the Temple of the White.

He wished the High Priestess could be convinced of this as well.

The young priest waited until they noticed him and motioned him over before making his way over to them. As he walked over, he could hear the end of the conversation. He caught the word Willowdale, but that was all he was able to make out. He was familiar with the twice dead city because of his studies, but he did not know why the Blademaster was discussing it. It did not bode well, though. There were prophecies centered around the twice dead city. He did not know what those prophecies meant, but some of the prophecies he'd read that mentioned Willowdale or, as it was most often referred to in the prophecies, the twice dead city, truly scared him. He knew that dark times were ahead. Everyone in the Temple of the White knew that Thraal had been freed from his prison in Limbo and that he would probably resume his attempts to conquer all of Calthea.

Some of the prophecies he read indicated such an attempt might be launched soon.

"Is the High Priestess on her way?" Alana asked softly. She did not want to use the voice of command on the young priest a second time. "We are in a bit of a hurry today."

"The High Priestess will be with you shortly," the priest bowed slightly at the waist. "I'm afraid the High Priestess does not have as high an opinion of the Blademasters as others in the Temple of the White do."

"What is your name, young priest?" Colwyn smiled at the young man. "You seem to have a good head on your shoulders."

"I am Martin Faolin," the priest could not meet Colwyn's eyes. "It has been less than a year since I ascended to the title of priest from acolyte."

"Martin, there is no need to fear Colwyn or myself," Alana smiled at the young priest. She had liked the young man immediately. There was something true and honest about the priest that she respected. "We serve Lord Taelin just as you do."

"But you are a Blademaster, Lady Alana," Martin protested. "You are Lord Taelin's chosen."

"I'm just a woman," Alana laughed heartily. "I am a woman who was blessed with the ability to find and hold onto true love. But I'm just a woman, nonetheless."

"If you say so, Blademaster Alana," Martin said, his head still bowed. He just could not meet her eyes.

"Martin, if you are going to go with us, and I suspect you will be, you had best learn to look up," Alana smiled. She placed her finger under his chin and lifted it so he was looking in her eyes. "I can't have a priest with us that can only look at his own shoes. He will be forever walking into things. How can such a man help us if he keeps knocking himself out by hitting his head on something he would have seen had he only been watching where he was going?"

"I go with the Blademaster?" Martin raised both eyebrows in surprise. "What makes you think that the High Priestess would even allow me to go?"

"Just a hunch," Alana smiled. "You'll find that my hunches are usually fairly accurate."

The three of them stood chatting about Taelin's wisdom. Slowly, the young priest began to loosen up around the Blademaster and her Protector. He started to slowly open up and talk about himself. Alana learned about his training and about his childhood. She was saddened to learn of how he had been orphaned and raised by the church. By the time the High Priestess had arrived in the great hall, Alana had learned enough about the young man to be comfortable with him were he to join them on their journey. Colwyn had remained silent during most of the conversation, and Alana could tell that he had some reservations about the young man's inexperience.

The High Priestess of Taelin came regally swooping into the great hall, her robes fluttering behind her. She stopped to talk to various acolytes and priests, the High Priestess looking after her flock. The message to Alana and Colwyn was clear to them. *I am the High Priestess and this is my temple. I will see you when it is convenient for me. I will not put off the business of this temple just because you have requested to see me.* Alana was amused by the display, but she could tell that Colwyn was getting angry.

She touched Colwyn on the arm to calm him. He looked at her and bowed his head slightly in response. She smiled at him telling him that they had to play the High Priestess's game for now.

Eventually, the High Priestess made her way over to where Alana and Colwyn were standing. The woman's regal bearing did not falter as she walked over to them. Her posture was one of defiance. Alana knew that Naomi had resented the summons, but there had been no time to make an appointment. She supposed that they should have made the request for a priest of Taelin to accompany them before now, but they had thought there would have been a little more time to prepare before they embarked on another journey.

"You have asked for an audience with the High Priestess of Taelin?" Naomi said haughtily as she stopped before them. Colwyn stifled a smile at the use of the word asked. Alana never asked when she could help it. "It is quite bold of you to ask for an audience with me after refusing to come see me when I sent for you."

"We cannot accept a mission from the Temple of the White at this time," Alana said softly. She had to fight the urge to use the voice of command on the pompous woman. She knew that it would not work on Taelin's High Priestess even were she to use it. "We have recently been contacted for help, and we have decided to grant that help."

"Without consulting the Temple of the White first?" Naomi raised one delicately manicured eyebrow.

"I did not realize that we needed permission of the Temple of the White to provide aid and succor to an oppressed people," Colwyn fumed. He turned to Alana. "This is a waste of time, Alana. This woman won't help us. We need to finish getting ready so we can be on our way."

"Peace, Colwyn," she smiled at him. She turned to face the High Priestess. "And we will be going. Just as soon as the High Priestess assigns us a priest to go with us."

"I cannot," the High Priestess shook her head. "We have no experienced priests that we can send on a prolonged journey with you. Were you to accept the mission I have for you, I am sure something could be arranged. But there is simply no one to send."

"We can't go into Willowdale without a priest, Alana," Colwyn grunted. He turned to leave. He stopped when Alana put a hand on his arm. "It's already feeling like it might be too much for us even if we had one."

"Willowdale?" Naomi's eyes flew open wide. "You cannot go to Willowdale. I forbid it."

Alana had had enough. She held up her hand and stopped the High Priestess from speaking. "I will say this one time, Naomi Mastairs," the Blademaster said in a soft voice, letting every ounce of authority she possessed ring through with each word. "There is a young man at the Lucky Minotaur who asked for my help. He risked everything he cared about, his wife and his daughter, to find me and bring me to Willowdale. Not for himself but for all the people of Valendale who have been taken to that gods forsaken city. I promised him that I would do what I can to save them. You will send a healer to see him. And you will send a priest to go with us or I will see you strung up by your heels and removed from your position as the High Priestess of our Lord Taelin. I doubt Lord Taelin would look kindly upon your turning your back on an entire people."

The High Priestess hung her head, chastised greatly by the Blademaster's words. She sighed and nodded.

"I will send a healer to visit this man who risked so much," she said finally. "As I said, I have no one experienced that I can send with you. But you can take Martin Faolin. He is not very experienced, but I believe he will serve you well. I wish him out from this Temple of the White anyway. Maybe time with you will straighten him out a little."

The High Priestess of Taelin stalked out of the great hall, not looking at anyone as she left. Alana watched as the woman kept clenching and unclenching her fists as she stormed out.

"I do not think we've heard the end of this, Alana," Colwyn said softly.

"I think you might be right, Col," Alana sighed. She turned to Martin. "Martin, go get what you need for the journey. We have supplies for you already. Just get whatever personal items you need. Meet us at the Lucky Minotaur in an hour. It has become tradition for us that we have a large breakfast on the morning we leave on a new journey. As you are one of our companions now, you should be a part of that meal."

"I will be there, my lady," Martin bowed low and headed off to his dormitory room.

"Gods above, he's so young," Colwyn grumbled. "Are you sure about this, Alana?"

"He will do fine, Colwyn," Alana smiled at him. "I don't know what it is about young Martin Faolin, but I see something in the young man. We could have received worse. He will do just fine."

"I hope you're right, my love," Colwyn shrugged. "I'll meet you at the Lucky Minotaur. I need to pick something up at the house."

Alana arrived at the tap room while Albert was still preparing their traditional send off feast. Colwyn was not far behind her, carrying a sheathed dagger in his hand. Gwendolyn White was setting the table that had been readied for them. Alana noted that there were several small sacks of provisions waiting for them there at the table. She smiled when she saw them. Once again, Albert had provided for all their needs.

Gwen smiled when she saw them and raced over. She hugged Colwyn and then Alana in turn. She grabbed their hands and dragged them over to the table.

"Albert has gotten everything together for you," she said. "He may have gone a little overboard. I think he takes it personally what happened to that poor innkeeper's family. Albert will do anything he can to help them."

"Albert always did have a kind heart," Colwyn laughed heartily. "It's one of the reasons we keep coming back here."

"That and the chocolate pie," Alana piped up. "Still the best chocolate pies in the entirety of the Southern Dales."

"Alana would know," Colwyn quipped. "She's tried practically every single one." He ducked as Alana took a half hearted swing at him. "What? It's true!"

"Albert made sure you had some of his chocolate pie in your provisions, Alana," Gwen winked. "William and Meryn will be along momentarily."

Alana and Colwyn went through the provisions making sure everything they needed was in the sacks. Checking the provisions was merely a formality, because they knew that Albert would have been thorough in putting the sacks of provisions together. They packed the sacks away in the companions' packs which were also already there. A brand new pack and bedroll had been added to the normal collection of stuff. Somehow Alana was not surprised that Albert had known to provide them for the new priest. Colwyn placed the dagger he had brought on the priest's pack.

They had just finished packing their provisions when the door to the tap room opened. They looked up in surprise when they heard the jangle and clanging of full plate armor. Two armor clad knights had entered the tap room and were headed towards the Blademaster and her Protector. Alana looked at Colwyn with a confused expression on her face. Colwyn had paled. He knew the insignia on the tabards that the knights were wearing meant that these knights were part of the personal ring of protection around the King himself.

Colwyn did not understand what the King might have wanted with Alana, but he had a feeling that they were about to find out.

The two knights came up to Alana and Colwyn and, as one, dropped to one knee. It was a display made far more impressive considering that the two knights were wearing full plate mail and that kneeling as they were was not easy wearing such armor.

"The King sends his deepest regards to Blademaster Alana Steeldrake and Protector Colwyn Starseeker," the knight on the left said after removing his helmet. The knight had dark brown hair and a pair of long flowing bars to his moustache. He had hazel eyes and held Alana's gaze unwavering. "He bids you to come see him before you leave on your journey. We are here to act as escort for you to His Highness."

Alana and Colwyn looked at each other. Colwyn hefted his bow off his shoulder and hooked it on his chair. He unhooked the scabbard strapped across his back and left it along with the quiver on his chair at the table. Alana, surprised at his actions, followed suit and laid both of her scabbarded swords on her own chair. Her various knives appeared and were laid on the chair as well. Gwen came by and assured them that their weapons would be there and safe when they got back.

"We obey His Highness's request and follow, Sir Knight," Colwyn said softly. "Lead us on to the palace, please."

The knights stood and nodded. The knight who had removed his helm put it back on his head before they turned and led the way out of the tap room.

"Why did we leave our weapons behind?" Alana asked Colwyn quietly.

"One does not appear before his King with weapons," Colwyn shrugged. "It isn't proper and would be considered a threat to him. It would not do to threaten the King."

"You make a good point," Alana nodded sagely. "Let's go see the King."

Colwyn led the way following the knights out of the tap room.

Roland Stonehammer had been the King of the Southern Dales ever since his father, Antonius, had passed into his walk with Taelin twenty years before. King Roland was a well loved King and he was known not to abuse his power. He was considered as fair ruler as his father had been before him. Like many of the people of the Southern Dales, King Roland had grown up with stories of the Blademasters. He had not thought that he would actually meet one, as no one believed the Blademasters would be reborn. And yet, here was a Blademaster within his very own capitol city.

Willowdale

He had waited for the Blademaster to pay her respects to him, and he was sure that she would have eventually done so. The situation with the people of Valendale had prompted him to seek her out rather than wait for her to come to him. He knew about the innkeeper's arrival at the Lucky Minotaur, and he knew that the Blademaster and her companions were about to set out on a journey to attempt to rescue the people of Valendale.

He wanted to see her before she left.

He wanted to offer her his every assistance. There was not much that he could offer her that would help her, but he had to make the offer. If the rumors his advisors had passed on to him were true, the Southern Dales were surely in need of the Blademaster and her companions.

King Roland waited for the Blademaster and her Protector in his private library in the palace in Ravendale. He wore a simple pair of black breeches, soft black leather boots and a white tunic laced up to just below his neck. He did not wear his royal cape or his crown. He was a ruggedly handsome man, standing six and a half feet tall with broad strong shoulders and a thick barrel chest. He had long flowing brown hair and a full beard. A few slight wisps of grey had begun to creep into the corners of his moustache and at his temples, but they looked distinguished on him. His eyes were a dark and piercing brown color. He looked to be a kindly man, and he knew that most people thought him such. He smiled easily and often, something that made him very popular with his subjects.

He was looking over a map of the Southern Dales, the map divided into the individual territories controlled by the First Lords. He was staring at the northeast corner of the map which was a part of the Southern Dales that lay fallow and uninhabited save for the lowlifes and cutthroats that had made that area their home. It was what used to be the Willowdale Territory. He had long wanted to send troops into that territory to tame it and make it once more a livable and viable area. He had not been able to convince the First Lords to commit troops to the cause, however.

He was still studying the map when the two knights he had sent to bring him the Blademaster brought her and her Protector into the library to see him. He did not look up from the map but had noted their presence.

"That will be all," he said, his rich voice soft in the stillness of the library. "I do not believe that either the Blademaster or her Protector mean me any harm."

"Of course, my liege," one of the knights said. Both knights pressed their right fist against their hearts and turned on their heel, leaving Alana and Colwyn alone with the King.

King Roland stood up from where he was looking over the map and looked at the two of them, getting a feel for the couple. He had been surprised to learn that it was a Starseeker that had become the young woman's Protector. The Starseeker line was deep in the nobility and the king knew that the marriage would be trouble for the young man.

The King, of course, had no objections to the marriage, knowing, as he did, that it was a marriage blessed by the gods themselves. Who was he to break them apart if the gods put them together?

"Blademaster Alana Steeldrake," the king said softly. "Protector Colwyn Starseeker. It is good of the two of you to come."

Colwyn and Alana both sank to their knees in the presence of the king out of respect for his office.

"We serve the king," they said in unison.

King Roland laughed heartily and motioned for them to rise. "Of all the people that live in the Southern Dales, you two are the only two who do not, in fact, serve the King. Colwyn, how fares your father?"

"Lord Dargan is as healthy as always, my liege," Colwyn shrugged. "We don't talk very much. I'm afraid he doesn't like the choices I have made in my life. I dare say the choice of my wife is going to cause further problems between us."

"Yes, I am afraid you are likely right," the King nodded. "A pity. Alana Steeldrake, you are the first Blademaster in three hundred years."

"I am," Alana nodded. She turned to face Colwyn, a quizzical look on her face. She turned back to the King. "My liege, if I may ask, why are we here? We are headed out on a rather important errand of mercy."

"I am aware of the young innkeeper's request for help," the king said. He smiled as he walked over. He took the Blademaster's arms in his hands and stared deep into her eyes. "And I know that you two have felt honor bound to accept his plea. I would do nothing to change your minds on this. The people of Valendale are my responsibility. It does my heart good to know that you are going to go bring them home."

"But why are we here?" Alana asked. "I'm very confused by our presence here."

"It's very simple, my dear Blademaster," King Roland smiled broadly at her. He dropped to one knee and took her hand. "As the Kings did during the time of your predecessors, I pledge the support of the Southern Dales to the Blademaster Corps. May the light of the Blademasters guide us through the dark times that are to come."

Alana and Colwyn looked at each other. This was new to them. There was much that they still did not know about the Blademasters and every time something new came at them it caught them off guard. But to have the King of the realm kneel before them... this was completely unprecedented!

"Please do not kneel to me, my liege," Alana said, her voice barely above a whisper. "I've done nothing to deserve your allegiance."

"And yet you have it," the King said as he stood. "As time goes by, if you or Colwyn need anything, you have but to let me know. Colwyn, you remain heir to your father's title, correct?"

"Yes, my liege," Colwyn nodded, smiling wryly. "One day, hopefully many years from now, I will serve you as the First Lord of Arvendale. It is a day that I hope takes a good long time to arrive."

"Indeed," the King nodded. He scratched his chin and moved back over to the table and pulled out a fresh sheet of parchment. He pulled a quill and dipped it in ink. He began to write quickly, stopping periodically to dip the quill back in the ink. When he finished writing, he put the quill in the ink bottle and read over what he had written. Smiling, he pressed his signet ring into wax to forge his seal on the document and handed the letter to Colwyn. "When you see your father next, give him this letter. My seal is on it. It should help you."

Colwyn took the letter and read it.

First Lord Dargan Starseeker,

I, King Roland Stonehammer, have reviewed the matter of the marriage of Colwyn Starseeker, heir to the title of First Lord of Arvendale, and Alana Steeldrake, chosen by our Lord Taelin to be the first in a new line of Blademasters. I have found that this marriage is valid and binding.

This letter, signed by myself with my seal, shall serve as all the documentation required for this marriage to be permitted. No attempt to break this marriage apart will be tolerated by the throne.

The light of the Blademasters is one that is sorely needed in the dark times that are to come. All of the nobility must stand behind the Blademasters and their Protectors. They have been chosen for a reason. None of us can say what that reason is, but we must trust that Lord Taelin and Lady Laeyra are indeed wise in their decisions.

Signed by my own hand,
Roland Stonehammer
King of the Southern Dales

Colwyn folded the letter and gently put it in the inside pocket of his tunic. He bowed his head to the King and looked back at him, a tear rolling down his face.

"My liege, this means more to me than you could possibly know," Colwyn's voice cracked. "I do not know how to repay you for your kindness."

"You have but to do one thing to repay me, Sir Colwyn," the King smiled broadly. He placed his hand on Colwyn's arm. "Promise to always love and protect this woman. If the advisor and mages I have in my court are correct, the world is going to need her more than ever very soon."

"That is a promise I can easily make, my liege," Colwyn smiled back. He looked at Alana and the King could easily see the love they shared with each other. "I have never loved anyone as I have this woman. I truly doubt that any man has ever loved a woman as much as I love Alana."

"Then there is nothing more I could ask of you, Sir Colwyn," the King nodded. "I believe that Lord Taelin has chosen well for his new Blademaster. And I believe that she has chosen well for her Protector."

"Thank you, my liege," Alana smiled her special slight little smile that she reserved for Colwyn. "I am still new to everything that goes with being a Blademaster."

"You will do fine," the King laughed. "I wish that you two would come by and speak to me whenever you are in town. I would hear of your adventures during those visits. Dark times are coming. I need all of the information I can get if I am to lead the Southern Dales during those dark times."

"We have felt the darkness coming on for some time, my liege," Colwyn said softly. "Is there anything you can tell us about what is to come?"

"War," King Roland said softly, sadly. He sounded tired. "I have been studying the prophecies. I know that the sage gave you one of the core prophecies about the coming war. Unfortunately, if you are successful in your current task, it means that war will come and soon."

"*When the twice dead city falls empty a third time, the storm clouds will gather and sabres will rattle in their scabbards. The blight of war shall be upon the land and only the one born of the light can lead the charge against the darkness,*" Alana repeated the prophecy that Isaiah had given her. She did not mention the prophecy that said someone would betray her. "I will not leave the people of Valendale in the hell they are in just to avoid war."

"Nor would I ask you to do so," the King nodded. "You must prepare though. You must lead the forces of the light in the coming war. Or else all will be lost. I am sorry to put this on your shoulders, Alana Steeldrake. Know that if I could carry the weight myself, I would."

"I have broad shoulders," Alana smiled weakly. "And I do not have to carry the load alone, my liege. That is, as I have come to understand, one of the reasons that Lord Taelin in his wisdom forces the Blademasters to be married." She reached over to take Colwyn's hand. "That way we always have someone we can turn to in our times of need or when the burden becomes too much for one person to bear."

"Indeed. Lord Taelin is wise," the King smiled broadly. He turned back to his map and sat back down at the table. "I will not keep you from your farewell meal. Be safe, Blademaster Alana and Protector Colwyn. Return the people of Valendale to where they belong. Please. Save my subjects for me. And remember, if there is ever anything you need, you need only ask it of me."

It was a memorable breakfast. Albert had, as usual, outdone himself. The companions had eaten until they were close to bursting. Alana knew that it probably wasn't a good idea for them to eat so much before flying on Cobalt's back, but none of them could help themselves. The Blademaster simply hoped that no one would be sick during the flight. That could get spectacularly messy.

After they finished eating, Alana led the companions outside of the Lucky Minotaur and called for Cobalt. Albert and Gwen had come out to see them off.

"Albert, thanks again for getting everything we needed," Alana smiled at the older innkeeper.

"You are welcome, my dear," the old man smiled broadly. "You have made me very proud, you know."

"What do you mean?" Alana cocked her head slightly.

"It is a very rare person that will drop everything to go to another's aid, Alana," Albert explained. "You heard Marcus's story and immediately started planning how to go help him. There aren't many other people who would have. I am proud that you are that type of person. And I am honored to know you."

"You can thank us by taking good care of Marcus until we free his wife and daughter," Alana smiled broadly at Albert.

"I think that can be easily arranged," Albert smiled back. "He will be well taken care of when you send for him. I can promise you that."

"The High Priestess of Taelin will be sending a priest over to attend to his wounds," Alana said. "Give the priest anything he wants to eat or drink while he's here and put it on my tab. I shall repay every penny when we return from Willowdale."

"No you will not," Albert crossed his arms. "As far as I am concerned, anything the priest needs will be part of Marcus's food and lodging, and, thus, free."

Alana hugged the innkeeper. "You are a good man, Albert. I am honored to know you too."

Cobalt took that opportunity to gently land with the soft whisper of his wings. Alana walked over and rubbed the dragon on the side of his snout. Colwyn came over and stood next to her and scratched Cobalt on the bottom of his chin. The dragon rumbled contentedly.

"Go, Alana," Albert said softly. "Go save those people. And know that my prayers and thoughts go with you."

"Thank you, Albert," she smiled. She went over and kissed the old innkeeper on the cheek. Then she turned back to her companions. "OK. Everyone on the dragon."

Alana was the last one to climb up on Cobalt's back. She waved to Gwen and Albert as Cobalt launched himself into the air. The innkeeper and the barmaid watched as the dragon soared higher and higher into the sunlit sky. They kept watching until the dragon disappeared in the distance.

"I hope they'll be all right," Gwen said softly.

"They will," the old man smiled broadly. "It will be difficult, but they will persevere. Alana is a survivor. She'll be back. And she'll bring that young man's wife and daughter back with her. You'll see."

Alana and her companions flew on during the day, Cobalt's powerful wings guiding them forward. They were five hours into the flight when disaster struck. They had been flying steadily along and were making good time.

Alana figured that they would make it to Willowdale before the sun went down.

That is, they would have until they flew into the flock of thrynda birds.

It was a large flock of the birds that they flew into. Normally it would not have been a problem. Thrynda birds were generally harmless. However one of the birds managed to fly through the membrane of Cobalt's right wing.

The dragon screamed in agony and began to slowly circle for a landing. The landing was not the gentlest of landings, and all of the companions were jarred a bit in their seats.

"I am sorry, Blademaster Alana," the dragon hissed. "I cannot fly all of you with a rent in my wing."

"I can try to patch the rent," Martin offered. "I may not be the best as far as healing, but I will do what I can to at least speed the healing process for you, Cobalthaxillius."

"Do what you can, priest," the dragon nodded once. "I will be grateful for whatever aid you can provide."

Martin slid off the dragon and walked over to where the torn wing was laying on the ground. He gently laid his hands on the membrane and began to pray quietly. The membrane under his hands glowed softly. The tear in the membrane began to slowly close. It closed most of the way and the healing stopped. The young priest fell back into a sitting position and wiped his brow.

"I have done all I can, but he will still need time to heal," Martin panted. "There is only so much I could do."

"I will need at least a week to heal," Cobalt grunted. "But the priest sped the process up by several weeks. You did a good job, young Priest of Taelin."

"Thank you, noble dragon," the priest smiled weakly.

"All right," Alana said as she slid off the dragon. "We walk from here. We break for food and then start walking. Cobalt, how far do you think we are from Willowdale?"

"If you walk all day like you normally do, I think no more than a week."

"All right," Alana nodded. She rubbed the side of the dragon's snout. "You stay here and heal up. Join us when you can. We'll walk the rest of the way from here. If we absolutely need you, either Colwyn or I will summon you. We'll try not to, though."

"Thank you, Blademaster Alana." The dragon closed his eyes and laid his head on the ground.

The companions ate a quick meal of dried meat and trail biscuits. When they were ready, Alana led the way down the road towards Willowdale. They were in a hurry, so they did not stop until late that evening.

The companions had walked for most of the morning. The road they were on would lead them into Willowdale by the middle of the afternoon. The companions stopped on the side of the road for a meal break. Colwyn passed out strips of dried meat and hard rolls to each of the companions. It was standard travel fare, but by then all of the companions had become sick of the hard rolls. They knew, though, that since they were so easily portable, it was the best for them right now.

As they finished their meal and were packing back up to continue their journey, they heard a rustling in the trees nearby. William vanished within a cloak of invisibility that he cast around himself. The other companions came to a ready status with weapons drawn. They knew that they were near an enemy camp. Their alertness had been roused, and caution was easily exercised.

The rustling continued and suddenly a young silver haired woman appeared on the road. She was wearing a long white robe, much like William's. There was some odd writing stitched into the collar, cuffs and helm of the robe. Alana had never seen the like. The young woman's long silver hair was worn straight back over her shoulders. Her eyes were a deep unearthly sea blue under pencil thin silver eyebrows. Alana imagined that she could bewitch a man with those eyes. The woman looked sad, though, and Alana wished she could see what the woman looked like if she smiled a true beaming smile.

"Go back," the young silver haired woman said softly, pointing directly at Alana. "Go back the way you came!"

Part II
Willowdale

Chapter VII
Silvestra Knightwing

"Go back the way you came," the silver haired woman said a second time. "There is nothing for you in Willowdale. Turn back now while you still have a chance."

"We are here to help," Alana said softly. "My companions and I are here to bring the people of Valendale home."

"The people of Valendale are lost," the silver haired woman wailed softly. "Go back before you are too."

"Alana speaks the truth," William said as he dropped his cloak of invisibility. He stepped forward, making sure the young woman could see him clearly. "Hello, Silvestra."

"William? William Stonehands?" Silvestra looked at the mage with an odd expression. "Is that really you?"

"It would appear that fate has conspired against Eliazar's wishes to bring you once more into my life," the mage shrugged. "Yes, it's me. I have been travelling with the Blademaster for some time. We have come to free the villagers of Valendale."

"Blademaster," the woman dropped to her knee and bowed her head. No matter how many times Alana saw someone drop to their knees in front of her, it still made her uncomfortable. "Willowdale is lost. I fear that not even the power of a Blademaster will be enough to free the people here."

"I have to try," Alana smiled at Silvestra as she helped the other woman to her feet. "Who are you? It seems that William knows you."

"He should," Silvestra smiled. It was a true smile that transformed the young woman's face. "Come, I will take you somewhere safe and I will tell you my tale. At the very least, I'll tell you the parts of my tale that are mine to tell."

Silvestra started off down a poorly marked trail that led away from the city of Willowdale. William knew and trusted the woman and did not hesitate to follow her. Alana looked at Colwyn. The ranger shrugged and motioned for Alana to follow the mage. Colwyn ushered the priest and the halfling down the trail in front of him.

The companions followed Silvestra, carefully keeping on the path she walked on. The path slowly wound around one of the mountains that surrounded Willowdale. The path was a poor one, barely cleared. Colwyn did not think anyone had been up the path anytime recently. He doubted that anyone would be able to follow them up the path. He did not like to gamble Alana's life on such a guess, but there was no way to obscure the trail more than it already was.

When the companions reached a cave entrance about halfway up the mountain, the woman stopped. They'd been walking for about an hour and a half, and they were happy to stop. Silvestra sat down on a rock just outside the cavern's entrance. She was not quite winded, but it was clear that she wanted a break before going into the cave.

"There is something I must tell you before we go any further," she said quietly. "William knows what I am about to tell you already. This is not my true form. I have held this form for too long and need to transform to my natural form once we enter the cavern. I know that there will be questions for me. I would ask that you save your questions until after I've told my tale. I believe that most of your questions will be answered as I tell my story. I am afraid that my story is a sad one."

"If you are not a human like you appear, then what are you?" Colwyn asked.

"You will soon see, Protector," Silvestra smiled. Unlike her earlier smile, this one was tinged with sadness. "Follow me into the cavern. But keep near the entrance until I am done with my transformation."

The silver haired woman led the way into the cavern. At a word of magic from her, the torches along both sides of the cavern roared to life, brightening the cave immensely. It was a much larger cavern than it had first appeared to be from the outside. As the woman had requested of them, the companions stopped just inside of the cavern, while the silver haired woman walked all the way to the very center of the cavern.

The woman turned her back to the companions. They watched as she threw her head back and closed her eyes. Carefully, she stripped off her clothes. After another whispered word of magic, she started to grow in size. As she grew in size, her skin began to grow silver colored scales and her hair flowed together to become hard spines. Her face elongated into a long snout. Wings sprouted from her back and grew in long and graceful lines. A tail started to grow out from the junction of her lower back and her buttocks. As she grew in size, she leaned forward so she was on all fours.

It took just shy of five minutes for the woman to complete her transformation. With the exception of her eyes, which bore a striking resemblance to those of the woman that had walked into the cavern, the mighty silver dragon in front of them resembled nothing of the woman that had been there previously. Had they not witnessed the transformation, the companions, save for William, would not have believed that the dragon before them was the same creature as the woman known as Silvestra Knightwing.

William had known what to expect, of course, having known the silver dragon for years. He leaned against the wall of the cavern and watched the woman take her dragon form. He knew the others would be surprised at the transformation, but he did not care about seeing their reactions. The young mage's mind was in turmoil over what he was seeing. He pulled a small amulet from around his neck and looked at it. The ruby colored stone on the end of the chain had long since lost his light, which had caused him a lot of pain. And considering what he had just seen, he did not understand why the amulet was dark. He put the amulet back around his neck and inside his robes where no one else could see it. He knew that the others had seen him looking at the stone from time to time, but he had never told them what it was. The memories were still too painful for him to tell his companions about. Even now that Silvestra was seemingly back in his life.

"You're a silver dragon," Alana said in wonder after the dragon had settled on her haunches in front of the companions.

"Yes, I am," the dragon said softly. Her voice retained much of the tonal quality of the silver haired woman that she had transformed from. "I know you have your questions. Let me tell you my story first though."

"Tell your story," Alana nodded. She motioned for the other companions to sit before sitting herself. "We will ask any questions we have after we've heard what you have to tell us."

"Thank you, Blademaster," the dragon nodded. "You are truly as wise as a Blademaster should be." Silvestra lowered her neck so her chin was resting on the ground. She sighed slightly. "As I told you, my story is a sad one, I'm afraid. I cannot tell you the whole story. Parts are for others to explain. I will tell you what I can though. I studied at the Tower of the White. That is where I met William. As I'm sure you've figured out, William and I know each other fairly well. That is the part of my story that I will not tell. If William wishes you to know his part of the story and of how we know each other, he will tell you himself."

Alana looked at William, but the mage merely shrugged and motioned for the dragon to continue.

"After I left the Tower of the White, I returned to the Isle of Dragons, for the Dragonic Council had summoned me," Silvestra continued. "I did not have a choice but to go, so I went. The Dragonic Council was livid with me. I had defied them. Eliazar, the ancient gold dragon who is one of the three leaders of the Dragonic Council, was particularly irate with me. He felt that my actions in the Tower of the White were inappropriate for a dragon."

"Er, excuse me," Alana interrupted. "What actions at the Tower of the White."

"Let Silvestra finish her tale," William said quietly from where he was standing by the entrance to the cavern. It was clear that he was not ready to tell his part of the story.

Alana looked at William oddly, before turning back to Silvestra. She caught the look in the dragon's eye as she looked over at the mage and understood all that had been left unsaid. It was the look she had in her own eyes whenever she looked at Colwyn.

"Never mind," Alana nodded. "Sorry for interrupting."

"It's all right," the dragon smiled slightly. "I don't blame you for being confused. You are coming into the tale somewhere in the middle, I am afraid."

"As you said, part of it is not your tale to tell," Alana shrugged. She reached over and touched the dragon on the snout. It was a touch meant to comfort. The dragon's eyes met hers. "I understand your pain."

"Yes, Blademaster," the dragon nodded and turned her eyes away from Alana. "I suspect you do at that."

"Please, Silvestra," Alana smiled. "Finish your story."

"As punishment, I was sent to the city of Valendale," the dragon sighed. "I was not permitted to return to my dragon form while in the company of anyone from the town, nor was I able to use any dragon magic. I could use any human magic that I knew, though, which made me happy. I had studied so well while I was at the Tower of the White. I was looked on as an eccentric by the people of Valendale. I made a living as a medicine woman. I made potions to help people. I made all kinds of potions from poultices and antidotes to love potions. It kept food on my table and it kept me in Valendale where I needed to be.

"Every time you came through Valendale, I wanted so much to come out and meet you. But I was forbidden. You were not yet mantled as a Blademaster, and I am forbidden from seeing William again." The dragon smiled broadly. "And I'm rather happy to violate that prohibition now. If you can help rescue the people of Valendale than I will happily accept the censure I will receive from the Dragonic Council for seeing you again."

"Once we have a good idea of what we're facing, we'll figure out how best to rescue the people of Valendale," William assured her. "Now, please, continue with your story."

"I lived in Valendale for almost seven years. It was peaceful for the most part," the dragon sighed. She rearranged herself before continuing. "It wasn't the life I wanted, but there was nothing I could do to change it. I had my duty. Oh, how I hate that word now. All duty has done is cause me pain. When the citizens of Valendale are freed, I will no longer be bound by my duty to the Dragonic Council. The only voice I shall heed is that of Lord Taelin's."

"That's going to cause you some problems," William laughed. "I doubt Eliazar will be overly thrilled to hear that."

"I don't care," Silvestra snorted, a puff of smoke rising from her nostrils. "He has seen fit to ruin my life with his edicts. Because I followed his edicts, I was forced to watch and do nothing as the Zeraphim invaded Valendale."

"We know what happened when the Zeraphim came to Valendale," Alana said softly. "I don't think any of us need to hear what happened again."

Alana looked at Colwyn and she knew that he was thinking about how the First Lord of Valendale and his daughter had been slaughtered by the Zeraphim. She knew that he did not want to hear about that again either. She hadn't told the others that part of the story. She would be happy if she could save them the pain. She wished she hadn't known about it herself.

"I wish I could say I fought them," Silvestra sighed. She closed her eyes and slowly transformed back into a woman. It took some time, but she made herself back into the form that she had been when they'd met her. She put her robes back on and sat with the companions. "In this form, though, there was little that I could do. William will tell you that there's only so much that can be done with the limitations built into human magic. I can do a great deal with magic as a dragon, but I'm still relatively new in the study of human magic. I'd say that William and I are about the same level with our abilities. He might be a little ahead of me when it comes to human magic, actually."

"You guys know I have to constantly replenish my magic spell components," William explained. "And that I can only cast spells as I have the energy to. If I try to do too much, I will die. It is the same for Silvestra. If she had attempted to take on the number of soldiers that were there, she would have expended all of her energy and probably died in the attempt. Or she would have been killed by the soldiers. She can be a great help to us now, so I think it was wiser for her to not make the attempt."

"Of course," Alana nodded. "What has life been like here in Willowdale?"

"It has been terror," Silvestra whispered. A shudder ran through the young woman's body. "The Zeraphim have kept us separated as much as they can. Some wives and husbands have not seen each other since we left Valendale. The children are kept apart. They are kept hostage to keep the men and women working. It is a sad thing when people use children as a weapon like this."

"Indeed," Colwyn said softly, a single tear rolling down his cheek. Alana knew that he was remembering what happened to the First Lord's daughter. They would both have nightmares of that story for the rest of their lives.

"I've used my human magic to keep myself apart from the rest of the citizens," Silvestra explained. "I've been living in this cave since we got here. I interact with the Resistance as much as I can. I run errands and carry messages. There is little else that I can do to help them."

"If we are to rescue the people of Valendale, we may need your help, Silvestra," Alana said softly. "Will you help us?"

"I am forbidden from using dragon magic," Silvestra shrugged. "Although I no longer feel beholden to the Dragonic Council, my word is binding. I will find myself in deeper trouble if I break my word. But what skills I have in this form are yours to command, Blademaster. You have my word that I will do whatever I can to help the people of Valendale."

"Thank you, Silvestra," Alana smiled. "I know that this has been very difficult for you, but we are all happy to have you with us."

"There is one other thing you must know, Blademaster," Silvestra said suddenly. "And I can tell you nothing more than what I am about to relate. Three weeks ago, a woman appeared in the palace at the heart of Willowdale. It is said that she now controls the Zeraphim. No one from Valendale has seen her and lived to tell what they saw."

"I see," Alana frowned. "Well, I guess we're going to have to find out more about our mysterious woman before we plan out our attack, then."

"I will try to find out what I can," Silvestra nodded.

"Tell us about the Resistance," Colwyn said. "You mentioned that you run errands and messages for them. Can they help us?"

"Whether they actually can help you or not, they will try," Silvestra smiled. Her smile faded quickly though. "Unfortunately, the Resistance is made up of small cells spread out all over the city. Not much communication actually happens between each cell. I'm the only communication many of those cells have with the rest of the Resistance. Very few members of the Resistance are trained fighters. Most of the members of the Resistance are shopkeepers."

"Shopkeepers can be vicious if their shops are in danger, Silvestra," Alana smiled. "We could do worse."

"It's also possible that the Resistance will not help," Silvestra closed her eyes. "Four weeks ago a man named Marcus Whelan left Willowdale in the middle of the night.

His wife and child have been held in the dungeons, and they are scheduled to be executed in three days' time. The night Marcus disappeared, the Zeraphim came upon a meeting of a Resistance cell. The cell was led by a man named Carl Kavanaugh."

"I know Carl," Alana said. A dagger appeared out of nowhere. Colwyn knew that it had come from between the hollow of her breasts, but no one had actually seen her draw the blade. "He made this special for me over a year ago. It has served me very well since."

"Carl stood up to the Zeraphim that night and was killed for his trouble. The rest of the Resistance cell was publicly executed the following morning as an example of what happens to people who continue to resist the Zeraphim. It was a very convincing example."

"Can you take us to the Resistance, Silvestra?" William asked. "If we can talk to them, then maybe we can convince them to help us help themselves."

"I will show you the city of Willowdale tomorrow. From there, we will contact the Resistance," Silvestra nodded. "For tonight, consider my cave your home. Rest and make yourselves ready. The next few days will be very hard for all of us. And I know that your travel here must not have been easy."

"My nathair an aeir a chosnaíonn carried us part of the way. It cut two weeks off our travel time," Alana said. "But it was still not an easy journey."

"Well, then," Silvestra said softly. "Rest, Blademaster. You are safe here. You need not keep watch. Nothing can come into my cave without my permission."

"Thank you, Silvestra," Alana smiled.

Alana and the others began to unroll their bedrolls. They put their bedrolls in a rough circle, although there was a good amount of space between them. Alana and Colwyn put their bedrolls right next to each other as they always did.

William carried his bedroll off to the far side of the cavern. Meryn started to follow him, but a sharp look from the mage stopped her in her tracks. It was clear that the mage wanted to be alone. He put his staff on the ground next to the bedroll and sat on his bedroll with his back to the rest of the companions. He pulled the stone from inside his robes and sat staring at it, a look of complete confusion on his face.

Alana and Colwyn sat next to each other on their bedrolls. They were gently holding each other's hand. Their eyes were both closed, and anyone watching the two of them would simply think they were two lovers enjoying each other's company. But it was more than that. They were taking comfort from each other. They were also sharing and building each other's strength. They had both taken a pounding in their psyches with the news of how the people of Valendale were captured. The part of the tale concerning the death of the First Lord's daughter had been the hardest. They needed to comfort each other. They knew how the other was hurting.

"Colwyn, after we get in touch with the Resistance and start to make plans, I want you to take Cobalt and fly to the Temple of the Blades," Alana said softly.

"If you are trying to protect me, I'm a big boy, Alana," Colwyn growled. "I can't protect you if I'm not with you."

"Colwyn, I need answers," Alana touched his cheeks. "You're better at getting answers from the Legacy of the Blademasters than I am. I feel silly talking to them. It's like talking to a mirror."

"Promise me that you won't get in trouble while I'm gone to the Temple of the Blades," he held her chin between his finger and thumb. "Promise me."

"I promise you," Alana smiled, a twinkle in her eye. "I will not get in trouble while you are at the Temple of the Blades,"

"Thank you," Colwyn nodded. "I'll go and get you your answers."

"Thank you, Col," she smiled her special smile at him.

They lay down together arm in arm and stared at the ceiling, simply enjoying the feeling of each other beside them. It brought the both of them a great deal of peace. They soon fell asleep in each other's arms.

Some time after the rest of the companions had fallen asleep, William stood up from his bedroll and made his way to the cavern entrance. It had gotten dark and very little light came in from the entrance. There was not a cloud in the sky though, and the moon was near full, so he knew he would have enough light for a walk outside the cave. Silvestra had noticed his movement and came up to where he was standing.

"I'm going to replenish some of my spell components, Silvestra," he said quietly, not looking at her.

"I would go with you, William," she replied just as quietly. "We need to talk."

"I have nothing to say right now," William turned away before she could see the tears start to fall. "Thank you for not telling Alana how we know each other."

"I suspect she knows anyway," Silvestra shrugged.

"If she does, she will keep her own counsel," William started out of the cave, but she put her hand on his arm to stop him.

"I could show you where you can find what you are looking for," she pleaded.

"I need some time to think," he growled. "Alone. Finding my spell components has always been my way of thinking. You of all people know that."

"I suppose you're right," she let go of his arm. "This isn't over though, William. You know the time will come when we will talk."

"I know," he nodded. "But that time is not tonight."

He made his way out of the cave and down the mountain. The dragon woman watched him make his way down the mountain side and sighed deeply. She had not known how she would feel upon seeing William again. The way he brushed her off hurt her more than anything Eliazar and the Dragonic Council could have ever done to her. She knew that her heart still belonged to William.

She was in deep trouble, and she knew it.

Willowdale

Chapter VIII
Willowdale

The next morning, the companions awoke in confusion. It took several minutes for each of them to remember where they were and why they were there. Alana was the first to come to full awareness and she slumped back in her bedroll with a groan. Colwyn opened one eye and looked at her quizzically.

"We're actually here, Colwyn," she said softly. "This wasn't just a bad dream."

"No, I'm afraid it isn't a nightmare, my love," Colwyn touched her arm. "At least it's not one for us. The people of Valendale are living a waking nightmare every day, though. That's why we're here. You know as well as I do that we can't leave them here."

"I know," she groaned again. "I just was kind of hoping that this was just a very bad dream."

"I know what you mean," Colwyn took her in his arms.

"So, what do we do next?" Alana asked as she buried her head in his chest. "How do we save them?"

"First things first," Colwyn stroked her hair. "Silvestra will show us the city of Willowdale today. Once we see what the city is like, we will have a better idea as to what we can expect. We'll be able to plan from there."

"One of these days, we'll get an easy assignment," Alana mumbled into his chest.

"Somehow, I think the missions we take are only going to get harder," he sighed softly.

"You mean we will do things harder than sacking an entire city by ourselves?" Alana raised her head to glare at him. "You are a glutton for punishment."

"I never said it was my first choice," Colwyn chuckled softly. "I just said that I had a feeling that our job is going to get tougher as we go along."

"Isaiah and the King have both said that a war is coming, Colwyn," Alana said softly. "The Southern Dales hasn't been through a war in over four hundred years. I'm not sure the people will be ready."

"They'll have to be," Colwyn shrugged. "You will be too, my love. You are the one who must lead them. At least, that's what the prophecies have indicated."

"Gods damn the prophecies," Alana flopped on her back. "All the prophecies in the world have ever done is cause trouble."

"Yes, we all know how you feel about prophecy," Colwyn laughed. "If there is one thing that anyone can say about you, it is that you are definitely not fond of prophecy."

"Am I really that predicable, Colwyn?" Alana asked softly as she looked over at the man she loved.

"Only when it comes to certain things," Colwyn shrugged. He reached over and squeezed her gently. "We should probably get up soon. Silvestra is going to take us to show us what life is like in Willowdale."

"I don't think we're going to like what we see there," Alana heaved a deep sigh, looking back up at the roof of the cavern.

"I think you are probably right," Colwyn nodded. "It is what it is though. Come on. Let's get up. The others will be ready to go shortly."

The city of Willowdale spread out in front of the companions. The city looked like any other city in the Southern Dales, although it was the dirtiest city that they had ever seen. They had heard stories about how the city of Willowdale was a haven for criminals and cutthroats. As they looked over the dale, none of the companions had any doubts about the veracity of the stories

As the companions shuffled through the gates, they each slouched a bit as if they had been holding the weight of the world on their shoulders for years. The dragon woman had shown them how the people of Valendale walked and she wouldn't agree to bring them into WIllowdale until they had mastered the walk. She'd only take them into Willowdale if they could blend in with the citizens of Valendale as much as possible. Anything out of the ordinary would be enough to raise the alarm.

The guards did not give the companions a second glance. Since the six of them looked as if they were any other citizens, the guards simply waved them through the gate. Silvestra had been right about their needing to look slouched and bedraggled.

It was especially difficult for Colwyn to play the part. As a noble, he was not used to appearing any way other than looking his best. He had the most difficult time picking up the walk and mannerisms of the oppressed. Even now, he was having trouble staying hunched over. His natural noble bearing was still showing through somewhat despite his best efforts to appear otherwise. He felt lucky that he was able to get by the guards without them noticing his bearing.

"Do all of you have your ration chits?" the silver haired dragon woman said softly.

The others nodded. SIlvestra had gotten ration chits for each of the companions so that they could go to the market and experience what life was like for the people of

Valendale. Alana had agreed to this, although she knew that none of them were going to like the experience.

They shuffled their way through the city towards the market in the center of the city. No one gave them any notice. It felt odd to be so invisible to all of them except the halfling.

When they got to the market, they found a large crowd that formed a very long and ragged line. The companions shuffled to the end of the line. Silvestra motioned for the companions to keep silent while they were in the line. They slowly shuffled forward, inch by inch, as the line slowly snaked through and people got their rations.

Alana and Colwyn kept looking at each other, but they did not say anything. Nothing needed to be said. Neither of them could believe that the people of Valendale had to live like this. It was just one more thing that underscored why they were trying to help free the people of Valendale.

It took almost three hours for the companions to work their way through the line. By the time it got to be their turn in line, it had gotten to be past midday. It had turned into a very warm day and the companions, who had all decided to wear their armor under their peasant clothes were sweating profusely by the time they had gotten through the line. The Zeraphim soldier sitting at the table did not give the companions a second look. He looked bored and leaned his head on a gauntleted hand.

"Ration chit?" the bored Zeraphim officer droned to Alana as she stepped up to the table.

Alana handed over her ration chit to the Zeraphim officer. The officer reached into several bins and deposited a crust of bread, a small wedge of cheese, and an apple that looked suspiciously like a worm had made its home in it.

"This bread has mold on it," Alana complained in a soft voice.

"You're lucky to get that, slave," the soldier grunted. "Now get out of here. There is a sizeable line still and you're holding it up."

Alana started to say something, but she felt the dragon woman put her hand on her arm. Alana nodded and shuffled off taking the food with her. She waited for the rest of her companions to join her.

"How can the people of Valendale live like this, Silvestra?" Alana asked the silver haired woman when she got to where the companions were gathered.

"They are not living, Lady Blademaster," Silvestra sighed deeply. "They are merely surviving. That is why the need your help."

"Well, we are here and we will do whatever we can to bring these people home once more," Colwyn smiled at Silvestra.

"Take this food to a family that needs it, Silvestra," Alana said as she gathered together the breads, cheeses and apples that the companions had gotten. "It's not much and the food may not be all that good, but I am sure that it will help someone out."

"I know of a family that was denied their ration chits for this week. They will be extremely grateful for your kindness," Silvestra nodded.

"Why were they denied ration chits for this week?" Alana asked, horrified at the thought of a family going hungry.

"The father was too sick to work this week," Silvestra sighed. "The rule in Willowdale is that if you do not work, you do not eat."

"That's horrible!" Colwyn thundered.

"Sadly, that's life in Willowdale, Colwyn," Silvestra shrugged.

"Then bring us to where you are going to have the Resistance meet with us" Alana said, her eyes blazing in anger. "Let's get these people home."

"Follow me, then." Silvestra nodded.

Willowdale

Chapter IX
The Resistance

Ilvestra had led the companions to an abandoned warehouse near the eastern walls of the city. The location of the warehouse meant that they would have to go through the entire city if they were to leave where they came in. Or they'd have to sneak out through the eastern gate and travel all the way around the city to get back to the cavern they'd been staying in.

Neither option thrilled Alana.

"Please wait here, Blademaster Alana," Silvestra said softly. "I will bring one of the leaders of the Resistance to see you."

"How long will you be?" Colwyn asked.

"It will take as long as it takes," Silvestra said with a slight shrug. "We have to be careful. The Zeraphim will kill anyone they believe to be in the Resistance. It may take several hours to get back here. There is a trap door to a basement. It is very well hidden. You can go down there if the Zeraphim come by."

"I can always make us invisible," William shrugged indifferently.

"There are rumors that the Zeraphim can see through the invisibility spell we use, William," Silvestra said softly. Her voice was tender whenever she talked to William. Alana knew that the situation between William and Silvestra would need to be resolved and soon. "Be careful. I do not know if they can see through the invisibility spell or not. It is probably better to just use the basement and hide that way."

"We will be careful," Alana nodded. She looked over at William, but the young mage had already turned away and was investigating the trap door that Silvestra had mentioned. "Please don't take too long. We need information if we are going to help these people."

"It will take as long as it takes," the young dragon woman said again and slipped out of the warehouse.

Alana walked over to the dirty window and peeked out. She had decided that she should keep watch. Someone should keep watch at least. She felt Colwyn come up behind her and she smiled back at him. He put his arms around her and they both watched out the window to make sure none of the Zeraphim patrols surprised them.

Alana wondered once again at the comfort she was able to draw from a simple embrace. She knew that true love was like that, but she had never thought she would be able to ever experience such peace and happiness. She still didn't believe that she and Colwyn had been allowed to marry each other after all that they had been through. It was a dream come true, and she feared that any day it might come to an end. She could bear it if it ended.

She thought about the dragon woman.

What must it be like to see her true love with another woman?

How would Alana react herself if Colwyn were with another woman? She did not think she would react to that well at all. She felt sorrow for the young woman. There must be a way to get William and Silvestra back together.

She knew William still loved her. She could tell by the way he avoided her gaze whenever Silvestra was around. She knew that many people thought that a Blademaster could read the truth in someone's eyes just by looking into theirs. It was clear that the mage thought this was true. She didn't have that ability, but the mage's avoidance told her everything that she needed to know.

And she knew that Silvestra was still hopelessly in love with William. As much in love with William as she was with Colwyn. She thought about the First Law of the Blades, which she had to live by every day. She knew that the words of the First Law of the Blades held the key to solving the mystery of William and Silvestra.

She repeated the words of the First Law of the Blades over and over again, a slow sad mantra in her heart. Each time she repeated it, she thought that she might be closer to unlocking the secret to Silvestra's problem.

You are commanded to love. Love your friends. Love your enemies. Love without reservation. Love without hesitation. Love without condition. Love without expectation of return. If you must fight, then fight with love in your heart. If you must kill, then kill with love in your heart. Never kill or fight with hate or anger in your heart. Hate leads to impotence, but love brings power. This is the law a Blademaster must live by more than any other or else she will be powerless to serve as she should. It is the First Law of the Blades because it is the most important. Live by it, or you will die.

It was the most sacred of the Laws of the Blades. It was the core law by which the Blademasters had to live. It was also perhaps the most important law of life as a whole. What could be more important than true love? Colwyn had once joked that true love did not happen every day. When someone finds true love, he had said, they need to grab onto it and hold on tight.

There were a lot of competing problems that Alana felt that she needed to work on. She knew she needed to focus on the Zeraphim problem, but the problem of what to do about William Stonehands and Silvestra Knightwing kept dominating her thoughts. Frustration set in that she could not focus on the problem that had brought her all the way to Willowdale.

She looked back at Colwyn and watched him watching out the window. She needed his strength. She needed him to help keep her focused. He had joked once that Lord Taelin and Lady Laeyra made the Blademasters marry because they knew the Blademasters would sometimes be flighty lassies and need to be brought down to the ground to walk amongst the regular folks.

There might be some truth to that, she mused.

She did know, for a fact, that if it weren't for Colwyn, she never would have gotten as far as she had. He was her rock. She would be lost without him.

It was for that reason that she decided that she would find a way to bring Silvestra and William back together. Meddling in another's life wasn't something she felt comfortable doing. There just was something *right* about William and Silvestra being together.

Her only concern was the halfling.

Meryn viewed William as her true love. Now that Alana had seen Silvestra, she knew without a doubt that Meryn was not William's true love. The halfling would be hurt in the process. She hoped that Meryn would forgive her for what she felt she had to do.

"Someone's coming," Colwyn said suddenly, rousing Alana from her thoughts about the mage and the young woman. He peered closer out the window. "It's a patrol. Quick. Everyone go to the basement."

The companions moved quickly, getting themselves through the trap door as quickly and quietly as possible. Colwyn was the last one through the trap door.

As soon as Colwyn was down in the basement, William cast a wizard's lock spell on the trap door. He hoped that it would be strong enough to keep the Zeraphim out of the basement. It was a complicated spell that he had never cast before, so he could not even be sure that he had cast it correctly. It had been in one of the new books he had picked up prior to their journey to Valendale during the fateful journey to the Temple of the Blades.

He prayed to all three of the gods of magic that it would hold.

They heard the sound of heavy boots on the floor boards above their heads. The five of them held their breaths. Colwyn had his hand held over Meryn's mouth to make sure she did not say anything. He felt it a sensible precaution.

"Search the building," one of the guards that had entered the building said. "I thought I saw someone in the window."

"Yes, Captain," three other soldiers said, more or less in unison.

The guards spread out and began to methodically search the warehouse. Based on the way that the guards were searching the warehouse, Alana knew that, had they depended on William's invisibility spell, they would have been caught. Alana looked at the mage who simply shrugged as if to say he was glad they heeded Silvestra's warning.

The companions were nervous, though. One of the soldiers was searching near the trapdoor. Colwyn wondered how well their tracks had been covered. Could they see tracks leading to the trap door? Would they be given away?

"Captain, it looks like there's a trap door here," the guard near the trap door announced. "They may have gone down to the basement."

"Then get that trap door open," the captain of the patrol ordered.

They heard the guard grab onto the side of the trap door. They could hear him grunt with the effort of trying to open the door. All five of them were now praying to the gods of magic that the wizard's lock would hold. The Zeraphim would find them and kill them if it didn't hold.

"The trap door is not budging, Captain," the guard said. "It may have been rusted closed, or it may not even really be a trap door."

"All right," the captain said. "It looks like there's no one here. Let's go."

The companions held their breaths as they listened to the guards march out of the warehouse above. They heard the door slam closed, but still they waited. They waited for what felt like an hour but it was actually only about ten minutes. The last thing they wanted was to be taken prisoner. They still had so little information to go on. They had so little idea of how to free the people of Valendale.

"I think they're gone," Colwyn said softly, not wanting to speak too loudly in case he was wrong.

"I'll go look," William nodded.

The mage waved his hands and disappeared. The companions looked at each other then watched as the trap door slowly cracked open enough for the mage to look out into the inside of the warehouse. When he was satisfied, he opened the trap door far enough so that he could climb out of the basement. He gently lowered the trap door closed again.

"Have you noticed that our little mage is getting more powerful?" Colwyn observed. "That trick with the door, he wouldn't have been able to do even a month ago."

"You sound like you're concerned," Alana stroked his arm.

"Not concerned, per se," Colwyn put his arm around his wife. "But it could be cause for concern if he grows too powerful too quickly. I wonder if he'll be able to handle it."

"William is one of the straightest players I have ever known," Alana laughed. "I don't think he is anyone we have to worry about power corrupting."

"We once said that would be the case about anyone who became the High Priest of Taelin, Alana," Colwyn reminded her. "Look how that turned out."

"If it makes you feel any better, I will have a talk with William, my dear," Alana chuckled softly. "I really don't think you have anything to worry about, though."

"I hope you're right," Colwyn smiled. He kissed her hair. "I truly hope that I am worrying over nothing."

The trap door opened and William came back down into the basement. He was no longer hiding under his invisibility spell. Alana and Colwyn both felt that that was a good sign.

"They're gone," William confirmed. "I don't know if they'll be back or not, though. I think we should stay down here just to be safe. If I lock the trap door again, Silvestra should be able to open it up when she gets here. Her magic is in tune with my own."

Colwyn and Alana exchanged looks. It had been the closest that William had come to admitting that he had had a prior relationship with the dragon woman. Both Alana and Colwyn wanted to explore that knowledge, but neither knew how to proceed.

"Go ahead and lock the trap door then, William," Alana nodded finally. "We'll wait down here for Silvestra and the leader of the Resistance she's gone to find."

William nodded and went back to the trap door and made sure it was securely closed. For the second time in an hour, he wove the complex wizard's lock spell. Colwyn and Alana could both tell that the mage was beginning to tire, and he would need to rest soon. Alana sincerely hoped they would not need his help any more before he had a chance to rest.

Alana found herself a somewhat comfortable seat on a large crate. There was easily enough room on the crate for two people. Alana patted the part of the crate next to her and Colwyn joined her, putting his arms around her. She leaned into him and rested her head against his chest. He stroked her hair gently, the slight motions comforting her and bringing her a little peace.

"We really need information, Col," she whispered softly into his chest.

"I know, my love," he kept stroking her hair. "After we get through this meeting with this leader of the Resistance, I will summon the dragon and fly to the Temple of the Blades to get you what answers I can."

"Do you think the Legacy of the Blademasters will be able to help us?" Alana asked. She looked up at him. "I mean, do you think you'll be able to get the answers you need from them? I know that you don't always get to talk to the member of the Legacy that has the answers you need."

"I will get your answers, Alana," Colwyn smiled. "Now hush and stop worrying."

"I'm always going to worry," she chuckled at him. "But nice try."

"Can't blame a guy for trying," he squeezed her gently.

He held her tight stroking her hair for several long minutes, although they did not feel like long minutes to either of them. They simply enjoyed the closeness. And, just for a moment, Alana forgot all of her worries as she snuggled under his arm.

"I wonder how much longer Silvestra is going to be," Alana said after a while.

"Well, we know the Zeraphim are about, so they have to be careful," Colwyn rubbed her arm as he held her.

"I know, but I hate waiting," Alana complained softly. "I really hate waiting. I just wish they'd get here already."

"They'll be here soon, I'm sure," Colwyn laughed and squeezed her again. "Then we can find out what we need to know to save the people of Valendale."

"Why do you think the Zeraphim took the people of Valendale?" Alana asked after a few moments of thought.

"I don't know that we'll ever really know the answer to that," Colwayn said. "I doubt the Zeraphim are going to tell us why."

"It just bothers me," Alana grunted.

"It bothers me, too," Colwyn nodded. "A lot of things about this bother me. The fate of the First Lord of Arvendale and his daughter bothers me. The condition Marcus Whelan was in when he got to us bothers me. The fact that people we know and care about were abducted and made slaves bothers me. The fact that no one knew what had happened for three months truly bothers me."

"So what do we do about it?" she asked softly.

"The only thing that we can do," Colwyn shrugged. "Help them."

"That's one of the things I love about you, Colwyn," Alana smiled up at him. "You always find a way to boil it down to the simplest answer for me."

"What other answer is there?" Colwyn kissed her hair. "We help them. We bring them home. And we make sure that this never happens to anyone else."

"What about the prophecy that the King and Isaiah told us about?" Alana changed the topic suddenly. "What do we do about that?"

"Not much we can do about it for now but to get ourselves ready for it," Colwyn sighed and hugged her closer. "And we depend on each other. We depend on our friends to help. And we believe that Lord Taelin and Lady Laeyra will be wise enough to send us help."

"That just doesn't seem like enough," Alana mumbled.

"We could always go back to Ravendale and forget about saving the people of Valendale," Colwyn poked her in the arm. "Remember, the prophecy specifically said that the twice dead city had to fall empty a third time. So if we don't rescue the people of Valendale and the city of Willowdale stays full, no war."

"I can't believe you just said that," Alana stared up at him. "We can't leave those people there and you know it."

"I was simply pointing out the only way to truly avoid the prophecy," Colwyn said softly. "I never said I wanted to do so."

"So long as that's settled," Alana settled back down against his chest. "We're helping these people and let the consequences be damned."

"I rather think that they will be, if it be war that comes as a result," Colwyn said in a hushed whisper. "Maybe the Legacy of the Blademasters can shed some light on this war that's supposed to be coming."

"You'd be the one who could get those answers, not me," Alana laughed. "The girls seem to like you." She looked over him with a lusty eye. "Not that there's a problem with that. There's a lot to like."

"Alana!"

"What?" Alana looked at him innocently. "I'm sweet and innocent."

"Not. Buying. It," Colwyn grunted.

Alana pouted and then poked him in the belly. Colwyn returned the favor by tickling her ribs. She squealed and pulled away. William and Meryn both looked at Alana and Colwyn like they were little children. Alana looked back at them, pouting slightly.

"Maybe they're right," Alana said as she slipped back under Colwyn's arm. "Maybe now isn't an appropriate time for tickling."

"I suppose you're right," Colwyn chuckled softly.

They went back to leaning against each other, holding each other tenderly. They waited well over an hour in silence. Alana began to worry more with each passing minute. The Blademaster began to mull over the thought of when she felt they would need to head back to Silvestra's cavern to regroup. She did not want to do so, but if the dragon woman did not arrive with her friend from the Resistance soon, they would have to accept that maybe Silvestra and the Resistance leader had been taken prisoner.

"They should be here by now," Colwyn said, concern in his voice. "How much longer do we wait?"

"Give it another hour, Colwyn," Alana said into his chest. "If they're still not back by then, we'll leave and regroup at Silvestra's cave."

They sat like that for another twenty minutes before Colwyn roused himself. He had heard something in the warehouse above them. He had heard the door opening. He extricated himself from Alana and walked over to the trap door, listening carefully. He knew that they could be in deep trouble if the Zeraphim had returned. He did not want to think about them being dragged into a dungeon. He was afraid of what would happen should they be caught.

He listened carefully, and detected two different sets of foot falls. One was very light, and he thought he recognized it as the young dragon woman's. The other was a sturdier step, and he figured that she had a man with him. That would certainly track. He expected that the leader that she would bring to see them would be a man. He nodded to William and he released the wizard's lock spell on the trap door.

The young mage pushed the trap door up enough to be able to look around. There was no way that William could mistake Silvestra's legs for anyone else. When he saw her legs in the crack he'd opened, he pushed the trap door all the way open and led the way out of the cellar. Silvestra smiled at the companions as they arrived in the warehouse from the cellar below.

"Blademaster Alana Steeldrake," Silvestra bowed slightly. "I am sorry it took so long for me to return to you. It took me some time to find this man. And once I found him, it took us some time to get back here. I am afraid there are a large number of Zeraphim soldiers out and about in the streets of Willowdale. We had a rough time avoiding all of them."

"We know," Alana nodded. "A patrol came in here. Had William not been able to lock the trap door with a spell, they would have found us. These Zeraphim are a lot smarter than I had originally thought. They knew about the trap door, and they knew about the cellar. They suspected we were there. But when they could not open the door, they left. I suspect that they will be back soon."

"Indeed," SIlvestra nodded. "We should make this quick then. This man is Arun Jossun."

"I remember you," Colwyn said suddenly. "You run that grocery store two streets over from the White Horse Inn." He turned to Alana. "We have been in his store many a time."

"Indeed, I remember you as well, Lord Colwyn," Arun smiled slightly. "You were always kind and generous in my store. I had no idea that I had been provisioning the Blademaster and her companions for years."

"To be fair, Arun," Alana chuckled softly. "We had no idea I was a Blademaster until just recently. But you were always fair with us. All of the people of Valendale were. That is why my companions and I are here. We know what happened to your people. We are here to do something about it."

"I do not know what can be done, Blademaster Alana," Arun said. His voice was tired. "The people of Valendale have been oppressed for so long. We know no other way to be, anymore. I do not know if you can help us or not."

"We aim to try," Alana smiled at the grocer. She walked over and put her hands on his arms. "But we will need your help. Can you get the word out to the other leaders in the Resistance to meet with us?"

"Of course," Arun nodded. "We'll do whatever we can to remove the yoke of the Zeraphim from our necks. I do not know about the others, but I will do whatever it is you ask of me, Blademaster. I am tired of the life we lead here. I want to go back to my grocery store and sell my simple wares once more."

"We will do whatever it takes to make that happen," Colwyn said to the grocer. He moved up to stand beside Alana. "You have our word that we will see you all home."

"How is it that you came to know of our plight?" Arun asked. There were tears running down his face. He was truly overjoyed to think that he might soon get to go back to his home once more. "Many of the others, like myself, have long feared no one would come to help us."

"Marcus Whelan was told where to find me," Alana smiled. It was a strangely sad smile. There was really no room for mirth with what the companions were facing. "He risked everything to find me. He came at the risk of having his wife and daughter executed for his actions. Marcus has long been our friend as have many of the people of Valendale. When we heard what happened, we came just as soon as we could. After hearing Marcus's tale, nothing could have kept us from coming."

"I am overjoyed to see you, Blademaster," Arun whispered, his voice choked with tears. "You will never know how much what you are doing means to us."

"So long as we are able to save all of you, I do not think that we need to," Alana smiled. "We will do whatever it takes to bring you all home safely."

"Thank you, Blademaster," Arun started to weep openly. He fell into her arms. "You have given an old man true hope."

"I do what I can," Alana smiled. This time, it was a genuine full smile. It was good to hear that she was appreciated. "Arun, you should go before we leave. Go, and quickly. I need you to get in touch with the other leaders. Tell them to meet with us. Silvestra will come to all of you with the time and the location. Two days hence we will meet with you. Two days hence begins the end of the Zeraphim's hold on the people of Valendale. We will see you then, Arun. Now, go. Before the Zeraphim come back."

"You have my deepest gratitude, Blademaster Alana," the old grocer wiped tears from his cheeks. "Whatever you need when we return to Valendale, it is yours. You and your companions will never need to pay in my store again It is the least that I can do for what you and your companions are doing for us now."

"You don't need to do that, Arun," Alana shook her head. "We do this because it is the right thing to do."

"It is already done," Arun smiled. "And there's not much you can say to change my mind. Now I will go and talk to the other leaders. You will see us two days from now."

The old man carefully slipped out of the warehouse, leaving the companions by themselves. Alana and Colwyn held each other as they watched the old man go. They were pleased that they could help the people of Valendale, but neither was comfortable with the kind of gesture that the old grocer had just made. Alana sighed softly.

"I suppose that if we're going to keep saving people's lives, we're going to have to keep dealing with gestures like that," Alana said softly.

"I suppose," Colwyn nodded. "I don't think I will ever be comfortable with things like that happening."

"Me either," Alana smiled up at her husband. "At least we know that they appreciate what we're doing for them."

Colwyn hugged her closer and they waited for a little while before leaving the warehouse themselves.

Willowdale

Chapter X
Captured

The Nightstalker paced back and forth in the quarters that she had appropriated for herself when she had arrived in Willowdale, waiting for a patrol to report in on the location of the Blademaster. They were the quarters that belonged to the First Lord of Willowdale. The commander general of the battalion of the Zeraphim in the city had protested at first. He had protested her taking command of the battalion as well. But she had convinced the commander general that she would be taking over. It had only cost six good men their lives. She had asked him to pick his 6 toughest soldiers and fought them all at once. When she bested all six without taking any serious injury, the commander general conceded his authority to her.

She knew that the Blademaster was coming to rescue the people of Valendale. She honestly didn't care one way or the other for the sniveling slaves of the Zeraphim. All she wanted was her chance to kill the Blademaster. She believed that the Blademaster had already arrived, although she had no proof. She had sent patrols out to find her. So far, none of them had.

It was just a matter of time. She knew that the Blademaster would not let the people of Valendale stay in the clutches of the Zeraphim. It was too much of a wide reaching problem for the Blademaster to resist. And she had studied the Blademaster from afar. She knew that the Blademaster had a special place in her heart for the people of Valendale. It was the perfect trap for the Blademaster and it would be sprung soon.

She ached to be out there tracking down the Blademaster herself. It would not do for her to do so, however. For now, she was content to let the Zeraphim do her work for her. She would let them track down the Blademaster and take her and her companions prisoner. And then she would personally remove the Blademaster's head.

She walked over to the window and looked out over the city. She did not like the cities of the Southern Dales. They always felt so crowded. She did not like cities at all. She lived in a small village outside of Tornith. She was amused to think that the people of that village had no idea that a killer lurked within their midst. But they left her alone. It was peaceful. As peaceful as anything in her life could be. She craved the hunt, though. Craved the hunt and wanted to kill. It had become her nature. She knew it had not always been that way, but she did not care. She was who she was now. Nothing could change that.

Just as nothing could change the Blademaster's fate. It was sealed as soon as Kera Rayden had first decided that it would be her who beheaded the Blademaster.

"Soon, Blademaster," she whispered. "Soon, my pets will bring you to me. And then that will be it for you. There will be no more Blademasters and nothing will stop my Lord from rising to his full power."

Alana led the way out of the warehouse, carefully. The companions had a long way to go to get out of the city, and they needed to be careful. There were a lot of people in the streets of Willowdale, and the companions knew that they could use that to their advantage. They needed to get lost in the crowd somewhat. The problem was that they stuck out from the rest of the people in Willowdale. They did not completely share the downtrodden appearance that the citizens of Valendale wore all the time. And they bore their weapons with them, something that none of the citizens of Valendale did.

Alana was afraid that they would get caught because of the differences in their appearances to the rest of the people of Valendale. She wanted to be wrong. She wanted them to get out of the city as quickly as possible without any confrontations with the Zeraphim.

But the Zeraphim were everywhere. She knew it was only a matter of time before they ran into a Zeraphim patrol. If they did, she knew that they would be in distinct trouble.

Alana moved them through the city as quickly as she could. With the traffic in the streets, their progress was slow going. She could only hope that when they got on the other side of the palace their progress would move a little faster.

The dragon woman stumbled slightly, and Colwyn was there to catch her. Colwyn and Alana both looked around to see if the stumble had brought any attention to the little band of companions. They could not see any extra attention coming their way because of the stumble. They continued their way around the palace, working their way around several blocks away from the palace, hoping that the Zeraphim presence would be lessened the further away they got from the palace.

Alana caught sight of a Zeraphim patrol several streets over and she pulled her cloak tighter around her and hunched over, approximating the walk of the downtrodden citizens of Valendale. She watched as the others followed suit. She and the others were not comfortable walking like that, but if it fooled the Zeraphim, then the discomfort would be worth it. Alana kept an eye on the Zeraphim patrol as they walked past. The Zeraphim did not turn and look at them as they went by, and Alana let out a quiet sigh of relief. It had been a close call, but they had gotten lucky. Alana could only hope their luck would hold up.

They got about halfway around the palace before their luck changed.

Alana had not seen the Zeraphim patrol as they came around the corner and none of the companions had had a chance to slouch more convincingly into the walk of the oppressed. Alana cursed under her breath as she saw the Zeraphim soldiers watching them. She knew the Zeraphim would stop them. She did not know what would happen when they did though.

The Zeraphim watched the companions closely, but did not stop them right away. They watched as the companions slowly made their way around the building they were walking by. As soon as the companions were out of sight of the Zeraphim, they broke into a run, running as fast as they could. They did not get far, though, as other Zeraphim patrols caught sight of them. The companions were quickly corralled, all of them, including the silver haired woman, were brought into a circle of Zeraphim steel. Alana thought that they might be able to fight their way out, but she also thought that if they tried one or more of them would be hurt or possibly even killed.

It was not yet time to fight back, but the time would come. Alana promised herself that they would fight back and they would fight hard. But they needed some more information, and being captured might give them that opportunity.

Alana held her hands out in front of her to show that she was not carrying any weapons openly. One of the Zeraphim grabbed hold of her wrists and twisted them behind her, tying them roughly with a woven cord. The others were quickly subdued and likewise bound.

"For crimes against the One God, you are hereby under arrest," the leader of the Zeraphim patrol intoned in a deep baritone. "You are to be judged and executed in the morning."

"What crimes are we accused of?" Alana asked, her voice bold and strong.

The Zeraphim officer slapped her across the face with the back of his hand. "You will speak only when you are spoken to, woman," he said. "Your crimes will be told to you during your trial. You will accompany us to the dungeon, and you will do so quietly. The first of you that utters a word, dies."

The companions all nodded their understanding and fell into step behind the Zeraphim patrol. They walked to the palace and were led up the steps to the front archway and then inside. They walked down several halls and came to a grate on the floor. One of the guards opened the grate and shoved the six companions inside the dungeon, forcing them to jump down into the hole without the use of a ladder.

"You may talk amongst yourselves while you wait to die," the guard bellowed down to them. "There is no hope for escape for you."

They listened as the guard laughed and left the corridor above.

Alana looked around at the dungeon room that they had been shoved into. The room was about twenty feet square. From the floor to the ceiling was about ten feet, and there were no easy handholds to climb the walls. Water dripped down the walls and rats scurried around in the corners. It was not a pleasant room, but then, Alana supposed, most dungeons weren't.

The Zeraphim had made a mistake though. They had not taken the companions weapons or packs. Alana wasn't sure how this would help them in the long run. She slipped the summoning statue for Cobalt out of her pack and handed it to Colwyn.

"If we can figure out how to get out of here, use the statue and get out of here," she said softly to him. "Get to the Temple of the Blades and get the information I need."

"What about you?" Colwyn asked. "I don't want to leave you down here."

"If one of us can get out, we can all get out, Colwyn," Alana smiled. "But I'll need you to go get the information I need."

"Yes, Alana," Colwyn nodded.

They waited in the dark dungeon for a long time. They could hear people walk in the corridor above them, but no one opened the grate and no one called down to them. They wondered if anyone would come to them before their trial and execution that had been planned for the following morning.

They had to get out of there before that.

Alana began to think about how they might get out of the dungeon. Whatever they tried would be risky though. But the alternative was not an option. They would have to take the risk and hope for the best.

Alana and Colwyn stared at the grate that they had been thrown down into the dungeon through. They stared at it long and hard in the hopes that some kind of a solution would come to them. Colwyn wasn't sure either of them would be able to get their hands through the holes in the grate. He wasn't even sure that Meryn could. He thought that maybe William could unlatch the grate with magic, but he wasn't sure. He did not know enough about magic to know if that was possible.

They were still staring at the grate when the holes of the grate went dark. They could tell that someone was standing right over the grate, although they could not tell who it was. They heard the rattle of the grate being unlatched and light flooded into the dungeon as the grate was opened. A ladder was thrust down into the dungeon.

"You, warrior woman," the Zeraphim guard said. "Our mistress will see you now. Get up here."

Alana scooted up the ladder. Colwyn tried to follow but he was shoved backwards into the dungeon when he got to the top. He landed on his back and watched as they took the ladder back up out of the dungeon. He had a last view of Alana being led away before the grate slammed shut, and he heard the slide of the latch being locked again.

Colwyn groaned as he heard the guards dragging Alana off towards gods only knew where. He rubbed his head and sighed deeply. He only hoped that he would see her again. He fingered the summoning statue that she had given him, wondering if the dragon could get them out of the dungeon. It was something that he knew he would have to give a serious amount of thought. He thought the dragon would have to tear apart the palace to get to them, but maybe that wouldn't be too bad so long as the castle didn't collapse into the dungeons and kill the companions while he did so.

"Where are you taking me?" Alana demanded as the two guards dragged her down the hallway. "I demand to know where you're taking me."

"Shut up," one of the guards said as he back handed her. "You have no rights, slave. You only speak when we ask a question. Remember that."

Alana glared at the guard, promising herself that she would personally kill the arrogant guard. She wanted to rub her cheek where the back of his hand had slapped her hard, but they had tied her hands behind her. It was probably better that she didn't rub her cheek anyway. Better to not show weakness in front of the Zeraphim. When it came time to launch the assault, she did not want them to think her weak. She wanted them to run from her. She wanted them to fear her.

She could be fearsome. She had to be fearsome for the people of Valendale. So much rode on her shoulders. Sometimes she hated the burden placed on her shoulders. But she would not trade her life for any other. She knew that there would be other missions. She knew that those missions would be tougher. She thought about the war that the sage and the King had promised was on the way. She feared for the people of the Southern Dales.

She feared for them all.

The guards led her down hallways in the palace that in other palaces in the Southern Dales would lead to the First Lord's compound, the place where he and his family kept their quarters. She wondered who was making those quarters their home in this palace. She assumed she was going to meet the commander general of the Zeraphim forces in Willowdale. She did not know what this meeting was about, but she hoped to get some intelligence about the Zeraphim forces so that she could form her attack plan.

She had no idea what to expect and was very surprised when she was shoved through the door to the First Lord's private quarters.

"You may leave us now," the woman that was standing there said. "Cut her hands free and remove her weapons. Then go."

"As you command, Mistress Kera," the guard bowed low.

The guards ripped her scabbards off her back and took her knives. Then one of the guards cut the rope binding her hands. The Blademaster glared at the guards as she rubbed her wrists.

The woman in the room motioned for the Blademaster to sit. Alana, defiant, stayed standing where she was. The woman, who was wearing all black leather, shrugged and lazily sat in a chair, one leg hanging over the arm of the chair.

"You are here because I wished to meet you before your execution," the woman said. "You see, I know who and what you are, Blademaster. I will succeed where that idiot Drakkhous failed."

"You followers of Thraal are all the same," Alana snorted. "All bluster and no action."

"Oh yes, I know you think that now," the woman said. She pulled a peach out of a bowl on the table and took a bite, juices flowing out over her leather clad hands. "But you have never met anyone like me before, Blademaster."

"You sound like all the others," Alana snorted again. She crossed her arms over her chest. "The lich Drakkhous kept bragging about how he would sacrifice me to Thraal. I severed his head from his shoulders. Sorry if I don't take you too serious, precious."

"You have not seen anything like me before," the woman said again. She threw the peach pit into a bucket nearby and stood, her leather creaking as she moved. "You see, I am you. Only better. I am Lord Thraal's perfect creation. But so we are properly introduced, you are Alana Steeldrake, the soon to be dead Blademaster. I am Kera Rayden, the Nightstalker. And I am your executioner. I will be the one to personally remove your head from your shoulders in the morning."

"What makes you think I'll be here in the morning for you to execute?" Alana raised an eyebrow. "I don't plan on being here."

"Oh, I truly hope you try to escape," Kera laughed. "That will just make it that much more fun for me. In fact, there is a part of me that hopes you succeed. I would much prefer to meet you on the field of battle. How much more demoralizing would it be for you and your precious Taelin for me to best you in battle?"

"Why don't you give me my swords back and we can settle this right now?" Alana sneered. "Say, winner take all. I best you, the people of Valendale will go free. You best me, you get to kill me and have the glory of ending the line of the Blademasters before it really gets going."

"Tempting, but I think not," Kera laughed harder. "I really think it's best to just kill you in the morning. Yes, I think that would be far better."

"I'm not that easy to kill," Alana took a step closer to the Nightstalker. "Just ask your last High Priest. Did you know that I was naked when I killed him? It was so easy. I leapt right off the altar he had me pinned down on, grabbed my swords and severed his head. Even a lich can't live without his head. Imagine, a naked woman killing the high and mighty High Priest of Thraal."

"You caught him by surprise," the Nightstalker held her ground in front of the Blademaster. She was fighting to not rise to the bait. "But what you fail to understand, Blademaster, is that I am you in every way. Lord Thraal took what Taelin and Laeyra created in the Blademaster and modified it to his purpose. I am the result. I am more powerful and a far better fighter than you will ever be."

"And yet, instead of proving it, you're choosing to simply cut off my head in the morning," Alana took another step closer. Soon she would be in striking range. She did not have her swords, but she knew that her hands could be just as powerful a weapon. All she had to do was get her hands around the other woman's neck. "You're really proving just how much better you are. Yes, indeed. I'm sure Thraal will be pleased that you're taking the easy way out."

"Don't think your baiting will work, Blademaster," the Nightstalker held up her hand, momentarily freezing Alana in her tracks. "You are to die in the morning. If you do not stop walking towards me now, you will die where you stand. It matters not to me either way."

"Now is not the time for us to do battle, Kera Rayden," the Blademaster stopped walking and crossed her arms again. "But I promise you, the time will come soon when we will do battle. And I will best you and set the people of Valendale free."

"A noble boast, but a futile one," Kera shrugged. "The guards will take you back to your little hole in the ground now. Enjoy your last few hours with your precious companions."

The guards came back in and roughly pulled her arms behind her back. They tied her wrists together once more with the rough cord that they used. They marched her out of the First Lord's quarters. Alana watched the Nightstalker's face as she left, memorizing every detail of the other woman's face. She watched the Nightstalker until they turned a corner and she could no longer see the mysterious woman in black.

Chapter XI
Prisoner Escape

olwyn had been waiting for Alana to come back. He did not know where she had been taken, nor if he would ever see her again. The worry bothered him. He was her Protector. She should not have been so easily taken from him like she had been. But there had been nothing he could do.

He resolved that he would free her from the dungeon.

Far more immediately concerning to him, though, was that he needed to leave the dungeon himself so that he could keep his promise to get the information she needed in order to be able to plan the assault on the Zeraphim. He had every intention of leaving on that journey soon. He had held the summoning statue in his hands, wondering what to do with it. Could he use it in the dungeon? Would Cobalt even respond to his summons if he used the statue? He wasn't sure. Alana was convinced that he could use the statue the same as she could, but they had never tested that theory.

He had kept away from the other companions, but he had watched them. Silvestra had gone over to talk to William twice, but the young mage had rebuffed her both times. The young woman was sitting in the corner of the dungeon looking absolutely miserable. Colwyn felt for the young woman, but there was nothing he could do for her at the moment. He knew that Alana had planned on having a talk with her, but he knew that they had not had a chance to talk. He did not think that it would be his place to have the talk for her. But he wished that there was something he could do to comfort the young woman.

He worried about William. The young mage had displayed great power over the last few weeks. He knew that the young man had great untapped potential, but he was afraid that the power would corrupt the young man. He liked William and he always had. But he worried that the mage's thirst for power would turn him to the side of evil. He did not want to see the corruption that power could cause visit the young man. In part, that was why he had wanted to get Silvestra and William back together. He felt that the young dragon woman might have a chance in succeeding where no one else might be able to in keeping William from letting the quest for power corrupt his kindly nature.

Colwyn turned his attention to the young priest that had joined them on this journey. Colwyn had had some reservations about the young man. He did not know if young Martin Faolin would be able to hold his own on such a difficult journey. The young priest had not once complained about any of the difficulties that they had faced. Indeed, the young man had been stoic and stuck to the matter at hand. Colwyn was finding that he was coming to respect the young priest. He did not understand why the High Priestess found him to be a troublemaker. Colwyn did not see how the quiet young man could cause much in the way of trouble. In fact, he had come to realize that the young priest fit in quite well with the companions.

Maybe that was why Naomi didn't like him.

The last member of their party was the halfling. Meryn Swiftfoot had long been a thorn in Colwyn's side, but, by the same token, Meryn had saved all of their lives in Tornith. She had removed the binding spell that had held all of them, freeing Alana to kill the lich. She had proven her worth to Colwyn time and again. The problem was that the young woman was a thief and a liar. And she was very annoying.

All of the members of their party, including Alana and Colwyn himself, were very different. And each of them served a definite purpose in the group. The problem was, he did not yet know how the six of them could get out of this dungeon and escape the executions that had been planned for the following morning. It was something he was still trying to work out in his head. He kept running escape plans through his mind, but each time he did not know that he could make it work.

He wished Alana would get back. He missed her terribly. He also worried about her deeply. He did not think that she had been taken to be killed. The Zeraphim had been clear that they would be publicly executed the following morning. Where, then, had she been taken? The Zeraphim guard had said something about their mistress. Colwyn pondered about that for a few minutes, wondering who the Zeraphim could be working for. He also wondered why they were working for anyone. It was a difficult thing to ponder. The Zeraphim did not serve any of the Calthea gods, so who could they be working for?

Could the Zeraphim be working for Thraal? That was a scary thought, but one that they definitely needed to consider. After all, the Dark God did not like the companions, especially after what had happened in Tornith. More, the Dark God did not like the Southern Dales as a whole. He had waged many a war on the southern part of the continent. The Dark God did not like the freedom that the people of the Southern Dales savored. It meant that anyone who lived in the Southern Dales was a prime target for the Dark God's wrath. And an entire noble city of the Southern Dales had been kidnapped to work for the Zeraphim.

Colwyn did not think that it was a coincidence that it had happened so soon before Thraal had been returned to Calthea.

Colwyn looked up at the grate in time to see that the small openings had gone dark. He heard the latch being unlocked and he watched as the grate was taken away. Alana was shoved forcefully into the dungeon, and Colwyn moved quickly to try to catch her. He did not quite make it, though and she hit the ground hard. He was helping her up when they put the grate back on the entrance to the dungeon.

"Enjoy your last few hours together, love birds," the guard taunted. "We will be back soon to take you to your executions."

Colwyn helped Alana out of the bindings that they had put on her and held her close. She wrapped her arms around him and kissed his cheek. He stroked her hair, just happy to have her back. He hated whenever they were apart. He knew they would be parted again soon. She had to stay and help coordinate the plan of attack while he went and got the information she needed from the Legacy of the Blademasters.

"Colwyn, there's one more thing I need you to get me information on when you go to the Temple of the Blades," she whispered in his ear. "I think we have a bigger problem than just the Zeraphim."

"What do you mean?" he asked as he held her close.

"They took me to meet their leader," Alana said. She pulled back from him slightly so she could look in his eyes. "Or at least I presume she is their leader. They were very deferential to her at any rate."

"Something about this woman bothers you?" he met her gaze boldly. He was the only one who could meet her gaze for any length of time. It was, he knew, because of the love he shared with her.

"She called herself a Nightstalker," Alana said. She slipped from his arms and found something to sit on. He came and sat beside her. "She said that she was Thraal's solution to the Blademasters. She said that Thraal had taken everything that a Blademaster was and made it his own. That she was the result. She said she was stronger and a better fighter than I was. When you go to the Temple of the Blades, you must find out everything you can about the Nightstalker."

"Of course I will," he nodded. He held her close. "But before I can go to the Temple of the Blades, we need to get out of here."

"I know," Alana nodded. "I've been thinking about how we can do that. Do you think Meryn can reach her hand through the holes in the grate?"

"No, I think the holes are too small even for her hand," Colwyn grunted. He turned and called out to the mage. "William, could you and Silvestra come here for a moment? I have an idea, but I don't know how well it will work. I think you two are the best people to ask, since you two would be the ones who would have to do it."

"What do you have in mind?" William asked as he joined the other two where they were sitting.

"Do you think you could do anything to that grate with magic?" Colwyn asked. "Either you or Silvestra?"

"Well, we could certainly blow it off its hinges," Silvestra said as she examined the grate. "That would probably make a lot of noise, though, and it would probably alert the guard."

"Is there a way that either of you could unlatch the lock on the grate?" Alana asked. "I thought maybe Meryn's hand might fit through the holes in the grate, but I agree with Colwyn. I think the holes are too small for that."

"Maybe," William said softly. He studied the grate and the latch carefully. "It would be a tricky spell. I'm not sure I can handle it. I'm good with raw power. This is a finesse spell. Silvestra might be better suited for it. Her magic has always been more finesse than power."

"I can probably do it," Silvestra nodded. "It will weaken me greatly. It's a very complicated spell. I will need a little time to prepare."

"Start," Alana nodded. "The sooner you are ready, the sooner we can get out of here. The sooner we get out of here, the sooner we can get to planning how to save the people of Valendale."

"I will begin preparing at once, Blademaster," Silvestra nodded.

The dragon woman walked a few feet away and sat cross legged on the floor. She closed her eyes and began to chant softly. Colwyn and Alana did not recognize the words. William did not recognize many of the words, which troubled him somewhat. He knew that it was a ritual to prepare for a spell. He thought that he knew all the words to such rituals. His frown deepened as he realized what he was hearing.

"She's not using human magic for this, Alana," the mage said softly. "This is a dragon spell. This could cause a great deal of trouble."

"For her or for us?" Colwyn asked.

"For both," William took a moment before answering. "She is forbidden from using dragon magic in Willowdale. And Eliazar is not overly forgiving of transgressions. As you remember from hearing Cobalt's story."

"This is bad," Alana nodded. "Is there anything you can do to stop her?"

"Not at this point," William shook his head. "She's already begun the process. If I interrupt her now, she could get hurt. I won't do that to her. She needs to finish the preparation and cast the spell. We will all have to deal with the consequences later."

"Consequences be damned," Alana shrugged. "If we don't get out of here, the consequences are our necks on the chopping block. I'd rather be alive and face the wrath of the Dragonic Council than be dead."

"I would tend to agree," William smiled slightly. "I am just telling you that there will be consequences to our escape. And they will not be pleasant ones either."

"We will deal with whatever comes in time, William," Alana smiled at the young mage. "Meanwhile, I would speak with you. There is something that has been troubling both Colwyn and myself."

"I know," William said softly. "You are both worried about the increase in power I've been showing lately."

"In a word, yes," Alana nodded. "It's not that we don't trust you, because we do. We trust you with our lives. You would not still be travelling with us if that were the case. We are concerned that the new strength of power you have been showing might be too much for you to handle."

William looked away from the two of them, and Alana could tell that he was trying to carefully word his response. She reached out and placed a hand on his arm. He turned back to look at her, his eyes sad. She knew, then, that it was a concern the mage had for himself as well.

"I worry about that every day," the mage said in a whisper. "It is something I fight with every time I cast a new spell and make it my own. The mage lock spell I cast today was the strongest spell I have ever cast. It should be beyond my level of ability, and yet I was able to cast it easily. I worry about what it is that I am turning into, for I feel that I am rushing towards something more than what I am. I have no idea what my destiny holds. Even the Mages of the Inner Circle had no idea what I would become."

"William," Colwyn put his hand on the mage's shoulder. "One thing Alana and I do know is that we will be with you on your journey. You helped us on our journey to discover our destiny. It is only fair that we join you on yours. You are our friend and our companion. We would help you through this. And if we feel you slipping into the power too far, we will be there to drag you back out."

"I appreciate that, Colwyn," the mage smiled. "But I am afraid that you may not be able to walk down the path with me when it comes time to find out what my destiny is. When a mage discovers his exact destiny, it is a solitary quest. I feel like that quest is coming for me soon. I think it is coming very soon. I feel like Silvestra reappearing in my life may be a signpost towards where I go next, although I don't yet know where it will lead. I do not know what the future holds, my friends. But I do know that I am honored that you two care enough about me to worry about me. It means a great deal to me that I have people that do care like this."

"No matter what happens, William," Alana hugged him. "We will be there for you for it. I can promise you that."

"Thank you, Alana," William's smile grew a little broader. "We will take it one day at a time. I promise you that if I start to feel the power taking over, I will come to you for help."

"You do that," Alana winked.

The three friends turned and watched the dragon woman as she continued to prepare the spell that she would cast to quietly open the door. Neither Alana nor Colwyn had ever seen dragon magic, so this was new to the both of them. William had seen the young woman cast dragon magic before. The wild dragon magic was far different from the human magic that William knew and used. It was far easier to get out of control. William was concerned that she was casting dragon magic in human form, but there was no way she would be able to transform into dragon form to cast the spell. He hoped that she would be able to contain the energies of the spell in her human form.

Even though he was still confused about what to do about the two women in his life, he knew for sure that he did still love Silvestra Knightwing. He did not want her hurt. He did not know what would happen, and he was not ready to talk to her about it, but he knew that it was a conversation he would not be able to put off for too much longer. He was at a crossroads in his life in more ways than one, it seemed. He did not know too much about either of the directions he could take. It was a difficult choice that he would have to make. And he knew that that decision point was coming very soon, possibly even within hours.

He reached up and touched the amulet he wore beneath his robes. The amulet and what he saw in front of him confused him. There was something strange at work here, and he did not know what it was. He knew what he knew and what he now saw was different than what he knew.

And that was where the confusion was coming from.

He wondered if any of what he had been told over the last seven years about this woman was the truth. Had he known the truth, he knew, there would be no question about which direction he would take at this crossroads. But he had been lied to, repeatedly. The great gold dragon,

Eliazar, had done everything he could to make sure that this decision would never come.

And yet, here it was.

He hated the gold dragon for the pain he had caused in both his and Silvestra's life. His life had been far easier. He had been assigned to watch over the Blademaster, and he had done so, although it was, in a lot of ways, a bit of pure luck that he had even found her. No one had known who she would be, just that a new Blademaster would be discovered in Ravendale.

William had sensed something special about Alana when they had first met. Without being told, he had known that Alana was the Chosen of Taelin. How could he not know? Alana was special in every way. There had been no doubt in his mind as to Alana's true destiny. He wished he had been able to tell her all along. But the Law of the Blades was specific. No one could tell her before it was her time to discover the truth.

He hoped that Alana would never find out that he had known all along. He did not think he could bear the distrust she might have for him if she ever found out.

He was impressed with Alana. He did not know much about the Blademasters of old, but if they had half of her character, they must have all been very special ladies. The thing that impressed William, however, was how Alana had been very careful in choosing her companions. The four people that travelled with her, Colwyn, William himself, Meryn and now Martin, all brought different talents and abilities to her aid. They were all important to her, and he knew that she was happy to have each and every one of them along.

He wondered if Silvestra would become one of her regular companions. He did not know what role she could fill. Alana already had a nathair an aeir a chosnaíonn. He did not think that Eliazar would allow her to travel with the Blademaster at any rate. Not if William was still with the Blademaster.

It was a puzzle to be solved on a different day. William was more concerned with getting out of the dungeon and helping Alana to solve the mystery of how to save the people of Valendale.

Silvestra stood suddenly. She walked over to stand directly under the grate and extended both hands towards the side of the grate where the latch was. She closed her eyes and whispered words in the dragonic language that none of the others could hear. William winced at the light coming from her hands as she finished the spell.

There was a soft but audible click as the latch slid free of the lock.

The rest of the companions joined Silvestra under the grate. She started to fall, dazed, but William caught her. Colwyn motioned for the halfling to join him.

"I'm going to boost you up, Meryn," Colwyn said. "I want you to get out and get the ladder so we can all get out of here."

"Don't worry, I can do it, Colwyn," Meryn nodded.

Colwyn knelt down and made a stirrup with his hands. Meryn put one of her small feet in his hands and held on to him around his neck as he stood up. He pushed her up until she almost hit her head on the grate. She shoved upwards on the grate and it moved enough for her to be able to squeeze herself out.

She went to where they kept the ladder and dragged it over to the grate. She quietly opened the grate all the way and slid the ladder inside. The companions took no time in climbing out of the dungeon, William carrying the unconscious dragon woman. The spell to release the lock had taken a great deal out of her. Colwyn silently wondered if she had been getting enough rest prior to making the attempt to open the grate like she had.

The companions quietly made their way down the hallway towards the exit. Having never been in the palace, the companions did not really know how it was laid out. Colwyn had lived in Connemara Castle in Arvendale his entire childhood, though, and he knew that all of the palaces in the Southern Dales were laid out similarly. There were differences from city to city, though, based on whoever it was that designed the palace in the first place. Colwyn tried to use that knowledge to guide the others out of the palace. He was clutching the summoning statue, praying that the dragon would heed the call and be there when they got out of the palace.

His plan was a simple one. As soon as they left the palace, they would get on Cobalt's back and fly up to the cavern they were using as a base. The rest of the companions would stay there while he and Cobalt flew off to the Temple of the Blades. It was a sound plan in his mind, and he prayed fervently to Taelin and Laeyra that it would work out the way he wanted it to.

They got about a third of the way from the dungeon to the front gate before they were spotted by Zeraphim soldiers.

"Run for it," Colwyn shouted. "Cobalt will be outside the front gates. We'll fly to safety on his back."

The companions split up, each going down a different hallway. Colwyn quickly lost sight of all of the others. Alana had not gone the same way that he had. There was nothing he could do about it, however. He simply hoped that she would make it safely out. He knew the direction he was going would take him out of the palace very quickly. He hoped that the others could find their own way safely out.

He was challenged by a Zeraphim guard as he came around a corner, but he had drawn his sword and charged at the man. The guard brought his own sword up, but he wasn't in time to deflect Colwyn's charge. Colwyn's bastard sword sliced through the guard like a hot knife through butter. The big ranger stopped long enough to rip off the emblem on the soldier's cloak, but did not otherwise slow down in the slightest, running right through the body. He bolted down the hallway, running just as hard as he could. He prayed the dragon would be there. He had not prayed so hard as he did now while running out of the palace in Willowdale.

He turned the corner and found himself staring at the archway that led to the outside. He could see the body of the great gold dragon sitting out in the courtyard of the palace, and he breathed a huge sigh of relief. He dashed out the archway and down the steps, stopping only when he stood beside the gold dragon.

"Thank you for coming, Cobalt," the ranger panted. "I wasn't sure you would come if I used the summoning statue instead of Alana."

"You called, and I came, Lord Colwyn," the dragon's voice was soft. He craned his neck around so that his head was right next to the young ranger. "I can only assume that you are in trouble."

"We were captured by the Zeraphim,' Colwyn said, scratching the dragon on his chin. "We just escaped the dungeon and were hoping that you could give us a ride out of here."

"Where are the others?" the dragon asked.

"We got separated," Colwyn sighed as he slumped against the dragon's body. "I don't know if they made it out."

"Let us see," the dragon rumbled.

He lowered his head to the ground and whispered a word of magic. A fog began to appear. Shapes began to appear in the fog. The shapes began to look like figures. Colwyn recognized his companions. They were surrounded by Zeraphim soldiers, and they were being herded back towards the dungeons. He saw the strange black leather clad woman that Alana had told him about leading the group towards the dungeons.

Colwyn's heart sank. He was the only one that had gotten out of the palace.

"It would appear that the others were recaptured," Cobalt hissed. "We could go after them."

"No, Cobalt," Colwyn said quietly after a few moments of watching the image in the fog. "I'm afraid we can't. Alana has ordered me to go to the Temple of the Blades. As much as I want to go in and rescue her, I need to give her the answers she needs. We fly to the Temple of the Blades. We need to be there and back before the morning."

"Then climb on my back and let us fly," Cobalt roared.

Colwyn took one last look at Alana being herded by the Zeraphim and sighed. He climbed on Cobalt's back and held on tight as the great gold dragon launched himself into the sky.

Alana groaned softly to herself. She had known that it was possible that they wouldn't make it out of the palace, but she had hoped that they would. She was crowded in with the others and headed back to the dungeon. Everyone except Colwyn was there. She fervently hoped that her husband had made it out of the palace. She also hoped that Cobalt was waiting for him out there. She wondered if he would do the right thing and go to the Temple of the Blades rather than trying to rescue them now. She calculated the time it would take to fly to the Temple of the Blades. She knew that they could be there and back before morning without any problem.

"It was a nice try, Blademaster," the Nightstalker said, breaking her out of her thoughts. "But not good enough I'm afraid you will still be here for your execution in the morning."

"My husband is free," Alana reminded the Nightstalker "He could still rescue us."

"I doubt that," the Nightstalker laughed. "He was seen flying off on a dragon. He has left you behind. That just proves how little he cares for you."

Good for you, Col! She thought. Aloud she said, "He'll be back in time to take me from the dungeon. You'll see. You'll come by in the morning to execute me, and I will be gone. I promise you."

"We shall see," the Nighstalker shrugged. They stopped at the grate to the dungeon and she motioned to a guard. "Open it. Push them in. Make sure the mages are unconscious when they go in."

One of the guards pulled the grate open and started to shove the companions inside the dungeon. Alana was the last to be shoved in. She looked up as the Nightstalker looked down at the companions.

"I will see you in the morning, Blademaster," the Nightstalker said. "It will be my deepest pleasure to take off your head."

"You're all talk, Kera Rayden," Alana smiled. "I told you. I'm not that easy to kill."

"It will be all too easy," Kera Rayden smiled broadly as she slammed the grate closed. "Enjoy your last few hours."

They heard the latch slide home in the lock and footsteps leading off from the grate. Alana slumped to the ground and sighed.

"Come back with the answers I need, Col," she said softly. "Come back quickly."

Chapter XII
Elvish Temptation

obalt flew Colwyn to the edge of the Elven Woods. When the dragon landed, Colwyn slid off his back and patted the dragon on the side. The great gold dragon hunched down on the ground.

"This is as far as I'll go," the dragon rumbled. "While Blademaster Alana has been kind enough to accept me as her nathair an aeir a chosnaíonn, I am not comfortable going to the Temple of the Blades. You'll have to walk from here, Lord Colwyn."

"That's all right, Cobalt," Colwyn assured the dragon. "I know these woods very well. Nothing will attack me here."

"If you are sure, Lord Colwyn," the dragon huffed. "If you need me, you do have my summoning statue. Do not hesitate to use it. I will come if you call."

"Thank you, noble dragon," Colwyn smiled. "I do not expect to need you, so rest. But be alert. The strangest things seem to happen around Alana and I."

"So I have noticed," the dragon rumbled with a laugh. "That is why I enjoy being her nathair an aeir a chosnaíonn. It is anything but a boring job."

"We aim to please," Colwyn rolled his eyes. "I'd like my life to be a little more boring myself these days."

"Humans," Cobalt rolled his eyes and blew a puff of smoke. "No sense of humor."

Colwyn laughed and cinched his bag on his shoulder. He made his way into the Elven Woods, stopping at a clearing not far inside the woods to wait for the Forestwalker Elves. Even though Queen Mirian had promised that the Blademaster and her companions would have free passage through the Elven Woods, Colwyn still felt like he could not just walk through the woods without giving his respects to the elves themselves. It was improper and he knew that Alana felt the same way. That she understood was one of the things he loved about her.

Colwyn sat down on the ground and crossed his legs. He knew that it would take a little time for the elves to get to him, and so he made himself comfortable. He closed his eyes and tried to force himself into a state of stát ndoimhneacht na tsíocháin inmheánach. He knew he did not have time to settle into the full deep state of stát ndoimhneacht na tsíocháin inmheánach, but he would settle for a touch of the deep inner peace from the technique.

He was too unsettled knowing that Alana was still being held prisoner. He wanted to fly back to Willowdale now and break her out of her prison. He knew that he could not do so, however. He had promised her that he would get her answers, and this was the only place he could go to do that. And he would get the answers she needed, he promised himself that. The unsettled feeling stayed, however, and he could not get any of the inner peace that he was looking for.

And it did not matter, for the elves had arrived. He opened his eyes and saw Otan Kovalani standing over him. The master ranger had an amused expression on his face. The ranger offered Colwyn a hand, and Colwyn took it, standing up. The elves towered over Colwyn, as most elves did.

"Bhuel le chéile, mo dhearthái," Otan said in his rich baritone voice.

"Well met, Otan Kovalani," Colwyn said softly bowing slightly at the waist.

"The Queen wishes to see you before you continue onto the Temple of the Blades," Otan said. His face looked slightly pained as he switched back into elvish before continuing. "Cibé rud a tharlaíonn, deartháir, tá a fhios go bhfuil mé go raibh aon pháirt ann."

"What do you mean?" Colwyn frowned.

He had never been able to fully understand Otan. It was one of the reasons that Otan had been so frustrated with Colwyn during his ranger training. And yet, Colwyn had become one of Otan's favorite pupils. Or at least so Otan had said. He had not taken it as a personal affront when Colwyn had taken up with his sister, Mirian, who was now the queen of the Forestwalker Elves.

"You will see," Otan rumbled in his chest. He turned to Colwyn and smiled as they started out of the clearing. "I heard you have married your Blademaster, Colwyn. You are to be commended. She is an excellent match for you."

"Thank you, Otan," Colwyn smiled back. "I am truly happy with her as my wife. You will be glad to know that I finally experienced stát ndoimhneacht na tsíocháin inmheánach while in the Temple of the Blades."

"Really?" Otan shot an eyebrow up. "I am impressed. What memory did you use?"

"It was the memory of the day that I met Alana," Colwyn smiled. "The High Priestess of the Blades explained to me that the reason I was able to enter stát ndoimhneacht na tsíocháin inmheánach with that memory is that Alana is my true love. Is it true that only a memory of my true love would allow me to enter stát ndoimhneacht na tsíocháin inmheánach?"

"It is a popular theory amongst my people," Otan shrugged. "I happen to believe it myself. I take it you no longer feel anger towards the Council of Elders for their decision to part you from my sister?"

"I feel relief towards them, actually," Colwyn shrugged. "Whether they knew it or not, they did me a very great favor by doing what they did. They have allowed me to find true love. I never thought I would. As you know, I am a noble. We are supposed to marry for political reasons, not for love."

"Humans," Otan snorted. "I have never understood your ways. Elven ways are so much better."

"I do not disagree, my friend," Colwyn laughed. "Why do you think I'm here and not at Connemara Castle with my father droning in my ear about duty and honor and finding me a bride who would be a good political fit for me?"

"Because you have seen the light, of course," Otan smiled. "After all, you were my student for seven years. I'm glad to know that I knocked some sense into you during your lessons."

"You knocked something into me all right," Colwyn grumbled, remembering all the times Otan had ended up planting Colwyn on his back during their sparring sessions. "I never could best you."

"And yet you kept trying," Otan grinned. He clapped Colwyn on the shoulder. "Even my own men stopped trying after I beat them ten times, Colwyn."

"What can I say?" the human sighed. "I'm a human. We're stubborn like that."

"Indeed," Otan chuckled.

The two friends walked for several minutes thinking about the past. Neither wanted to break the silence. It was a peaceful and beautiful day in the Elven Woods. Birds were fluttering around and singing their merry songs. Squirrels chattered in the trees as they hid their nuts for the winter. Nature was singing its most beautiful song, and Colwyn was glad to once more be listening to the symphony.

"I always forget how beautiful it is here, Otan," Colwyn said softly. "Alana and I do so much running around and fighting. I have seen so much death. I think maybe that's why Taelin put the Temple of the Blades in these woods. He knew that his Blademasters and their Protectors would need a reminder of nature's beauty."

"That would not surprise me," Otan laughed. "Taelin is the god of Wisdom after all. He had to know that surrounding the Blademasters with the beauty of nature would only help them. Just like the Blademasters needing to know how to love and having a spark of true love in their lives is an important component to balance the Blademasters, the need to be surrounded by beauty when surrounded by so much ugliness is just as important Taelin knew exactly what he was doing when he put the Temple of the Blades here."

"I never thought about the true love requirement of the Blademasters being a balance before," Colwyn rubbed his chin. "I shall have to think on that some more."

"Do you mean to tell me that you have not heard of the Eighteenth Law of the Blades?" Otan raised an eyebrow. "I thought I had trained you better than this, Colwyn. Really, you must learn all of the Laws if you are going to continue to be her Protector."

"The only one I know is the First Law of the Blades," Colwyn shrugged. "It's the most important one, apparently, so it's the only one I've learned."

"Listen carefully, mo dheartháir, for I will only say this once," Otan said softly. "It is not for outsiders to know the Law of the Blades. I was taught this one Law because it seems the High Priestess of the Blades knew that you would never learn it on your own. I will tell you the Eighteenth Law of the Blades this one time. After that, you are on your own. I ngach den saol, ní mór go mbeadh cothromaíocht. A chailleadh go bhfuil cothromaíocht a cuireadh chaos agus bás isteach Ní mór máistir na lanna a bheith i gcónaí ar comhardú i di féin agus ina cuid déileálacha le daoine eile. Sin é an fáth go bhfuil an dlí chéad cheann de na lanna chomh tábhachtach sin. Ní mór an grá roinneann sí lena fear céile bás caithfidh sí a chothromú déileáil ina seasamh. You understand, yes?"

Colwyn mulled the translation through his head for several long minutes. *In all of life, there must be balance. To lose that balance is to invite chaos and death in. A Blademaster must always be in balance in herself and in her dealings with others. That is why the First Law of the Blades is so important. The love she shares with her husband must balance the death she must deal in her position.* After he felt that he understood what the other man was trying to tell him, he nodded once and smiled.

"I will never forget that one," Colwyn nodded. "I believe that this is not the first time you've tried to teach me that particular truth."

"The life of the ranger is a life of balance, Colwyn," Otan groaned as he slapped his forehead with the palm of his head. "Of course, I have tried to teach you that truth before. It is the center of all your learning during your time here."

"Perhaps I did not learn as much as I thought I had during my time here," Colwyn grunted.

"And perhaps that is the smartest thing I have heard you ever say," Otan laughed heartily.

"We have a saying in Arvendale, Otan," Colwyn growled. "Nobody loves a smartass."

That made Otan laugh all the harder. The two friends walked deeper into the forest, heading towards the Forestwalker clan's city in the trees. Colwyn had spent a great deal of time among the Forestwalker Elves and he knew that the elves were nearing one of their times of celebration. He could almost see them preparing for the celebration, preparing decorations for their trees and houses. He knew that strands of gold and silver would line all of the trees in the city.

He also knew that the time must come soon for Queen Mirian to choose a mate. He found that he bore whoever was chosen no ill will. After all, Colwyn had found his true love. He only hoped that Mirian would find some trace of the happiness that Colwyn himself felt whenever he looked at Alana. She deserved as much for all the sadness that she had had in her life. The life of the Queen was not an easy one.

"Otan, why does Queen Mirian want to see me?" Colwyn asked softly.

"That is for the queen to say, Colwyn," Otan said equally as softly. Colwyn could tell that there was a bitter note in the other man's voice. "Even if I wanted to tell you what madness is to come, I have been forbidden to."

"Forbidden by whom?" Colwyn raised an eyebrow. "Other than the queen, I can't imagine anyone who could forbid you to do anything."

"That is for the queen to tell you, mo dheartháir," Otan sighed. "I have said too much already. You are headed into something dangerous. I can be of no help to you. Impigh mé de tú maithiúnas a thabhairt dom, mo dheartháir. Tá a fhios agat an grá agus meas agam duit féin agus do na mná grá agat. Ba mhaith liom rudaí a bhí difriúil ná ní mór cad a tharlóidh. Tá tú i gceannas ar feadh trialach nach raibh ach is féidir leat duine. Ní mór duit i réim. Gach ár saol ag brath air. Is é an meáchan ar an domhan ar do ghualainn. Tá eagla orm go bhféadfadh sé a bheith i bhfad ró-a iompróidh. Cuimhneamh nach bhfuil rudaí i gcónaí mar atá siad."

Colwyn mulled that over. He had heard that phrase before and he thought that maybe it might be a Law of the Blades. It was one more thing he would have to ask when he consulted the Legacy of the Blademasters. He had so many questions, and so few answers. And yet, that seemed to be the way that he and Alana lived their lives. They never had all the answers. But they always seemed to find the answers that they needed when they needed them the most. He knew he needed to get some answers for her. He wished that he could bypass the Forestwalker Elves and just head straight to the Temple of the Blades.

Something was telling him that he should do that very thing.

It would not be proper is what he kept telling himself. He was a noble. Propriety was everything in the nobility, and a queen was certainly nobility. It went against everything he believed to just skip the meeting with the queen. And yet, everything inside him was screaming to just tell Otan to lead him to the path to the Temple of the Blades and bypass the city of the Forestwalker Elves altogether.

Colwyn generally trusted his instincts. But he could not make himself bypass the Elven city and go straight onto the road to the Temple of the Blades. He had a feeling he would come to regret his nobility. He just couldn't shake the feeling that he should just go. He was sure that if he asked Otan, his friend would guide him to the road to the Temple of the Blades.

"Otan, why do I feel like I'm about to walk into a trap?" Colwyn said softly as they kept walking towards the Forestwalker Elves' city.

"I know not what you are referring to, mo dhearthái," Otan said quietly. There was something in the way that Otan said it that gave the human ranger pause.

"I have never known you to lie to me, Otan," Colwayn's voice was barely above a whisper. "Please do not dishonor me by starting now."

"If I could, I would take you straight to the Temple of the Blades to avoid what is about to happen," Otan said sadly. "There is nothing I can do to stop it. Even if you tried to go there on your own and try to get away from us, I would be honor bound to stop you and bring you to the Queen. I am sorry, Colwyn. Tread lightly when you are in with the Queen. That is all I can say."

"It's all right, Otan," Colwyn smiled weakly. "I'd hate to start getting straight answers now after all this time. I'm not sure I would be able to handle it if someone were to just tell something without the riddles for a change."

"You have been deeply hurt by the process of joining to the Blademaster," Otan nodded. He clapped Colwyn on the shoulder. "But she is quite a woman, mo dhearthái. You are a very lucky man."

"She is indeed," Colwyn's smile grew broader. "I love her, Otan. More than I've ever loved anyone else. Even more than I loved Mirian."

"Remember what you just said, Colwyn," Otan said mysteriously. "Remember that when you are in with the Queen. It may save you if you keep it in mind."

"You're making me nervous, Otan," Colwyn's smile faded. "Mirian is up to something, isn't she?"

"That is for the Queen to say, Colwyn," Otan sighed. "You will find out soon enough."

Sure enough, as he said that, the city of the Forestwalker Elves came into view. Colwyn never got tired of the city in the trees. Tree bridges stretched from great redwood trees. The trees held houses in their thick leafy branches. The houses were well crafted to be hidden in the foliage of the trees. Had Colwyn not spent so much time in the home of the Forestwalker Clan as he had, he might not have made out the houses. Even the tree bridges were artfully hidden. Despite the fact that Ravendale was where he made his home now and despite the fact that one day he would have to return to Connemara Castle in Arvendale and take up the mantle of the First Lord of Arvendale, the Elven Woods would always have a special place in his heart.

"I never get tired of seeing this, Otan," Colwyn smiled.

"And we never get tired of having you here, Colwyn," Otan smiled back. It was a smile tinged with sadness though. "Is cuma cad a tharlaíonn sa lá atá inniu, tá a fhios go mbeidh tú féin agus an Alana Lady a bheith i gcónaí fáilte roimh chách sa chathair sna crainn, le haghaidh an banríon gheall an dílseacht na clan go siúlóidí i measc na foraoisí ar an máistir na lanna agus an ceann a chosnaíonn di."

"Thank you, Otan," Colwyn clapped his friend on the shoulder. "I think I can find my way from here. I should not keep the Queen waiting any longer than necessary."

"Be careful, Colwyn," Otan warned. "There is something at work here in the Elven Woods today that could cost you everything. I warn you now in defiance of the Queen's orders. Be careful when you meet with her. And remember. Things are not always as they seem."

"Thank you for the warning, Otan," Colwyn nodded. "I shall take it to heart."

Otan watched as his friend climbed the ladder to the rope bridges.

"Féadfaidh an ádh ar Laeyra agus an eagna Taelin leanann tú, mo dheartháir," Otan whispered. "You will need both."

Alana was sitting by herself in the dungeon. She wished Colwyn was back. She missed him terribly, but she knew that he was going to get the answers that she needed in order to free the people of Valendale. She hoped that he would be able to get those answers and get back in time to rescue them from the dungeon.

She had no doubt that he would make it back in time. She had to believe he would. Her love for him was all that was sustaining her in the dungeon. She could feel the power of his love for her burning through her body as if he were sitting right there holding her. It was a feeling she always loved to have. He was the only one who had ever made her feel that way and she would do anything it took to keep feeling that way for the rest of her life.

She could not stop thinking about the Nightstalker. The Nightstalker had intrigued her, and even scared her a little. Kera Rayden was cool and confident. Maybe a little too confident. There was something about the woman that really bothered her. She could feel the evil and the hate flowing off the young woman. She could still see the woman's icy blue eyes staring coldly at her. She shivered slightly thinking about those eyes.

There were footsteps in the corridor above the dungeon, and Alana looked up at the grate expectantly. She hoped it was Colwyn coming back to rescue them. But instead it was a guard that opened the grate. He slid the ladder down and pointed at Alana.

"Mistress Kera wishes to see you, Blademaster," the guard announced. "Move it. It's best not to keep the Nightstalker waiting."

Alana shrugged and climbed up the ladder. The guards roughly dragged her down the corridor towards the quarters of the First Lord. Alana knew that the woman with the icy blue eyes was waiting for her.

Colwyn stood on the tree bridge. He was in between two trees, and he found he could not move any further. It was strange. Once upon a time, nothing could keep him from moving so easily through the city in the trees. But something was troubling him. The closer he got to the home of the Queen, the harder it was for him to go any further. He could not allay his fears that he was walking into a trap. He could not help but feel that something truly bad was about to happen.

But how could something bad happen in such a beautiful setting?

It was a question he kept asking himself. And yet, his instincts were telling him that something was off in the Elven Woods. Something was wrong.

Something was about the happen that he would regret.

He forced himself to continue across the tree bridge He knew that there was no way he could prevent what was to happen. Otan had already told him as much. He knew that if he tried to avoid this confrontation, Otan's rangers would simply drag him back through the Elven Woods to meet with the Queen anyway.

He felt trapped. And he knew that the trap had not even sprung yet. There was a deep uneasiness about this meeting with the Queen. Otan had said that there was something at work in the Elven Woods today that could cause him to lose everything. The statement had been a simple one, and yet, Colwyn wondered about it. He knew that only one thing truly mattered and that was his love for Alana.

Could that be what Otan had been referring to?

"Oh, Mirian," Colwyn whispered. "What are you up to? You gave your word and your vow to Alana. Don't break it now."

He could not put it off any longer. Slowly he brought himself to the door of the Queen's house. He raised his hand to knock and paused. He thought about running. He thought about trying to just leave the Elven Woods and having Cobalt fly him into the clearing of the Temple of the Blades. He sighed, knowing he could not do that to the poor dragon. He knew that Cobalt could not bring himself to enter that clearing. And Colwyn would not be the one to make him.

He knocked and heard an acknowledgement for him to enter. He took a deep breath and opened the door to the Queen's house. He hesitated on the threshold and then stepped inside.

The living room of the little house was just as it had been the last time he had been there. The room was tastefully done in rich greens and browns. Artistically carved chairs and tables were carefully placed around the room. The hardwood floors were bare and polished to a muted shine. A hall leading off to other rooms left through an opening in the wall to the right. On the wall in front of them was the room's only window. Queen of the Forestwalker Clan, Mirian Kovalani stood in front of the window, gazing outside, just as she had been when Alana and Colwyn had visited the Forestwalker Elves on the day they were married in the Temple of the Blades. Even with her back to the door, she knew who it was that had entered the house.

"Colwyn Starseeker," she said softly, her musical voice betraying the smile she wore. She turned around and strode across the room towards him. She placed her hands on his shoulders and smiled broadly at him. "You are just in time, my dear one. You are just in time for my wedding."

"Who is to be the groom, Queen Mirian?" Colwyn asked, his eyebrow raised in surprise.

"Why, you are, of course!" the Queen beamed.

Alana stumbled entering the quarters of the First Lord. Something was deeply wrong, and she did not know what it was. She carefully straightened and strode purposefully into the room. She chose to maintain her dignity, although inside she was deeply concerned. She tried to figure out what it was that did not feel right, but she could not make out what the problem was. She was afraid. She did not want to face Kera Rayden like this.

"What is it you want, Nightstalker?" Alana ground out through clenched teeth. "I'm too busy to deal with your nonsense."

"Too busy getting ready to die?" Kera raised one delicately manicured eyebrow. "Too busy praying to your pathetic Lord Taelin to take your soul when you die in the morning? That's what you should be doing, you know. You should be praying that he will accept you after I prove just how weak you are."

"I keep telling you, I'm not going to be here in the morning for you to kill," Alana crossed her arms. She fought to keep her face straight as she felt a twinge deep in her core. "I'll be gone and you'll have to fight me one on one in due time."

"So you keep telling me," the Nightstaler said. She stood up and crossed over to where the Blademaster was standing. She started to slowly circle Alana like a cat circling a mouse. "I think there's something wrong with you. Something deep inside doesn't feel right."

"I don't know what you're talking about," Alana ground out. The twinge inside her core was getting harder to ignore. It was starting to become painful.

"I think your god has forsaken you," Kera grinned wickedly. She reached out and trailed a finger along Alana's body as she moved around her. "I think your Protector is dead and you are feeling your powers fading away. I think that very soon, you will be powerless to do so much as pull a knife from a sheath."

"My Lord Taelin will never forsake me," Alana gritted her teeth. The pain was getting almost unbearable. "And my Colwyn will be back for me soon. You will see."

"No," Kera smiled wryly. "I don't think you will be saved. I think you are quite, quite doomed."

Alana couldn't take it anymore. She doubled over in pain and fell to her knees. She screamed in pain, a primal deep scream that hurt the Nightstalker's ears.

"Lord Taelin, help me," the Blademaster gasped weakly.

"No one can help you now, child," Kera said, her face right by Alana's. She slapped Alana across her face with the back of her glove, leaving a deep red mark on the Blademaster's cheek. "You are as helpless as a child." She stood up and addressed the guards that had brought Alana to her. "Guards, throw this pathetic wretch back in the dungeon. See how the high and mighty Blademaster has fallen."

The guards picked Alana up and carried her out of the First Lord's quarters. The Blademaster moaned pitifully all the way back to the dungeon. She could not fight back. The pain inside her core was too intense. It was as if she had had a part of herself ripped out of her. She could not even focus enough to wonder what could have caused such a thing.

She lay where they threw her in the dungeon. She did not even see the guards take the ladder away and close and latch the grate. She simply moaned. Martin Faolin came over and tried to tend to her, but there was nothing the young priest could do other than comfort her. He stroked her forehead and whispered prayers to Taelin over her.

"What happened to Colwyn?" she whispered weakly after a few minutes. "Why do I feel like he is gone?"

"I don't know, Lady Alana," Martin said gently, his fingers gently tracing her hairline in an attempt to relax her. "I don't know."

"Well, say something, Colwyn," Mirian crossed her arms. The smile had faded from her face when Colwyn did not reply to her pronouncement. "You are to be my husband. I have chosen you over everyone else."

"You must be joking, Queen Mirian," Colwyn whispered. He strode over to the window and looked out over the Elven city. "I cannot marry you. The Council of Elders would never approve. To say nothing of the fact that I am already married."

"The Council of Elders has already approved of my choice," the Queen came up behind him and put his arms around him. "And as for your marriage to the Blademaster. Well, you are ill suited for her. You are nobility. She is a simple common swordswoman. You must marry within your class."

"Mirian, we cannot be," Colwyn pulled away from her. It wasn't as easy to pull away as it should have. "You know I have committed myself to the Blademaster. Alana is my true love. I cannot abandon that."

"But I desire you as I always have," the Queen spoke. She came around to stand in front of him. She reached out and traced her fingers against his cheek. "We were meant to be together. Did you not say that once?"

"Once upon a time I believed that," he pulled away again. It was becoming harder and harder to pull away from her. Something about the way she was talking was breaking down his defenses. "I love Alana. I must be with her."

"No," Mirian smiled at him. "You must be with me."

She leaned up and kissed him on the lips. Sparks of electricity crackled through him, and he felt himself returning the kiss with equal passion. Something was preventing him from pulling away. Slowly, he stopped fighting and fell into the kiss.

It was wrong though. He did not love Mirian, he knew. He was kissing the wrong woman. But it felt so right to kiss her. He had wanted to kiss her like this for such a long time.

Suddenly, his brain flashed on something that Otan had said during their walk to the city in the trees.

"You have been deeply hurt by the process of joining to the Blademaster," Otan nodded. He clapped Colwyn on the shoulder. "But she is quite a woman, mo dheartháir. You are a very lucky man."

"She is indeed," Colwyn's smile grew broader. "I love her, Otan. More than I've ever loved anyone else. Even more than I loved Mirian."

"Remember what you just said, Colwyn," Otan said mysteriously. "Remember that when you are in with the Queen. It may save you if you keep it in mind."

With an effort, Colwyn broke the kiss. Gently, he pushed the Queen away.

"No," he said softly. "This is not right. You have to stop, Mirian. I cannot be your husband. I am Alana's husband and that is all I need and want to be. Do not ever try to change that again."

"If that is your wish," Mirian nodded. "I had to try."

"No, you didn't," Colwyn turned away. He let tears flow freely for what he had almost done. "You almost caused me to betray the woman I love with all my heart. You almost caused me to betray something so beautiful. I loved you once, Mirian. How could you do this? How could you hurt me like this?"

"I had to," Mirian said. She turned to stare out the window again. "Go, Colwyn. Your Blademaster needs answers. You should go and get them."

"If it weren't for being so in love with Alana, I would be with you, Mirian," he said softly. "You have to know that."

"Just go, Colwyn," she whispered. "Just... go."

Colwyn bowed slightly and made his way out of the house. He sat on the steps leading up to the Queen's house. He put his face in his hands and started to weep.

The pain was getting worse. She had been screaming so loudly that she had gotten hoarse. She wondered if she would ever know what it was like to live without the pain inside her core once again. It was getting so hard to breathe. The pain was overwhelming.

And then, it was as if the pain were never there.

She opened her eyes and gasped at the cessation of pain. She began to breathe slowly and evenly. She looked up at the priest who was still stroking her forehead.

"What... happened?" she asked weakly.

"I have no idea," the priest frowned down at her. "We were all worried about you though. How do you feel?"

"It was weird," she said. "The pain was like something was being ripped from me. It was as if something reached inside and was literally ripping out my core. It was getting to be unbearable at the end. And now it feels as if everything is normal."

"I have never heard of anything like this happening to a Blademaster before," Martin admitted. "I think it would be best if you tried to sleep. You have been through quite the ordeal. I have some herbs that might help you sleep."

"Thank you, Martin," she reached up and placed her hand against his cheek. "Thank you for being there for me."

"It is my job, Lady Blademaster," the young priest smiled down at her.

Colwyn was trying to leave the city without anyone seeing him. He did not want to talk to anyone after what had happened with the Queen. He knew, though, that he would not be able to just disappear. He had just finished climbing down the ladder to the floor of the forest below the city when Otan caught up with him.

"Allow me to escort you to the Temple of the Blades, Colwyn," Otan said softly as he fell into step with Colwyn.

"Thank you for the help, Otan," Colwyn would not look at his friend. "But I wish to be alone in my journey to the Temple of the Blades."

"Wait, mo dheartháir," Otan said. He put his hand on Colwyn's arm and spun the human around. "You will hear me before you leave."

"Take your hand from me, Otan," Colwyn's voice was quiet. "What has happened today puts bad blood between me and the Forestwalker Elves. You would be best served to leave me be."

"I warned you that something bad was in the city today," Otan said. He dropped to his knees before Colwyn. Mo dheartháir, le do thoil logh dom. Bhí mé ina páirtí do pian. Rinne mé rabhadh duit, ach tú a bheith gortaithe ar aon nós. Impigh mé de tú maithiúnas a thabhairt do mo mhuintir an pian go bhfuil muid ba chúis agat. Más rud é go mbeadh sé éasca do pian, a chur ar mo shaol mar íocaíocht as an méid atá déanta againn a thabhairt duit."

"Get up, Otan," Colwyn said, his voice angry. "I'm not going to take your life. Your Queen would be best served to stay away from both Alana and myself however."

"Queen Mirian asked me to relay a message to you," the elven ranger said softly. "She begs your forgiveness. She asks that if you can find it in your heart to forgive her for what she has done to you today, that you do so."

"I forgive her, Otan," Colwyn nodded. He turned away towards the direction he had to go to get to the Temple of the Blades. "But I do not forget. The time will come when she will have to pay for what she has done. That day is not today. Nor will I be the one to set the price. She will one day have to face Lord Taelin. I hope that when she does, the Lightbringer will be forgiving of her."

"Thank you, mo dheartháir," Otan smiled sadly. "Turas go maith duit, an ceann a chosnaíonn sí an máistir na lanna. Go dtí go mbeidh níos mó ná uair ár cosáin trasna."

"Good journey to you, Otan Kovalani," Colwyn nodded. "Until next our paths shall cross."

With that, Colwyn set off towards the Temple of the Blades by himself.

Willowdale

Chapter XIII
Consulting Raven

It took Colwyn several hours to reach the Temple of the Blades after leaving the Forestwalker Elves. He wasn't sure that he would ever be welcome back in the home of the elves after he spurned the queen as he had. But he had been tempted. That was what hurt him more than anything. He had come far too close to giving in to that temptation and losing the woman he loved forever. That he had not given in did not mitigate the pain he felt. He could only hope that Alana would forgive him for even thinking about the temptation.

He stopped at the edge of the clearing where the Temple of the Blades rested in the heart of the Elven Woods. He stared at the marble walls and heaved a great sigh. He sat in the grass and rested before continuing. He wasn't sure he was ready to go in just yet. After what had happened in the Elven Woods, he knew that he would have a great deal of questions to answer before he would be able to get his own questions answered.

He pulled a piece of dried meat from his pack and started to nibble on it as he thought about what had happened and about what he needed to find out from the Legacy of the Blademasters.

He found that he could not think about the questions he had while he worried about what to do about what had happened in the Elven Woods. He did not understand why Mirian Kovalani had tried to tempt him into breaking his vows to Alana. It did not make sense. Mirian had known what he was to become when they came through the Elven Woods weeks before when Alana became the Blademaster. He knew that she knew what kind of a sacred bond that was. He did not understand why she insisted that they break the bond and be together.

He did not love her the same way he loved Alana. For that matter, he could love no one the way he loved Alana. What he and Alana shared was true love. He would never have anything like that with anyone else. Nor did he want anyone else.

So why had he been tempted?

Of course, he found the elven woman attractive. Who wouldn't? She was an exquisite beauty, to be sure. But there wasn't anything more than that in Colwyn's mind. And for Colwyn, there had to be more than just physical attraction for there to be love. Now that he had experienced true love as he had with Alana, he understood that the Council of Elders had actually done him a favor by forbidding his romance with the Queen. It was odd. At the time, he had mourned the loss of that relationship. But now that it was put into perspective, he knew it was a blessing. Such a romance between them would have never worked anyway.

So why had he been tempted?

He should have known that something fishy that was going to happen as soon as Otan Kovalani had greeted him. The master ranger had specifically told Colwyn that he had had no part in anything that was about to happen. That should have been enough to alert Colwyn that danger was ahead. He should have seen the trap before it had wrapped around him.

So why had he been tempted?

He kept asking himself that question, but he had no answers. It was as if the temptation had been arranged somehow, but he did not know why he would be tempted in such a way, nor did he have any idea who would be responsible for such a temptation.

It was a mystery that he knew he would never be able to solve by himself. He did know that he had jeopardized what might be the most important relationship in the world today. He could only hope that he would be able to find a way to tell Alana just how sorry he was.

Colwyn sat in the grass outside the Temple of the Blades, idly chewing on the piece of dried meat as he tried to sort things out in his own mind. He knew that he loved Alana, and he knew that she loved him. He could only hope that it would be enough to save their relationship.

He felt secure in the clearing, so he did not keep his attention focused around him as tightly as he normally did. He was too focused on working through the trouble of his almost betraying the love of his life to care about anything going on around him. He was secure enough that nothing dangerous would find its way into the clearing housing the Temple of the Blades to hurt him. If he had stopped to remember the story of the Great Purge, he would have remained alert to his surroundings.

"Why so sad, Colwyn?" Solara Moonfire, the High Priestess of the Blades, asked when she found him sitting there in the clearing outside the Temple of the Blades. She had come up on him without his noticing, which disturbed him a little bit. He was normally a lot more observant than that.

"I almost betrayed my Alana on the way here, Solara," Colwyn said, his voice above a whisper. "I almost lost the one person who means more to me than anyone else in my life. For nothing."

"Come on inside, Colwyn, there is something I must tell you," Solara smiled sadly at him. She took him by his arm and brought him to his feet.

Colwyn slowly followed her up the steps of the Temple of the Blades. He stopped before the great plaque by the door and ran his fingers over the letters like he did the first time he had stood of it.

Thiocfaidh sí a anseo chun aghaidh a thabhairt ar ndán di dul isteach le croí mór íon. Ní mór di troid i gcomhréir le prionsabail na Taelin agus Laeyra. Ní mór di cloí le Dlí na lanna má ghlacann sí a ndán. Chun é sin le bás a theipeann. She who enters here to face her destiny must enter with a pure heart. She must fight according to the precepts of Taelin and Laeyra. She must abide by the Law of the Blades if she accepts her destiny. Failure brings death.

He hadn't understood why those words were there before. He understood now. Their lives had changed irrevocably when they had walked through these doors just a few months before. He was surprised to realize that it had only been a few short months since Alana had accepted her burden as the Blademaster. Had he known exactly how much his life would have changed... He let that thought trail off because he knew full well that even had he known what was going to happen, he would have done the same thing all over again.

He would have done anything to be with his Alana.

Solara watched him trace the letters of the plaque without comment. It was almost as if she knew what he was thinking. With the way the Legacy of the Blademasters was, he did not doubt that she could read anyone's mind inside the Temple of the Blades. She seemed to have some kind of supernatural sense about everything that happened inside the Temple. It was an uncanny sense. It was as if she had a far heightened form of the enhanced senses that rangers often displayed.

Colwyn stepped inside the Temple of the Blades without a word and made his way into the Great Hall. He strode to the altar and took a knee before it, bowing his head. He said a silent prayer of thanks to Taelin and Laeyra for putting Alana in his life and keeping her there.

"You seem very troubled, Colwyn," Solara said after watching him for a few minutes.

"I came seeking answers from the Legacy of the Blademasters," Colwyn said without looking up. "I find that I will have more questions than before I came, however."

"Ah, yes," Solara sighed softly. "You refer to the situation with the Elven Queen on your way here."

"Why am I not surprised to know you know what happened?" Colwyn grunted as he stood and faced the High Priestess of the Blades.

"Because I am responsible for it," Solara moved to the other side of the altar.

"What?" Colwyn thundered. "You were responsible for Mirian trying to tempt me away from Alana?"

"Of course," Solara nodded. "I needed to know that you were completely sure about your path."

"Are there going to be any further tests of my faithfulness or my love for Alana?" Colwyn demanded angrily.

"You have every right to be angry, Colwyn," the priestess sighed as she perched on the edge of the altar. "But no, there will be no further tests. You must understand. So much rides on you and Alana. I had to be sure that I had the right Protector for her."

"The Test of the Blades wasn't proof enough?" Colwyn crossed his arms.

"We have always done this for the most important Blademasters," Solara crossed hers in return. "Just to make sure. Fear not, Colwyn. You have proven yourself beyond any shadow of a doubt."

Colwyn stormed away from the High Priestess of the Blades. He stormed his way out of the Great Hall and worked his way through the corridors until he found himself in the little room that he had used while waiting for the Test of the Blades to begin. He sat on the bench in the room and closed his eyes. He struggled to control his anger. He focused on that perfect memory of his first meeting with Alana and felt himself falling into a state of stát ndoimhneacht na tsíocháin inmheánach. Instantly, his anger faded away.

"So sad for one so handsome," a familiar voice said from next to him. "Solara was not right to do what she did. But she meant well."

"I only hope Alana can forgive me for being tempted," Colwyn said. He opened his eyes and looked at Raven Windrider, the very first Blademaster. "Did she do this to you and Richard as well?"

"She did," Raven nodded. "And I forgave Richard. Just as your Alana will forgive you. After all, you did not betray her. But someone from your party will."

"What do you mean?" Colwyn turned to face her fully. "Someone who's been traveling with Alana and I will betray her?"

"So it is written," Raven said sadly. "The sage Isaiah tried to warn her, but she refused to listen. And so I must tell you. You will be betrayed by one of your friends. I do not know who. I know only that it will not be you. Well, that is something to know at least. A small comfort, at any rate. I know you have questions, Colwyn. I also know some of the answers. They will not be easy ones."

"The important answers never are, Raven," Colwyn closed his eyes and leaned his head back against the wall. "When we were taken prisoner in Willowdale, we met this strange woman in all black leather. She called herself the Nightstalker. I got the feeling that she was like a dark version of Alana."

"That's about as accurate a description as any of us have been able to come up with for the Nightstalker," Raven nodded. "None of us know exactly what the Nightstalker is capable of. I don't think even the Dark God knows. By tempering the Blademaster's powers through the strength of her love for her Protector, Taelin and Laeyra, in essence, created an upper limit of power for the Blademasters. The Nightstalker is made of pure hate. There is little that can limit that."

"What can we do to stop her?" Colwyn asked.

"You must believe in the First Law of the Blades," Raven said simply. "The only thing that can counter hate is love. Her love for you is the only thing that can save her when she faces the Nightstalker."

"She almost lost that."

"But she didn't, Colwyn," Raven smiled at him. She reached over and touched his cheek. "Never forget that. She still has you. And you must continue to love her as you always have. There is great magic in that love. And you must always protect that magic. It will save both of you many times as you go through your adventures."

"Thank you for reminding me of that, Lady Raven," Colwyn turned away from her and stared at the far wall.

He continued to look at the wall for several long minutes. Raven kept looking at him to see if he was still awake. She could see that he was working through some things in his head. She simply let him. She knew that he had more questions. She knew that he would ask them when he was ready. She stood up and stretched her legs, turning every now and then to watch him.

"Is é sin é! Is é sin an réiteach!" Colwyn exclaimed suddenly.

"What is it, Colwyn?" Raven raised an eyebrow. "What have you figured out?"

"Something Otan Kovalani told me while I was in the Elven Woods on the way here," Colwyn said excitedly. "Before I met with the queen, we were talking about the beauty of the woods. I mentioned that I thought that putting the Temple of the Blades in the Elven Woods had been a wise move. He said something about balance. He said, 'the Blademasters needing to know how to love and having a spark of true love in their lives is an important component to balance the Blademasters.' That's what she needs to know in order to defeat the Nightstalker. The Nightstalker isn't in balance like the Blademasters are."

"That is a very astute observation," Raven smiled broadly. She cocked her head to the side. "But can Alana apply that revelation during her battle with this Nightstalker?"

"I believe that she can," Colwyn nodded. "I think that knowing that may well tip the scales in my Blademaster's favor."

Colwyn turned back to face the wall again, stroking his chin thoughtfully. After a few minutes, he pulled a piece of cloth from inside his tunic and threw it on the bench. Curious, Raven walked over and picked it up. As soon as she saw what was on the cloth, she hissed and threw it back on the bench.

"What is it?" Colwyn asked, standing in a hurry.

"Great evil," Raven wrapped her arms around herself. "An unnatural great evil." She shivered. "It should not be in here. Take it away."

"I took this off one of the Zeraphim soldiers, Raven," Colwyn said as he tucked the cloth back in his tunic. "What can you tell me about the sigil on the cloth?"

"It belongs to a god not of our world, Colwyn," Raven hissed again. "It is an abomination. And it portends dark things for our world in the future. Some of those things you will not deal with in your lifetime, but you will need to pass on to other Blademasters. When the time is right, I will tell you about the One God. You do not need to know now for the task ahead."

"What do I need to know?" Colwyn asked. He could tell that Raven was terrified but he had to keep pressing. "The soldiers wearing this sigil have abducted the citizens of an entire town and Alana and I are fighting for our lives to free them."

"You must get the citizens of Valendale to rise up against their captors. It's the only way that they can be freed," Raven sat back down on the bench, still clearly shaken by what she'd seen. "The soldiers of the One God do not follow the same rules as the people of this world do, Colwyn. Their mages are not bound by the same rules. They are far more powerful than your mage friend, Willaim Stonehands, is now. He will have to grow and evolve before the final battle with the One God. Fortunately for him, that time is far in the future."

"You're not making much sense, Raven," Colwyn sat back down beside the young Blademaster. He looked at her face and saw that it was pained. "I'm sorry, Raven," he added quietly. "I don't mean to push, but the woman I love is currently being held prisoner by the Zeraphim. I can rescue her and the others, but what is the point of rescue if there's no hope of defeating them. She is depending upon me to find the answers."

"I know, Colwyn," Raven nodded. She let her hair fall in front of her face. She buried her face in her hands. "I was so shaken when I saw the sigil of the One God. I did not think we would see it so soon. I know you came here for help. I will give you what I can."

"What can you tell me of the Zeraphim?" William asked.

"Not much, I am afraid," Raven replied. "We have not had much information come into the Temple of the Blades about them. They serve a god not of this world. It would appear that it is the One God based on what you have shown me. Other than that, I'm afraid there isn't that much I can tell you about them."

"Is there anything else you can tell me about what is going on in Willowdale?" Colwyn asked.

"There is a great abomination there," Raven said, pain evident on her face. "I cannot tell you much about it. One of your party will fall to it, I am afraid. I do not know who."

"Surely not Alana?" Colwyn asked, a terrified note in his voice. "I could not bear that."

"That much I can tell you," Raven said softly. "Alana will face the Nightstalker. Whether she defeats the Nightstalker or not, I cannot say. But she will live to see that battle."

"Thanks for that," Colwyn slumped against the wall. He went back to staring against the far wall.

"Something else troubles you, Colwyn?" Raven asks.

"Silvestra Knightwing. Can we trust her?" Colwyn asked after a moment's pause. "Her sudden appearance in our lives is a bit of a shock. And I don't believe in coincidence."

"Silvestra has had a difficult few years," Raven started after taking a deep breath. "She was parted from her true love and was made to believe that she would never see him again. So was he."

"William," Colwyn said, understanding rushing in on him. "Oh, that explains a lot."

"I always knew you were smart, Colwyn," Raven smiled at him. "Yes, William is her true love. And his loss has haunted her for years. The leader of the Dragonic Council, Eliazar, has done everything that he could to prevent the two of them from being together. It has been very difficult on both of them. I dare say that Silvestra has taken it harder, though."

"So how did Eliazar break them apart?" Colwyn asked softly. "And what would happen if they were to get back together?"

"Eliazar convinced William that Silvestra was dead. How he accomplished this, I do not know," Raven sighed. "It's very difficult for any of us in the Temple of the Blades to hear about two people who share true love being broken apart. You know as well as I do that the Blademasters and our Protectors hold true love to be a sacred thing. None of us would be who we are without it."

"I am rather fortunate to share true love with someone. I could not bear if I lost it," Colwyn nodded.

"Cherish that love, Colwyn," Raven smiled at him. "It will sustain you on the darkest nights and it will keep you alive when nothing else will."

"Thank you, Raven," he smiled slightly. "I will do so. Is there anything else you can tell me?"

"Nothing that would be of help, I'm afraid, Colwyn," the first Blademaster said softly. "And a great deal that will not help you at all. I wish I did know more to help you."

"That's all right," he smiled. "You've actually been a rather big help."

"Good," Raven smiled. "I tried to be."

"There is one more question I have actually, Lady Raven," Colwyn said softly. "Do you know if there's a Law of the Blades that contains the words *things are not always as they appear?*"

"It is the Fourteenth Law of the Blades," Raven said softly. "A tricky law, that one. There are many things in life that are but mere illusions. Things are not always as they appear. A Blademaster must depend on the wisdom of Taelin to understand what is real and what is an illusion. Confusion brought on by false realities can lead to a gruesome death. Always remember to let Lord Taelin be your guide in everything you do. Remembering this will cause you to see through any illusion that is in your path."

Colwyn stood and slung his pack over his shoulder. He cinched the pack tight and bowed to Raven. "Until next I see you, Lady Raven."

"Until next we meet, Lord Colwyn," Raven said with a twinkle in her eye.

Raven Windrider and Richard Kale watched from the door of the Temple of the Blades as Colwyn made his way out of the clearing and into the Elven Woods. They gently held each other's hand, knowing that trouble was coming.

"You didn't tell him about the prophecy," Richard said softly.

"It's not for me to tell him," Raven said softly. "It is for someone else to tell him."

"The prophecy still scares you, doesn't it?" her Protector took her in his arms.

"I have no idea what it means," she admitted. "That's what scares me so. *On the rising of the dark tide comes the invasion. If the child of he who sought the stars with the dragon of steel by his side does not lead the Blademasters against the darkness, then all of Calthea will be washed away by the dark waters. With the invasion, the dragons withdraw from the field of battle and old enemies join forces under the banner of the champion of the light.* What could that possibly mean?"

"I don't think we'll ever know," Richard shrugged.

"He had a cloth bearing the sigil of the One God with him, Richard," Raven said, her voice quavering. "Things are going to be very difficult for that young man and his family for a long time."

"You're sure it was the sigil of the One God?" Richard held her tighter.

"I could never forget such evil, my love," she rested her head on his chest. "Never."

"I know," Richard stroked her hair. "All will be all right. You'll see. Colwyn and Alana will figure things out."

"Yes, you're right of course," Raven smiled up at him. "They'll figure it out. They have to."

Willowdale

Chapter XIV
The Rescue

Olwgn waited until he had reached a clearing far enough away from the Temple of the Blades before he summoned the dragon. He knew that Cobalt did not feel comfortable landing in the clearing where the Temple of the Blades was and he tried to respect that. But he also knew that he was running out of time. He knew that the woman he loved was to be executed upon the rising of the sun. That left him with little time to get back to Willowdale and get his companions out of the palace.

He waited patiently for the dragon to arrive. He knew that the summons had gone through. He knew that it was a matter of time for Cobalt to get there, but he hoped the dragon would arrive quickly. He feared they would not get back to the palace in Willowdale in time for him to rescue the woman he loved.

He thought back once more to the temptation that he had faced in the Elven Woods. He knew that he would have to face Alana and tell her what had happened. But he knew that he had not betrayed her. He had held true to the love that he had for her. He hoped that she could see that and forgive him for wavering. It was important to him that she know that he had stayed true.

It bothered him that he had even been tempted. Even worse was the knowledge that there would still be a betrayal before this mission was over. He could not fathom which of their companions might betray Alana. He knew that it had not been him. He knew that he would never betray the woman he loved. And yet someone in Willowdale would.

He immediately thought of Meryn. He still did not completely trust the little halfling despite her having saved all of their lives atop the ziggurat of Thraal in Tornith. Despite there being something he did not trust about the halfling, he could not accept that she would betray Alana. There was something about the way the young halfling looked at Alana that bordered on love. As much as he did not trust her, he knew that Meryn would never intentionally betray Alana.

He wondered about Martin. He did not know much about the young priest. He did know that he was completely dedicated to his god, Taelin. Would a priest so completely dedicated to Taelin betray Taelin's chosen? Colwyn didn't think so, but that did not allay his concerns about the young priest. They knew so little about him. And yet, Alana had instantly trusted the young man. She had clearly seen something in the young man that no one else had. Maybe it had to do with the intense dislike that the High Priestess of Taelin had for the young man. Colwyn did not know what she had seen in him. Alana had not yet shared her thoughts about the young man with Colwyn.

Maybe it would be William. Maybe the power would overwhelm the young man and corrupt him. He did not think that was likely. The young mage was one of the most centered people that Colwyn knew. It would take a great deal to corrupt the young mage. And he and Alana were both watching the mage closely.

Maybe it would be one of the dragons that betrayed Alana. Silvestra had already gone against edicts that had been put in place for her. Granted they were edicts put on her by the Dragonic Council, but if she could go against their wishes, could she go against Alana's? He did not know. He knew that William trusted Silvestra implicitly, but he did not think Silvestra was the same person that William had been in love with when they were at the Tower of the White. And even if she was the same person, could they really trust her? Silver dragons were not always the most trustworthy of the good dragons. They had flights of fancy that they followed whenever they came to them.

Cobalt had already betrayed one Blademaster, Colwyn knew. But he did not think that the great gold dragon would betray Alana. It was his chance for redemption before he passed into the walk with Taelin. He was sure that Cobalt would not do anything to jeopardize his redemption.

There was no one left for Colwyn to consider. And yet, he knew that one of his companions would be the one to betray Alana.

But who would it be? And what would the betrayal entail?

It was the one answer he wished that he could give Alana. Maybe it would make the coming battle easier if they knew who would betray them and how.

The great gold dragon dropped from the sky and into the clearing that Colwyn was waiting in, causing Colwyn to drop his line of thought about whom amongst his companions would end up betraying the rest of them. Colwyn moved away so that he could give the dragon room to land. When the dragon was settled in the clearing, Colwyn went over to him and scratched him on the chin like the dragon liked.

"Did you get your answers?" Cobalt asked.

"Some," Colwyn nodded. "I have enough for now. But I still have questions that Alana and I need the answers to."

"You humans are all the same," Cobalt snorted. "Always wanting to know all the answers."

"Are you ready to fly hard, Cobalt?" Colwyn refused to rise to the baiting. "We must be back in Willowdale before the sun rises to save our friends."

"Then what are you doing talking and wasting time, Lord Colwyn?" the dragon blew a puff of smoke. "Get on my back and we shall fly like the wind."

Colwyn climbed up on the great gold dragon's back and held on tight to the neck spikes as Cobalt launched himself in the air. Colwyn closed his eyes and let the dragon fly hard. He did not want to watch the ground go by, for he knew that the dragon would be covering ground faster than he would like. He would be sick if he watched the ground flying by that fast.

The flight from Willowdale to the edge of the Elven Woods had taken just under seven hours to complete. The great gold dragon had flown leisurely on the way there. He did not fly leisurely on the way back. They were able to shave two hours off their flight time. There were no incidents on the way from the Elven Woods to Willowdale, and Cobalt flew hard the entire time.

"Land where you picked me up earlier, Cobalt," Colwyn yelled up to the gold dragon. "And wait for me while I get the others."

"I will be there when you come out with my Blademaster, Lord Colwyn," The dragon roared.

The dragon made a hard bank and came around the city of Willowdale. He circled the city three times before coming in for a landing just outside the palace. Men went running out of the courtyard, screaming and running at the sight of the massive gold dragon landing. Colwyn waited until the dragon landed and then slid off his back. Without stopping to make sure the dragon would be all right, he dashed up the stairs and into the palace.

Colwyn slowly made his way through the corridors of the palace. He knew he did not have much time, but he would not be well served by getting caught. Care was needed. He loosed his sword in its scabbard and drew it, knowing that he would need it soon. He could hear the echoes of armored footsteps elsewhere in the palace.

He came up to a cross corridor and he carefully made his way up to the cross in the corridor, sliding against the wall. He had a good view of the corridor going in one direction, and it was clear. He risked peeking around the corner in the other direction, and it too was clear. He carefully crossed the hallway, praying silently to himself that no Zeraphim would come down the cross corridor at that moment. He moved as quietly as he could. Idly, he wished that Cobalt could have come in with him, but he did not think the dragon would have been much help in his human form and there was no way he could have fit inside the palace in his dragon form.

Colwyn knew where he was going. He remembered the path he had taken when he escaped and he was doing his best to work backwards to the dungeon grate. It was too slow going, though, as he had to keep watching for Zeraphim patrols.

Colwyn finally came to the corner that led to the hallway with the entrance to the dungeon. He peeked around the corner and saw that there were two guards standing over the grate. They were looking down the hallway in the opposite direction. He leaned against the wall he was standing by and closed his eyes. Quietly, he put his sword back in its scabbard and pulled his bow over his head. Quickly, he nocked an arrow.

He had spent time during his training as a ranger perfecting a quick shot. The elves he trained with were notably better at that type of shooting, but he was a fairly accurate shot in his own right. He was grateful for that training now. He took a deep breath, and drew the string of the bow back as he rounded the corner. He fired as soon as he had jumped into the corridor. He jumped back out of the line of sight as soon as he had fired.

"What the--?" one of the guards said.

Alana awoke suddenly. She had thought she heard something in the hallway above. There was something about the sound that she knew. She heard one of the guards yell and then she heard the sound again.

It was the sound of an arrow striking home in armor.

Quickly she woke the rest of the companions. She knew that if someone was firing arrows at the guards, it could only be Colwyn. He had to be there to rescue them. The others rose groggily, and she had them standing and ready to leave by the time Colwyn opened the grate.

Colwyn smiled down at Alana and it was one of the most beautiful things she had ever seen. She knew that everything would be all right. She waved and he waved back. He moved out of her view and soon came back, sliding the ladder down into the dungeon.

Alana had the rest of the companions climb up the ladder in front of her. She was determined that all of the companions got out this time, not just Colwyn. William carried the still unconscious Silvestra up the ladder. The young woman had not yet regained consciousness from the spell she had cast to unlock the grate the day before. Alana was growing concerned about the dragon woman. She did not understand how one spell could cause her to be so drained. She hoped Silvestra would wake soon.

Colwyn hugged Alana fiercely as soon as she stepped out of the dungeon. She knew something was wrong, but she also knew not to ask about it until they were free. There would be time enough for questions when they were all safely back in Silvestra's cave. She hugged him back and then motioned for the companions to start moving.

"I thought you might be needing these," Colwyn said as he handed her a familiar pair of long swords. "I found them hanging on a hook right over the dungeon. They look better on your back than on that hook."

"Indeed," Alana smiled as she strapped the swords on her back. "Ah, yes. That does feel much better. Thank you, Col."

"Anytime," Colwyn smiled. He led the way down the hallway. "There is a large and angry gold dragon waiting outside. Next stop, Silvestra's cave."

Colwyn lead the charge down the hallway, the companions following close behind. The ranger had his big bastard sword out and ready to swing at anyone who got in their way. He was not letting anyone keep them from getting free this time. It had been hard enough on him to leave the woman he loved behind the last time. He would not do that again.

They did not meet any Zeraphim patrols on their way from the dungeon to the front gate. Colwyn was concerned about the lack of Zeraphim guards, but he was happy to be able to get his companions and himself out without a fight.

The companions burst out of the front gate and skidded to a halt by Cobalt. They climbed up on Cobalt's back, William still holding the unconscious Silvestra. Cobalt craned his neck and peered at the young woman.

"She used her dragon magic in her human form," Cobalt said softly, his normal deep rumble showing his tender side.

"Yes, Cobalt," Alana nodded. "She hasn't woken up since."

"Very dangerous for her to do what she did," Cobalt sighed, a light puff of smoke blowing from his nose. "I will see what I can do when we get you all back to her cave. I have treated this condition before. I believe that I can help her. It will be hard on her. And on me."

"Thank you, Cobalt," William said softly. Alana looked at the mage, but the mage had made his face as unreadable as possible.

The Blademaster thought she had detected a note of pure concern and love in the young mage's voice. Maybe there could, indeed, be a future for the two of them to be together again. She would figure out how to broach the subject with Silvestra. If Silvestra ever woke from her unconscious state, that is. She was worried about Silvestra and hoped that Cobalt could help her.

She smiled over at Colwyn as he climbed up onto Cobalt's back. He chose to sit right behind Alana and wrap his arms around her. Something had changed in the man she loved while he was at the Temple of the Blades. She did not know what it was, but she knew they would have to talk about it soon.

Deep down, there was some fear about whatever it was that caused him to seem so sad since he came back. She hoped that it was something that the two of them could work through. She hoped that it wasn't anything too serious.

Once everyone was on the dragon's back, Cobalt roared and blew a long plume of flame in the air. He launched himself and soared out of Willowdale towards the cave that Silvestra had been calling her home.

Kera Rayden watched from her window in the First Lord's quarters as the great gold dragon launched into the sky. She knew that the Blademaster and her companions had escaped. She did not know how it happened, but she vowed that there would be repercussions for the Zeraphim responsible for letting them get away.

Two Zeraphim soldiers stood in the quarters along with her. They watched her as she watched out the window. She stood there until the dragon was nothing more than a dot in the sky. She turned to the two soldiers and crossed her arms.

"They escaped," she said softly. The two soldiers could tell she was angry despite her soft words. "I told you all that they were not to escape, and yet they just flew out of Willowdale on that infernal gold dragon."

"We will get them back, Mistress Kera," one of the soldiers said.

"No, you will not," Kera shook her head. She strode towards them and back handed each of them in turn. "We will wait. They will come back to us. Their work isn't done yet. Not until the fools you enslaved are freed. We will wait. But the Blademaster is mine."

"Of course, Mistress," the soldier that had spoken earlier said stiffly. He did not rub his jaw, she was happy to note. "None of the men would ever presume to kill the Blademaster in your stead."

"As it should be," Kera nodded. She turned away from the soldiers. "Leave me. I have work to do."

The two soldiers bowed and quickly made their way from the quarters. She did not watch them go. She had no need to. The Zeraphim were a useful tool, but they were, unless she required something of them, beneath her notice.

"Soon, Blademaster," she said softly as she looked once more out the window. "Soon, it shall come down to you and me. One shall stand. One shall fall. And I will not be the one to fall, I can promise you that."

Cobalt knelt down next to Silvestra in her cavern. He had changed to his human form. It was easier for him to tend to her while she was in her human form if he was also in his. He had asked for complete privacy, for the rituals involved to heal this kind of sickness were not for humans to know. While he had his problems with the Dragonic Council, this was one thing in which he agreed with them on. It would not do for humans to know too much about dragons. Not even humans who were in love with a dragon.

William had argued fiercely about leaving, as Cobalt had expected he would. Cobalt had known that William loved the dragon woman from the moment he had met him. Even in his exile, he had heard of the silver dragon that had fallen for a human mage. Cobalt was not stupid. He had seen the stone hanging around William's neck and he knew it for what it was. He had respected William's unspoken wishes and not said anything to anyone about it.

Cobalt had insisted that even William leave, and the young mage had eventually left Cobalt to his work. The gold dragon had promised the mage that he would let William know just as soon as he knew whether or not Silvestra could be saved. But it would take time. Healing the imbalance caused by casting dragon magic in human form was a difficult and time consuming process. And it was very risky for Cobalt. Cobalt ran the risk of causing a similar imbalance in himself should he err in the process. Cobalt was a far older and, he hoped, wiser dragon than Silvestra was and he knew that he could handle the forces involved with the spell that he needed to cast.

He slowly began to prepare the young dragon woman for what he had to do to her. It would take several hours for him to correct the imbalance the proper way. He slowly worked his way from her head to her feet. His hands were just a couple inches away from her body. His eyes were closed and he was feeling the balance within the young woman. He frowned as he felt how deep the imbalance ran in Silvestra.

He had more work to do than he first thought. He started to fear that it might be too much work to fix for one dragon.

He put that thought from his mind and focused on what he needed to do. He began to slowly chant in the draconic language, slowly dragging out each phrase. He felt power slowly seep into the young dragon woman from his hands. Each time he uttered a phrase, he felt a tiny bit of balance return to the dragon woman. Then he would move to another part of her body and repeat the process.

Silvestra groaned and moaned as he worked. He knew that it caused her pain to be put back in balance, but it was a necessary pain. There was nothing he could do to ease her pain without stopping. And he was at a point that he was not sure he could stop without hurting her more.

He kept working for several long hours. Each time he muttered the words, her pain eased just slightly as another touch of power eased into her body and brought her closer to perfect balance once more. Finally, after working for several hours, he sat back on his heels and wiped his brow. He let himself rest for a few minutes before going back out to where Alana and William were waiting to see what the result of his work would be.

"How is she, Cobalt?" Alana asked softly. She looked in to where the silver haired woman was resting.

"She will be fine," the dragon said wearily. "I have fixed the imbalance. It took far more of my strength than I expected it to. I must go and hunt. I need a good meal to replenish my energy. Healing her took a lot of my extra reserves. I will go now. I will come if you need me, but try not to need me until I've had something to eat."

"Go and eat, noble dragon," Alana smiled. "I don't believe we will need you until later today or tomorrow at any rate."

"Thank you," Cobalt smiled at his Blademaster, thankful that she was so understanding.

Cobalt made his way out of the cavern and Alana watched him go. William smiled at her as she watched him.

"I think Eliazar made a mistake with that one," William said softly. "Cobalt may have made a mistake three hundred years ago, but he is truly one of the best gold dragons I have ever known."

"I think you might be right, William," Alana laughed.

The Blademaster walked over to where Silvestra was lying and sat next to her. She took the young woman's hand and stroked the back of her hand with her thumb. She could feel the energy in the young woman returning. Before Cobalt had healed her, Alana could feel almost no life in her hand when she had held it. Now she could feel life flowing deep inside the young woman. It was good to feel. She hoped that the young woman would return to consciousness soon.

Silvestra's eyes opened half an hour later. Alana was still sitting next to her when she awoke. Alana squeezed her hand to let her know she wasn't alone.

"Where am I?" Silvestra asked weakly. She rasped her tongue over her lips to wet them.

"You're in your cavern," Alana said softly. "We brought you here when we escaped. You've been unconscious for almost a day. When you cast the spell to unlock the grate, it caused a severe imbalance in your system. My nathair an aeir a chosnaíonn had to heal you. He's been at it all morning."

"Where is he so that I may thank him?" Silvestra asked. She tried to sit up, but Alana would not let her.

"Rest, Silvestra," Alana smiled down at her. "He went to hunt. He used a lot of energy to heal you. He needs to eat so that he can be ready to help us again when we need him. You should eat and rest as well. We will likely need you before this is over."

"I am yours to command, Blademaster," the silver haired woman smiled. Her voice was already starting to get stronger. "I will be ready when you need me."

"Rest, Silvestra," Alana squeezed her hand again. "We'll try not to need you until you are ready."

Willowdale

Part III
A Clash of Swords

Chapter XV
Scouting the Enemy

olwyn Starseeker stood at the entrance to Silvestra's cave. He was looking out over the city of Willowdale. He had not spoken to anyone since they had returned to Silvestra's cave after the rescue. He had simply kept watch on the path leading up to the cave. He knew that Silvestra had been healed and had woken. But he could not convince himself to go in and be with the others.

The events of the day before in the Elven Woods were firm in his mind.

He knew that he and Alana would need to have a nice long talk about everything that had happened while he was in the Elven Woods and the Temple of the Blades. He was not looking forward to it at all. He had decided that the best thing he could do was to be honest with her about what had happened in the Elven Woods. Their love was too important for him to try to hide the truth from her. Not being honest would hurt her more than the truth would.

He knew that for sure. He figured that there was a Law of the Blades about honesty. There seemed to be a Law of the Blades about everything. If there was such a Law, he did not care what the text of it was.

He was afraid he would lose her over the near betrayal in the Elven Woods. The betrayal had been a near miss. Looking back, he realized that the Queen of the Forestwalker Elves had probably used some of her magic on him to make the temptation that much harder to resist. He had not even given Queen Mirian much of a passing thought since finding Alana. It bothered him that a woman he did not even think about could cause him to consider straying from his vows to the woman he loved.

For neither the first nor the last time, he prayed to Taelin and Laeyra both that Alana would find it in her heart to forgive him for what had happened. And he vowed to himself that if she did forgive him, he would never stray from her side.

He felt a light touch on his arm, and he looked over to see Alana standing by his side. She was not looking at him, simply standing beside him with her hand on his arm. She smiled when she felt him watching her.

"I suppose we need to talk, Alana," he said softly. "There are things you need to know in order for us to do what we need to in Willowdale."

"You've been very distant since you came back, Col," she looked at him. There was a slight sadness in her eyes. He knew that this mission had not been an easy one for her. He knew that it would not get any easier. "It's not like you to be distant from any of us. Did something happen at the Temple of the Blades to upset you?"

"Not at the Temple of the Blades, no," he sighed. "I did get the answers you needed though. Well, some of them, at any rate."

"Tell me what you found out," Alana smiled at him. She had known that he would have found out what she needed to know.

"First, let me tell you of the Nightstalker," Colwyn said. "She is the one that you will have to fight in the end. The key to defeating the Nightstalker is the Eighteenth Law of the Blades. I ngach den saol, ní mór go mbeadh cothromaíocht. A chailleadh go bhfuil cothromaíocht a cuireadh chaos agus bás isteach Ní mór máistir na lanna a bheith i gcónaí ar comhardú i di féin agus ina cuid déileálacha le daoine eile. Sin é an fáth go bhfuil an dlí chéad cheann de na lanna chomh tábhachtach sin. Ní mór an grá roinneann sí lena fear céile bás caithfidh sí a chothromú déileáil ina seasamh. Otan was the one to tell it to me, and he told it to me in Elvish."

"What does it mean, Col?" Alana frowned.

"In all of life, there must be balance. To lose that balance is to invite chaos and death in. A Blademaster must always be in balance in herself and in her dealings with others. That is why the First Law of the Blades is so important. The love she shares with her husband must balance the death she must deal in her position," Colwyn responded. "It's what you need to know to defeat the Nightstalker. She's not in balance. She's powered by hate and because of that does not have the powerful force of love to counter the killing she does. You have to use that when you fight the Nightstalker."

"I will keep that in mind," Alana nodded. "I'm not sure how much that actually helps me though."

"Raven said you would be able to figure it out," Colwyn smiled. It was a sad smile, and Alana could tell that something was deeply troubling Colwyn. She did not ask him about it, because she was afraid to know what it was.

"What of the Zeraphim?" Alana asked.

"Raven actually could tell me little about the Zeraphim," Colwyn sighed. "She freaked out when I showed her the sigil that the Zeraphim wore. Apparently, they revere this deity called the One God. The One God is not from Calthea. I have not seen the Lady Raven terrified like she was when she saw the sigil. She told me that we have to get the people of Valendale to rise up against the Zeraphim. That the soldiers of the One God do not fight by the same rules that we do. Apparently their mages are not subject to the same limitations that ours are. It will be a very difficult battle even with the help of the people of Valendale."

"Well, we knew that we would need their help," Alana nodded. "There are way too many of the Zeraphim for just the seven of us to handle."

"It will apparently be six before the end," Colwyn said bitterly. "Raven foretold that one of us would fall during this battle. She did not think it would be you or I, but she believes one of us will die. There is some kind of abomination in Willowdale that will end up killing one of our companions. Abomination was the exact word she used. She had no idea what it was, though."

"Did she give you anything else that was useful?" Alana asked in a whisper.

"I asked her about the silver dragon," Colwyn nodded. "It is as you suspected. She deeply loves William. In fact, he is her true love. Eliazar meddled. He meddled to the point where there was no way they could continue the relationship. He made William think she was dead."

"Well," Alana frowned. "That certainly explains a lot about the situation. I think that if Eliazar can meddle in their relationship, then perhaps I should meddle as well."

"Just be careful, Alana," Colwyn smiled sadly. "No matter how you handle the situation, someone will get hurt."

"I know." She turned to face him fully. "Now, are you going to tell me why you've been so distant since you came back from the Temple of the Blades?"

"As I told you, nothing happened at the Temple of the Blades to cause this pain," he sighed deeply. He walked over and pulled a large rock over so the two could sit down next to each other. "But something did happen while I was parted from you that you need to know about. And you need to hear it from me."

"Col, you're scaring me," Alana held his arm tight. "What happened?"

"Apparently, the Test of the Blades was not the last time I had to prove my love for you in the eyes of Solara Moonfire," Colwyn looked back out over the city of Willowdale. He could not meet her eyes. "She set something up for me... a test of sorts."

"What kind of test, Colwyn?" Alana asked softly. She was afraid she already knew what he was going to say. "What exactly happened?"

"Cobalt would not fly all the way to the Temple of the Blades," Colwyn began to explain. He closed his eyes and fought the urge to cry, but tears leaked from his eyes without his wanting them to. "He does not feel comfortable landing there considering what happened to his last Blademaster. I had him land at the edge of the Elven Woods, figuring I would just hike in. It's not that far, and we did have a promise of safe conduct from the Forestwalker Elves."

"Did something happen among the Forestwalker Elves that has you crying, Col?" she gripped his hand tight.

"Otan tried to warn me that something was going to happen," he said, his voice quavering slightly. "Every instinct in me was telling me not to go to the Forestwalker Elves. Every instinct told me to break propriety and just go straight to the Temple of the Blades. Something felt like it was terribly wrong. But I could not make myself violate the rules of noble propriety. I supposed that for a flaw, always wanting to do the right thing isn't a bad one."

"No, it isn't, my love," she squeezed his hand. "What happened?"

"Otan tried to warn me," he repeated. "He even told me part of the Fourteenth Law of the Blades, although I don't think he quite knew what he was telling me when he said it. There are many things in life that are but mere illusions. Things are not always as they appear. A Blademaster must depend on the wisdom of Taelin to understand what is real and what is an illusion. Confusion brought on by false realities can lead to a gruesome death. Always remember to let Lord Taelin be your guide in everything you do. Remembering this will cause you to see through any illusion that is in your path."

"Colwyn," she said sharply. Her tone of voice told him that there would be no more putting off telling her what happened. "Stop stalling and tell me what happened."

"When I got to the city of the Forestwalker Elves, the Queen requested my presence before I went off to the

Temple of the Blades," Colwyn said, still unable to meet her eyes. "I thought nothing of the request. After all, I was a guest of the Forestwalker Elves for a long time. I should have listened to what Otan tried to tell me. *Things are not always as they appear.* That was what he said. I should have listened."

"What happened? Alana asked again.

"The Queen of the Forestwalker Elves tempted me," Colwyn whispered. "She tried to do whatever she could to get me to turn from you. I know she tried to use her magic to enchant me. Alana, I fought it for all I was worth."

"Did you give in?" she asked, her voice barely above a whisper.

"No," he said after a few moments. "But it was so hard. All I wanted was to get out of there. I couldn't. I almost betrayed you in the Elven Woods, Alana. And my heart has been breaking ever since. All I want is to hear that you forgive me for almost giving in. It was so hard to resist her. It would have been so easy to just stay amongst the trees that I love so much. I almost gave up everything."

"Colwyn," she said softly. He turned to look her in the eyes. "I do not know what I can say. I need to think about this. And we have work to do."

"Right, we need to get more information about the Zeraphim," he brought himself out of his dark mood. "That is more important than anything else."

"We will talk about this later, though," Alana said, her voice brooking no nonsense. "Let's go back in and discuss what we need to do to get the information we need."

Alana had had the companions go do various scouting amongst the people in the city of Willowdale. She had sent each of her companions to check on specific things that she needed to know in order to plan out the assault on Willowdale. She was depending on all of them to get her the information she needed about the specifics in the city. Silvestra had insisted on taking an assignment as well. Alana had not wanted to let the dragon woman put herself in danger after her ordeal, but Silvestra was not taking no for an answer. Alana had to smile in spite of herself and had let the young dragon woman go and get some information for her.

Alana was the first to return, and she had made lunch while she waited for the others to get back. She had made a delicious smelling stew. The others were in for a surprise she thought to herself. Colwyn had taught her how to cook trail food and she was getting quite good at it. Colwyn had praised her recent attempts. She hoped that he would like what she had made this time. She figured all of the companions would be hungry when they got back from the scouting missions they had gone on.

Silvestra and Martin were the next to return. They both plopped near the cook fire and took in the smells of the stew. The young priest rubbed his belly in anticipation and the dragon woman shrugged and closed her eyes after sitting. Alana was happy to see Silvestra return safely. She had worried about sending the young woman off on a mission so soon after her return to consciousness, but Silvestra was proving to be tougher than everyone was giving her credit for.

Meryn was the next to arrive back in the cavern and the little halfling had to be held back from the cooking pot. She was clearly hungry and Alana was highly amused by her antics. She scolded the halfling, telling her that they would eat when everyone got back. Meryn pouted but sat down and waited with her arms across her chest.

William came back soon after the halfling did. He simply placed his staff against the wall of the cavern and laid down on his bedroll until lunch was ready. He closed his eyes, but Alana doubted that the young mage was actually going to sleep. He did need to rest though. She knew he would expend a lot of magic over the next couple days, so she did not begrudge him any opportunity to rest.

Colwyn was the last to arrive, and he was longer in returning than she had expected. She was starting to worry a little when he finally appeared in the entrance to the cavern. He was sweating and looked like he had had to run hard for at least once during his scouting mission. He plopped down a little ways away from her, a distance she could not help but notice. She frowned at the distance but he was looking down at the floor and did not notice it.

"I made lunch while I waited for you all to get back," Alana announced. The companions cheered at the thought of food. She dished a bowl full of the stew out to everyone. "While we're eating, I'll listen to what each of you found."

The companions ate hungrily for several minutes, each of them simply enjoying the food that had been made. Alana let them. She could tell they were all hungry. She could wait. She knew they would not be able to launch an attack until the next day anyway, so a delay of a few minutes would not matter.

She watched her companions eat for several minutes. They all agreed that the stew was fantastic. She was happy to hear they liked her cooking. She was feeling more and more confident in her cooking abilities, although she knew she would never be as good a cook as her husband was.

She kept looking over at Colwyn, but her Protector was not looking back at her. She did not know what was going through his mind. She was afraid, though. She was afraid that this Elvish temptation may well cause her to lose the man she loved more than anything. She could only hope that she could find a way to keep that from happening.

"We need to start," she said softly. "Silvestra, I did not want to send you out after your ordeal. You insisted that you could do a good job though. I sent you and Martin out to check patrol patterns and troop strengths."

"We were able to find out a lot," Silvestra nodded. "The Zeraphin patrol in five man patrols. Each patrol covers several city blocks, and there is some overlap with each pair of patrols. There are a hundred patrols working their way around the city at any given point in time."

"There are well over fifteen thousand Zeraphim troops in the city," Martin added. "There are a lot of foot soldiers and they appear to be well trained. I saw a squad of soldiers running drills in the palace courtyard."

"They're well disciplined in patrol," Silvestra continued. "I don't know how they'll do in battle, but my guess would be that if they're as disciplined in battle as they are in patrolling, I think the people of Valendale will have a difficult time of it in the coming battle."

"Thank you, Martin and Silvestra," Alana smiled at them. "William, I sent you to try to find out what their mages are capable of. What did you find out?"

"I did not really get to observe any of their mages in action," William shook his head. "I can tell you, though, that I felt their power. I don't know if Silvestra and I will be enough to counter them. I felt power such as I have not felt on Calthea."

"When I was at the Temple of the Blades, Raven told me something that might help you, William," Colwyn said softly. "She said that the mages in service to the Zeraphim do not adhere to the same rules as you and Silvestra do. They don't have the same built in limitations. She said that because they are not believers of any of the gods of magic from the Calthea pantheon, they would be more powerful as they did not have the same limitations."

"If they do not draw power from the gods of magic then where do they draw their power from?" Silvestra asked, her brows furrowed. "The gods of magic are the only fount of magic on Calthea."

"That we know of," William reminded Silvestra. "Remember, there have long been theories among the Inner Circle of wild magic. If the Zeraphim mages can tap into that, it will make them very dangerous. I'm afraid that you may have to use dragon magic during the battle, Silvestra."

"If I must, I must," the dragon woman shrugged. "Eliazar can be no more angry at me than he already is. And I have to tell you, I feel no longer beholden to the Draconic Council. After all that Eliazar has done to me, I will no longer live by his edicts. If I had been able to use the dragon magic all along, these people would not be here now."

"No one blames you, Silvestra," Alana said quietly. She reached over and laid her hand on top of the dragon woman's. "You've done everything you could within the rules you have to abide by. None of us could have done any better were we in your position."

"Thank you for saying that, Lady Blademaster," the dragon woman's voice was subdued. "I wish that there were more that I could have done. Taelin knows I would have done more were I able to."

"He does," Alana smiled at Silvestra. She turned to Meryn. "Meryn, what did you find out about entrances to the city?"

"There are gates on all four sides of the city," Meryn began. "Each of them is sealed save for the main gate to the west of the city, which is the gate closest to us. There are guards at all four gates. We're either going to have to breach the other gates or have all of our forces pour in through that one open gate. Either option has its own set of problems we'd have to overcome. We will have to be very careful either way. There is a small door on the western wall of the city that they use to bring corpses out to be buried in the graveyard. But it's only big enough for a single person to go through. It won't help get our forces inside."

"Do you, by chance, have a map, Meryn?" Alana smiled, knowing the halfling would have made one. If there was one thing that Meryn liked more than shiny things, it was maps.

"Right here, Alana," she said as she pulled a folded piece of parchment from one of her pouches. She pointed to the main gate and the other gates. "These are the four gates into the city. Guard posts are on either side of the gate."

"This is the door they use to bring the corpses out?" Alana asked as she pointed to another spot on the map.

"Yes," the halfling nodded. "It's locked, but the Zeraphim don't keep a guard on the door."

"That's my way in then," Alana stroked her chin as she studied the map. "Colwyn, what did you learn about the Zeraphim?"

"Well, from what I've learned, this is only a small portion of the Zeraphim," Colayn sighed as he reported. "No matter what happens in Willowdale, we will not have seen the last of the Zeraphim. The forces here are lead by one of eight Zeraphim commander generals, a man by the name of Arven Trimmack. He's going to be the one I'll end up facing. From what I've been able to gather, he is a brutal warlord. He's also, from what I hear, the next in line to take over the overall command of the Zeraphim. He sends daily reports back to Zhentaril Keep."

"How did you find this out?" William asked.

"I'm a noble, William," Colwyn winked. "You think I don't know all the secret ways into one of the palaces in the Southern Dales?"

"I knew all of you nobles were deceitful buggers," William grumbled.

"There's one other thing you need to know, Alana, and it's something very troubling," Colwyn's voice turned serious again. "It seems that this was an experiment to judge you."

"Me?" Alana raised an eyebrow.

"Apparently, the Zeraphim knew about the Blademasters being returned to Calthea even before we did," Colwyn nodded. "This has been set up to determine whether or not you are a threat to the Zeraphim."

"I can assure you, I am," Alana nodded. "They're going to find I'm far too much for them to handle."

"Trimmack had orders that if you did not respond within six months, he was to kill all the people of Valendale and then start over with another town. They would have captured Solvendale next," Colwyn said, a tear rolling down his cheek.

"Like hell," Alana growled. "This ends here and now. I cannot allow this to happen to anyone else, Colwyn."

"I know," Colwyn nodded. "We'll stop them."

"I need some time to think," Alana said, standing up. She looked at each of the companions, one after the other. "Good work, all of you. I should be able to come up with a good plan with what you all have found out for me."

She walked away from them and moved to gaze out of the mouth of the cavern. She was soon lost in thought about what to do next.

Willowdale

Chapter XVI
Dragon Flight

The companions were in Silvestra's cave. They had finished eating lunch and Alana had been staring out towards the town for the past fifteen minutes. She had heard all the scouting reports from her companions. Still, she couldn't help but feel that there was something missing. Something about the situation did not fit in her mind. She knew that missing a piece of information could result in the difference between successfully rescuing the people of Valendale and the death of her and her companions. She trusted her instincts that she was missing something important.

"Stay here," Alana commanded to her companions. "I'm going to fly around on Cobalt and see what it is that I am missing."

"Hang on," Colwyn called. "I'll go with you."

"Not this time, Col," she shook her head. He stopped in mid rise. "I need you to guard the others while I'm gone."

She was gone before he could protest. She had told him the truth, but not the whole truth. She did need him to protect the others, but even more than that, she needed some time to herself to work through what he had told her about what had happened while he was in the Elven Woods. She knew he was hurt by her forcing him to stay behind. It hurt her to have him stay behind, but she needed to work through this by herself.

She slowly made her way down the mountain to where Cobalt would be waiting for her. She had summoned the dragon and directed him to meet her at the bottom of the mountain. She did not think that it would be a good idea to have the two dragons meet just yet. She had the feeling she could trust Silvestra. She did not really know the silver dragon, though. She knew William loved her, but she also could tell there was a great deal of pain there. Maybe she would have a talk with the dragon woman when she got back to the cave.

She made her way carefully down the path. Lessons learned from Colwyn in the course of their travels allowed her to move quickly and safely. The thought of not being able to face him if she fell and broke her ankle made her chuckle. She was too well trained for that, though. Colwyn's instructions had only made her more nimble than she already was.

She could see the gold dragon waiting for her, his long serpentine neck snaked out on the ground. He appeared to be asleep, but Alana doubted that he actually was. She finished the trek down the mountain to where the dragon was. She slowly walked around the dragon, running her hands along his scales. She walked all the way around his tail and back up his other side. She stopped near his wing and frowned.

"Cobalt, you are missing a few scales right near your wing," she remarked. She traced the gap where the missing scales were. "What happened?"

"I am getting old, Blademaster Alana," the gold dragon sighed. He arched his head around to look at the bare patch on his side. "When dragons get older, some of them start losing their scales. Now that I've started losing them, I will start losing more and more of them as time goes on. Very soon, I will no longer be able to serve as your nathair an aeir a chosnaíonn, I am afraid. When I lose too may scales, it will be impossible for me to protect you."

"Noble dragon, you have served me well," she kissed him on the cheek. "Whatever happens, I want you to know that."

"That means a great deal to me, Blademaster Alana," the old dragon croaked. "You have honored me by allowing me to serve as your nathair an aeir a chosnaíonn. You've given me back my honor. I thought that I would die in dishonor. When I die, I will go to a place prepared for me to rest with Lord Taelin."

"As you should," Alana tweaked his cheek. "Now, my friend, it's time to fly. There is something about this situation that bothers me still. I'm hoping that the two of us can find out what it is."

"Then let us fly," the dragon hunched down so she could climb on his broad back. "Let the wind flow through your hair, my Blademaster. Let the joy of flight ease all of your burdens."

"Thank you, Cobalt," Alana said as she climbed on his back and secured herself for the flight. She grabbed a hold of one of his neck spikes and called out. "I'm ready to fly, my friend."

"Then let us be off!" Cobalt roared as he launched himself off the ground.

The great gold dragon soared into the sky, his huge wings beating steadily as he rose and banked in a circle around the city of Willowdale. The wind blew Alana's hair back and she shouted with delight at the feeling of weightlessness that flying with Cobalt always gave her.

She held on to the spikes on Cobalt's back and the centrifugal force of his banking around the city kept her glued to his back. It was an amazing feeling that she loved every time she flew on his back.

Although she had not known the great gold dragon for long, she had already found that flying with the dragon allowed her to think clearly, sometimes far more clearly than she did at any point when she was on the ground. It was for that reason that she had decided to fly on Cobalt's back to try to figure out what she was missing about the situation in Willowdale. She hoped that she would get some clarity on the situation in Willowdale as well as the situation between herself and Colwyn.

She did not know which situation she wanted clarity about more.

Cobalt soared above the cloud cover and the sun warmed Alana's face. She closed her eyes and held on tight. She felt elated. The wind whipped through her hair, but was not too much for her to be able to maintain her hold on Cobalt's neck spikes. She kept her eyes closed and allowed her mind to wander, knowing that the answers she sought would come to her.

She thought about Colwyn. He hadn't betrayed her. She knew that he hadn't. But he had been tempted. And while he had not given in to that temptation, she knew that he had wavered. It did not change her love for him at all. She was afraid, though. She was afraid that he would be tempted again. She was afraid that the next time that he was tempted, he would give in. She did not want to lose him. Even more, though, she knew that losing him would mean losing her abilities as a Blademaster. Too much rode on her shoulders for her to even contemplate that.

She thought about something that she had heard from Lord Taelin when she had met Darius Redwind. He had mentioned the Second Law of the Blades. *True love breeds true forgiveness. Nothing is more powerful than the ability to forgive the one you love. And nothing brings you closer than the forgiveness of your own misdeeds.* She wasn't even completely sure there was actually something to forgive Colwyn for. But she knew that when she landed, she had to go to him and forgive him for his temptation. As she made the decision, she smiled to herself. She already felt better knowing that they would become closer from this.

Now that she had decided what to do about Colwyn, all that remained was to think about what was missing in her intelligence about the city of Willowdale.

The first thing she thought about was the Nightstalker. She had only seen the mysterious woman in black a couple of times during her time as a prisoner in Willowdale. There was something odd about the strange young woman. There was a power coming off of the Nightstalker in waves. Alana could feel it. She thought that the Nightstalker might be able to feel the same kind of power coming from her. There was no mistaking what the Nightstalker was. She was clearly meant to be the counter to the Blademaster. The thought filled Alana with a little bit of dread. She was not sure if she would be able to take the Nightstalker out. She did know, however, that she was the only one that had a chance of doing so.

She needed to know more about the Nightstalker, that was for sure. But she did not think that she would find anything more about her before it was time for her to fight her. And she knew that it would come down to a one on one fight between the two. One would stand. One would fall. She was determined that it would not be her that would fall. Colwyn had told her about the Eighteenth Law of the Blades. He had said it was the key to defeating the Nightstalker. She mused on that Law one more time as she thought about how to defeat this Kera Rayden.

In all of life, there must be balance. To lose that balance is to invite chaos and death in. A Blademaster must always be in balance in herself and in her dealings with others. That is why the First Law of the Blades is so important. The love she shares with her husband must balance the death she must deal in her position.

She did not know how it would help her, but she kept focused on that nugget of knowledge, hoping that, in the end, it would be the key to the Nighstalker's undoing. She knew that in the battle ahead, the Nightstalker was her responsibility and hers alone. She knew that she was the only one who could actually kill the arrogant young Kera Rayden. And she realized that the main difference between the two women was that Alana did not relish the killing that she had to do as part of her job.

The Zeraphim troubled her. Colwyn had told her that they did not believe in any of the gods of Calthea's pantheon. She did not know who they worshipped. Further, she did not understand how they could be taking orders from someone who was so clearly the champion of one of the gods that they did not believe in.

They were a puzzle. And there were a great many of them. The six of them would not be able to fight the Zeraphim by themselves. They would have to find a way to arm the men of Valendale. Colwyn would have to lead them into battle while Alana fought the Nightstalker. The two dragons could help the people of Valendale and might just be able to turn the tide against the Zeraphim.

Alana suspected that part of what she was missing had to do with the dragons. The Nightstalker had to have something that would be able to counteract the dragons. There had to be something that would be dangerous for the dragons in Willowdale. But then, the Nightstalker probably only knew about Cobalt. Maybe the fact that Silvestra was there would tilt the balance back in Alana's favor. Of course, in order for the dragon woman to help them, she would have to go against the edict of the Dragonic Council. Alana knew that that would cause no end of trouble for the silver dragon. Alana would have to talk to Silvestra and see what she would be willing to do in order to save the people of Valendale.

She felt sure that she could defeat the Nightstalker. She also felt sure that Colwyn and the people of Valendale could defeat the Zeraphim. Her only question remained what surprise did the Nightstalker have in store for Cobalt. She was sure there was something.

"Cobalt," she called to the dragon as her eyes snapped open. "We're focusing on finding anything that might be a danger to a dragon. I'm sure that the Zeraphim and the Nightstalker have some kind of surprise for you. Thraal had to tell the Nightstalker about the nathair an aeir a chosnaíonns."

"I'm sure he did," Cobalt replied. "And you're right. She had to have planned for that. Let's see if we can find what the Nightstalker has come up with."

Cobalt took a wide bank around the city and came up to the mountains near where Silvestra's cave was. Staying away from the mountain that Silvestra had made her home in at Alana's request, Cobalt flew around the other mountains, investigating little nooks and crannies. They found a very large cavern near the summit of one of the mountains.

Alana directed the gold dragon to land near the cavern so they could investigate it. Cobalt whirled around and came in for a gentle landing on the outcropping of stone that signaled where the cave was. Alana slid off the gold dragon's back and rubbed his neck.

"I think it's large enough for us to both investigate, my friend," Alana scratched the patch of scales right under Cobalt's ear, just like the gold dragon loved. "Let's go see what surprises our Nightstalker has for us."

"I have a bad feeling, Blademaster Alana," Cobalt said suddenly as they crossed the threshold of the cave. "There is something not right about this cave. I cannot tell you what that might be, however."

"I understand, Cobalt," Alana nodded. "Please, keep your eyes peeled. I'm not sure what we'll be seeing in here, but this is clearly what we've been looking for.

They crept slowly forward, knowing that they could be walking into a trap. They both extended their senses as far forward as they could. Alana immediately began to feel shivers running up her spine. She knew what Cobalt had meant about the cave not feeling right. The cave felt like pure evil and hate. She knew that she wouldn't be able to stay in the cave for long. But they needed to stay in long enough to find out what the cave was.

Alana slowly made her way deeper into the cave. Cobalt lifted his hand and said a word. A globe of light appeared over the palm of his hand lending some light to the cave. There was not enough light to light the cave completely, but it was enough for the two of them to be able to see where they were going. As they made their way slowly in, they could tell that this cave was a far larger one than the one Silvestra had made her home in.

Alana wondered if that meant that the inhabitant of the cave was likewise far larger than Silvestra. Perhaps the owner of the cave was even larger than Cobalt. It was a scary thought for her. She wondered if Cobalt could handle something that appeared to be much larger than he was.

After several long minutes, they got to the main room of the cave. It was enormous, easily two hundred feet in circumference. Clearly a very large creature called this home.

"This is a dragon cave, Alana," Cobalt sniffed. "It's a dragon cave that has very recently been used. I dare say a very large dragon is using this cave. I can't tell you what kind of dragon it is though. I am having trouble picking up the scent. There is very little in the world of dragons that I cannot handle, however. Fear not, my lady. This will not be a problem for me."

"Are you sure about that, Cobalt?" Alana looked a little worried. "Whoever lives here looks to be a good deal larger than you are."

"You know what they say, Blademaster Alana," Cobalt said with a wry smile. "The bigger they are, the harder they fall. And I can promise you that whatever dragon calls this lair home will fall."

"Let's go back, Cobalt," Alana said suddenly. "This place is giving me the creeps."

"I can understand," Cobalt nodded. "Straight back or do you want to fly around some more?"

"One more time over the city," Alana requested. "I want to see troop arrangements from the air so I can see the whole city at once. The more information I have, the better I can make a plan."

"Very well," Cobalt said as he transformed back to his dragon form. "Once more around the city it is."

Alana climbed back onto the dragon's back and they launched back into the air. She loved the feel of wind in her hair as they flew high into the sky. It was a joy for her to fly. It relaxed her and helped to clear her head. She wondered if that was a part of the reason that Taelin had deemed that all Blademasters have a nathair an aeir a chosnaíonn. She would not have put it past the God of Wisdom to have considered that such a thing would be needed.

As they flew high over the city, Alana looked down and watched the soldiers of the Zeraphim as they marched through the city. She thought she could see patterns in the way the soldiers marched and patrolled the city. She made a note of any patterns she thought she noticed. Anything she could use in the plan against the Zeraphim was welcome.

They circled over the city four times before Alana was content that she knew how the Zeraphim had arrayed their forces. She patted Cobalt on his flank and motioned for him to land. He began to bank slowly around the city so that he could slowly lower himself and land gently. It took several circles around the city before he was able to touch down.

Cobalt landed softly on the ground under the cave where Silvestra and Alana's companions waited. He hunkered down so that Alana could slide off his back. He stretched and slowly started the long transformation to his human form.

"Follow me up to the cave, Cobalt," Alana said. "But wait outside until I can talk to Silvestra about you. She, like you, isn't exactly one of the best loved dragons on the part of the Draconic Council. She's a little skittish about other dragons."

"I understand," Cobalt nodded when he finished his transformation. "Let me guess. She's had some trouble with Eliazar."

"You got it in one," Alana laughed. "He has kept her apart from her true love and made her life miserable over the last seven years."

"That sounds about right for Eliazar," Cobalt sighed. "Very well, I will wait outside. I have no desire to make another dragon nervous."

"Thank you, Cobalt," Alana smiled at the dragon man. "You're a good friend."

Cobalt grunted once and followed Alana up the path towards the cave.

Alana let her mind wander once more as she made her way up to where her companions were waiting. She had more to go on towards making the plans for repelling the Zeraphim. She knew that it was not going to be easy. She also knew that the lives of many people depended on her.

The lair that they found troubled her. She did not know what called the lair home. Cobalt had suggested that it was a dragon's lair, but he couldn't tell her what kind of dragon. That didn't help her plans. She knew that Cobalt felt sure that he could handle the dragon, but Alana could not help but worry. Cobalt had become her friend over the past few weeks, every bit as much a friend as Colwyn and William. She did not want him to be hurt for her sake. She was afraid that she would lose him in the coming battle. Worse, she almost felt like it was destined to happen. She would not tell him that. He might pull back from what he needed to do and lose his last chance at redemption.

She could not do that to him.

She also wondered what to do about Silvestra. Her mind was troubled about the young silver dragon. Alana could tell that Silvestra was still on the young side for a dragon. She knew that silver dragons were known for having something of a stubborn streak. If Alana could harness that stubbornness and channel it, then Silvestra could indeed be quite a weapon against the Zeraphim. She worried about what the arrival of Silvestra into their lives would mean for her companions. She knew without a doubt that Silvestra loved William. That, of course, would lead to trouble. She knew that the halfling truly loved William as well. She had done some soul searching about the matter and decided that Silvestra really needed to talk to William before Alana could even begin to worry about what affect Silvestra would have on the party.

She turned her mind to the question of the plan of attack to get the people of Valendale away from the Zeraphim. She turned the matter over and over in her mind and came to one conclusion.

There were too many question marks in her plan, and she did not like that.

The biggest question mark in her mind was with the people of Valendale themselves. She knew that she would have to somehow convince them to pick up arms against the Zeraphim. She knew that they would rebel at the idea at first. She knew they would feel that they were putting their loved ones in danger by taking up arms against their oppressors. But it needed to be done. They would not be able to escape from the Zeraphim without helping themselves. Alana and her six companions, counting Silvestra, just weren't enough to remove the Zeraphim yoke from the necks of the people of Valendale. They had to learn from the example of Marcus Whelan who risked everything by escaping and bringing Alana to Willowdale to rescue his people.

He could have lost his wife and daughter.

Alana had checked around and knew that Jenny and Lisa Whelan were still alive and well, but they were scheduled for execution in a few days. While she was not happy to hear that they were slated to be killed, the fact that they were still alive eased her mind heading into this showdown. And a showdown she knew it would be. There was no question that when it came time to fight the Nightstalker, she would be in for the fight of her life.

And of course there was the question of the mysterious dragon lair. She knew that this would have a big impact on the coming battle, but she had absolutely no idea how to plan for it. She could only hope that Cobalt and Silvestra could handle whatever dragon it was.

She sighed and focused on where to put her feet. It would not do to break an ankle before the battle. It took about an hour for Alana to work her way up to the cave. Since she had made the journey twice before, she knew what to expect so she could move a bit faster than she had the first time.

When she got to the cavern mouth, she again motioned for Cobalt to wait for her before going inside. She went over to the dragon woman and pulled her away from the rest of the companions. Silvestra went with Alana with a raised eyebrow.

"I would speak with you privately, Silvestra," Alana said softly. "And if I find out that William is listening, I will personally rip his ears off. And he knows I will too."

She heard a gulp coming from William and she knew he had heard her and would stop listening in. She chuckled softly and turned back to Silvestra. The dragon woman looked amused, a small smile playing across her face.

"It's been some time since I've seen someone put William in his place," Silvestra chuckled a little. "I saw it happen once at the Tower of the White and not since. You know he could probably rip you apart with his magic."

"But he would have to expend all of his energy in doing so and then would have to deal with Colwyn without magic," Alana raised an eyebrow. "Or Colwyn would get in the way and William would expend all his energy and then he'd have to deal with me without magic. Either way, it would not go well for him."

"You make a good point," Silvestra nodded. "What did you wish to speak with me about, Blademaster Alana?"

"There are two things," Alana said. She sat on the ground, motioning for the dragon woman to follow suit. She waited for Silvestra to sit before continuing. "The first is my nathair an aeir a chosnaíonn is waiting outside. I asked him to wait before coming in to join us, because I know you have had problems with the Draconic Council. I wanted to tell you that he has too."

"Who is he?" Silvestra asked with a raised eyebrow.

"Cobalthaxillius," Alana responded. When she saw Silvestra's shocked reaction, she smiled. "I see that you know the name."

"Cobalt isn't exactly welcome among the Draconic Council," she smiled broadly. "In fact, I believe he was banned from the Isle of Dragons altogether."

"I believe I had heard that yes," Alana chuckled. "Eliazar does not like him. My Lord Taelin has given Cobalt a chance to redeem himself. I have agreed to have him serve as my nathair an aeir a chosnaíonn, although I do know what happened to the last Blademaster he served in that position for. I believe that everyone deserves a second chance. Don't you?"

Alana caught the quick glance to William. She'd been watching for it.

"What do you mean, Blademaster?" the dragon asked.

"You love William Stonehands," Alana smiled. "Don't try to deny it. I could see it in your eyes from the very first moment you looked at him when we arrived outside

Willowdale. I know that look well. I see it in my husband's eyes whenever he looks at me."

"It's far too complicated," Silvestra turned away.

"Look at me, Silvestra Knightwing," Alana commanded softly. She did not have to raiser her voice. She let her authority as the Blademaster ring in every word. "Look at me. Look deep into my eyes and tell me the truth. You love him, correct?"

"I do," Silvestra said softly, a tear running slowly down her cheek. "But too much has happened."

"I think you're just frightened," Alana said. She caught the tear on her finger and flicked it away. "I think you're afraid that, when all is said and done, he doesn't love you back."

"You might be right," Silvestra hung her head. "He is with another now though."

"Silvestra, do you know what the First Law of the Blades is?" Alana asked. She knew that the dragon would know. It was something that all dragons were supposed to know.

"Yes, Blademaster Alana," the dragon woman said, still looking down at her lap.

"Repeat it for me now, then," Alana commanded.

"This is the First Law of the Blades. You are commanded to love. Love your friends. Love your enemies. Love without reservation. Love without hesitation. Love without condition. Love without expectation of return. If you must fight, then fight with love in your heart. If you must kill, then kill with love in your heart. Never kill or fight with hate or anger in your heart. Hate leads to impotence, but love brings power. This is the law a Blademaster must live by more than any other or else she will be powerless to serve as she should. It is the First Law of the Blades because it is the most important. Live by it, or you will die." Silvestra repeated it word for word as the High Priestess of the Blades had told it to Alana and Colwyn on the night of their wedding.

"What do you think you should do, knowing the First Law of the Blades?" Alana demanded. It was like teaching a young child was what she thought. She knew that Silvestra could be led to the right answer.

"I don't know if I can," the dragon woman said weakly, her voice barely above a whisper.

"William wears a gemstone on a chain around his neck. I've seen him looking at it when he thought no one else was looking," Alana said after a moment of thought. "It looks to me like a half of a heart. I've seen a heartstone before. I know what it means. I know that whoever he gave the other half to still means a very great deal to him."

Silvestra pulled her half of the heartstone from inside her tunic. Alana had seen the pulsing red gem very briefly when Silvestra had morphed into her dragon form earlier. She had known then what it was. And she had known then that William was at a crossroads that he may not have even known he was at just yet.

"William made this the last time I saw him," Silvestra whispered. "It was over seven years ago. When Eliazar saw it, he flew into a rage and demanded that I stop wearing it. He forced me to throw it away. After I had arrived in Valendale, Talonwing, the silver dragon on the Dragonic Council arrived. She had this chain and gave it back to me. She told me that true love should never be ignored. It was the single nicest thing that any member of the Draconic Council has ever done for me." She looked up and met Alana's eyes. "And here I am ignoring Talonwing's words again."

"You know what you have to do," Alana smiled. It was a sad smile. She knew what it meant to be separated from someone you loved. She had almost felt that separation because of the Law of the Blades. She hoped that Silvestra and William could recover their love.

"I will talk to William," Silvestra nodded. She reached over and clasped Alana's hand, a small smile playing across her face. "Thank you, Blademaster Alana. You have given me a great gift today."

"I have done nothing other then tell you what you already know, Silvestra. It is on you to do what you need to do with that knowledge."

"Well, thank you anyway, Blademaster," Silvestra's smile grew.

"You're welcome, Silvestra," Alana stood up. "Don't forget the truth again."

"I won't," Silvestra said to Alana's back as the Blademaster went outside the cave to bring Cobalt in with the rest of the companions. "I'll never forget again, thanks to you."

Willowdale

Chapter XVII
The Plan

Colwyn stood in the entrance to Silvestra's cave staring out over the city of Willowdale. He had been watching the city for the past hour. The ranger had gotten up before the sun and had watched the sun slowly climb the sky on the far side of the city of Willowdale. It had been an impressive sight, the sky turning blood red.

He hoped that it would not be a sign of things to come.

He was trying not to think of Alana. For the first time in a long time, they had not slept next to each other. Colwyn had moved his bedroll away from her so that the woman he loved would have time to think on her own. He had cried himself to sleep, knowing that he had caused her a great deal of pain. He had never intended to do so, but he had nonetheless.

He was surprised to find a touch on his arm. He looked over and saw Alana watching him, her hand on his arm. He fell to his knees in front of her and bowed his head.

"Mo ghrá, Tá brón orm má ba chúis agam ort pian," he said softly

She placed her fingers under his chin and raised his eyes to look at her. Tears streamed down his face. She wiped some of them away.

"My love, do you know the Second Law of the Blades?" she asked softly.

"No,' he shook his head. "I'm afraid I don't."

"This is the Second Law of the Blades, Colwyn: True love breeds true forgiveness. Nothing is more powerful than the ability to forgive the one you love. And nothing brings you closer than the forgiveness of your own misdeeds," Alana explained. "I could not love you as much as I do and not apply this law to you. I love you now and always, Colwyn. You did not betray me, no matter how much you were tempted, so there is nothing to forgive. But if it will ease your pain, my forgiveness is yours anyway."

"Thank you, my love," he smiled. Tears continued to flow down his face. "Is breá liom tú go mór, Alana Steeldrake."

"That better mean that you love me, Colwyn Starseeker," Alana smiled her special smile at him. "And if you ever move you bedroll away from me like that again, I will melt your sword down and make a cooking pot out of it!"

"It does, and you're not melting my father's sword!" Colwyn protested.

"Then don't move your bedroll away like that again!" Alana punched him in the arm.

"Ow," he rubbed his arm.

"Serves you right!" Alana laughed. "You should know better than to make me angry at you, Col."

"I promise not to do so again," Colwyn groaned, rubbing his arm where she'd hit him.

"Don't make promises that you can't keep, Colwyn Starseeker," Alana warned. "You're a man. It's your job to make me angry at times!"

Colwyn chuckled and turned back to continue to watch the sunrise. He felt Alana wrap her arm around his and he smiled softly. Her touch had always been magical to him. Today was no different.

"Colwyn, how much trouble can we expect from your father about our marriage?" Alana asked after a few moments.

"Oh, I expect he'll be furious. He'll definitely give us a hard time and try to nullify our marraige," Colwyn sighed. He turned to face her and took her in his arms. "Unlike me, my father is very old fashioned when it comes to the nobility. He believes that nobles should only marry nobles. The fact that our marriage has been sanctified by Lord Taelin will mean nothing to him. He will want to know your noble heritage."

"And since I don't know who my parents are, I can't give him that," Alana frowned. "What do we do about this?"

"Well, the letter that the King gave us will help, I hope," Colwyn smiled. It was a sad smile though. "But I believe that my father will still be very resistant to the marriage. I do not know how to get through to him."

"What about the other members of your family?" Alana asked. "How will they react?'

"My mother, Serina, will go along with whatever Lord Dargan says," Colwyn shrugged. He held her close. "My sister, though..."

"What about your sister?" Alana looked up at him.

"Bella is what you might call a wild child," he smiled down at the woman he loved. "She's a bit of a rebel. I don't think she'll have a problem with our marriage. Especially since it will go against tradition. And she will enjoy that it will upset our father."

"This is something we're going to have to deal with soon, Colwyn," she said softly. She leaned her head onto his chest. "I don't know my family, but I can't let you be alienated from yours because of me."

"Don't worry about that, Alana," Colwyn chuckled softly. "I've already managed to alienate myself from Lord Dargan. We don't speak to each other much anymore, and when we do, it's mostly to yell at each other. Neither of us knows how to communicate with each other. I wish we did."

"That's terrible!" Alana said into his chest. "Is there nothing you can do to get back in his good graces?"

"The only thing he would accept would cause me to lose you," Colwyn sighed deeply. "I would have to give up my position as your Protector and settle down and prepare myself to take over as his successor."

"But you are his successor anyway," Alana looked up at him.

"Indeed," he nodded. "But he does not, at this time, see me as a fit successor as I have not sat down and let myself be trained. Right now, he does not feel comfortable with the thought of my ruling the Arvendale territory after he passes into his walk with Taelin."

"I think you're ready, though," Alana smiled her special smile at him.

"I am," he smiled back. "That being said, I hope that it happens many years from now when you and I are both ready to settle down. I can't abandon my duties to you, Alana."

"And I cannot allow you to abandon your responsibilities to the people of Arvendale, Colwyn," she leaned up and kissed him on the cheek. "When the time comes for you to ascend to the title of First Lord of Arvendale, I will simply have no choice but to put my swords aside and stay by your side, just as you have stayed by mine."

"What did I ever do to deserve a woman like you, Alana Steeldrake?" Colwyn kissed her forehead. "Whatever it is, I should do it more often."

"Just be yourself, my love," Alana laughed lightly. "May I see the letter from the King? You read it when he gave it to you and put it inside your tunic. I never read it."

"Of course," he nodded.

He pulled away from her so that he could reach into his tunic. He pulled the letter out and handed it over to her. He knew what the letter said word for word despite having read it only the once.

"*First Lord Dargan Starseeker,*

I, King Roland Stonehammer, have reviewed the matter of the marriage of Colwyn Starseeker, heir to the title of First

Lord of Arvendale, and Alana Steeldrake, chosen by our Lord Taelin to be the first in a new line of Blademasters. I have found that this marriage is valid and binding.

This letter, signed by myself with my seal, shall serve as all the documentation required for this marriage to be permitted. No attempt to break this marriage apart will be tolerated by the throne.

The light of the Blademasters is one that is sorely needed in the dark times that are to come. All of the nobility must stand behind the Blademasters and their Protectors. They have been chosen for a reason. None of us can say what that reason is, but we must trust that Lord Taelin and Lady Laeyra are indeed wise in their decisions.

Signed by my own hand,
Roland Stonehammer
King of the Southern Dales"

It had meant a great deal to Colwyn that the King of the Southern Dales would take such an interest in their marriage. But take an interest, the King had, and he had done all he could to made sure that the marriage would be observed by all. Colwyn hoped and prayed to Taelin and Laeyra that the letter would be enough to convince his father to let the marriage be as it was. He knew in his heart, though, that Dargan Starseeker would not give in so easily. It was going to be a difficult road.

But it would be a road that he got to walk with the woman he loved. That made it all the easier.

Alana read the letter silently twice and then handed it back to Colwyn. She watched him as he gently folded the letter back up and put it back inside his tunic. His eyes found hers as she watched him. He patted his breast where the letter was and smiled at her.

"All safe," he winked.

"Good. Now, let's go make breakfast for the others and start thinking about how we're going to free the people of Valendale from the Zeraphim," Alana smiled at the man she loved.

Colwyn and Alana worked through the morning on the plan to save the people of Valendale. No matter how they worked it, there would be no easy way for them. And every plan they came up with centered around the people of Valendale joining into the fight. There did not seem to be any way around it. Alana hated depending on the people of Valendale themselves, but the scouting reports on the enemy showed that there were just too many of the Zeraphim for the companions to be able handle them on their own.

They would need the people of Valendale to fight for themselves.

Alana was not sure how they could convince the people of Valendale of the need for them to fight, but she knew that success would come down to whether or not they could. She would have to put a great deal of thought into how to get the people of Valendale to join the fight. She would meet with the leaders of the Resistance the following day, but she knew she needed to be thinking about it.

They took a break for lunch, leftover stew from the day before, reheated with some extra meat and vegetables. The companions all ate together. When the dishes were cleared away, Alana asked Meryn for the map of Willowdale. She spread the map out on the ground.

"All right, this is the city of Willowdale," she began. "We all know what the objective is."

"Kill the bad guys, save the good guys," Meryn volunteered.

"That sums it up admirably, Little One," Colwyn laughed.

"Good," Alana nodded, smiling. "Now, this is where we are now." She pointed to a point on the map not far from the city. "Colwyn and I have worked on a plan of attack for how to do this. It's not going to be easy and we will need the help of the people of Valendale to accomplish what we need to do."

"Alana will be speaking to the leaders of the Resistance tomorrow," Colwyn added. "She'll get them to join the cause."

"I've met with my contacts in the Resistance," Silvestra piped up. "They've all agreed to meet you. You will have all of the leaders there tomorrow."

"Good," Alana nodded. "That just leaves me with how to convince them to join the battle."

"It's not going to be easy," Silvestra sighed. "These are scared people, Alana. They don't believe that they can win if they take on the Zeraphim directly."

"Without our help, they might be right," Colwyn frowned. "Even with our help it's going to be difficult. The Zeraphim soldiers are trained fighters. We don't have enough time to train the people of Valendale completely."

"We're going to have to make do," Alana sighed softly. "They're all that we have. They'll have to gather whatever weapons that they can and when they take out a Zeraphim soldier, equip with their weapons."

"We're talking about having them fight swords with pitchforks and shovels," William grunted. "I don't like their chances.'

"We don't exactly have a whole lot of choice in the matter, William," Colwyn shrugged. "We don't have enough weapons to equip all of the people of Valendale with swords. They'll have to fight with whatever they can find and make the best of it."

"I don't like it any more than you do, William, but it is the only way we can free the people of Valendale," Alana slumped a little where she was sitting. "If you have any other way to do this, put words to it."

"I wish I did," William sighed deeply. "I know you're right. I just don't like it."

"Here is the main entrance," Alana said pointing to the map. "Colwyn, you'll lead the charge from here. Give no quarter. The people of Valendale are to do whatever it takes to finish off soldiers quickly. I don't want them spending any time on each individual battle. It will simply tire them out. Move quickly from soldier to soldier trying to take out as many as you can."

"This is a good location for Silvestra and I to coordinate the magical attacks against the Zeraphim," William pointed to a location just inside the city walls. "We will climb onto the roof there and we should have good cover to launch our magical attacks without being too open to mundane weapons from the enemy. That location gives us a pretty good vantage point of the whole city. Or it will give us a good vantage point on this side of the palace. And that's really all we'll need to focus on."

"Agreed," Alana nodded. "Meryn, there are plenty of nooks and shadows that you can hide in. You should be able to find a number of good locations to launch sneak attacks on the enemy."

"You can count on me, Alana," the halfling smiled. "I will get as many of the Zeraphim as I can."

"I know you will," Alana smiled. She turned to the priest. "Martin, I know you didn't sign up for a full scale war. I want you running around the battlefield tending to the wounded. Don't engage the enemy unless you absolutely have to. I know that you're one of the more skilled healers that Lord Taelin has, although healing is not one of my Lord's strong points. I want you trying to help as many people as you can."

"Of course," Martin nodded.

"Cobalt, you'll wait here," Alana pointed to another point on the map, this one just outside the city walls. "I suspect that the Nightstalker has some kind of surprise in store for me that I'll need your help with. You saw the cavern we found. You know what I want you on the lookout for."

"You know I have your back, Lady Alana," the dragon man nodded. "I will be there when you need me."

"I have no doubt of that," Alana smiled at him. She pointed to the small door that Meryn had pointed out for her. "This door is where I will enter the city. My job is to take out the Nightstalker. I'm not going to mess around with any Zeraphim soldiers that get in my way. My plan is to run through the city until I'm at the palace. You guys need to keep the Zeraphim busy so that they don't harass me on my way to take on the Nightstalker."

"They'll be far to busy to worry about you," Colwyn grinned. "Just be careful with the Nightstalker, Alana. She gives me an odd feeling."

"I'll be careful," she promised. "You need to be careful leading the people of Valendale as well, Col."

"I will be safe, Alana," Colwyn laughed. "I promise you I will come back."

"How are you going to convince the people of Valendale that they need to fight, Alana?" Silvestra asked.

"I suppose that I will have to figure that out by tomorrow," Alana shrugged. "The wisdom of Taelin will guide me as it always does."

"Let's start getting everything ready for the coming battle," Colwyn said softly.

Alana smiled at him as he stood and pulled out his bastard sword to make sure it was in good shape. The rest of the companions followed suit, checking and rechecking all of their weapons.

Willowdale

Chapter XVIII
Midnight Betrayal

William stood on a rock overlooking the companions' camp. The mage had taken the first watch. He was leaning against the trunk of a tree, his wizard's staff resting in the crook of his left elbow. Although his pose appeared to be casual and one where he looked to be a great deal less than alert, he was ready to alert the others at a moment's notice with a spell that he had prepared. He only needed one word to trigger the spell should someone come up the path towards the camp. From where he was standing, he would easily get that spell off before anyone coming up the path would see him standing there.

Colwyn had wanted to take the first watch but William had insisted. He knew that Colwyn and Alana had needed some time alone. It was time much needed after he had nearly betrayed her in the Elven Woods. Besides, the solitude offered by the watch was good for William. It would give the young man a chance to think. The events of the previous few days had thrown him for a loop, and he needed to take some time to finally sort through his feelings.

It was *her* reappearance in his life that had done it. He had never forgotten the lovely Silvestra Knightwing, but at the same time, he had never thought that he would ever see her again. For her to just turn up again so suddenly was a shock to his system.

Unbidden, the memory of that last meeting at the Tower of the White leapt to the forefront of his mind.

The young mage put the white robes of a full mage of the white for the first time. The crushed velvet felt good against his skin, especially after wearing the scratchy brown wool of the apprentice robes for the previous eight years. But this was the day he would finally become a full mage and leave the Tower of the White.

When he had woken up, he'd found that his brown apprentice robes had all been taken away and replaced with the white velvet robes that would mark him as a mage of the white sometime while he was sleeping. The bright velvet shone in the morning light pouring through the windows. It had been his final conformation that it was time for him to leave.

There was a knock on the door as he was tying his long hair back with the white velvet band that the woman he loved had given him. He finished tying his hair back and opened the door.

"I wanted to see you before you went to your appointment with the Inner Circle," Silvestra said when he opened the door. "I don't think we'll get a chance to see each other afterwards."

"Why do you say that, my love?" he asked as he took the dragon woman in his arms. "I'll always have time to see you, Silvestra."

"They're going to send you somewhere, William," Silvestra looked up at him, her eyes large and glistening with tears. William was shocked to see those tears streaming down her beautiful face. He'd never seen her cry before. "I overheard one of the mages of the Inner Circle talking to the

sage Isaiah. Isaiah told the mage that a Blademaster was soon to be revealed in the city of Ravendale. He implored the Inner Circle to send a mage out to Ravendale in an effort to help protect her."

"And they're sending me" William said softly. He brushed a lock of her hair away from her eyes and gently kissed her. "You could come with me. I'm sure they'd send us both if we asked."

"I cannot come with you, my love," she pulled away from him and went over to look out the window. "I have already received word from the Draconic Council that I am to return home." She turned back to face him. "Something larger than you and I is about to happen, and I will be sent somewhere."

He walked across the room and took her back into his arms. She laid her head on his chest and he gently stroked her hair.

"I will always love you, Silvestra," he said softly. "I do not wish to be parted from you."

"Nor do I wish to be parted from you, my love. But we have our duties," she pulled back and placed a hand on his chest. "We must attend to those duties. Maybe, one day, our duties will allow for us to be together again. But for now, I am afraid that we must be parted. No amount of wishing otherwise can change that."

"This is true love, Silvestra," he smiled sadly. "Do you think this happens every day? I will always come for you should you need me. When you need me the most, I will be there for you."

"Don't make promises that you can't keep, William," Silvestra pulled away from him. She turned away and lowered her head. "I'm sorry, but you can't walk this path with me. At least for now, your life is down another path."

"Well, I won't give up on us, Silvestra," he kissed her hair. "Surely, something can be worked out for us to be together."

"Maybe someday, my love," she smiled sadly at him. "But for now, we must part. I shall not see you again before you leave the Tower of the White."

"I will not say goodbye, Silvestra," he let her go.

He raised a hand, palm upward, and he whispered a word of magic. The air above his palm began to glow with a pale red light. The light began to grow in brightness, and it began to expand. After a few moments, the glow faded out to nothing once more. A perfect heart shaped ruby lay in the palm of William's hand. He uttered another word of magic, and the ruby split into two parts. He took half and handed it to Silvestra.

"A heartstone?" Silvestra raised both eyebrows, impressed with the magic the young mage had just crafted. "I did not know you were that strong a mage, William."

"Nor did I," William shrugged.

She peered deeply into his eyes. "Clearly the Inner Circle does not know what they have in you just yet." She laid her hand against his cheek. "You are indeed headed down a difficult path, my love. I know now which path your journey will take. I doubt anyone else does."

"Will you tell me?"

"I cannot," she shook her head sadly. "You know as well as I that it is for you to discover on your own."

"I believe that my path will again one day include you, Silvestra," he said quietly as he placed the half of the stone he kept for himself in a pouch. "I give you this half of the heartstone as a pledge of my love for you now and forever. Never again will my heart be whole until we are once more together like the two halves of the heartstone."

"Nor will mine," she replied as she conjured two chains into being. She attached her half of the heartstone to the chain and handed him the other chain to do the same. She put the chain with her half of the heartstone around her neck. "I must go now, my love. The Draconic Council awaits my arrival on the Isle of Dragons. Until we meet again in this life or the next, know that I love you."

"I love you too," he said to her back as she slipped out of his quarters.

It would be seven years before he would once again see the woman he loved.

William snapped out of his reverie with a start when he heard someone coming up on his position from the direction of the companions' camp. He tensed and readied the magic word to release his alert spell, but he relaxed when he recognized the soft footfalls of Silvestra Knightwing.

"I was hoping to have some time alone with you, William," she said softly as she came up by the rock. "We have not been able to speak since you and the others arrived in Willowdale. I think we need to talk."

"I think you're right," he nodded. "It's been a long time since we saw each other. A lot has happened to both of us in seven years."

"Indeed," she nodded sadly. "We have both been surrounded by so much death."

"We are on the brink of war," the mage sighed deeply. "I don't think either of us has seen the last of death's dark spectre in our lives."

She climbed up to where he was standing and leaned against the trunk right next to him, her side pressed against his side. She reached over and took his right hand in her left. He looked over and she smiled at him, her smile melting his heart as it always did. He smiled back at her, but his smile was tinged by sadness. A single tear rolled down the young mage's face.

"I thought I had lost you, Silvestra," he said softly. "I received word four years ago from Eliazar of the Dragonic Council that you had been killed during a mission. I truly thought you dead."

"The heartstone you made should have told you differently, William," she whispered. "He should not have been able to deceive you like that."

William did not say a word. He simply reached inside his robes and pulled the chain the hearstone was attached to free so she could see it. The once bright ruby hung dark and dead on the chain. No light came from the stone at all. Silvestra stared at the dark gem for several long minutes. She looked him in the eyes, a look of pure disbelief on her face.

"Yes, Silvestra," he said sadly. "My half of the heartstone went dark not long before I got the message from

Eliazar. Thus, I did not doubt his words. As much as I wanted to."

She pulled her half of the heartstone from where she wore it around her neck. Her half of the heartstone pulsed with a warm ruby light. She reached over to where his half of the heartstone hung dark on its chain. When she touched her half of the heartstone to his, there was a sharp flash of ruby light, and his half of the heartstone began to pulse with the same light and pattern as her half.

"Eliazar never approved of our relationship, William," she smiled sadly. "He once told me that he would do whatever it would take to break us apart. Clearly, he tried his best."

"I thought you were dead, Silvestra," he turned away from her. A tear rolled down his cheek. "I moved on."

"I know," she put her hand on his arm. "I saw how you looked at Meryn. But I never stopped loving you."

William stepped away, putting a little distance between the two of them. He bowed his head and sighed.

"You cannot fight true love," he said softly. He lowered his head to his chest and closed his eyes.

"William?" Silvestra asked. "Are you all right?"

The mage opened his eyes and looked at the heartstone. He watched the light pulse deep in the stone for a few moments and sighed softly. William looked back at her, pain in his eyes. "You are my one true love, Silvestra Knightwing. You always have been. You always will be. This will end up breaking Meryn's heart though."

"That's going to make life with your companions a little difficult," SIlvestra reminded him softly. "And these are the people you need to be with."

"Yes, I need to be with them," he nodded. He walked back over to her and put his arms around her. "But I can't be without you either. I knew as soon as I saw you again that things were about to get complicated."

"If you are sure that this is what you want, my love, I will be with you," she smiled at him. "So long as you are aware that there will be consequences."

"There are always consequences, Silvestra," he kissed her hair gently. "Whatever consequences come from this, we will deal with them together."

"Then if you will have me, I will be yours, my love,' Silvestra said quietly, love in her eyes as she looked at him. She reached up and touched his cheek. "Now and forever, I am yours. Our paths have finally come back together. They shall not part again. As you once said would happen.'

He did not respond with words. He leaned down and found her lips with his. She wrapped her arms around him and melted into his kiss. She closed her eyes and returned the kiss with fiery passion. They stayed in that warm embrace for several long seconds before he broke it. Neither wanted to be the one to part from the kiss first.

"I'll take that as a yes," her voice came in ragged breaths.

"Am I interrupting something?" Colwyn asked as he stepped up to the tree they were leaning against. "It's my turn to take watch."

"Did you and Alana get to work things out?" William asked.

"Let's just say that Alana is very satisfied with our resolution. And that she's going to sleep *very* well the rest of the night," Colwyn grinned at his friend. "Now, I think that you two should go, ah, resolve some issues yourselves."

"That sounds like a good idea," Silvestra grinned and winked at William.

William returned the grin then closed his eyes. With a bit of intense concentration, the mage released and regained the energies that he had gathered for the spell. He waved at Colwyn and they walked off towards the camp. Colwyn watched them walk back to the camp, grinning broadly at them, knowing that his friend had finally found the kind of love that he shared with Alana. He turned back to monitor the path leading up to the companions' camp, happily convinced that something good had happened tonight.

Willowdale

Meryn Swiftfoot ghosted away from where she had been watching the tree where Colwyn was now keeping watch. She had been there long enough to watch the conversation between William and the silver haired woman. She felt her heart breaking as she watched the two of them kissing. She pawed the tears off her cheeks and growled softly.

"If I can't have you, no one will, William," she growled bitterly.

Upset, the halfling made her way back to the companions' camp and quietly packed her gear. She looked over at where William lay sleeping next to the dragon woman. She wanted to go and fight for him, but she knew she had no chance to best a woman born of dragonkind, least of all one that was trained in both human and dragon magic.

Once all of her belongings were all packed up, she made her way quickly and quietly back to where Colwyn was keeping watch. She crept through the bushes until she could see him. Where she was crouching, she knew that Colwyn could not see her hiding there in the bushes watching him. Yet she knew that his senses were heightened due to his training as a ranger. She knew that she could get away without alerting those heightened senses, but it would take careful action to accomplish.

Even the most alert ranger could not catch a halfling that did not wish to be detected. She backed herself back into the bushes, moving so subtly that not even a leaf rustled. Colwyn never noticed her movements, which made her smile slightly. She tracked through the bushes until she reached the point where the trail leading to the companions' camp from the town turned a corner and was out of sight of the ranger keeping watch.

Once back on the road, she could move much faster. She scuttled quickly down the road towards the town. She dared not enter the town through the main gate, though, as they would undoubtedly be guarded. During the companions' tour of the city, the halfling had noticed a small door on the west wall of the city. When she'd asked about it, she'd been told that it was the door by which corpses were taken out of the city to be buried in the cemetery that was about a mile west of the city. She knew the door was kept locked, but no lock was safe from a determined halfling.

Just before she came in sight of the gates to Willowdale, Meryn slipped back into the brush and made her way around the city to the door she intended to enter the city by. It took her over an hour to get to the door, because she was moving cautiously and stopping at the slightest bit of movement. By the time she got to the door, she was tired. She paused to nibble on a bit of dried meat before tackling the lock on the door.

Examining the lock told her that it would be easy for her to pick. She took an extra moment to check for traps, and, finding none, she set to work. The lock gave way in under a half a minute. She opened the door and slipped into the city.

Meryn knew that things would get difficult for her now. She glided through the city, making sure she avoided the Zeraphim patrols. The patrols were all over the city but the halfling used the shadows to her advantage.

She worked her way through the city towards the palace. She knew that was where the Nightstalker and the captains of the Zeraphim were. She wasn't yet sure how she was going to get into the palace or what she would do exactly but she knew that she had to get into the palace undetected. If she could get inside without being detected, she knew she could get to the Nightstalker.

At that point it would be all too easy to do what she needed to do. Once she figured out what that would be.

Her steps were light and silent as she worked her way through the city, ducking into alleys from time to time to avoid the guards. As she came into sight of the palace, the patrols grew more and more frequent. She worked her way around the palace while still several blocks away so that she could move a little more freely. When she got around to the back of the palace, she crept slowly forward towards the servants' entrance.

No one noticed the halfling as she entered the palace by the servants' entrance. She had a vague idea of where she was going in the palace, but she wasn't fully positive. She lifted her little dagger a little ways out of its sheath and let it slide back in to make sure that it was clear in the sheath. She had watched Colwyn and Alana perform the same ritual hundreds of times before going into a battle. She wasn't sure why they did it, but it was something they always did, so Meryn thought that maybe it was something that just had to be done before someone went into any battle.

And no matter what happened in the next few minutes, the halfling knew that she was definitely in for a battle of some kind.

She crept through the corridors of the palace, figuring that the Nightstalker would be in the quarters of the First Lord of Willowdale. It would be a simple matter to sneak into those quarters if she could avoid the Zeraphim on the way. She had to duck into a room several times on the way to the First Lord's quarters to avoid Zeraphim guards.

Finally she got to the First Lord's quarters and she slipped inside. She took several seconds to let her eyes adjust to the near darkness of the First Lord's quarters. When her eyes adjusted, she crept towards the bedroom. The door to the bedroom was slightly open, and Meryn could make out the form sleeping on the bed. The woman on the bed was clothed head to do in black leather. She had dark hair that flowed loosely across the pillow. She looked peaceful, but Meryn knew her to be as lethal as Alana was. But this woman was without the honor and mercy that the Blademaster displayed.

Meryn slipped inside the bedroom and ghosted over to the bed. She soundlessly slid her dagger out of its sheath and leaned over the sleeping woman. She gently placed the point of her dagger against the woman's breast and closed her eyes. She had just started to push downward when her wrists were captured in an iron grasp.

"My, my, my," a soft voice laughed, forcing Meryn to open her eyes. The woman on the bed had opened her ice blue eyes and had fixed her gaze on the halfling. She had also captured Meryn's wrists in her gloved hands. "The little sneak thief thought to kill me in my sleep?"

"I was thinking about it, yes," Meryn gulped.

"What shall I do with you?" the Nightstalker smiled. She disarmed the shaking halfling and threw the dagger into the far wall. The dagger stuck with a thud and the hilt quivered in the air.

"You could let me go," the halfling suggested with a whimper.

"You tried to kill me." Kera snarled. "No, I don't think I can let you go. I think I should give you to the Zeraphim as a toy."

"I can tell you what Alana is planning," Meryn squealed.

"Oh, yes. I'm sure you can," Kera smiled wickedly. She lowered her face so that it was mere inches from Meryn's, her ice blue eyes boring into Meryn's hazel ones. "Before this night is over, I will know everything you know about the Blademaster and her plans to rescue the poor pathetic people of Valendale."

"But—"

"Enough!" Kera bellowed. "Guards, take this little sneak thief to the dungeons. Show her what happens to people who oppose the will of Thraal."

The halfling squealed in protest as she was dragged out of the First Lord's quarters to the dungeons. Kera smiled wickedly as she crossed the room to look out of the window towards where she suspected the Blademaster and her companions were camped.

"Soon, Blademaster," she said softly. "Soon, you shall die at my hands."

Willowdale

Chapter XIX
Discoveries

"The halfling is gone, Alana," Colwyn's voice was harshly cross as he woke Alana up.

"What?" Alana came to full awake in an instant, her auburn hair in a disarray around her face.

"Meryn," Colwyn repeated. "She's missing. She packed her belongings and left sometime during the night. She wasn't in her bed when I went to start my watch, but her belongings were here. I never saw her leave, and I didn't think to check to see if she was here when I got back to the camp after my watch was over."

"Well, this is unexpected," Alana frowned. "Where do you think she might have gotten off to?"

"I don't know," Colwyn sighed as he sat down next to her. "I suspect she left because she overheard William and Silvestra talking last night."

"What do Silvestra and William have to do with it?" Alana frowned. She thought for a second and Colwyn could see the light suddenly go on with the expression on Alana's face. "Oh. Oh, dear."

"What did you do, Alana?" Colwyn said softly.

"I reminded Silvestra of the First Law of the Blades," Alana slumped back in her bedroll. "I told her that she should tell William how she feels about him. Oh, Lord Taelin, what have I done?"

"It sounds like you've given two people who love each other a new chance at a life together," Colwyn lay down next to her. "I saw the two of them when I went up to take my watch. You should see the way they look at each other, Alana. You did the right thing, no matter what the consequences might be for everyone involved."

"Did I, Colwyn?" Alana opened an eye and looked at him. "Meryn's gone. We need her. There's no way of knowing just what trouble she will get into without us around."

"She's a big girl, Alana," Colwyn reminded her. "She did fine before she met up with us the first time. She'll do fine without us now."

"What if she goes to the palace and gets caught, Colwyn?" Alana asked. "What if she decides that the only way to get William back is to try to capture the Nightstalker on her own? She'd be killed. There's no way she can stand up to Kera Rayden on her own. Hell, I don't even know if I can stand up to her."

"This could be a problem," Colwyn nodded. He slapped a hand over his eyes. "This could be a big problem."

Colwyn and Alana got up and rolled up their bedrolls. They went looking for William. The mage and the dragon woman were sleeping side by side, a peaceful look on both of their faces. Alana couldn't help but smile at the two of them. Colwyn looked at Alana and grinned wickedly. Alana knew what he was thinking and shook her head.

Colwyn grabbed a small bucket of water and splashed the contents on William. Some drops fell on Silvestra too.

"Wake up, William," Colwyn announced. "We have trouble."

"What?" William sputtered and shook water out of his hair. "Col, you really need to find another way to wake me up. What do you mean we have trouble?"

"Look around. See anything or anyone missing?" Alana asked.

"Oh, gods," William slumped back in his bed as soon as he realized who was missing. "She must have heard Silvestra and I talking. Oh, this can't be good."

"Can you scry for her and see where she is?" Alana asked.

"I can't," William shook his head. "I don't have enough power for such a complex spell."

"I can do it," Silvestra said. "But not in my current form. I'd have to use dragon magic. Which I'm forbidden to do."

"That's all right, Silvestra," Alana held up a hand. "I suspect I know where she is anyway. There has to be a way to tell if she's still alive though. That's all I really need to know. If she's alive, I can get her."

"That I can do with human magic," Silvestra said softly.

Silvestra closed her eyes and held her hands out. They glowed softly with a faint blue light. She held her hands with the palms up and the glow intensified. She whispered a few words in the elven language, but neither Colwyn nor Alana could tell what they were.

"She is alive," Silvestra said softly, her voice slightly strained. She dropped her hands to her side and the blue glow went away. "She is alive and in the city of Willowdale somewhere. More than that, I cannot say."

"She's in the dungeons then," Alana nodded to herself. "Very well, after we talk to the people of Valendale, I'll have to go in and get her."

"That's suicide, Alana," William thundered. "You are too important. Let Silvestra and I go get her. It's our fault she's in there in the first place. If she hadn't overheard us talking she never would have gone off."

"And if I hadn't reminded Silvestra of the truth of the First Law of the Blades, she would not have worked up the courage to talk to you, William," Alana said softly. "It's every bit as much my fault. This is something I have to do."

"No, William is right, Alana," Colwyn said, as he put a hand on her shoulder. He looked her square in the eyes, and she met his gaze and held it. "You need to prepare to fight Kera Rayden. You can't go off and rescue Meryn. You don't have enough energy to do both."

"You're right, Colwyn," Alana said softly. She turned to William. "Can you and Silvestra get her out?"

"It won't be easy and we might have to tap into some of our reserves in the battle as a result, but yes we can," Silvestra answered for William. "We have to do this, Alana. I told you there would be consequences."

"There are consequences to everything we do, Silvestra," Alana smiled.

"I know," the silver haired dragon woman sighed. "But why is it that sometimes the consequences for what we do hurt someone else and not us?"

"I've never understood that, Silvestra," Alana laid a hand on the silver haired dragon woman's shoulder. "If you ever figure out the answer to that, let me know."

"I'll be sure to," Silvestra nodded. She turned to face William and shared a smile with the young mage.

William smiled back at Silvestra and stroked her hair. He turned to Alana and his smile faded.

"Alana, I found something while I was exploring the cave yesterday," he said softly. "I don't quite know what it means, but I believe that what I found was a book of prophecy. I don't know what the prophecies are, as I cannot read any of the languages in the book, but I believe that it's actually the same set of prophecies written in several languages."

He went over to his belongings and pulled the book out. He brought it over to Alana and handed it to her. The Blademaster took the book and leafed through the pages. She stopped suddenly, a look of mild surprise on her face.

"I think this might be Elven, Col," she said softly as she handed the book to him. "Can you read it? What does it say?"

Colwyn took the book from Alana and studied the words that she pointed out to him, frowning slightly. He read over the prophecy several times, making sure he made out all of the words correctly. He translated the prophecy in his head and sighed deeply.

"It is, indeed, Elven," he said quietly. "It's a long and complicated prophecy. Let me read it to you."

"*Tá an tuar an cogadh mór anamacha*

Tar éis trí chéad bliain ar fud an domhain a thagann an Aois dorchadais. Beidh an Dia olc ar ais chun tús a conquest an domhain arís.

Sna laethanta tosaigh an Aois dorchadais, tar éis na máistrí na lanna ar ais go dtí saol na Calthea, déanfaidh an arm na marbh chun cinn i seirbhís an Dia olc. Déanfaidh an marbh ardú agus cogadh pá ar fud an aghaidh Calthea.

Nuair a thiteann an chathair faoi dhó marbh folamh ar feadh uair an tríú, beidh an scamaill stoirme a bhailiú agus beidh an claimhte fuaime i gcuid truaillí. Déanfaidh an dúchan cogaidh a bheith ar an talamh agus ní féidir ach an ceann a rugadh ar an bhfianaise an cúiseamh i gcoinne an dorchadas mar thoradh.

Ní mór don arm an solas scaoilte an draíocht na bean sidhe dul ar ais ar an dorchadas. An ceann a rugadh ar an cheo solais mar thoradh ar an oidhreacht na máistrí na lanna isteach ar an réimse an cath.

Nuair a ghlaonn an anam an bean sidhe a gabhadh amach, beidh na clocha ar an daingean ar an bhfianaise a bhriseadh agus titim ar a chéile. Beidh an bhiotáille an roghnaithe de Taelin uair níos mó a chur ar an réimse an cath i Cruinniú w i gcoinne an dorchadas.

Déanfaidh an tine an ghrian agus an ghealach dim agus céimnithe chun dorchadais. Ní mór don duine a rugadh ar an solas ag siúl amach as an scáth an tine an ghrian agus an ghealach agus an roghnaithe de Taelin mar thoradh.

Beidh an Dlí is Fiche ar an Tríú na lanna a shárú, i gcás roinnt de na roghnaithe de Taelin.

Mura ndéanfaidh an ceann a rugadh ar an bhfianaise thoradh an cúiseamh i gcoinne an arm na marbh, beidh an domhain titim isteach i dorchadas a bheidh gan deireadh. Ní féidir ach an cumhacht ag an Dlí Chéad na lanna threorú láimh an ceann a rugadh ar an solas.

Sa chath mar atá i ngach daoine eile a mbeidh an ceann a rugadh ar an solas troid, ní bheidh aon ráthaíochtaí. Ní ghlacfar ach le méid seo a leanas an eagna Taelin agus ag an ádh de Laeyra an ceann a rugadh ar an solas i réim.

Ba chóir an ceann a rugadh ar an bhfianaise a bheith rathúil i gceannas ar an fórsaí an tsolais, beidh an domhan beo go buan coibhneasta ar feadh tamaill, ach ní bheidh ach ar feadh tréimhse chun a Dhia olc a thabhairt ar a thóir suas.

Más mian leis an duine a rugadh ar an bhfianaise a Cealaigh an damáiste de bharr an anam glaoch ar an bean sidhe a gabhadh, ní mór di teacht ar an Solas de Taelin agus a chuid draíochta a úsáid chun aon uair amháin níos mó a thógáil an daingean ar an solas.

Sna blianta tar éis dheireadh an chogaidh mór anamacha ba chóir, an ceann a rugadh ar an solas i casadh ar ais ar an dorchadas ar feadh tamaill, beidh sí a leathnú trí solas huaire. Ach leis an tríú, beidh sí a hionad i measc na spioraid na roghnaithe de Taelin.

Mar sin deireadh leis an bhfocal an tuar deiridh Bahala, an fíodóir de greams. Leis an gifting an tuar, cas mé an maintlín de chumhacht an fíodóir an aisling thar a fíodóir nua agus i bhfad níos óige an aisling. Creid na focail seo, beidh ar gach a bhfuil scríofa anseo teacht chun pas a fháil.

Is féidir na focail seo lá amháin a mbealach chun an ceann a rugadh ar an solas. Beidh an té a chosnaíonn a bheith in ann aistriú na focail seo a son, cé go mbeidh a fhios ag an bhrí nach taobh thiar de na focail nuair a fhaigheann siad iad.

Scríofa ag mo lámh,

Bahala Maranal, an fíodóir an aisling

Tríocha seacht mbliana anuas an bás mór de na máistrí na lanna."

"What does it mean, Colwyn?" Alana asked. "It sounds somewhat ominous."

"It is," Colwyn nodded. "I don't quite understand what it means. We've heard part of this prophecy before though.

The prophecy of the Great War of Souls

After three hundred years of peace in the world comes the Age of Darkness. The Dark God will return to begin his conquest of the world once more.

In the early days of the Age of Darkness, after the Blademasters have returned to the world of Calthea, the army of the dead shall arise in service to the Dark God. The dead shall rise and wage war across the face of Calthea.

When the twice dead city falls empty for a third time, the storm clouds will gather and the sabres will rattle in their scabbards. The blight of war shall be upon the land and only the one born of the light can lead the charge against the darkness.

The army of the light must uncork the magic of the bean sidhe to turn back the darkness. The one born of the light must lead the legacy of the Blademasters onto the field of battle.

When the soul of the captured bean sidhe wails, the stones of the stronghold of the light will shatter and crumble upon one another. The spirits of the chosen of Taelin will once more take the field of battle in the war against the darkness.

The fire of the sun and the moon will dim and fade to darkness. The one born of the light must walk out from the shadow of the fire of the sun and the moon and lead the chosen of Taelin.

The Twenty Third Law of the Blades will be violated for some of the chosen of Taelin.

If the one born of the light does not lead the charge against the army of the dead, the world will fall into a darkness that will be without end. Only the power of the First Law of the Blades can guide the hand of the one born of the light.

In this battle as in all others the one born of the light will fight, there will be no guarantees. Only by following the wisdom of Taelin and by the luck of Laeyra will the one born of the light prevail.

Should the one born of the light be successful in leading the forces of the light, the world will live in relative peace for a time, but only for a time for the Dark God shall never give up his quest.

If the one born of the light wishes to undo the damage caused by the wailing soul of the captured bean sidhe, she *must find the Light of Taelin and use its magic to once more build the stronghold of the light.*

In the years after the end of the great war of souls, should the one born of the light in turning back the darkness for a time, she will extend the light three times. But with the third, she will take her place among the spirits of the chosen of Taelin.

So ends the words of the final prophecy of Bahala, the Dream Weaver. With the gifting of this prophecy, I turn the mantle of power of the Dream Weaver over to a new and much younger Dream Weaver. Heed these words, for all that is written here shall come to pass.

May these words one day find their way to the one born of the light. The one who protects her will be able to translate these words for her, although neither will know the meaning behind the words when they find them.

Written by my hand,
Bahala Maranal, the Dream Weaver
Thirty seven years past the Great Purge."

He lowered the book and looked at Alana. He could see pain in her eyes from the translation of the prophecy. While he knew that neither of them could know exactly what the words of the prophecy meant, they both could see that it meant that the next few years would be very difficult for them as they went forward.

"There is that prophecy again," Alana frowned deeply. *"When the twice dead city falls empty for a third time, the storm clouds will gather and the sabres will rattle in their scabbards. The blight of war shall be upon the land and only the one born of the light can lead the charge against the darkness."*

"There is nothing that can be done about it, Alana," Colwyn said sadly. "We have to do this."

"I know," Alana put her hand on his arm. "It makes me sad that we are causing the events that will lead to war."

"Can we do anything else?" William asked. "The people of Valendale deserve to be home where they belong."

"I know, William," Alana nodded. "There is nothing else we can do."

The four friends looked sadly at each other, knowing that war was about to come to the world they loved so much. And there was nothing they could do to prevent it. All they could do is help keep the people of Calthea safe when the war came.

"Nothing is ever easy," William sighed deeply.

"This war that we seem to be headed for sounds like it will shape things to come for us," Alana said quietly after a long silence. "It also sounds like it's going to change the nature of the world."

"You cannot read too much into prophecy, Alana," William cautioned. "As easy as it would be to make changes to what you will do based on what you hear, you must not. You must proceed as you normally would as if you hadn't heard this prophecy. The truth is, no matter how much you think you understand it, things never work out exactly as a prophecy would lead you to believe. Things are not always as they seem. If you would alter what you would do to avoid what you think might come from this prophecy, you will actually make things worse. Trying to keep the things in the prophecy from happening will be far more difficult for you and for the world than the consequences you are trying to avoid."

"I already told the King that I would not change what we were about to do just to prevent the coming of this war," Alana's voice was barely above a whisper. "That is a commitment I intend to keep."

"Good," William smiled at Alana. "Just remember, Alana. You're not going to be leading the forces against the darkness by yourself. Colwyn, Martin, Silvestra and I will all be with you. I promise you that whatever comes, we will face it together."

"Good," Alana nodded, smiling slightly. "I must admit that the knowledge that the world is going to rest on my shoulders is a bit of a burden. Less so if I don't have to shoulder the burden by myself, though."

"That's one of the reasons you have me, Alana," Colwyn smiled a cockeyed smile at Alana. "I will always be here for you."

"Of course you will, Col," Alana smiled her special smile at him. "For now, though, let us concentrate on the task at hand. Colwyn, you and I have to go meet the leaders of the Resistance. We'll talk to whichever members of the Resistance show up. William, you and Silvestra should go and try to free the halfling. We'll meet back here afterwards. Hopefully, we will all have success in our tasks."

The other three nodded assent at her suggestion. Colwyn followed the woman he loved out of the cavern towards the meeting with the leaders of the Resistance.

Chapter XX
Taunts

Meryn Swiftfoot wished she had never left the companions. She was alone in her cell in the dungeon of the palace of Willowdale. There was no worse feeling for a halfling than being locked up. She knew that the end to her confinement would likely come soon. She wondered if she would have a chance to ask for Alana's forgiveness before she died. For betraying Alana, Meryn truly felt bad. Guilt was not a normal feeling for a Halfling to have. Meryn was typical of that.

Alana had become a very special person to Meryn though. Most people viewed Meryn with intense distrust because she was a halfling. She was used to it. Alana, however, had befriended the halfling and even trusted her. Alana had saved her life, and Meryn had, in turn saved Alana's. She had saved all of the companions at the top of the ziggurat of Thraal. Alana had repaid Meryn with a deep and intense trust.

Meryn had repaid that trust with betrayal.

No matter how she rationalized her actions, the end result was the same. She had betrayed her friend Alana. Alana had been the only person outside of the halfling nation that had treated her as a person and not as a potential source of trouble. Meryn cried softly to herself as she realized the pain she had caused her friend.

She had to make it up to Alana somehow.

Meryn hoped that Alana would think to make changes to the plan after she realized Meryn had gone. She believed that the Blademaster was smart enough to realize that she could have given the Nightstalker the attack plans.

Meryn went over the attack plan in her head again and realized that there really wasn't anything Alana could do to change the plans. The thought made her even more depressed, knowing that the Nightstalker knew exactly how the Blademaster would be attacking the city. And Meryn knew it was all her fault.

Meryn hoped that everyone in the party would survive the attack. She hoped she would see them again before she was killed. She hoped she could apologize to William and Silvestra. She hoped she could beg Alana for her forgiveness.

She thought about William and Silvestra. That was why she had done what she had done. The more she thought about it, however, the more she realized that she had no right to be jealous over the silver haired dragon woman. The two of them had loved each other long before Meryn had met William.

In the end, William's happiness was all that was important.

Meryn pictured the dragon woman in her head. She smiled slightly. William certainly knew how to pick them. Silvestra was a beauty. And she was smart. Meryn was not sure that she could have competed with her even if she had wanted to try.

She hoped that Silvestra would make William happy. He deserved some happiness in his life. She knew that he had been sad for a long time. And now, she thought she might just understand a little bit why he had been sad for so long. If she had lost her true love like he had, she would be too.

With a jolt, she realized that she had not. William was not her true love, no matter how much she might want that to be the case!

Meryn wondered if she would ever meet her true love. She wondered if she would ever get out of the cell she was in.

A plan began to form in the young halfling's head. She knew that she would have to get out of the cell on her own. She wasn't sure yet how she would accomplish that, but she knew that if she could get out of the cell, she could get back to the companions and warn them that the plan had been compromised.

And ask for forgiveness.

The Nightstalker sat in the quarters that she had appropriated. She was eating cherries out of a bowl. She ate one cherry at a time, savoring the succulent fruit. She was watching two guards who were watching her. She had one leg slung over the arm of the chair she was sitting on.

"What have you gotten out of the halfling?" she asked between cherries. She spit the pit out into the bowl next to the one containing the cherries. "You assured me you would have the Blademaster's entire plan by now."

"The halfling isn't talking," one of the guards said "Anything more we do to her in order to get her to talk may well damage her beyond the ability to heal."

"What does that matter?" Kera raised an eyebrow. "She is to die with the rest of her companions anyway."

"Of course, Mistress Nightstalker," the guard bowed slightly.

"Bring her to me," Kera ordered. "I could use a little entertainment this evening."

"As you command, Mistress Nightstalker," the guards bowed and left the room.

"A halfling that doesn't talk," Kera Rayden laughed heartily. "Now I have heard everything."

Meryn was moaning to herself, crying really, when she heard the guards walking in the corridor above her cell. She knew that they were back to torture her some more. She did not care. Despite her original intentions when she left the companions' camp, she had no desire to betray her companions anymore. All she wanted was to go back to them and beg for forgiveness.

She scrunched into a corner as they opened the grate, hoping that they wouldn't see her.

"Halfling, your presence has been requested by the Nightstalker," one of the guards bellowed into the dungeon. "You do not want us coming down after you. Now climb the ladder, little one. Climb it quickly."

Meryn unballed herself from the corner and made her way slowly over to the ladder. She tentatively climbed it, thinking that this would be far worse than torture. She remembered how Alana had been a little disconcerted after meeting the Nightstalker the first time. She was not all that excited about the prospect of seeing Alana's evil counterpart a second time. The little taste she'd had when she'd been captured had been more than enough.

As soon as she reached the top of the ladder, the halfling was grabbed roughly. She squeaked in protest, but she was bound hand and foot anyway. She knew that there was nothing she could do to help herself. She only hoped that she could hold out and not tell them anything before she was rescued. Or died if it came to that. She had decided that she would die before betraying Alana.

They dragged the halfling down the corridor like a piece of meat. She tried to kick and scream, but bound and gagged as she was, there was little she could do to struggle. She could not see where they were dragging her, but she knew that they were taking her to the Nightstalker.

She struggled in her bonds, but it was no use. They were going to take her to see the Nightstalker whether she wanted to go or not. It was not going to be fun for the halfling, she knew.

After what seemed like hours to the poor halfling, she was thrown into the quarters that the Nightstalker had claimed for her own. She hit the floor with an oof of expended air. She slowly sat up, still bound. The halfling caught sight of the Nightstalker and wriggled back towards the door.

"There is no escape for you, little one," the Nightstalker said softly. "Ungag her. She can't answer me if she can't talk." She moved over so that her face was right next to the halfling's. "And trust me, my little sneak thief. You will talk to me. You will tell me everything I want to know before this night is over. And then, when your pathetic companions attack tomorrow, you will die."

"I think you have it backwards," the halfling squeaked out. "When Alana comes, you're going to be the one to die."

"What did you just say to me?" the Nighstalker backed up. "How dare you insinuate that the accursed Blademaster is my better?"

"Because she is your better," Meryn barked out. She was starting to feel a little more confident with her words. "She fights for the people. What do you fight for? You fight for a dark and stupid god. All Thraal wants is to create chaos and make the world fall into darkness. How can you be a part of that? What happened to you to make you fall so far into the darkness?"

"Silence," Kera roared. She slapped Meryn across the face with the armored back of her glove.

"I thought you wanted me to talk," the hafling stared at her. Her cheek was reddened, but she did not rub where the glove had hit. "Make up your mind. Either I talk or I don't talk. You can't have it both ways, you know."

"Halfling, I am warning you," Kera raised her hand to strike again. "You will tell me the Blademaster's plans or my hand will fly again."

"I don't think that even if I told you what she's planning it would help you," Meryn crossed her arms. "As I said, she's better than you. She has this very well planned out."

"You were warned," Kera snarled. Her hand flew and slapped the halfling across the other cheek. "Now, little sneak thief. You will tell me what the Blademaster is planning or I will gut you where you stand."

"If you gut me then you will never get the answers that you want, and then where will you be?" the halfling continued to taunt her.

"I will have the satisfaction of ending your life, little sneak thief," Kera leaned back down and put her face right next to the halfling's. She pulled a knife from her belt and waggled it just inside the halfling's vision. "Now. Are you going to tell me what I want to know or do I get to read the answers in your steaming entrails?"

"She's going to get the people of Valendale to rise up against you," Meryn said, instantly hating herself. But she resolved herself to not tell the whole plan. "She's going to lead them into a frontal assault against you. Her nathair an aeir a chosnaíonn is ready to take on the surprise that she knows is waiting for us. And we have two mages that will provide magical support."

She did not tell the Nightstalker that one of the mages was also a dragon. She left a lot of the plan out. She also knew that she would likely not be alive to take part in the plan.

"A frontal assault?" Kera raised an eyebrow. "Such a foolish plan. She will, of course, be killed before she even gets to me."

"I've told you what you want to know," Meryn whimpered. "Now let me go."

"Oh, I don't think so, little sneak thief," Kera laughed. You get to watch as the foolish Blademaster fails to rescue the people of Valendale. You will get to watch your precious Blademaster die." She motioned for the guards. "Guards, deposit the little sneak thief back in her little hole. She can rot there for all I care."

The guards grabbed Meryn and dragged her out of the room. The Nightstalker did not watch her go. It did not matter at this point what the halfling did. Even if she were to escape, there was nothing she could do to stop the destruction of the Blademaster. As far as Kera Rayden was concerned, the Blademaster's fate had been sealed as soon as the Nightstalker had arrived in Willowdale. All that Kera had to do was to wait for the Blademaster to come to her. It would be so easy for her to kill the Blademaster. She would make her High Priest and her god proud.

"Soon, Blademaster," Kera whispered to herself, as she had so many times before. "Soon you will die by my hand. I will bring honor to the Dark God once more.

The halfling grunted as she was thrown back into the dungeon. She landed flat on her back and her head hit against the cold stone of the floor. She looked up at the guards that were still standing over the entrance to the dungeon. They seemed to be laughing at her, but she could not hear them through the rush of blood in her ears.

She watched as they slammed the grate closed and slid the bolt home, locking her once more in her prison. Only then did she sit up.

She brought her knees up under her chin and wrapped her little arms around her knees. Then she buried her head between her knees and started to cry, tears continuously rolling down her face.

The only comfort that the halfling took was that she did not tell the Nightstalker everything. She hoped that that little bit of advantage would be enough for the Blademaster to survive.

Willowdale

Chapter XXI
The Wisdom of Taelin

Alana and Colwyn were alone in the clearing where they were going to meet with the leaders of the Resistance. All of the leaders had agreed that they would come. It would be a large meeting, and, Alana hoped, a productive one. She could only hope that the men from Valendale would realize the words she would tell them were the truth.

She had no idea what those words would be, however.

They had a half hour before the time they had set for the meeting. Alana had wanted the two of them to get there before the others so that they would both have time to ready themselves for the task of convincing the leaders of the Resistance of the need for action.

Alana knelt down in the middle of the clearing and drew one of her swords. She drove the tip of the sword into the ground and grabbed the hilt with both hands. She leaned her head on the pommel and closed her eyes.

"Lord Taelin, please hear the prayer of your humble servant," she said softly. She could feel her words flowing out of her as energy, and she knew that her god was listening to every word she said. "I know that I do not always do things as you wish I might. You gave me the free will to pursue things as I saw fit. But you also know that I always depend on you and the Lady Laeyra for everything I do. It is in your power that I succeed at anything I do. I ask now for your guidance and wisdom. Give me the words to say to these men who have been held under the oppressive thumb of the Zeraphim for these many long weeks. I do not even begin to understand what they have gone through. And yet, in order to save them, I must convince them to take up arms against their oppressors. I do not have the words to tell them what they need to do. I ask you for your wisdom and your guidance. I know that this is what you wish for us to be doing and I know that I need your help. Please come, my Lord Taelin. Please help us help these people."

She stayed in that position for several long minutes before opening her eyes back up and standing. She pulled her sword from the ground and wiped it clean before putting it back in its scabbard on her back.

"Do you think Lord Taelin heard you?" Colwyn asked softly.

"He heard me," Alana nodded. "The question is what will he do to help us?"

Colwyn took her in his arms and held her while they waited. They stood like that for several minutes. A slight wind began to blow in the clearing, lifting strands of Alana's auburn hair behind them as they stood. The wind began to grow in speed and pitch. There was a bright flash of light and a woman stood in the clearing where they were.

Neither Colwyn nor Alana had ever seen the woman before, but they both knew exactly who it was. The woman had long golden hair and pale icy blue eyes. Her eyes matched the pale blue of the robes she wore. Her face appeared to be chiseled from marble, not an imperfection in sight. She had a small nose and thin ruby red lips that contrasted from her pale white skin. Her hair hung in golden ringlets that framed her face.

There was no doubt that the woman was the Lady Laeyra herself.

Both Alana and Colwyn fell to their knees before the goddess. Laeyra laughed and motioned for them to stand.

"My child, you need never bow to me," Layera laughed again. Her voice was musical and sweet. Comforting and haunting at the same time. "Nor need you, my brave young man."

"Lady Laeyra, you honor us with your presence," Alana said after standing. "How may we serve you?"

"You serve me by living, my child," Laeyra smiled at Alana. She came over and traced her fingers over Alana's cheek. "Indeed, you are far more than I expected you to be. I am pleased with how you have turned out. And your Protector, noble and wise, strong yet gentle. Indeed, my husband and I have outdone ourselves with you two. You will do great things for us, yes? You already have. And the world will be far better for your being in it."

"I need Lord Taelin's wisdom, Lady Laeyra," Alana cried softly. "This is too difficult for Colwyn and I to do by ourselves. We need the help of the men of Valendale if we are to have any success in freeing them."

"And she knows when to ask for help," Laeyra smiled in wonder. "My husband has heard you and he is coming I wanted to see you for myself, my child. I have heard Taelin speak of you and I have watched you from afar. I felt it was time to meet you myself. Know that you can call on me at any time and I will aid you in your journeys."

"It is said that Blademasters are the children of you and Lord Taelin," Alana said. She reached up and covered the goddess's hand on her cheek with her own.

"Yes, I have heard that said many a time," Laeyra nodded.

"I do not know my parents. Is there anything you can tell me about them?" Alana asked softly, almost pleading for the answers.

"I cannot answer your question, Alana," Laeyra said sadly. "You are not ready for the truth of who you are. But one day you will be. When you are, my child, my Taelin and I will answer all your questions. But that day is not today."

"Please, Lady Laeyra, I need to know who I am," she pleaded. Tears leaked from the corners of Alana's eyes. Not knowing who her parents were had always caused Alana a deep pain, one she never let show to anyone but Colwyn. But this was one of the two deities she served in her duties as the Blademaster. She was able to be free with her feelings with the goddess.

"I promise you that one day you will know the truth," Laeyra said softly. She kissed Alana on the forehead. "For now, my child, forget your pain and focus on the task at hand. Even with my husband's help, you have a difficult task in front of you."

"I am sorry for showing weakness, Lady Laeyra," Alana bowed her head. "Thank you for your help, now and always."

"We have indeed done well with you," Laeyra smiled broadly. "I am well pleased with you, Alana Steeldrake. And with you, Colwyn Starseeker. You were indeed a fine choice for my Blademaster's Protector. I leave you now. My Taelin is coming to you soon. Heed his words as you always do."

Laeyra kissed Alana on the forehead a second time, then walked over to Colwyn and kissed him on the forehead as well. Both felt instant peace spread out over their bodies starting from where the goddess had kissed them. She stepped back and disappeared in a flash of light.

Alana and Colwyn continued to hold each other, drawing comfort from each other after the strange experience with the Lady Laeyra. Alana hoped that Taelin would arrive before the Resistance leaders got there so she could talk to him about what to say to them. She hoped he might also be able to shed a little light on what Laeyra had said.

"There you are, my children," the Lightbringer called from behind them. "You have called for my help?"

"Yes, Lord Taelin," Alana bowed low. "I need your wisdom. I need to know how to get the people of Valendale to join the battle to save themselves."

"Such wisdom you show," Taelin nodded. "You are correct. You will not be able to save the people of Valendale without their own help. One cannot help someone who does not wish to help themselves."

"I do not have the words to convince them of that," Alana said softly. "I am no speaker. I'm a fighter. This is more of something that Colwyn would normally know how to handle, but even he is stumped as to how to convince them."

"You will have the words when they get here," Taelin smiled at her. "And I will be here to help you in convincing them. I am very proud of the way you have turned out. Not all of the Blademasters of old would have come to Willowdale like you did. Some would have. They were my favorites. I think you will surpass them all."

Alana walked over to Taelin and put her arms around the old man. It was something she had wanted to do since the first time she had met her god. She did not know why she gave in to the temptation at this time, but it felt right. She leaned her head on his broad chest and let herself cry gently. Colwyn moved beside her and put his hand on her back. The god put his arms around Alana and patted her back gently. He stroked Alana's long auburn hair and tried to give the young woman what comfort he could.

"I'm so scared all the time, Lord Taelin," she whispered into his chest. "I know that Colwyn and I are the front lines in the battle against the darkness. But I fear that we will fail. I fear that we will fail you and fail Calthea."

"My dear child," Taelin kissed her hair. "You cannot fail me so long as you try your hardest in whatever you do. You and Colwyn are both very special to me."

"Thank you, Lord Taelin," Alana's voice cracked. "I hope I can live up to your faith in me."

"I have no doubt that you will," Taelin smiled. He held her out at arm's length. "We have certainly done well with you. Now dry your eyes. The leaders of the Resistance will be here momentarily. Fear not. I will be here by your side if you need me. I am always by your side, my child."

Alana smiled at her deity and pulled away from him. She turned to Colwyn and touched his arm. Colwyn smiled broadly at her.

"Lord Taelin, when this war ends, I would speak with you," she said softly. "There are answers I need about my life if I am to be an effective Blademaster."

"The war never ends. Only the battles change." Taelin said sadly as he looked at the Blademaster and her Protector. "It is the Twenty Third Law of the Blades. I am afraid it is all too true. But I promise you that I will give you your answers, Alana. You certainly deserve to know the truth about yourself."

"Is there a full set of all the Laws of the Blades written down somewhere?" Colwyn grumbled. "Or are we destined to learn them as we go?"

"All Blademasters learn them as they go, I am afraid, Colwyn," Taelin sighed softly. "You will learn them all in time. You might even write some new ones."

"You do know it's a little frustrating to be learning as I go," Alana snorted.

"My child, we are all learning as we go," Taelin smiled broadly. "Even I learn something new every day. That is the true price of wisdom."

Colwyn cocked his head to the side, frowning slightly. He drew his sword and stepped in front of Alana, shielding her from the entrance to the clearing.

"Someone comes," he said softly. "Several someones from the sound of it. I do not hear armor." He relaxed slightly. "I believe it is the leaders of the Resistance."

"Put your sword away, Colwyn," Alana said gently. "We need their help. Not to scare them."

Colwyn put his sword back in its scabbard on his back and carried the log he had shaped earlier to where Alana was. He laid it on its side, and Alana and Colwyn stood tall on the log. This way they could see all of the Resistance leaders. Taelin found himself a small log on the side of the clearing to sit on. It was time for him to watch his Blademaster at work in person. She was a wonder to him.

She had done so much in so little time. And yet she had not even reached the true height of her power. He did not think the world was ready for her to really let loose and assume the full authority that was at her disposal.

She would have to in the months that were to come however.

Alana had closed her eyes, preparing herself for the coming encounter. She knew the men of Valendale would be difficult to convince to join the battle against the Zeraphim. She knew that after the deaths that they had already suffered, they would not wish to risk any further trials. They had no choice, however. It was going to be a difficult battle. She knew that many of the men she was about to speak to might not even make it home.

When she heard the men enter the clearing she opened her eyes and looked at each individual leader in the Resistance, meeting each of their eyes.

"Hear me and heed me," she cried out, using the full voice of her authority. "I am the one spoken of in prophecy. The one born of the light. I am the bright star in the darkness. I am the slim blade of truth and justice. I am the chosen of Lord Taelin and Lady Laeyra. I am the Blademaster and you will hear me."

The men in the clearing looked at each other in confusion. This was certainly not what they had expected to hear. They had expected to hear... Actually, if they thought about it, none of them knew what to expect by this impromptu meeting. They hoped that it would be the beginning of the end for the Zeraphim oppression. But how that would happen, none of them knew.

"We hear you," one of the men yelled.

"Almost two weeks ago, a young man came to see me," she began. "That young man told me a tale that angered and upset my Protector and myself. Marcus Whelan and his family are friends of Colwyn and myself, as are many of you. We have been through the city of Valendale many a time in the past. While we consider Ravendale to be our home, Colwyn and I have always had a special place in our heart for the city of Valendale.

"When Marcus Whelan told us what happened to the people of Valendale, it broke our hearts. We felt the need to act. We came here to Willowdale to do what we can to free you and the rest of your people.

"We have been arrested and tortured. I have been betrayed by one of my own and almost been betrayed by another. I have made new friends, and before this battle is over, I will undoubtedly say goodbye to at least one person I know and love. This is not a battle that any of my companions will take lightly.

"We cannot help you if you will not help yourselves.

"I have brought you here today so that you will know what I expect of you. I expect you to join us in battle. We will lead you and guide you, but you must take up arms against the Zeraphim yourselves if we are to succeed. I cannot fight the Zeraphim myself. I will be fighting the Nightstalker. It will be a fight for keeps. Neither she nor I will have any intention of backing down from the battle.

"Colwyn will lead you. He has led men in battle before. He is a good man. I trust him with my life. More importantly, I trust him with yours.

"It will not be easy. Many of you may die. But if you do die, you will die knowing that the people you love will go free because of your sacrifice.

"I do not ask this of you. I demand it. If I am to help you, you must help yourselves."

When Alana finished her speech, the clearing was silent. She knew that she had reached them. The only thing that remained was whether or not they would rise to the occasion. She did not have long to wait before she would have her answer.

"To go up against the Zeraphim is suicide," one of the men said. The others yelled in agreement. "You ask us to lay down our lives so that you do not have to fight the Zeraphim yourself?"

"I ask you to lay down your lives for your people," Alana replied to the challenge. "You have all seen the Nightstalker. You know what she is capable of. I am the only one that even has a chance to defeat her. She must be defeated if you are to go back to your homes and your lives."

The men of Valendale continued to shout their protests against taking up arms against the Zeraphim. Alana let them rant for several long minutes. She looked to Colwyn, but he only shrugged as if to say he knew that it was going to be a difficult sell. Alana sighed and crossed her arms across her chest.

"Enough!" the old man at the side of the clearing thundered. Alana had forgotten that Taelin was still there. The god stood and strode over to where Alana and Colwyn were standing on the log. He touched both of them on the arm and smiled at them. "You have done well, my children. But they are too afraid of the truth. I will speak now."

The god turned to face the men from Valendale. The blood drained from their faces and they fell to their knees in respect to the God of Light.

"Lord Taelin, why have you forsaken us to the Zeraphim?" one of the men asked.

"Stand up, all of you," Taelin thundered. He waited until they were all standing. He met each of their eyes before continuing. "Why do you think I have forsaken you?"

"We have prayed and prayed to be freed from the Zeraphim," the man said, his voice cracking. "And yet we are still held captive."

"And had you only attempted to help yourselves, you might have been free," the god shrugged his shoulders. "But I have not forsaken you. I sent her, my chosen Blademaster, to help you. Oh, it was her choice to come, mind you, but I made sure she knew what had happened to you. Who do you think asked Isaiah Talon to mention to Marcus Whelan that there was a Blademaster and where to find her?"

"She asks the impossible," the man quavered. "We cannot rise against the Zeraphim. They will kill our wives and children."

"She asks no more of you than I do," Taelin smiled sadly as he touched the man on the shoulder. "She cannot help you if you refuse to help yourself. She is right on that."

"But what of our families?" the man asked. "They will be at risk."

"Then you must not fail," Taelin said softly. "Their lives depend on your success. You know that. If you truly wish to save your families, then you will pledge your swords to the Blademaster here and now. She is my chosen. You will heed her, or the people of Valendale are lost."

"But we are afraid," another of the men spoke up.

"Let me let you in on a little secret," Alana smiled as she hopped down off the log. She walked over to the man who had spoken of his fear and put her hands on his shoulders. She looked deeply into his eyes as she confided the truth to him. "I am afraid too. I am afraid for me and I am afraid for all of you. What we are about to do will not be easy. As I said, there is every possibility that one or all of you may die in the coming battle. There is every possibility that I will die in battle against the Nightstalker."

"It is not for everyone to know the Laws of the Blades," Taelin said softly, his voice carrying well despite the low volume. "But I think that you men should hear the Fifteenth Law of the Blades. And you and Colwyn as well, my Blademaster. In life as in battle, there are no guarantees. Victory and defeat teeter on the edge of a thin blade. It is belief in one's self that can make the difference between victory and defeat. A Blademaster must always believe in herself and be willing to seek the help of others in order to claim victory. This is the truth of life and battle. Live or die as you choose."

The men of Valendale looked at each other in wonder at the wisdom of their god. One at a time the men dropped to a knee in front of the Blademaster and pledged themselves to her.

"We heed and obey you, Lady Blademaster," they said when they were kneeling before her. "Command us so that we may be free from the Zeraphim."

"Colwyn will give you the instructions to relay to your cells," Alana ordered. "Go speak with him before you leave then go and coordinate your Resistance cells."

The men went to talk to Colwyn, the young Protector giving them their battle instructions. Alana went over to Taelin. The god took her in his arms and held her.

"I am sorry I could not convince the men without your help, Lord Taelin," she said into the god's chest. "Maybe I am not ready for the tasks that are ahead of me."

"They were afraid, my child," Taelin stroked her hair. "As are you. But you are ready for what lies ahead. Whether you believe it or not remains to be seen."

"I hope your faith in me is justified, my Lord Taelin," Alana sighed deeply.

"It is, my child," the god kissed the top of her head. "Now go prepare. The great battle with the Nightstalker is soon to come. You must ready yourself."

Alana let herself be held by the god for several more minutes before pulling away. She looked over at Colwyn and saw that he had finished giving the men of Valendale their orders. It was time for them to go back to the cavern and prepare for what was sure to be a fierce battle for the people of Valendale.

Willowdale

Chapter XXII
The Luck of Laegra

Silvestra Knightwing and William Stonehands looked out over the city of Willowdale from the entrance to her cavern. They were about to risk their strength reserves needed to save an entire city's worth of people to try to rescue one halfling. Both felt great sadness about the pain that they had caused Meryn. But they also knew that they needed to be together despite the pain it caused others.

Because they had caused this pain, they knew that they had to be the ones that rescued Meryn from the dungeon.

"I may need to use dragon magic over the course of the battle because of this, William," Silvestra said quietly. "I will have to answer to the Draconic Council. They will be less than pleased."

"I suspect Eliazar will already be less than pleased with us, Silvestra," William chuckled softly. "After all, he did say that we were never allowed to see each other again. And yet here we are, once more together and still in love. Somehow,

I doubt that anything that you will do to help save the people of Valendale will make any difference in the matter."

"You're probably right," Silvestra laughed. "The young halfling awaits our expertise. Let's go save her."

The halfling was crying in her cell. She had her knees tucked up under her chin and her arms were wrapped around her knees. She had cried most of the night after being deposited back in her cell after her meeting with the Nightstalker. Her eyes were puffy, and her cheeks were sore where the Nightstalker had struck her.

She had lost hope. She knew she would be killed soon. The only thing that she could think about was whether or not she would get a chance to ask for Alana's forgiveness before she died. It was important to her that she receive that forgiveness. But she did not think it was likely that she would even see Alana again. She hoped that when they both got to the other side and walked with their respective deities she would be able to get Alana's forgiveness then.

She buried her head in her knees as she cried. She was all alone in the cell, but she could hear other people crying and moaning in other cells. Even with that small amount of personal contact, she felt completely alone. She was sad that she would never see any of her companions again. Even Colwyn, who had never trusted her, she would miss. She wished she could make things right with William. She knew that he belonged with the silver haired dragon woman, but that did not keep her from being sad at losing him to her. One day, she hoped, she would meet her own true love.

Her head came up suddenly as she heard a strange noise in the corridor over her head. She stood up trying to make out what the sound was. It sounded like people falling. Could someone have actually come to rescue her?

Getting into the palace had turned out to be surprisingly easy for William and Silvestra. They had snuck right in the front door. No one had stopped them and no one questioned them. They made their way down various corridors slowly working their way into the palace.

William remembered the route that the companions had taken on their way out of the palace when Colwyn had rescued them. He knew that if he more or less followed that route, he would find the halfling. He could not be sure that they were keeping her in the same cell, of course, but he knew that if she wasn't in that one, she would be close by.

"Surprisingly, there's not a lot of guards out and about this morning, William," Silvestra hissed quietly. "I think we might be using up a lot of our luck with this rescue."

"We have the luck of Laeyra with us," William shrugged. "We're part of the Blademaster's company, so we must have the Blademaster's luck. Right?"

"If you say so," Silvestra chuckled softly.

They came to the cross corridor where the dungeons were located. William held up his hand to stop Silvestra from going around the corner. He carefully peeked around the corner and counted five guards standing over the grates to the dungeons. Wincing, William swung back into the corridor they'd walked down.

He held up five fingers, and Silvestra nodded. She cradled her head on her hands as if they were a pillow and William nodded. Putting them to sleep would be the easiest way to get them out of the way.

He reached into one of his pouches and pulled out some plain sand. He closed his eyes and whispered a few silent prayers to his god. He swung back into the corridor and blew the sand at the guards.

"Dormus," he said softly.

The effect was almost immediate. The five guards never knew what hit them. As soon as William had spoken, the sand started to sparkle as it flew towards the guards. By the time the sand had reached them, the magic was already starting to affect them. Before any of them could raise an alarm, all five guards fell to the ground, sound asleep.

William staggered slightly with the effort of putting all five to sleep, but he was able to right himself quickly. He noted that he was able to recover from heavy exertions of magic a little easier and a little quicker. He took a moment to wonder if that had something to do with this mysterious future he had heard was in store for him.

Now was not the time to worry about such things though.

They crept forward in the corridor to where the grate to the dungeon that Meryn was in. William peeked through the holes in the grate to make sure they had the right dungeon and then he released the latch to the grate and pulled it open.

Silvestra had found the ladder and they lowered it into the dungeon cell. The halfling immediately climbed up out of the cell. William could tell she had been crying, and both of her cheeks were bruised. He gently touched her on both cheeks and relieved the pain. There was nothing more he could do for her. But when they got her back to the cavern, he was sure that Martin would be able to heal her completely.

"You came for me," Meryn whispered hoarsely. "I didn't think anyone would."

"We were responsible for your running off, Little One," William looked down at her. He could not muster up a smile for the halfling though. "The least we could do is come to make sure you were all right."

"I owe you and everyone else an apology for what happened," the halfling said. "I never should have run off like that."

"You should have come and talked to us, Meryn," Silvestra knelt down next to the halfling. "Neither William nor I meant to hurt you."

"I know that now," Meryn hung her head. "You two love each other and should be together. I was angry and hurt though."

"And that is why we came to find you, Little One," William said. "We need to move, but before we do, I need to ask you one thing."

"What, William?" the halfling raised her head to look at him.

"Can you forgive us?" the mage asked. "Can you forgive Silvestra and I for causing you the pain we caused you?"

"Of course, I can, William," Meryn laughed. It wasn't a full laugh, more of a tiny tinkle of one, but it was music to William's ears. "Now can we get out of here? The Nightstalker really gives me the creeps!"

William and Silvestra laughed. William knelt by each of the guards and whispered a word of magic. When William was finished casting a spell of forgetfulness over the guards, the three of them made their way out of the palace and back to Silvestra's cavern.

Kera Rayden was livid.

Twice now, she had had prisoners escape from the dungeons. The Zeraphim were failing miserably at guarding the prisoners. She would have someone flogged for losing the halfling. Or killed. She wasn't sure which, but someone was sure to pay for this.

"How could she escape?" she thundered. She was facing the captain of the guard. "How EXACTLY could she escape? You assured me that there would be no repeat of the prisoner escape. Those were your exact words, Captain."

"I don't understand it, Lady Nightstalker," the captain of the guard rumbled. "There is no way she could have gotten by her guards. And yet, somehow she did."

"I want the guards that were on duty executed," she hissed. "Do it yourself, Captain. And then find me some guards that will not let a halfling escape."

"Lady Nightstalker, they have served the Zeraphim for years," the captain of the guard protested.

"Fool!" she thundered. She crossed the room and slapped him with the armored back of her glove. She grinned wickedly as a ribbon of blood leaked from the corner of his mouth. "Clearly they have not served the Zeraphim well if they can't even keep a halfling in their dungeon."

"Lady Nighstalker, I must protest their execution!" the captain of the guard rasped. "We cannot waste good men like that."

"You will execute the men yourself, Captain. And do you know why you will?" she asked. She moved forward until her face was right in front of the captain's face. She flicked her tongue out and lapped at the ribbon of blood on his face. The captain's face paled. "Because if you do not, I will kill you myself and bathe in your blood as I prepare for my battle with the Blademaster."

"Yes, Lady Nightstalker," the captain of the guard quivered. "I will see to it right now."

"See that you do," Kera backed away from him. "Bring me their heads."

"As you command," the captain bowed and made his way hastily out of the room.

"You have your little sneak thief back, Blademaster," Kera said softly as she looked out the window. "But I know exactly what you are planning tomorrow. And I have such a wonderful surprise for you that you can't possibly plan for. It will be so much fun killing you. I can't wait."

Alana and Colwyn were sitting in the cavern already when William and Silvestra returned with the halfling. The Blademaster and her Protector were discussing the best way to deploy the people of Valendale in the upcoming attack. William and Silvestra both went deep into the back part of the cave.

The halfling started to go towards where she would drop her pack away from the others, but stopped when she caught sight of the Blademaster. Alana did not give the halfling a glance, knowing that Meryn would come talk to them when she was ready to. She did not want to force Meryn to talk to them. And she thought for just a moment that she understood how Colwyn had felt when he had given her space to think about what had happened in the Elven Woods. She looked over at Colwyn and smiled slightly.

"I get it now," she smiled gently as she put her hand on his.

"Um, what?" he raised an eyebrow. "What are you talking about, Alana?"

"I get what it was like for you while you were trying to give me time to think," Alana smiled her special smile at him. "I imagine that it could not have been easy for you."

"All I wanted to do was take you in my arms and just hold you until you forgave me," Colwyn smiled back. "I didn't think you would appreciate that considering what I told you happened. But, you're right. It wasn't easy."

"Well, I thank you for your restraint," Alana laughed. "Even though I think I would have preferred you hold me than be distant from me."

Meryn dropped her bedroll and pack far away from everyone else's belongings then slowly made her way over to where Alana and Colwyn were sitting. She hung her head and watched her feet as she walked.

"Alana, I need to speak with you and Colwyn," the halfling's voice was barely above a whisper and Alana could detect a note of deep pain in the young halfling's voice.

"Please sit, Meryn," Alana said gently. "We would both like to speak to you as well."

The halfling sat close enough to Alana and Colwyn that they could talk but not so close so that she could run away if she so chose.

"Alana, I know I messed everything up," the halfling said softly. "If you want me to go, I will."

It was a testament to how upset Meryn was that that was all she said. The normally gregarious halfling was silent and sullen. Colwyn looked at Alana, the look on his face clearly expressing his concern about the halfling. Alana was surprised to see that her husband was concerned about Meryn. He had made no secret of his dislike and distrust of the halfling over the years. They had not talked about what they were going to do about Meryn, but she knew that Colwyn would go along with whatever Alana decided to do.

"Meryn, you may have caused a great number of people to be hurt tomorrow," Alana said quietly. "I understand why you did what you felt you had to do. You have to know that there will be consequences for what you've done."

"I know, Alana," Meryn hung her head. Alana could see tears rolling down the halfling's face. "If I could have it all to do over again, I would never have gone to Willowdale. I would have just left."

"You should have come talked to me, Meryn," Alana said. "I could have helped you through this."

"I couldn't bear to face any of you after what William did," Meryn turned away. "How would you have felt if you watched Colwyn with another woman?"

Colwyn and Alana looked at each other. None of the companions knew about how close Colwyn had actually come to betraying Alana. They had both agreed that no one needed to know. It was an episode that they both wanted to get as far behind them as they could.

"I can tell you I would not have been happy," Alana turned her focus back to the halfling. "But I would have talked to him about it rather than lashing out in an effort to hurt him."

"That's why I think I should leave, Alana," Meryn whimpered. "I don't expect you to ever forgive me for what I've done."

"If you were to stay, would anything like this ever happen again?" Colwyn asked. Alana looked over at him with a raised eyebrow. Colwyn just shrugged.

"I don't know if I could stay, Colwyn," she said sheepishly. "But I would never do anything to betray Alana again. That is one thing I can definitely assure you of."

"Very well," Alana said softly. When she continued, she let the full voice of her authority resound with every word. "I want you to listen to me closely, Meryn Swiftfoot. You are to continue on with us. I believe you can still be of use to us. I believe that you have a lot to give to the side of the light. I forgive you for betraying me. But you must never do so again. I will not be so forgiving a second time."

"I understand, Lady Alana," Meryn whimpered. "I hope I can prove worthy of your trust someday."

"Go, Little One," Colwyn said tenderly. "Go get some rest. We will talk more later."

Colwyn and Alana watched the halfling go over to where her bedroll was. She laid down and curled up in a ball facing away from everyone.

"She's going to have a long road ahead of her," Alana said softly.

"Is keeping her with us the right thing, though, Alana?" Colwyn asked. "I'm afraid that we're asking for trouble."

"Maybe we are," Alana shrugged. "But it's my risk to make. I meant what I said. I believe that she still has a lot to give. If we're going to make it through this coming war, we're going to need to take some risks. I believe that this is one of the risks we're going to have to take if we're going to be successful."

"Just the same, I will be keeping my eyes on her in the future," Colwyn sighed.

"I would expect nothing less," Alana smiled at him. "Now, let's get some sleep. Tomorrow is going to be a very long day."

Willowdale

Chapter XXIII
The Challenge

Alana sat with her legs crossed. Her swords were crossed on the ground in front of her. Her hands were palms up on her knees and her eyes were closed. Colwyn had seen her sit in that same position several times before. She was clearing her mind, preparing herself as best she could for the battle ahead. Whenever she had the chance to settle her mind like this before a battle, she took it. It was a part of her strategy for being ready. There were times of course when a battle came as such a surprise that she had no way to prepare for it. But when she could, she took the opportunity to prepare as it helped her in the long run.

Alana and Colwyn both knew that she would need every advantage this time.

Colwyn stood guard over her as she prepared, his giant bastard sword held at a ready position in front of him with the tip on the ground. He would be too busy leading the Valendale men into battle with the Zeraphim to be able to help her. His only consolation was that he could watch over her while she prepared. It was a small comfort, but it was a comfort nonetheless.

Alana took the comfort that was offered by Colwyn watching over her and cleared her mind. She wished she knew the elvish technique of stát ndoimhneacht na tsíocháin inmheánach, but she made do with what she could. At least she could clear her mind and focus on the one thing she needed to focus on, which was the love she shared with Colwyn. She knew that, in the end, that love and that bond with him was what would get her through the battle with the Nightstalker. She did not know what the Nightstalker was capable of, but she assumed that they would be evenly matched at the very least.

"There's something I must remind you," Colwyn said softly, trying not to intrude on what little peace that she'd been able to work up. "I'm not sure how it will help you. I told you about this once before, but when I told you, nether you nor I were able to figure out how it would help you. I'm still not sure if it will be of help, but it is something that I need to remind you of, as it may well be the key to your victory against the Nightstalker. I'm going to tell it to you again now, because I want to give you every advantage."

"What is it you are going to tell me?" Alana opened her eyes.

"When I was in the Elven Woods, Otan told me something very important," Colwyn said as he turned to face her. "It may or may not help you. He told me the Eighteenth Law of the Blades. In all of life, there must be balance. To lose that balance is to invite chaos and death in. A Blademaster must always be in balance in herself and in her dealings with others. That is why the First Law of the Blades is so important. The love she shares with her husband must balance the death she must deal in her position."

"Balance," Alana frowned. "How can that help me?"

"Raven said that the Nightstalkers feed on hate not love," Colwyn continued. "There is no balance in them. There is no counter for the death they deal. I'm not sure how that will help you, but I am sure that you can figure out a way."

"Balance," Alana said, her face brightening. "I think it actually does help." She stood and wrapped her arms around Colwyn. "I think you just gave me the solution, my love."

"I have?" Colwyn seemed stunned. "I suppose I have. Maybe. I guess maybe I don't know what the solution is?"

"I focus on the love I share with you while feeding her hate," Alana kissed him on the cheek. "I feed my balance and feed her imbalance. It's still not going to be easy, but I do think it is my only way to counter her."

"I am sorry I can't be any more help with the Nightstalker, Alana," Colwyn said softly.

"You are going to be very busy leading the charge against the Zeraphim, Colwyn," Alana smiled. "I need you to lead the men of Valendale. This is one battle you cannot protect me from. When I first met Kera Rayden while we were prisoners of the Zeraphim, I knew that this would end up coming down to her and me. I would not have it any other way."

"Do you ever think about what it will be like when the wars are all over and we can one day lay down our swords?" Colwyn asked softly. He caressed her cheek gently.

"You heard Lord Taelin, Colwyn," Alana returned the soft caress. "The war never ends. Only the battles change. I fear his words will ring true for us. I fear that even when we do lay our swords down in defense of Calthea, we will still have many battles to face."

"I fear you are right," Colwyn sighed. "I fear that we are going to have many political battles ahead of us."

"Your father," Alana nodded in understanding.

"My father," Colwyn nodded. "He's never going to accept you, even with this letter from the king."

"Well, we will just have to make the most of it, Col," Alana smiled her special smile. "I'm not going anywhere. You know that."

"Nor would I let you," Colwyn boomed a deep laugh. "You're stuck with me, Alana."

"There are worse things in life," she shared in the laugh.

Colwyn helped her to her feet and the two of them watched the sun rise in the distance. They knew that the time was nearing for the attack to begin. But they were enjoying the last few moments of peace before they had to join the others in the attack on the Zeraphim. Colwyn put his arm around her and held her close.

He lived for the peaceful moments like this. These were the moments when he knew that she could feel the love for her pouring from him. He knew that she savored those moments just as much as he did. From the moment they had met, Colwyn had known that she craved love. He did not know what pain in her past caused the young warrior woman to crave love like she did. It was ironic that the position of power that fate had conspired to give her gave her exactly what she needed the most. Since she was a Blademaster, she had to have love, the one thing that he knew she wanted and needed more than any other.

Of course, the more he thought about it, the less it struck him as irony. He knew that Lord Taelin and Lady Laeyra knew what they were doing. Both deities had shown an amazing capacity for reason and compassion. He knew that he and Alana were lucky that Lord Taelin and Lady Laeyra were their patron deities. He knew that Alana felt the same way.

"Alana, it's time," William said as he stepped up to where Colwyn and Alana were watching the sun. "We need to get down and get ready to launch the assault."

"A moment more, William," Alana said softly. "The sun rise is beautiful today."

"It is," William nodded. He pulled a jewel from his pocket and handed it to Alana. "This will only work this one time. Put it against your throat when you issue the challenge and your voice will carry all through the city of Willowdale. Everyone will be able to hear you."

"Thank you, William," Alana smiled at him. "I hope that this didn't take too much of your strength. You will need as much of your energy as you can muster during the coming battle."

"Silvestra made it actually," William smiled. "It's dragon magic. She figured since she was already about to disobey the Draconic Council, she may as well go all out with her disobedience. She's already where she and I will be working from."

"She's a very special dragon," Alana laughed deeply. "Tell her I appreciate her disobedience. I wish more dragons would disobey the Draconic Council and do what was right."

"Ha! That would cause a great deal of confusion and consternation on the Isle of Dragons," William threw his head back and laughed. "It's something I'd love to see. So would Silvestra, I am sure. I must go join her so we can be ready to launch our part of the attack. Good luck to you, Alana. You have the toughest job of any of us in this coming battle."

Alana watched William start down the path towards Willowdale and sighed softly. Colwyn squeezed her in his arms and smiled over at her.

"It's going to be all right, my love," he said softly and comfortingly. "We will get through this. We'll get the people of Valendale free and they'll be home soon."

"You told me that Raven foretold that one of our party would fall during this battle," Alana said quietly. Colwyn could see the tears in her eyes. He knew that it would be hard on her to lose one of her companions, but he also knew that if one of their companions were to die during the battle, it would be in battle trying to free the people of Valendale. "I wish you could tell me more about who we were going to lose."

"All I know is that Raven does not believe that it will be you or I," Colwyn wrapped both his arms around the woman he loved. "There is not much more we can do but pray that Lord Taelin will protect us all and keep whichever one of us does not make it."

"I wish all of our companions would live through this, Colwyn," she said into his chest. "I could not bear to lose any of you."

"I know, Alana," he patted her on the back. "I know. We will all do our best to make it through this battle." He held her at arms length and looked deep into her eyes. "This is your last chance to back out of this battle, Alana. Once we leave this cavern, there is no turning back."

"I know," Alana nodded. "And there is no way I could allow us to turn back now anyway. The people of Valendale need us to do this."

"In that case, one kiss before we go," Colwyn smiled. "For luck."

"I think I can be okay with that idea," Alana laughed.

Colwyn pulled her close and stared deep into her eyes. Their lips gently brushed against each other as they came together. They both fell deeply into the kiss, each of them drawing strength from the bond they shared with the other one. It was a deep and passionate kiss, pure and perfect in its simplicity. After several minutes, they pulled far enough away from each other that they could stare into one another's eyes.

"Is breá liom tú go mór, Alana Steeldrake," he said tenderly. "No one could ever love you as much as I do."

"I love you too, Colwyn Starseeker," she smiled her special smile at him. "And I know no one could ever love you as much as I do."

He leaned in and kissed her a second time. A short, gentle kiss this time. Then he pulled away from her and went over to pick up his sword.

"It's time, my love," he said softly. "Let's go save some people."

The Blademaster and her Protector left the cavern and headed towards where the leaders of the Resistance were waiting to get their final orders.

The leaders of the Resistance were waiting for them. Alana looked them over when they arrived and nodded, meeting each of the men's eyes. She knew that they were still scared. She was too, but none of them had the luxury of letting that fear get the better of them.

The leaders of the Resistance were all armed with whatever they could find. Most of them had clubs and staves. Some of them had blades of some form or another. A couple had pitchforks. She was afraid that the weapons that they had would not be enough to protect them for long, but she suspected that each of these men would end up with a sword before too long. They would take weapons from the men they killed in battle. She knew that that had been an expressed order from Colwyn.

But she could not worry about these men. They had to fight in order to free themselves and the people that they loved the most. And Alana could do nothing to help them. Her battle was with the Nightstalker. Only she of all the people that were going into battle for the people of Valendale had a chance of stopping the Nightstalker. It was not going to be an easy fight either. She knew that the Nightstalker was her match.

She could only hope that her Lord Taelin's faith in her was justified and that she was up to the challenge.

For now, all she could do to help these men would be to exhort them and make them feel like they could do this despite their fear.

She stood in front of the men and they quieted down to hear what she would say to them.

"Hear me and heed me," she cried out, using the full voice of her authority. "I am the one spoken of in prophecy. The one born of the light. I am the bright star in the darkness. I am the slim blade of truth and justice. I am the chosen of Lord Taelin and Lady Laeyra. I am the one who has come to lead the people of Valendale to their freedom. I am the Blademaster and you will hear me."

The leaders of the Resistance dropped to their knees at the power of her voice, but to a man, they listened silently.

"We are about to launch a fierce battle against the Zeraphim," she continued. She walked among the leaders as she spoke, touching each of them on the shoulder. "We are about to free your people from the oppressive yoke that the Zeraphim have lain on their necks.

"For too long have the people you love been held as slaves by the Zeraphim. For too long have you all lived in fear of what the Zeraphim will do to you. You have lost friends and loved ones. People you have known for years have been killed. Your First Lord and his daughter were slaughtered in front of you before you even left Valendale.

"We hold the Zeraphim accountable for their actions. They cannot be left to do this to another people. This ends here. This ends now.

"You have come here today to lead your people in this final battle. You have come here despite your fear. Despite your worry about what will happen to the others.

"I tell you now that you are the only hope your people have. You must stand and fight for all you are worth. You must join me and stand as the light against the darkness.

"My Colwyn has given you your orders. And now I tell you some more of what you must do. Do not take too much time in each battle. Use a minimum of energy in each battle. If you have a chance to knock a soldier out, take it. Take every opening you are given. Each time you fell a soldier, make sure you grab a weapon from that soldier. The weapons you carry will not last long.

"Think of your families and your loved ones as you fight. Think of the happy reunion you will finally have when the Zeraphim are driven from this city. You will all be able to go home to where you belong. Think of your homes, which you will get to live in again.

"Now go, all of you," she concluded, standing back in front of all of the leaders of the Resistance. "Go and join your forces. My Colwyn has told you where you should be. Go to them. Lead them. In one hour, I will give the signal to start the assault. There will be no question when you hear it. When you hear the signal, you are to launch your attack on the Zeraphim. I will be with you. Colwyn will be with you. Fight for all you are worth. Fight for your freedom!"

The leaders of the Resistance roared and ran off towards their respective groups of Resistance fighters. Alana and Colwyn watched them go. Colwyn put his arm around her as they watched. Alana felt good about the prospects of what was to come.

"You did well, my love," Colwyn smiled at her. "I think they actually are ready to fight the Zeraphim."

"I hope so, Col," she sighed deeply. "I fear that many of those men will die today."

"If they do, they will die as free men, Alana," he took her arms in his hands and looked deep into her eyes. "And they will do so because of you. Never forget that they are fighting for themselves and for their loved ones because you showed them how to get over their fear. No matter how this turns out, they will always remember what you have done here. And so will I."

"Thanks, Colwyn," she smiled at him. "You always seem to know just what to say to make me feel better. Now you better go get to your own place. The time comes close for us to launch the attack on the Zeraphim."

He kissed her gently then made his way out of the clearing towards where he would be in the assault force. She watched him go then closed her eyes, clearing her mind, and prepared for what was to come.

She did not know if she would ever be ready to face the Nightstalker. She did not even let on to Colwyn how scared she was about this battle with her evil counterpart. She suspected that he knew, however. He always seemed to know what she was thinking and feeling. It was one of the reasons that she loved him. One of many reasons.

She reached up and pulled slightly on her two longswords, making sure that they were clear in their scabbards. Satisfied that they were clear, she found herself a ledge near the city wall that she could see out over the whole city from. She was ready to launch the assault on the Zeraphim. She could only hope that everyone else was ready.

She watched the sun move lazily across the sky. When she judged that an hour had gone by, she took a deep breath and stood tall. The pulled the gemstone that William had given her from the pouch that she had put it in and placed it against her throat.

"Hear me and heed me!" she began. Her voice boomed out, magically amplified, and she knew that everyone could hear her, both the people of Valendale and the enemy. She let all of the power of her authority ring through in her voice. "I am the voice on the wind and the pouring rain. I am the voice of your hunger and pain. I am the voice that is calling to you. I am the voice and you will hear me.

"People of Valendale, the time has come for you to win back your freedom. It is time for you to stand up and cast off the yoke of oppression. The Zeraphim must be crushed beneath your heels. You must rise up with all that you are and throw off the oppression of the Zeraphim. Fight with the First Law of the Blades in your heart and you will succeed.

"You are commanded to love. Love your friends. Love your enemies. Love without reservation. Love without hesitation. Love without condition. Love without expectation of return. If you must fight, then fight with love in your heart. If you must kill, then kill with love in your heart. Never kill or fight with hate or anger in your heart. Hate leads to impotence, but love brings power. This is the law a Blademaster must live by more than any other or else she will be powerless to serve as she should. It is the First Law of the Blades because it is the most important. Live by it, or you will die.

"Soldiers of the Zeraphim, if you meet the people of Valendale in open combat, you will be given no quarter. We will not take prisoners. We will not show mercy. This is your last chance to leave Willowdale without penalty. Leave now. Let the people of Valendale go now. Or die. The choice is yours. But know now, this is the only chance for leniency that you will get. The people of Valendale are hungry for freedom, and they will do whatever it takes to win that freedom. You have been warned.

"Kera Rayden, know now that I am on my way to do battle with you. You are the only one I shall cross swords with. Anyone who gets between you and I will die. Quickly. The battle comes to you now. I promised you it would come down to you and me and so it shall. I am coming for you.

"I am the wind of death. I am the one spoken of in prophecy. The one born of the light. I am the bright star in the darkness. I am the slim blade of truth and justice. I am the chosen of Lord Taelin and Lady Laeyra. I am the voice that is calling you now. I am the one who has come to lead the people of Valendale to their freedom. I am the Blademaster and I have spoken. Heed my words."

She let the gemstone fall to earth when she finished speaking. The gemstone crumbled to dust, but she was not there to see it. She had drawn her swords and started running towards Willowdale.

The Nightstalker was standing on the parapet of the palace in Willowdale. She, like the Blademaster, had watched the sun rise. And she, like the Blademaster, was anticipating the battle. She did not have any thought that the battle would go badly for her. She knew she could beat the Blademaster in one on one combat. It was just a matter of waiting for that combat to start.

Kera Rayden was looking out over the city from the parapet. She was looking in the direction that she knew the attack was coming from. She knew that the Blademaster would launch the attack not long after the sun had fully taken the sky. She also knew that she would only have to worry about the Blademaster. She had her own surprises in mind for the battle. She could not wait to see how the Blademaster reacted to the dragon she had. The skeletal dragon, Calindilarin, would take care of the Blademaster's nathair an aeir a chosnaíonn. Then, all she had to do was wait for the Zeraphim to kill the Blademaster's companions.

It would be all too easy.

When the Blademaster's voice boomed from outside the city, the Nightstalker did not give her words much though, until she heard the Blademaster call her name.

"Kera Rayden, know now that I am on my way to do battle with you. You are the only one I shall cross swords with. Anyone who gets between you and I will die. Quickly. The battle comes to you now. I promised you it would come down to you and me and so it shall. I am coming for you.

"I am the wind of death. I am the one spoken of in prophecy. The one born of the light. I am the bright star in the darkness. I am the slim blade of truth and justice. I am the chosen of Lord Taelin and Lady Laeyra. I am the voice that is calling you now. I am the one who has come to lead the people of Valendale to their freedom. I am the Blademaster and I have spoken. Heed my words."

Willowdale

The Blademaster is so full of herself, the Nightstalker thought.   *It will be quite satisfying when I shut her up for good.*

"Bring it," Kera Rayden called out from the parapet. She knew that the Blademaster could not hear her, but she had to shout it out anyway.   "Bring the battle to me, Blademaster. It will be your last."

Chapter XXIV
Dragon Tears

Colwyn led the charge against the Zeraphim. He had managed to gather almost all of the able bodied men of Valendale together and gotten them armed as best he could. They were not the most tight knit fighting group that he had ever seen. He had not expected them to be. He would just hope that they would hold together long enough to get the job done. It would be a difficult battle. Many of the men might die. But the only way to rescue the people of Valendale was to have them join into the battle.

The great skeletal dragon caused mass panic when he appeared. Some of the men of Valendale dropped their weapons and ran from the field of battle, the Zeraphim soldiers chasing them, trying to stab them in the back. Even Colwyn and Alana were momentarily shaken when they saw the great beast. Alana grabbed the summoning statue from around her neck, hoping that Cobalt would be able to handle the massive skeletal dragon. She did not know how or even if Cobalt could handle such a monstrosity, but she hoped he could.

It did not take long for Cobalt to soar onto the scene. The skeletal dragon was easily half again the size of the gold dragon. It was not going to be an easy battle, nor would it be a pleasant one to watch. But knowing that Cobalt was attacking the great skeletal dragon, Alana and Colwyn were both able to turn back to their respective battles, wading into the fray. Alana's way was suddenly clear in front of her, and she dashed towards the palace, running as fast as she could so that she would not be stopped by the Zeraphim.

Cobalt had seen the giant skeletal dragon take the field. He kept his fear in check and forced himself to launch into the air to take on the giant bone dragon. It was a fearsome prospect. For the first time, he actually doubted the bravado that he had shown Alana in the skeletal dragon's lair.

Cobalt actually did not know if he could best such a beast.

There was nothing he could do but to try though. With a cry, Cobalt loosed a humongous blast of flame at the skeletal dragon as he soared towards it. The great gold dragon tried to show no fear. He knew that his Blademaster was counting on him to take on this abomination.

Cobalt quickly ran through what he knew about skeletal dragons as he flew towards the monstrosity. Unfortunately, that knowledge did not amount to much. He figured that the only way to really kill the creature, if that was even the appropriate word, would be to remove its head.

It sounded a lot easier than Cobalt knew it would be. He kept the torrent of flame going as he flew towards the skeletal dragon, hoping that the dragon would be afraid of the fire.

The skeletal dragon roared a challenge back at Cobalt and the two dragons flew towards each other.

As he approached the skeletal dragon, Cobalt noted that, although the dragon had no flesh, he still had very sharp teeth and talons. He would have to be careful as he knew that those talons could tear his wings as easily as a living dragon's talons could. He was afraid of what extra surprises might be in store for him with the dragon being undead.

The skeletal dragon was easily twice as long as Cobalt was. The bones were bleached white, not showing a single speck of dirt. The head was massive with a snout twice as long as Cobalt's. The talons were razor sharp and the skeletal dragon kept flexing his paws and Cobalt could imagine the talons ripping through his flesh.

It was not a feeling the great gold dragon had any desire to actually experience.

The skeletal dragon was coming from a higher level, so Cobalt swooped low under the great undead beast. He hoped that he could make his way under the larger dragon and swoop up over his back. The skeletal dragon seemed to know what Cobalt was planning though and twisted in midair so that his talons were facing up when Cobalt finished his maneuver.

Cobalt kept circling around the larger dragon, but the skeletal dragon kept barreling around so that his talons were always directed at Cobalt.

The gold dragon was getting frustrated. He did not want to get too close to those claws. He kept faking moves to try to get the skeletal dragon to drop his guard, but the undead beast seemed to know everything that Cobalt wanted to try even before the gold dragon did.

Cobalt blew a short burst of flame at the skeletal dragon. It hit the skeletal dragon's ribs, causing the larger dragon to roar, although Cobalt did not think that he felt pain.

Cobalt reversed direction and took to the air, putting distance between the two dragons. He was frustrated, but he refused to be forced into a hasty attack. Such an attack would not go well for the gold dragon, he knew. He had to find a weakness. By the same token, he was not sure that the skeletal dragon *had* a weakness. There was something very disturbing about the skeletal dragon.

Cobalt watched the skeletal dragon as it lazily flew a circle under him. The gold dragon wondered what kind of dragon it had been in life. From its size and shape, Cobalt supposed that the dragon had probably been a red dragon in life. It certainly had the arrogance of an ancient red.

What accursed magic could bring it back across the veil like this though?

What had the Dark God done to imbalance the scales to create something like this?

It was an abomination like nothing that Cobalt had ever seen in his life. All he could do is pray to Taelin that there were no other undead dragons like this one on Calthea. One was enough. More than enough, really. Despite his bravado to Alana in the creature's cave, he was not sure he could actually defeat this creature on his own. It was not in his nature to ask for help, however. It had always been one of his biggest flaws. That and his stomach.

He had to keep the skeletal dragon interested in him rather than the troops that were attacking the Zeraphim. He was afraid that if he did not kill this beast, then many of the people that his Blademaster were trying to save would die.

He could not allow that to happen.

He circled twice more then dove straight at the skeletal dragon.

It was a sudden dive and it had actually caught the skeletal dragon off guard, which was what Cobalt had hoped. Cobalt got to the skeletal dragon before he could shift, and the great gold dragon latched his jaws onto a rib.

The skeletal dragon howled, and this time, Cobalt knew that the larger dragon actually felt pain. The gold dragon stayed with it, keeping his jaws locked onto the rib. He twisted his head, trying to jerk the rib free. He had decided that it might be easier to pick off individual bones this way rather than try to go for a killing blow. It would be harder, he felt, to latch onto the neck of the dragon. The larger dragon was proving to be far more maneuverable than he had at first expected.

With a last wrench, the rib came free. Cobalt dropped it from his jaws as the skeletal dragon howled in pain. The larger dragon craned his neck trying to reach Cobalt, but the smaller dragon did his best to keep out of reach of the massive jaws of the skeletal dragon. It was not an easy task, and the larger dragon kept trying.

Cobalt lashed out with a blast of fire aimed directly at the head of the skeletal dragon. The fire seemed to be doing nothing to the skeletal dragon, however. Despite that, Cobalt felt the need to keep at it in the hopes that it might distract the larger dragon at any rate.

The skeletal dragon proved to be too observant to be distracted by such ploys. Cobalt had all he could handle to keep himself out of the jaws of the larger dragon. It was not an easy trick, as the skeletal dragon was showing itself to be incredibly flexible. The skeletal dragon's massive jaws kept snapping at Cobalt, trying to latch onto anything that was vulnerable.

Cobalt knew that if the skeletal dragon got his jaws on him he was dead.

He could not die without being sure that his Blademaster would be safe. In this, though, he knew he was not alone. If for some reason he did fail in defeating the skeletal dragon, he knew that Silvestra would take his place in the battle. He did not want the young silver dragon to have to risk herself in that battle, however.

Cobalt broke off and flew high into the air trying to regroup. The skeletal dragon lazily swooped around in a circle below him, watching him. Cobalt hovered several hundred feet higher than the skeletal dragon. It was a height from which he could launch a devastating diving attack on the other dragon. He surveyed the skeletal dragon trying to figure out where the best place to attack the other dragon would be. He thought that maybe if he tried to sever the dragon's tail, the skeletal dragon would have a tougher time flying.

Quick as a flash, the great gold dragon dove at the skeletal dragon. The larger dragon knew what Cobalt was planning, however and was ready for the gold dragon. The skeletal dragon rolled on his back and let his talons rip along the gold dragon's sides. Cobalt screamed in pain and fury as drops of dragon blood fell on the battleground below.

Cobalt tried to latch his jaws on the skeletal dragon's tail, but the larger dragon kept it out of his reach.

Cobalt flew off to regroup. He surveyed the damage that the skeletal dragon had caused. Cobalt had lost a few scales and had some ragged gashes on his sides, but he was not heavily injured from the skeletal dragon's assault. He needed to be more careful in the future attacks he launched on the larger dragon. He had almost gotten caught by the great bone dragon's jaws.

He knew that the skeletal dragon was the better dragon on the battlefield, and that gave Cobalt pause. He knew that this would be his final battle. And that realization saddened him. He had simply gotten too old to be able to hold his own in battle.

Cobalt was desperate to end the battle quickly. He launched himself at the other dragon once more. The skeletal dragon caught Cobalt with a slash of talons across his right wing. Cobalt screamed in fury as his wing tore. He knew a torn wing was the one thing he could not recover from in the middle of battle. It was as good as a death sentence. He knew that he would not be able to carry his own weight for too much longer. He had to end it quickly.

He launched himself at the skeletal dragon and landed on the larger dragon's back. He tried to latch his jaws on the larger dragon's neck, but the skeletal dragon kept snaking his neck out of reach

It was then that the skeletal dragon got his jaws around Cobalt's neck.

Cobalt screamed in fury, but he knew that it was too late. The skeletal dragon closed his jaws around Cobalt's neck and slowly began to apply the pressure. It did not take long for the bones in Cobalt's neck to crack and splinter. The great gold dragon screamed one last howl of fury before he was incapable of such an expression.

I hope I have served my Blademaster well enough to find my redemption, was the gold dragon's final thought.

When Cobalt had breathed his last breath, the skeletal dragon opened his jaws, and the great gold dragon fell to the ground below them, knocking over several small buildings as he landed. The gold dragon twitched once and then was still.

The skeletal dragon roared in triumph and started circling the battlefield in search of easy prey.

Willowdale

Chapter XXV
A Clash of Swords

The Nightstalker stood on the parapets of the palace of Willowdale watching the battle below her. She had her swords drawn, the twinned scabbards on her back now empty. She knew that only one member of the opposing force would make it up to her. And it was the Blademaster that she wanted to face. She grinned in anticipation of the coming battle. Her mind was clear and she was focused. Her hate was boiling, and she knew that she would be able to best the Blademaster.

She let her arms fall by her sides, the points of her swords resting on the roof of the parapet. She could put herself into a ready position in a second from that position. She extended her senses out all around her and felt where the Blademaster was tearing through the Zeraphim to get to her. She touched the minds of the Zeraphim and moved them off to battle the people of Valendale that were attacking rather than trying to kill the Blademaster. She wanted to kill her by herself.

She touched the mind of Calindilarin and nudged the skeletal dragon into the battle. She felt the huge dragon take off and she knew that the Blademaster would have no help from her nathair an aeir a chosnaíonn. It would be a one on one battle with the people of Valendale as the prize for the victor.

Just the way the Nightstalker had wanted it.

Alana had found the door to the palace. She knew that the Nightstalker awaited her above. She decided that the Nightstalker would just have to wait for her. She took it slowly, building up her reserves so that she would not tire easily during the fight ahead. She did not want to wear herself out too early so that she would not be able to fight at all. It was a careful dance that she had to maintain, for she knew that the Nightstalker would be only so patient.

Alana found a stairwell leading up to the parapets, and took the stairs one by one, her swords leading the way. She took it slow, not wanting to rush the confrontation she was about to have. It would be an epic battle, and she could not afford to lose. She also knew that the Nightstalker would be playing for keeps. Alana frowned. She couldn't remember entering a fight that held more pressure for her.

"I hope she's ready for me," Alana growled softly. "I can promise her that I am ready for her."

The Blademaster finished the climb up to the parapet and eased her way out of the stairwell. The black leather clad woman known as the Nightstalker was waiting for her, watching her approach. Both of the Nightstalker's swords were at the ready and she looked amused at the appearance of the Blademaster.

Alana stopped just outside the stairwell and held her swords in front of her in a ready position. The Nightstalker watched her as she set herself. The two women appeared to be evenly matched in every way, and they both appraised the other.

"This can only end one way, Kera Rayden," Alana's voice was soft in the wind.

"With your death, Alana Steeldrake," Kera's voice rasped slightly but was equally as soft as Alana's. "Are you prepared to die?"

"I will not be dying this day," Alana smiled. She saluted the Nightstalker by touching the flat of one of her blades to her forehead. "But there will be a death on these parapets tonight."

"So you say," Kera Rayden snarled.

The Nightstalker launched a furious assault, her swords swirling in the air. Alana countered every attack, blade for blade, smiling all the while.

The final battle for the people of Valendale had begun.

Colwyn saw Alana make it into the palace safely, but he did not have time to watch and see if she was successful against the Nightstalker. The battle right in front of him was extremely fierce and he had to maintain his attention lest he fall to an unseen thrust. He was fighting hard, his large bastard sword cleaving through the enemy. There were too many targets for him to miss. The battle was wearing him down quickly. He longed for a short break, but he knew that such would not be forthcoming.

Every now and then, Colwyn would look up to see how the gold dragon was faring against the huge skeletal dragon. The two dragons had been locked in a fierce battle for what had seemed like hours. Colwyn wanted to watch the outcome of the battle, but he had to focus on the Zeraphim soldiers that seemed to be everywhere.

He heard the scream burst forth from Cobalt's throat before he felt the great gold dragon slam into the ground. He knew that Cobalt was dead, and he was afraid. He did not have time to mourn though. He could only keep swinging the bastard sword and hoping that something could be done about the monstrosity.

He heard Raven's words once more in his head

"Is there anything else you can tell me about what is going on in Willowdale?" Colwyn asked.

"There is a great abomination there," Raven said, pain evident on her face. *"I cannot tell you much about it. One of your party will fall to it, I am afraid. I do not know who."*

"Surely not Alana?" Colwyn asked, a terrified note in his voice. "I could not bear that."

"That much I can tell you," Raven said softly. "Alana will face the Nightstalker. Whether she defeats the Nightstalker or not, I cannot say. But she will live to see that battle."

"Thanks for that," Colwyn slumped against the wall.

Now he knew what the first Blademaster had meant. Poor Cobalt. He had died the way he wanted to at least. He had died protecting the Blademaster. That was all the gold dragon had wanted. Colwyn hoped that Cobalt would find his redemption.

He launched a renewed attack on the Zeraphim, roaring a challenge as he waded in. Soldiers fell under his renewed assault.

Silvestra and William were fighting with a force from Valendale. They were casting what spells they could, trying to conserve enough energy to be able to last the whole battle. They had been trying to cast simple attack spells. They knew the battle could last all day, and they did not want to tire before the battle was over.

"William, look," Silvestra pointed up at where the two dragons were fighting.

The mage looked up in time to see the great skeletal dragon close his jaws around Cobalt's neck. They heard the dragon's scream and watched as the great gold dragon seemed to fall to the ground in slow motion. The two lovers looked at each other. Neither could believe that the gold dragon was gone.

"He's gone," William said softly.

"William, I have to go up there," Silvestra said sadly. "I'm the only one that can face that monstrosity. If he's left unchallenged, he could wipe out everyone in a blink."

"Be safe, my love," William kissed her. "I've only just got you back. I don't want to lose you now."

"I promise you, I will do my best, William," she smiled at him. "But I have to do this. This is my battle. Just like the Nightstalker is Blademaster Alana's battle. I have no choice."

"I know," he held her for a moment longer. "Go and do battle. Do what you must. And come back to me."

He watched the woman he loved as she transformed into her dragon shape and launched herself into the air a roar of challenge issuing forth before her.

Alana Steeldrake and Kera Rayden were locked in combat. The two had been evenly matched from the start. It had been a difficult fight, as Alana had known it would be. Every attack that Alana launched, Kera seemed to have a counter for, but she also seemed to be able to counter everything that Kera launched at her in turn, so it was even.

"The battle does not go well for your companions, Blademaster," Kera smiled wickedly. "Your Protector is outnumbered. The mages are forced to cast simple spells so that they can be fresh for the entire battle. Your halfling seems to be lost in the crowd. Your priest seems to not know how to handle himself in battle. And your dragon is old and tired."

"They're still better then what you can throw at them," Alana gritted her teeth as she launched a complex series of thrusts and cuts at the Nighstalker. She was not surprised when Kera blocked each cut and thrust with one of her own blades.

"And you can't seem to get anything going against me," the Nightstalker laughed wickedly. "This is precious. I can't wait to see your life blood draining from your body."

"Not gonna happen," Alana grunted. She launched another series of attacks that Kera blocked with ease. "This can only end one way, Kera Rayden. I will best you and the people of Valendale will go free."

"Oh, you make me laugh, Blademaster," the Nightstalker laughed heartily. "You almost make me feel like you are a worthy opponent." They kept trading parries and thrusts, launching cuts and slices against each others. They both saw how easily matched they were. It was going to be a matter of who tired first.

The sound of Cobalt's scream filled their ears. They both turned and watched the great gold dragon fall to the ground. Alana's eyes went wide with surprise. She remembered what Colwyn had told her.

"It will apparently be six before the end," Colwyn said bitterly. *"Raven foretold that one of us would fall during this battle. She did not think it would be you or I, but she truly believes one of us will fall. There is some kind of abomination in Willowdale that will end up killing one of our party. Abomination was the exact word she used. She had no idea what it was, though."*

Now she knew what Raven had meant. She wondered if Lord Taelin would consider Cobalt to have earned his redemption, but she could not spare too much time to worry about it.

"Your dragon is dead, Blademaster," the Nightstalker said. "My Calindilarin will make short work of the rest of your companions. It's over. You may as well just give it up now."

Alana did not respond, she just renewed her assault on the Nightstalker, launching cut and thrust after parry and slice. She kept at it, always keeping an eye on where the skeletal dragon was. It was not long before she saw the silver streak come flying from the battlefield. She knew exactly what it was when she saw it, and she smiled broadly.

"I think your Calindilarin is in for a surprise," Alana swung a sword at Kera's head. The Nightstalker blocked it. "You see, I had two dragons with me today."

"No! It cannot be!" the Nightstalker thrundered. She looked out to where Silvestra had launched herself against Calindilarin, the skeletal dragon. "You cannot have had another dragon with you. We knew everything about your companions."

"Clearly not everything, or else you would have known that the silver haired woman who was taken prisoner with us was, in fact, a silver dragon,' Alana smiled. "Surprise!"

The Nightstalker launched a new attack at the Blademaster.

Silvestra examined the skeletal dragon as she flew towards it. The dragon was massive, far larger than she had first thought. She had no idea how she would be able to best it. Her only thought was that she had to keep out of the way of the massive jaws of the beast. If she could do that, she had a chance to survive.

She let off a blast of lightning to get the skeletal dragon's attention. The lightning did not connect with the dragon's bones, but it was not meant to. It was meant to get the dragon's attention, and it succeeded in doing so. The skeletal dragon roared in fury and started to chase the much smaller silver dragon. She prayed to Taelin that she knew what she was doing by taunting this evil monstrosity

She did not want to face the skeletal dragon right over the city. She was afraid that people she cared about might get hurt if she or the skeletal dragon fell to earth at the end of the battle. She did not want that to happen. She had not seen if there had been anyone under where the great gold dragon landed. She hoped there wasn't.

Her plan was simple. Get the skeletal dragon to follow her into the mountains. From there, she was not sure what the best course of action would be.

When she saw the skeletal dragon coming her way, she twisted her body and started to fly as fast as she could towards the mountains. She looked behind her several times to make sure that the skeletal dragon was, in fact, following her. She smiled grimly to herself when she realized that he was. The problem was that he was slightly faster than she was. She did not understand how that could be. He was far larger than she was, so she should be the faster of the two. She figured it had to do with how the skeletal dragon had been reanimated. There was clearly some evil magic at work here. She did not want to contemplate the kind of magic that went into creating such a creature.

She made it to the mountains before he did, though and so she whirled around a mountain so she could come at him from behind. She had timed it perfectly as she came around the mountain just as the skeletal dragon started to fly past the other side.

She let out another blast of lightning at the skeletal dragon, this time scoring a hit on the skeletal dragon's tail. The skeletal dragon roared and came at her. She used her smaller size to stay out of his way as much as she could, firing blast after blast of lightning at the larger dragon to keep him at bay and hurt him as much as she could before they closed in for the inevitable grapple.

Alana felt like she was losing the battle. The Nightstalker was every bit as good as she was with the blades, and she was feeling her strength starting to ebb while Kera Rayden seemed to be having no such problems.

Kera had pressed Alana up against a crenel of the parapet and was slowly inching her swords towards Alana's neck. Alana was pushing back for all she was worth, but she was slowly losing ground to the other woman.

"Give it up, Blademaster," Kera snarled in her face. "The time of the Blademasters is long passed. You need to pass with it. It is the time of the Nightstalker now."

"It's good to see that Thraal provides his Nightstalkers with ego strength," Alana grunted. Her muscles were straining, burning with the effort.

"It's not ego when you are clearly better than your opponent," Kera laughed. "And I am better than you, Blademaster. You just don't seem to be getting the message about that."

"You've got enough bluster for three Nightstalkers," Alana grunted. She put every ounce of strength she had in it and shoved Kera off of her. She swung out her swords to give her a moment to catch her breath. "That's all you are, though, is bluster."

With a yell, Kera renewed the attack, swinging both swords in an arc at Alana, one at her head and one at her side. Alana was expecting the attack and caught both swords on her own. She whirled around and tried to take off Kera's arm with a vicious cut while using her other sword to keep Kera's at bay.

Far above and far to the west of where the two women were fighting for their very survival, Silvestra and

Calindilarin were locked in heated battle, their jaws flashing at each other. Calindilarin was a little slower, having already fought one tough battle against Cobalthaxillius, but he was far larger, and he tried to use his size to every advantage. Silvestra writhed and twirled to keep out of the large skeletal dragon's jaws. She had seen what he had done to Cobalt and she was trying everything she could to keep the same thing from happening to her.

She had taken several bad cuts on her body during the battle though. The battle was wearing on both of them. They both knew it would have to end quickly or else neither of them would survive it.

Silvestra arced her neck and back away from Calindilarin and swirled away from him, flying slowly, turning lazily around. She sucked in a great breath of air and breathed a hefty bolt of lightning at the skeletal dragon. It struck home right in the skeletal dragon's ribcage, shattering two of the great ribs. Chunks of bone fell to the ground far below. Silvestra was thankful that they had moved away from the city. Someone would have been killed if they'd been hit by those chunks of bone.

The skeletal dragon screamed with agony and rushed Silvestra. She'd been waiting for the rush and flew to the side, raking her talons against the skeletal dragon's left wing, tearing large holes in the thin membrane and bone alike. Silvestra knew she had the advantage and that she had to press it while she had it. It would not do to gain the advantage and then lose the battle immediately following.

She waited until the great skeletal dragon had stopped spinning around and dropped onto his back, her talons digging into his ribs. She reached down and latched her jaws onto the vertebrae of the great skeletal dragon's neck. She held on tight as the great skeletal dragon bucked. She tried to close her jaws and sever the vertebrae she had in her mouth. The bone was rock hard though and she was afraid she would break her fangs if she did so.

So she did the next best thing she could think of. She twisted her neck with the vertebrae in her jaws trying to separate it from the next one in line. The skeletal dragon screamed with each twist of Silvestra's head.

Finally with a great wrench, she broke the connection between the two vertebrae. The neck of the skeletal dragon hung from her jaws and she spat it out. With a scream, she pulled her talons from the skeletal dragon's ribs, taking chunks of bone out when she pulled. She freed herself just before the great bone dragon fell to the earth with a jarring crash. The skeleton came apart as it hit the ground, and waves of released dark magic rushed out from the crash site. The waves of magic rushed all the way back to Willowdale, cracking foundations in the city's great walls.

Silvestra let loose with a howl of glee and a large bolt of lightning in celebration of her triumph than started to laboriously fly towards the palace at the heart of Willowdale to assist the Blademaster in the battle against the Nightstalker.

Colwyn had broken through the lines of the Zeraphim soldiers. He led a small group of men from Valendale forward. He had seen a glimpse of the commanding general of the Zeraphim. And he had a clear path to him.

With a yell, Colwyn led a charge towards the general. The general saw Colwyn coming with his small force and ordered some of his men to intercept Colwyn. Colwyn saw the Zeraphim coming and ordered the men with him to take care of them. He did not stop his charge, bearing down on the general. His thought was a simple one. Cut off the head and the body can't survive.

He launched a simple attack at the general, a large overhead cut with both hands, his bastard sword a blur as it arced towards the general's head. The general ducked under his own two handed blade and let the swords clash.

Alana hacked at the Nightstalker, trying to catch her off balance. Kera caught her blade on her own, locking their hilts together and stabbed with her other sword, aiming for Alana's stomach. Alana parried with an ease of movement she hadn't found much during the battle. She sidestepped with the parry and flicked the other sword out of Kera's hand.

Both swords dropped to the ground. Each woman now only had one weapon to fight with. That was enough for each of them. It was still an even match.

Kera launched a furious assault, Alana blocking each cut and thrust with her own sword. Alana used both hands to steady the sword she held as she blocked and parried each attack from the Nightstalker. Kera was slowly backing the Blademaster into a corner. Alana knew it but couldn't really do much to change the direction she was moving backwards.

Alana's back was against the wall, and she was doing her best to keep her sword moving. She took several cuts on her arms, but none of them were deep. She was able to keep Kera's sword from doing any real damage.

"You are mine now, Blademaster," Kera said softly. "You're tiring and my sword has tasted your blood. It's just a matter of time before I land a fatal blow. You're the best that that accursed Taelin can muster? This war will be quick indeed."

"You gonna fight or talk me to death?" Alana gritted her teeth. She kicked out with her right foot and connected with Kera's stomach, pushing the other woman back a few feet.

It was then that they heard the great crash of the skeletal dragon falling to earth and shattering followed by Silvestra's howl of triumph.

"No!" Kera shrieked. "It can't be."

"Yes, your pet dragon is dead," Alana smiled as she thrust her sword at Kera. "Mine is on the way back to help me."

"Ungh," Kera said as she blocked Alana's thrust. "This isn't over, Blademaster."

"It is over," Alana smiled. "Surrender now, Kera Rayden. You've lost."

"You've won this battle, Alana Steeldrake," Kera seethed. She made a motion with her fist, and a black portal of smoke opened behind her. "But it's only one battle in a much larger war. We will meet again soon."

Kera stepped backwards into the black portal and the portal flashed closed with a pulse of black light. The Nightstalker was gone.

Alana slumped to her knees with relief.

Colwyn had just taken a nasty cut on his leg from the general, but he wasn't letting it stop him. He just kept pressing the attack. They were evenly matched. What the general had as an advantage in technique, Colwyn matched with an advantage in imagination. It was an advantage he pressed, launching creative attacks that the general had to scramble to counter. Colwyn had landed several nasty blows on the general, though, and the general was starting to slow.

The general had just launched a counter attack when the dark light pulsed on the parapet above. They both instinctively knew what had just happened.

"Your mistress just left you, General," Colwyn grunted.

"So it would seem," the general sighed and lowered his weapon. "There is no point in continuing this. You can have these people back. They weren't doing a very good job for us anyway. We will go back to our Keep. But know this. This isn't over. You will see us again."

"So you nut cases always say," Colwyn grunted again. "Go home. Before I change my mind and cut you down where you stand."

Colwyn watched as the general gathered his troops and began to abandon the city. When the citizens of Valendale saw what was happening, they started to cheer. Colwyn didn't have the energy to cheer, he was so tired. He made his way up to the parapet where he knew that his wife had just won her own desperate struggle.

When he got to her, he dropped to his knees next to her and took her in his arms. He kissed her beautiful auburn hair and held her close.

"The Zeraphim are retreating," he whispered. "It's over. At least for now."

Chapter XXVI
The Return to Valendale

Alana and Colwyn sat silently on the parapets of the palace in Willowdale. The companions had gathered and then just sat where they were when the Zeraphim began to retreat. The sword fight with Kera Rayden had taken its toll on Alana. She had bested the Nightstalker, but not without taking some cuts of her own along the way. None of the cuts were particularly deep and they were already starting to heal.

Colwyn had also gotten hurt during the battle with the Zeraphim. He had suffered a deep gash on his left leg. Martin had done what he could to heal it. The bleeding had stopped, and Colwyn could walk on the leg without any problem. Colwyn looked over to where the young priest lay sleeping on the floor of the parapet, clearly exhausted and smiled. The young man had certainly made his god proud this day. He did not like the High Priestess of Taelin, even more he did not completely trust her. But he had to admit that she had provided more than adequate priestly support in the young Martin Faolin. The priest had been assigned to them as a punishment. Colwyn knew that there was more to the story of why they had been assigned the young priest than they would ever fully learn.

Alana looked over at Colwyn and smiled at him, a smile he heartily returned. They had been through so much over the past few weeks and they were stronger for it. He still hurt over nearly betraying her. He thought that he might never get rid of that pain. He once more vowed to never be tempted like that again. He knew he would never find someone as special as Alana was. She had forgiven him without reservation. She had told him that the Second Law of the Blades couldn't be ignored for someone she loved as much as she loved him. He'd felt tears welling up when she said that.

And it was why they had both been able to forgive Meryn for betraying them to the Nightstalker. They both understood the pain that she had suffered when Silvestra took William away from her. They knew why she had betrayed them. And they knew she did not mean to hurt anyone but William by it. And so they had both applied the Second Law of the Blades to her. He could still hear Alana's voice telling Meryn why she was being forgiven. *True love breeds true forgiveness. Nothing is more powerful than the ability to forgive the one you love. And nothing brings you closer than the forgiveness of your own misdeeds.* Meryn had cried for a long time after they talked to her. Colwyn had even started to feel bad for her. A fact that had greatly surprised him. He wasn't sure he would ever trust Meryn completely, but he was glad she was one of Alana's companions.

Colwyn stood and walked to the edge of the parapet and looked down. The citizens of Valendale were celebrating in the streets of Willowdale. They had been oppressed for so long by the Zeraphim, he did not begrudge them their celebration. The time would soon come where they would need to start the long journey back to Valendale. He wasn't sure how they would be able to get the entire population of the city of Valendale back home. He suspected that

Silvestra would get quite a bit of flying time ferrying people home along the way. He smiled at that. The dragon woman had proved her worth during the battle. He hoped that she would stay with the companions, especially with Cobalt dead. Alana would need a new nathair an aeir a chosnaíonn. He sincerely hoped that Silvestra would consider filling that position.

Colwyn's smiled faded when he thought about Cobalt. He could still see the body of the great gold dragon lying in the streets at the edge of town. Cobalt had given his life to protect Alana. It was a noble death worthy of a nathair an aeir a chosnaíonn. Even though he was severely outmatched against the skeletal dragon that Kera Rayden had sent against them, Cobalt had valiantly attacked the undead beast anyway. By doing so, he had allowed Alana to focus on fighting the Nightstalker. When Cobalt had fallen, Silvestra had immediately jumped into the fray and fought the undead dragon viciously, eventually killing it. None of the companions had had a chance to properly mourn the loss of the great gold dragon. He hoped that Cobalt had been able to finds his redemption and go to his eternal walk with Taelin.

He and Alana had sent Silvestra off to Ravendale. They had asked that the dragon bring Marcus Whelan back with her. Alana especially did not want the reunion between Marcus and his wife and daughter to be put off any longer. If Marcus had not come to find Alana, the citizens of Valendale would not be free now. Alana and Colwyn both felt that that effort needed to be rewarded. The best way they knew how to reward it was to bring his family back together.

"She should be back anytime," Alana said, reading his thoughts.

"Indeed," he smiled at her. "I can't wait to see Marcus kiss his wife hello for the first time in months."

"Me either," she winked. She leaned over and put her head on his shoulder. "Maybe we should get someone to go down and find Jenny and Lisa so they can be here when Marcus gets here."

"I think that would involve moving," Colwyn groaned. "I'm not sure I can do that right now."

"I know the feeling," Alana sighed. "This was almost too much for me, Col. We can't do this alone."

"I know," Colwyn kissed her hair. "I'm sure Lord Taelin already has something in the works. He can't be blind to the coming darkness."

They sat that way for several minutes. William came walking up to them. Of all their companions, William was the only one who had not seemed to be hurt in the battle. Alana knew that the mage had expended a lot of energy during the battle though. She wasn't sure how the mage was still able to stand, let alone walk around. In a way, she envied the young mage his resilience. Of course, he also had not fought a pitched hand to hand battle with someone of his equal either.

"You two look adorable together like that," William laughed as he plopped down next to them.

"Why thank you," Alana rolled her eyes. "We did a good thing here."

"Yes, we did," William nodded. "Very hard, though. What the hell was that woman you were fighting. I didn't think a Blademaster would ever have that much trouble in a one on one battle."

"She called herself a Nightstalker," Alana grunted. She put her arm around Colwyn to comfort herself. "Her name is Kera Rayden. Apparently, Thraal has decided to make it tougher for the Blademasters this time around. The Nightstalker was my equal."

"You bested her," William pointed out.

"She fled when her dragon was killed," Colwyn corrected the mage. "It isn't quite the same thing."

"Good point, Col," William frowned. "Do you think we'll see her again?"

"I think we'll see her sooner rather than later," Alana sighed. "And I suspect that now that Thraal knows how well his Nightstalker will do against me, he'll make more of them."

"Lord Taelin will have to give you some help," the mage observed.

"That's what we've been discussing," Colwyn nodded.

"William, can you do me a favor?" Alana asked the young mage. "Can you go find Jenny and Lisa Whelan for me? Silvestra should be back soon with Marcus and we'd like the three of them to see each other as soon as possible."

"Of course," William smiled broadly. "I can't wait to see that reunion myself."

"I think it's the reunion with Silvestra that you really can't wait for," Colwyn grinned at his friend. "You have to admit. You two do make quite a couple."

"We do, don't we?" William's smile grew even wider. "I can't believe she's back in my life. I thought I had lost her forever."

"Now we know how you've been feeling these last few weeks whenever you've looked at us," Alana grinned wickedly. "Absolutely sickening how you two carry on."

"Sickening how WE carry on?!" William looked shocked. "Gods, when you two kiss, I want to vomit. Of course, I suspect that neither you two nor Silvestra and I will be able to match the kiss Jenny is going to land on Marcus when he gets here."

"Just go get them," Alana laughed.

Colwyn and Alana watched the young mage make his way off the parapets. He wound his way down to the streets below. They lost sight of him when he got into the streets, but Colwyn and Alana both knew that he would not take too long to locate the innkeeper's wife and daughter.

Alana lay back on the floor of the parapet and stared up at the sky. There was not a cloud in the sky above them. She felt Colwyn lie down next to her and press up against her side. He took her hand and they stared up at the sky hand in hand like that for several minutes. Each let their mind wander, but neither of them thought anything of any lasting importance.

"Thank you for believing in me, Alana," Colwyn said softly after a while.

"What do you mean, Colwyn?" she looked over at him.

"You didn't have to forgive me," he looked back at her. "You could have held what happened against me. But you chose to forgive me instead. In doing so, you allowed me to regain my own confidence and be the leader I needed to be in the fight against the Zeraphim."

"I'll always forgive you, Colwyn," she laughed softly. "Because I'll always love you."

"I'll try to never give you a reason to forgive me again," Colwyn laughed slightly.

"Oh, you'll mess up again," she grinned wickedly. "You're a man after all. And a noble. Face it, Col. You're screwed."

"Great," he turned his head back to look at the sky. "You really know how to make a guy feel better about himself, Alana."

"Anytime, my love," she laughed.

They lay staring up at the sky for several minutes before William came back with Jenny and Lisa Whelan. The daughter, no more than six, was clinging to Jenny's skirts, still afraid of everything around her because of what happened. When Lisa saw Alana lying there, she squealed with glee and launched herself on top of Alana. Alana grunted as the child landed on top of her.

"You've gotten a lot bigger since the last time I saw you, Lisa," Alana groaned.

"Glad she landed on you instead of me then," Colwyn laughed heartily.

"Thank you for saving us, 'Lana," Lisa mumbled into Alana's chest. She'd always called Alana that, and it was something Alana treasured. "Thank you for driving off the bad men."

"That makes it all worth it," Alana said very quietly. She wrapped her arms around Lisa and held the child close. "You're welcome, Little One."

"I think I see something, Alana," Colwyn said suddenly. He stood and walked to the edge of the parapet and put his hand over his brow as he looked out towards the mountains. "It's Silvestra! She's on her way!"

Alana stood and picked Lisa up and carried her over to where Colwyn was standing. She looked out to where he was pointing and smiled. She looked down at Lisa and looked back out to where Silvestra was just coming into view. Her smile grew very broad and she hugged the little girl close.

"That's my friend Silvestra, Lisa," Alana said to the little girl. "She's bringing you a present."

"What kind of present, 'Lana?" the little girl squealed with glee.

"It's a surprise," Colwyn grinned, getting into the feel of it. "But I think you and your mommy will want this present very much."

The four of them watched as Silvestra slowly flew towards the palace of Willowdale. Her wings beat steadily and she grew in size as she got closer to them. As she got closer they could see that someone was pressed against her back. It was clear to Alana and Colwyn both that dragon flight did not really agree with Marcus Whelan. Although Alana and Colwyn knew who it was, Jenny and Lisa could not make out who was on Silvestra's back.

Silvestra swooped high over the palace and started to slowly circle around, flying a little lower with each circle. After what seemed like forever, Silvestra lightly touched down on the center of the roof of the parapet. She hunched down, and the poor innkeeper slid off her back. As soon as Marcus was off her back, she began to change back into her human form.

Alana looked at Marcus with some amusement. She could tell that he had had a rough flight. He was looking a little green around the gills as he turned around.

That was until he saw his wife and daughter racing across the parapet to hug him.

"DADDY!" Lisa squealed as she jumped into his arms.

Jenny Whelan was slower than her daughter but no less exuberant in her embrace. The three of them held onto each other as if they were afraid that the other would two would disappear if they let go.

"I thought I would never see you two again," Marcus said softly, tears rolling freely down his face. "I thought that none of us would ever escape from there."

"We missed you so much, Marcus," Jenny whispered as she kissed him.

Silvestra moved over to put her arm around William. The two couples watched the reunited family with broad smiles on their faces. Marcus put Lisa down and broke away to walk over to Alana.

"Blademaster Alana, you have my eternal gratitude," Marcus said as he took her hand. "What you have done here will never be forgotten. By any of us in Valendale. You will be forever welcome in Valendale as an honored guest. You will never have to pay for food or lodging as long as I own the White Horse. You or anyone with you."

"You don't have to do that, Marcus," Alana grinned. "Seeing the three of you back together is thanks enough. I had Silvestra get you because I couldn't wait for the three of you to see each other again. I think you'll find that you're going to be a hero to the people of Valendale yourself, my friend."

"I'm no hero," the innkeeper shook his head. "I don't have it in me to be a hero."

"Who was it that risked everything to come find me to rescue the people of Valendale, Marcus?" Alana raised an eyebrow. "I rather think that does qualify you as a hero."

"I guess when you put it that way, I am a hero," Marcus grinned sheepishly. "I did it for Jenny and Lisa though. There was no altruistic reason behind my actions. Isn't that what a hero is?"

Alana looked at Colwyn. Her husband looked back at her and the two of them laughed. William couldn't help but to start chuckling himself. Silvestra soon joined in.

"We've all found that being a hero usually means being scared to death as you do something that could be considered incredibly stupid," Alana explained.

"Ah," Marcus nodded in understanding. "That definitely explains how I felt."

"You're our hero, Daddy!" Lisa pitched.

"Marcus, enjoy being with your family," Colwyn said as he put his arm around Alana. "You've certainly earned it."

"Thank you, Lord Colwyn," Marcus bowed slightly. "More than you can ever know, thank you."

Colwyn and Alana watched as Marcus led his family down into the streets of Willowdale. People crowded around

Marcus and his family, offering the innkeeper their thanks for helping to save them.

"I think he'll be OK," Colwyn observed.

"Too bad he's not a noble," Alana shrugged. "They'd make him the next First Lord if he was."

"I wouldn't be surprised if they did anyway," Colwyn laughed. "That would be appropriate. I'm sure King Roderick would grant him noble status if you asked him for it."

"I don't know if I could do that," Alana looked at Colwyn. "I don't know if I could actually talk to the King like that. It made me extremely nervous when he fell to his knees to pledge his support. I would not want to feel like I was abusing my status as the Blademaster for personal gain."

"What's good about being a law unto yourself if you don't use that power to help someone like Marcus who's earned it?' Colwyn raised an eyebrow. "I think Lord Taelin would approve. And perhaps be highly amused by it."

"You may be right," Alana nodded. She smiled at her husband. "I'll think about it."

They watched the citizens of Valendale celebrating for several long minutes before Colwyn turned to Alana and kissed her gently.

"We need to get them organized and get them home, Alana," Colwyn said softly.

"Then let's get started," she leaned her head on his chest.

It took two weeks for them to organize but soon the companions were finally ready to start moving the people of Valendale back home. It would take several weeks, and Silvestra would fly whole families back as they travelled, but realistically, they could expect that the journey would take about three weeks. Alana wished she could just transport everyone home at once. Things just didn't work that way though. But at least the people of Valendale were going home. Most of them were at any rate. Some had died during the fight to free themselves from the Zeraphim. And then there were the deaths that came before they were brought to Willowdale.

They started the slow journey to Valendale. Marcus and his family were amongst the first to be shuttled back to Valendale on Silvestra's back. No one questioned that the innkeeper and his family should be amongst the first to go. The innkeeper, after all, had brought the Blademaster to Willowdale. Without the Blademaster, none of them would be going home.

Alana and Colwyn were the last ones to leave the city limits of Willowdale. As they passed the outer gates of the city, Alana turned and looked back at the city. She heaved a large sigh.

"What's wrong, love?" Colwyn asked. He turned to look where she was looking.

"Just remembering the prophecy the sage told me," Alana said softly. "Do you know one of the things that Willowdale has been called?"

"Admittedly, I don't know a whole lot about Willowdale, other than what we've seen over the last few weeks," Colwyn shrugged.

"Willowdale has been called the twice dead city," Alana said. She looked over at Colwyn. "You've heard the prophecy that Isaiah and the King both gave to me. It said: When the twice dead city falls empty a third time, the storm clouds will gather and sabres will rattle in their scabbards. The blight of war shall be upon the land and only the one born of the light can lead the charge against the darkness."

"Willowdale is now empty save for corpses," Colwyn said quietly.

"Which mean war is coming," Alana nodded. "We need to be ready."

"We will, Alana," Colwyn smiled. "Somehow, we will."

Alana took Colwyn's hand as they slowly started down the road that would lead the companions and the people of Valendale back home.

Epilogue
The Gathering of Storm Clouds, The Rattling of Sabres

he companions sat on rocks overlooking the city of Valendale, watching the citizens of that city walk down the hill towards their homes. The companions had walked with the beleaguered people all the way from Willowdale back to Valendale to make sure they all made it home alive. It had taken over a month to get all of the way back to Valendale.

The halfling was standing apart from the others. Even though she had been forgiven for her betrayal, Meryn still felt like she did not belong with her companions. At least for the moment. It would take some time for the wounds caused by her betrayal to heal. She feared that such wounds as she had caused might never fully heal.

Alana and Colwyn sat together on one large flat rock, simply holding each other's hand. They knew that the hard times were only beginning. Even without the prophecy they'd been given about the coming war, it had become clear to the both of them that a darkness was coming to cover all of Calthea.

"You have done some good work, Blademaster," a voice called from behind them.

Alana stood and whirled in one motion, drawing her swords as she moved. Colwyn shifted to his right and executed a similar turn, his bastard sword in his hand in a flash. As soon as they saw who it was behind them, they both relaxed and sheathed their weapons.

"My lord Taelin," Alana bowed to the elder god. "You once again honor us with your presence."

"Oh, stop the bowing, my child," Taelin laughed heartily. He reached over and put his hand on her arm. She felt instantly refreshed and invigorated by his touch. "You still have much work to do, my child."

"There's a darkness coming, Lord Taelin," Alana said quietly. "Colwyn and I both feel it."

"There is a great war brewing," Taelin nodded. "The Zeraphim and the Nightstalker are just a symptom of what is to come."

"What can we do?" Colwyn asked. "Surely there's an alternative to war."

"The only way that you can prevent yourselves from being involved in this war is to die now," Taelin shrugged. "There is no way to avoid it. The Dark God has pressed forth his plans to conquer Calthea. It will be up to you to stop him."

"We can't do it by ourselves," Alana shook her head. "The six of us against an army just isn't enough. And if the Dark God decides to create more Nightstalkers, it will be even harder. Kera Rayden was almost more than I could handle."

"And so you won't fight this battle by yourselves," Taelin smiled. "There are others. You were the first, Alana. You will certainly be the finest of them. You must find the others."

"How?"

Taelin lifted his hand and an amber stone on a chain appeared in his hand. The amber stone glowed softly. He took Alana's hand and motioned for Colwyn to join them.

When the two were standing side by side before him, Taelin wrapped the chain around their hands and placed the amber stone against their wrists. The stone pulsed once, almost too brightly to look at then returned to its previous brightness.

"This is the Bladestone," Taelin explained softly "Either of you can use its power. When it comes in contact with one imbued with the power of the Blademasters, it will grow bright and hot. There will be no mistaking the reaction. Guard the stone well."

"We will, Lord Taelin," Alana nodded.

The Lightbringer turned from Alana and Colwyn and walked over to where William and Silvestra were standing The wizard and the dragon woman noted his approach and bowed slightly in deference to the elder god.

"William Stonehands and Silvestra Knightwing," Taelin began. "I have a gift and some words of wisdom to share with you."

"We listen and obey, Master of the Light," Silvestra bowed her head, her silver hair covering her face.

"First the gift," Taelin smiled. "You two have been through great trials, and yet your love still burns strong. It is only fitting that you two marry. From this day forth, let all know that William Stonehands and Silvestra Knightwing are husband and wife. Let no mortal, man or dragon, tear asunder what I have put together."

William and Silvestra looked at each other and then looked at Taelin. They had no words for what the elder god had just done. William put his arm around Silvestra and held her close.

"Thank you, Lord Taelin," the young mage said quietly.

"Don't thank me just yet, William," Taelin smiled sadly "Neither of you will have an easy path to go down. I have put you together so that you each have someone to lean on as you go forward, much like I pair my Blademasters with their Protectors. Silvestra, I now have to ask you to do two very important things for me."

"You have only to ask, Lord Taelin," the dragon woman bowed low. "You have given me my heart's desire."

"Alana needs a new nathair an aeir a chosnaíonn now that Cobalthaxillius has gone to his walk with me. Thanks to Alana, my child has found redemption," Taelin informed her. He caught the look of relief on the faces of both Alana and Colwyn, causing the god to smile broadly. "I wish for you to take that position. You will get to spend more time with your husband this way."

"Of course I will accept," Silvestra smiled. "I have a great deal of respect for this Blademaster. She has taught me a great deal. It would be my honor to serve as her nathair an aeir a chosnaíonn."

"Good," the god smiled at the young dragon woman. "The second task I have for you will not be as easy, but is just as important. I wish for you to accompany me to the Isle of Dragons to convince the Draconic Council to provide more nathair an aeir a chosnaíonns. As you well know, Eliazar is a very stubborn old dragon."

"I do not think Eliazar will be too happy with what you have done today, my lord," William grinned wickedly. "He tried very hard to keep Silvestra and I apart."

"Let him be upset!" Taelin roared. "I will not allow two people who love each other as you and Silvestra do to be parted by him. But he will be hard to convince of the need of more nathair an aeir a chosnaíonns, I am afraid."

"I will do what needs to be done," Silvestra nodded.

"William, I believe that your path will be decided very soon," Taelin touched the mage on the arm. "You are far more than even you suspect, and far, far more than the Mages of the Inner Circle ever thought they would see go through the Tower of the White. I think that you will find what you are looking for not long after you and your companions return to Ravendale."

"I look forward to it," William nodded.

Taelin smiled at the mage and moved over to kneel in front of the halfling.

"Do not be sad, Little One," the god said reassuringly. "William was never really supposed to be on your path. But I can tell you that you will find someone who is perfect for you very soon. The Swiftfoot name is not yet done being an important part of history." He touched the halfling's face and her tears fell away instantly. "Good. You must help keep Alana safe for me. No more antics like the ones you showed during your time in Willowdale. I will not be so forgiving the next time you betray my champion."

"Yes, Lord Taelin," the halfling squeaked.

The god nodded and went to talk to his priest.

"Martin Faolin, you are assigned to the Blademaster as punishment by the High Priestess," Taelin looked at his priest with an amused expression on his face. "I do not think Naomi quite knew what she was doing when she assigned you. However, you are the right priest for the job. You have served me well."

"Thank you, my Lord Taelin," the priest bowed low, unable to look his god in the face. "I do what I can in your service."

"You have all done well," Taelin smiled at the companions. "Now, you should return to Ravendale and relax. But the time will quickly come for action. You will not be able to relax for long, I am afraid. The storm clouds gather. The sabers rattle. War is coming upon us all. Silvestra, if you will, I would ride on your back to the Isle of Dragons. It has been too long since I have felt the wind in my beard."

"It would be my honor, Lord Taelin," Silvestra nodded and began to change into her dragon form.

"You will have your wife back before too long, William," Taelin smiled. "And now, my children. Go home. Albert is waiting there for you with his spiced potatoes." Taelin climbed onto Silvestra's back and grabbed a hold on her slender neck spikes. "Oh, Alana, my child. You should listen to Colwyn and talk to the King about Marcus. I think it's time for some fresh blood in the noble ranks."

Alana's jaw dropped as Taelin winked at her. The companions watched as the mighty silver dragon launched herself into the air. Alana and William watched the dragon soar into the sky and fly off into the distance. When they could no longer see her, the mage sighed.

"Let's go home," Alana said quietly.

Willowdale

Appendix

Every effort has been made to keep things straight for the reader in the story, however, there are a lot of names and concepts. And so, I have provided this handy set of references for you. As the series grows, so too will this Appendix. I hope you all find this information handy.

The Appendix is divided into the following sections:

Deities
(Alignment of the Deity is in Parentheses) (G = Good Aligned, N = Neutral Algined, E=Evil Aligned)

Ana (*AH-nah*) (N) Goddess of History

Aram (*AH-rum*) (N) God of Balance

Ceres (*SER-ees*) (N) Goddess of Love

Chemish (*KEM-ish*) (E) God of Magic (for evil aligned magic users)

Ferrin (*FER-un*) (G) God of Magic (for good aligned magic users)

Isis (*EYE-sis*) (N) Goddess of Life

Laeyra (*lay-EHR-uh*) (N) Goddess of Luck

Raeven (*RAY-vun*) (G) God of Nature

Ranthos (*RAHN-thos*) (E) God of the Moon

Serrin (*SER-un*) (G) God of the Sun

Taelin (*TAY-lin*) (G) God of Wisdom and Justice, also known as the Lightbringer, the Lord of the Light, and the Bringer of Light

Terra (*TER-uh*) (G) Goddess of Healing

Thraal (*THRAHL*) (E) God of Chaos, often referred to as the Dark God or the Bringer of Chaos

Torval (*TOR-vul*) (N) God of Magic (for neutral aligned magic users)

Willowdale

Vash (*VAHSH*) (E) Goddess of the Seas

Veral (*ver-AHL*) (E) God of War

Xaria (*ZAHR-yuh*) (G) Goddess of Fertility

Zish (*ZISH*) (E) Goddess of Death

Places

The Southern Dales

The Southern Dales are the southernmost region located on the Continent of Calthea on the world of Calthea. Home to many races championed by the gods of good and neutrality, the Southern Dales are a region governed by a king who resides in a palace in Ravendale. Nobles known as the First Lords govern each of the ten territories reporting to the king. They rule fairly, the wisdom of Taelin guiding the leader's hands.

Arvendale – A medium sized city that is deep in the heart of the Southern Dales, on the other side of the Elven Woods from Ravendale and noble seat of the Arvendale territory. Dargan Starseeker, Colwyn's father, is the First Lord of Arvendale, and, although he does not necessarily recognize the fact, Colwyn is the heir to that title.

Attendale – A city on the eastern coast of the Southern Dales and the noble seat of the Attendale territory.

Barandale – A city on the western coast of the Southern Dales and the noble seat of the Barandale territory.

Darcandale – A small city in the northwest of the Southern Dales and the noble seat of the Darcandale territory.

Lovendale – A small port town on the southeast coast of the Southern Dales and the noble seat of the Lovendale territory.

Parciandale – A city in the north of the Southern Dales and the noble seat of the Parciandale territory.

Ravendale – The capitol city of the Southern Dales near the center of the Southern Dales and not too far from the Elven Woods. The noble seat of the Ravendale territory and home of the High Priest of Taelin.

Solvendale – A small town on the southwest of the Southern Dales and noble seat of the Solvendale territory.

Talondale – A small merchant city in the southern part of the Southern Dales and noble seat of the Talondale region. Alana's hometown.

Valendale – A town a week's ride south of Ravendale and the noble seat of the Valendale territory. Home to the sage Isaiah.

Willowdale – A city in the far northeast of the Southern Dales. Also known as the Twice Dead City, Willowdale was once the noble seat of the former Willowdale territory, but that area of the Southern Dales has become somewhat vacant. Willowdale is known from time to time to be home to various outlaws and cutthroats.

The Elven Woods – A dense forest to the southwest of Ravendale. Home to the Forestwalker clan of elves and the location of the Temple of the Blades.

The Temple of the Blades – The ancestral home of the Blademaster. Here, Blademasters learn what they are to become. The Test of the Blades and all Blademaster weddings happen here. In addition, the Temple of the Blades is the location of the Legacy of the Blademasters.

The Wilds

The Wilds are the lands between the Southern Dales and Dracomyr. Each of the town in the Wilds is its own little kingdom, governing over itself. Unlike the Southern Dales or Dracomyr, there is no central council or government for the region.

Vikerin – A small villaige in the Wilds that is home to the largest temples for Taelin and Laeyra in the Wilds.

Dracomyr

Dracomyr is the northernmost part of the continent of Calthea. Dracomyr is home to the shadow creatures and the undead that Thraal loves. The capitol city is Tornith.

The Stonegate Mountains – A mountain range not too far from the Wilds that is home to several large clans of goblins.

Tornith – The capitol city of Dracomyr. The High Priest of Thraal serves in Tornith

Outworld

Outworld refers to places that do not exist as part of the world of Calthea per se.

Limbo – Limbo is a prison where Taelin trapped the essence of the Dark God for several hundred years. It is protected by a multiheaded dragon known as Mahumet

The Isle of Dragons – The Isle of Dragons is home to the dragons of Calthea. The Dragonic Council meets here to oversee law and order for the dragon nation. Although the Isle of Dragons does actually exist as an island on Calthea, it is considered to be part of Outworld as it is inaccessible to any but the gods and the dragons.

Willowdale

People

Bothain, Albert – Proprietor of the Lucky Minotaur

Bunten, Hubert – A brute that occasionally can be found at the Lucky Minotaur

Dalphain, Caiaphas – High Priest of Taelin when the new Blademater, Alana Steeldrake, is born. Dies of old age

Darkholme, Adouon – High Priest of Thraal after the death of Drakkhous

Delwyn, Merinda – Priestess of Taelin sacrificed to Thraal and beloved of Balaam Otakis

Doilin, Altas – Legate of the Goblins in the Stonegate Mountains

Drakkhous – High Priest of Thraal. Killed by Alana Steeldrake

Faolin, Martin – Priest of Taelin assigned to Alana Steeldrake's party

Jana, Deera – An acolyte of Taelin that Alana Seeldrake finds to show some promise

Kale, Richard – Protector of Raven Windrider

Kovalani, Mirian – Queen of the Forestwalker Elves and former lover of Colwyn Starseeker

Kovalani, Otan – Trainer of rangers for the Forestwalker Elves and brother of Mirian Kovalani

Marant, Lilliana – Priestess of Taelin that dies of the wasting sickness in the wilds and beloved of Darius Redwind

Willowdale

Mastairs, Naomi – High Priestess of Taelin after Balaam Otakis dies.

Otakis, Balaam – High Priest of Taelin after Caiaphas Dalphain dies. Killed by Drakkhous in Tornith while protecting Alana Steeldrake

Rayden, Kera – The Nightstalker

Redwind, Darius – Priest of Taelin that becomes Drakkhous after he loses the woman he loves

Sapphire, Crystal – Last Blademaster named before the Great Purge

Starseeker, Colwyn – Protector to Alana Steeldrake and heir to the title of First Lord of the Valendale Territory

Starseeker, Dargan – First Lord of the Valendale Territory and Colwyn Starseeker's father.

Steeldrake, Alana – First Blademaster to be named in over 300 years.

Stonehammer, Roland – King of the Southern Dales

Stonehands, William – Mage of the White that travels with Alana Steeldrake

Swiftfoot, Meryn – Halfling thief that travels with Alana Steeldrake

Talon, Isaiah – A sage

Tencis, Olianna – Priestess of Taelin in Tornith

Thames, Mariska – Priestess of Thraal and beloved of Adouon Darkholme

Vilas, Arthais – Senior Priest of Taelin in Tornith

Whelan, Marcus – Inkeeper of the White Horse Inn in Valendale.

White, Ash – Stable boy at the Lucky Minotaur. Brother of Gwendolyn White

White, Gwendolyn – Waitress at the Lucky Minotaur. Sister of Ash White

Windrider, Raven – The First Blademaster

Willowdale

Dragons

(Type is in parenthesis)
Good dragons are Gold, Silver, Bronze, Brass, and Copper
Neutral Dragons are Diamond, Ruby, Emerald, Sapphire,
and Amethyst
Evil Dragons are, Red, Green, Blue, Black, and White

Alpharin (amethyst) Member of the Dragonic Council

Alpharis (bronze) Member of the Dragonic Council

Calindilarin (undead) Undead dragon in service to Kera Rayden

Centrus (brass) Member of the Dragonic Council

Cobalthaxillius (gold) Nathair an aeir a chosnaíonn to Alana Steeldrake.

Cyrus (green) Member of the Dragonic Council

Eliazar (gold) Leader of the Dragonic Council

Esmertas (emerald) Member of the Dragonic Council

Firegem (ruby) Member of the Dragonic Council

Mahumet (multi headed good dragon) Guardian of Limbo

Mintakis (diamond) Member of the Dragonic Council

Onyx (black) Member of the Dragonic Council

Pyrus (copper) Member of the Dragonic Council

Sephiras (sapphire) Member of the Dragonic Council

Shakaaris (red) Member of the Dragonic Council

Willowdale

Silvestra Knightwing (silver) Beloved of William Stonehands

Snowfang (white) Member of the Dragonic Council

Talonwing (silver) Member of the Dragonic Council

Trakkis (blue) Member of the Dragonic Council

The Prophecy of the Great War of Souls

Tá an tuar an cogadh mór anamacha

Tar éis trí chéad bliain ar fud an domhain a thagann an Aois dorchadais. Beidh an Dia olc ar ais chun tús a conquest an domhain arís.

Sna laethanta tosaigh an Aois dorchadais, tar éis na máistrí na lanna ar ais go dtí saol na Calthea, déanfaidh an arm na marbh chun cinn i seirbhís an Dia olc. Déanfaidh an marbh ardú agus cogadh pá ar fud an aghaidh Calthea.

Nuair a thiteann an chathair faoi dhó marbh folamh ar feadh uair an tríú, beidh an scamaill stoirme a bhailiú agus beidh an claimhte fuaime i gcuid truaillí. Déanfaidh an dúchan cogaidh a bheith ar an talamh agus ní féidir ach an ceann a rugadh ar an bhfianaise an cúiseamh i gcoinne an dorchadas mar thoradh.

Ní mór don arm an solas scaoilte an draíocht na bean sidhe dul ar ais ar an dorchadas. An ceann a rugadh ar an cheo solais mar thoradh ar an oidhreacht na máistrí na lanna isteach ar an réimse an cath.

Nuair a ghlaonn an anam an bean sidhe a gabhadh amach, beidh na clocha ar an daingean ar an bhfianaise a bhriseadh agus titim ar a chéile. Beidh an bhiotáille an roghnaithe de Taelin uair níos mó a chur ar an réimse an cath i Cruinniú w i gcoinne an dorchadas.

Déanfaidh an tine an ghrian agus an ghealach dim agus céimnithe chun dorchadais. Ní mór don duine a rugadh ar an solas ag siúl amach as an scáth an tine an ghrian agus an ghealach agus an roghnaithe de Taelin mar thoradh.

Beidh an Dlí is Fiche ar an Tríú na lanna a shárú, i gcás roinnt de na roghnaithe de Taelin.

Mura ndéanfaidh an ceann a rugadh ar an bhfianaise thoradh an cúiseamh i gcoinne an arm na marbh, beidh an domhain titim isteach i dorchadas a bheidh gan deireadh. Ní féidir ach an cumhacht ag an

Dlí Chéad na lanna threorú láimh an ceann a rugadh ar an solas.

Sa chath mar atá i ngach daoine eile a mbeidh an ceann a rugadh ar an solas troid, ní bheidh aon ráthaíochtaí. Ní ghlacfar ach le méid seo a leanas an eagna Taelin agus ag an ádh de Laeyra an ceann a rugadh ar an solas i réim.

Ba chóir an ceann a rugadh ar an bhfianaise a bheith rathúil i gceannas ar an fórsaí an tsolais, beidh an domhan beo go buan coibhneasta ar feadh tamaill, ach ní bheidh ach ar feadh tréimhse chun a Dhia olc a thabhairt ar a thóir suas.

Más mian leis an duine a rugadh ar an bhfianaise a Cealaigh an damáiste de bharr an anam glaoch ar an bean sidhe a gabhadh, ní mór di teacht ar an Solas de Taelin agus a chuid draíochta a úsáid chun aon uair amháin níos mó a thógáil an daingean ar an solas.

Sna blianta tar éis dheireadh an chogaidh mór anamacha ba chóir, an ceann a rugadh ar an solas i casadh ar ais ar an dorchadas ar feadh tamaill, beidh sí a leathnú trí solas huaire. Ach leis an tríú, beidh sí a hionad i measc na spioraid na roghnaithe de Taelin.

Mar sin deireadh leis an bhfocal an tuar deiridh Bahala, an fíodóir de greams. Leis an gifting an tuar, cas mé an maintlín de chumhacht an fíodóir an aisling thar a fíodóir nua agus i bhfad níos óige an aisling. Creid na focail seo, beidh ar gach a bhfuil scríofa anseo teacht chun pas a fháil.

Is féidir na focail seo lá amháin a mbealach chun an ceann a rugadh ar an solas. Beidh an té a chosnaíonn a bheith in ann aistriú na focail seo a son, cé go mbeidh a fhios ag an bhrí nach taobh thiar de na focail nuair a fhaigheann siad iad.

Scríofa ag mo lámh,
Bahala Maranal, an fíodóir an aisling
Tríocha seacht mbliana anuas an bás mór de na máistrí na lanna.

The prophecy of the Great War of Souls

After three hundred years of peace in the world comes the Age of Darkness. The Dark God will return to begin his conquest of the world once more.

In the early days of the Age of Darkness, after the Blademasters have returned to the world of Calthea, the army of the dead shall arise in service to the Dark God. The dead shall rise and wage war across the face of Calthea.

When the twice dead city falls empty for a third time, the storm clouds will gather and the sabres will rattle in their scabbards. The blight of war shall be upon the land and only the one born of the light can lead the charge against the darkness.

The army of the light must uncork the magic of the bean sidhe to turn back the darkness. The one born of the light must lead the legacy of the Blademasters onto the field of battle.

When the soul of the captured bean sidhe wails, the stones of the stronghold of the light will shatter and crumble upon one another. The spirits of the chosen of Taelin will once more take the field of battle in the war against the darkness.

The fire of the sun and the moon will dim and fade to darkness. The one born of the light must walk out from the shadow of the fire of the sun and the moon and lead the chosen of Taelin.

The Twenty Third Law of the Blades will be violated for some of the chosen of Taelin.

If the one born of the light does not lead the charge against the army of the dead, the world will fall into a darkness that will be without end. Only the power of the First Law of the Blades can guide the hand of the one born of the light.

In this battle as in all others the one born of the light will fight, there will be no guarantees. Only by following the wisdom of Taelin and by the luck of Laeyra will the one born of the light prevail.

Should the one born of the light be successful in leading the forces of the light, the world will live in relative peace for a time, but only for a time for the Dark God shall never give up his quest.

If the one born of the light wishes to undo the damage caused by the wailing soul of the captured bean sidhe, she must find the Light of Taelin and use its magic to once more build the stronghold of the light.

In the years after the end of the great war of souls, should the one born of the light in turning back the darkness for a time, she will extend the light three times. But with the third, she will take her place among the spirits of the chosen of Taelin.

So ends the words of the final prophecy of Bahala, the Dream Weaver. With the gifting of this prophecy, I turn the mantle of power of the Dream Weaver over to a new and much younger Dream Weaver. Heed these words, for all that is written here shall come to pass.

May these words one day find their way to the one born of the light. The one who protects her will be able to translate these words for her, although neither will know the meaning behind the words when they find them.

Written by my hand,
Bahala Maranal, the Dream Weaver
Thirty seven years past the Great Purge.

The Elvish Language

(Author's Note: When I first decided that the Forestwalker Elves were going to have their own language and that it would be represented in the book, I thought I was going to make a language up. Then, I realized just how difficult that really is. I wasn't going to create a language for the Forestwalker Elves, but I still wanted to have a distinct language for them. Last year I hit on the perfect solution to my problem, and I put it into action.

The language for the Forestwalker Elves is the Irish language. I am currently learning the language. Those of you folks who speak Irish fluently (And I know there are, sadly, not that many of you) will most likely see that the translations are not very accurate. That's OK. They don't have to be. They just have to be good enough. And that's what I have.

Less than two million people worldwide speak the Irish language. I do not want the language to die as it is a truly beautiful language, which is why I'm learning it. My hope is that maybe some of my readers will see that this language is a beautiful language that needs to be saved. When I have children, I hope to pass the language down to them. But, for now, all I can do to save the Irish language is to use it. As the series goes on, I am sure this Elvish Language dictionary will grow. –Rick Bentsen)

An máistir na lanna – Blademaster

An té a chosnaíonn a – Protector

Bhuel le chéile – Well met

Cibé rud a tharlaíonn, deartháir, tá a fhios go bhfuil mé go raibh aon pháirt ann. – Whatever happens, brother, know that I have had no part in it.

Féadfaidh an ádh ar Laeyra agus an eagna Taelin leanann tú – May the luck of Laeyra and the wisdom of Taelin go with you.

feithidí – A type of insect that releases silk that is woven into clothing by the Forestwalker Elves.

I ngach den saol, ní mór go mbeadh cothromaíocht. A chailleadh go bhfuil cothromaíocht a cuireadh chaos agus bás isteach Ní mór máistir na lanna a bheith i gcónaí ar comhardú i di féin agus ina cuid déileálacha le daoine eile. Sin é an fáth go bhfuil an dlí chéad cheann de na lanna chomh tábhachtach sin. Ní mór an grá roinneann sí lena fear céile bás caithfidh sí a chothromú déileáil ina seasamh – In all of life, there must be balance. To lose that balance is to invite chaos and death in. A Blademaster must always be in balance in herself and in her dealings with others. That is why the First Law of the Blades is so important. The love she shares with her husband must balance the death she must deal in her position.

Impigh mé de tú maithiúnas a thabhairt dom, mo dheartháir. Tá a fhios agat an grá agus meas agam duit féin agus do na mná grá agat. Ba mhaith liom rudaí a bhí difriúil ná ní mór cad a tharlóidh. Tá tú i gceannas ar feadh trialach nach raibh ach is féidir leat duine. Ní mór duit i réim. Gach ár saol ag brath air. Is é an meáchan ar an domhan ar do ghualainn. Tá eagla orm go bhféadfadh sé a bheith i bhfad ró-a iompróidh. Cuimhneamh nach bhfuil rudaí i gcónaí mar atá siad. – I beg you to forgive me, my brother. You know I love and respect for you and the woman you love. I wish things were different than what must happen. You are headed for a trial that only you can face. You must prevail. All our lives depend on it. The weight of the world on your shoulders. I'm afraid it might be too much to bear. Remember that things are not always as they appear.

Is breá liom tú go mór – I love you very much

Is cuma cad a tharlaíonn sa lá atá inniu, tá a fhios go mbeidh tú féin agus an Alana Lady a bheith i gcónaí fáilte roimh chách sa chathair sna crainn, le haghaidh an banríon gheall an dílseacht na clan go siúlóidí i measc na foraoisí ar an máistir na lanna agus an ceann a chosnaíonn di. – No matter what happens today, know that you and the Lady Alana always be welcome in the city in the trees, for the queen has pledged the loyalty of the Forestwalker Clan to the Blademaster and her companions.

Is é sin é! Is é sin an réiteach! – I've got it! I figured it out!

mo dheartháir – my brother

Mo dheartháir, le do thoil logh dom. Bhí mé ina páirtí do pian. Rinne mé rabhadh duit, ach tú a bheith gortaithe ar aon nós. Impigh mé de tú maithiúnas a thabhairt do mo mhuintir an pian go bhfuil muid ba chúis agat. Más rud é go mbeadh sé éasca do pian, a chur ar mo shaol mar íocaíocht as an méid atá déanta againn a thabhairt duit. – My brother, please forgive me for my part in the pain you have suffered. Although I did warn you, you have been hurt anyway. I beg you to forgive my family for the pain we have caused you. If it would ease your suffering, I offer my life as payment for what we have done to you.

Willowdale

Mo ghrá, Tá brón orm má ba chúis agam ort pian –
My love, I'm sorry for the pain that I have caused you.

Múinteoir – A term of respect for a teacher of rangers in the
Forestwalker Elves.

nathair an aeir a chosnaíonn – The dragon assigned to
protect a Blademaster

**Ní mór di a rachaidh isteach anseo chun aghaidh a
thabhairt ar ndán di dul isteach le croí glan. Ní mór sí
ag troid i gcomhréir leis an idéalacha Taelin agus
Laeyra. Ní mór di cloí le Dlí na lanna má ghlacann sí
ndán di. Teip ciallaíonn bás.** – She who enters here to face
her destiny must enter with a pure heart. She must fight
according to the precepts of Taelin and Laeyra. She must
abide by the Law of the Blades if she accepts her destiny.
Failure brings death.

stát ndoimhneacht na tsíocháin inmheánach -- A
technique used by elven rangers that allows them to be in a
deep state of inner peace

**Sí nach bhfuil grá nach bhfuil a fhios Taelin chun é
Taelin ghrá.** – She who does not love does not know Taelin
for Taelin is love.

**Turas go maith duit, an ceann a chosnaíonn sí an
máistir na lanna. Go dtí go mbeidh níos mó ná uair
ár cosáin trasna.** – Good journey to you, Protector to
the Blademaster. Until next our paths shall cross.

The Laws of the Blades

The First Law of the Blades:

You are commanded to love. Love your friends. Love your enemies. Love without reservation. Love without hesitation. Love without condition. Love without expectation of return. If you must fight, then fight with love in your heart. If you must kill, then kill with love in your heart. Never kill or fight with hate or anger in your heart. Hate leads to impotence, but love brings power. This is the law a Blademaster must live by more than any other or else she will be powerless to serve as she should. It is the First Law of the Blades because it is the most important. Live by it, or you will die.

The Second Law of the Blades:

True love breeds true forgiveness. Nothing is more powerful than the ability to forgive the one you love. And nothing brings you closer than the forgiveness of your own misdeeds.

The Fourteenth Law of the Blades:

There are many things in life that are but mere illusions. Things are not always as they appear. A Blademaster must depend on the wisdom of Taelin to understand what is real and what is an illusion. Confusion brought on by false realities can lead to a gruesome death. Always remember to let Lord Taelin be your guide in everything you do. Remembering this will cause you to see through any illusion that is in your path.

Willowdale

The Fifteenth Law of the Blades:

In life as in battle, there are no guarantees. Victory and defeat teeter on the edge of a thin blade. It is belief in one's self that can make the difference between victory and defeat. A Blademaster must always believe in herself and be willing to seek the help of others in order to claim victory. This is the truth of life and battle. Live or die as you choose.

The Eighteenth Law of the Blades:

In all of life, there must be balance. To lose that balance is to invite chaos and death in. A Blademaster must always be in balance in herself and in her dealings with others. That is why the First Law of the Blades is so important. The love she shares with her husband must balance the death she must deal in her position.

The Twenty Third Law of the Blades:

The war never ends. Only the battles change.

Blademasters and Protectors

Over the years of recorded history on Calthea, many women have held the title of Blademaster. Obviously, not all Blademasters have been mentioned in this series, but as Blademasters and their Protectors are mentioned, they will be listed here.

Blademasters of Old:

Raven Windrider and Richard Kale (The first Blademaster and her Protector)
Alyssa Nesbitt and Michael Westlund
Maria Davalos and Tarvan Draderis
Crystal Sapphire and Markus Sharde

Blademasters of Now

Alana Steeldrake and Colwyn Starseeker

Willowdale

The adventures of Alana Steeldrake and her companions
will continue in

The Age of Darkness

Coming April, 2016

War is coming to Calthea.

With the defeat of the Zeraphim in Willowdale, the Prophecy
of the Great War of Souls has been invoked. In Tornith, the
army of undead has begun to form. Their goal is to assault
and conquer the Southern Dales.

Alana Steeldrake and her companions must prepare to lead
the charge against the darkness coming to the Southern
Dales. But they cannot lead the charge on their own.

The search for help takes them closer to home than any of
them realized it would and sets up an epic confrontation for
Colwyn Starseeker....

With his father...

TURN THE PAGE
For a preview of **The Age of Darkness,**
the third exciting book in
The Blademaster Chronicles

pROLOɔue
The ɔReam ɯeaveR

he old man had once been called by another name.

It had been many years, though, since anyone had called him by name. He was known only as the Dream Weaver. Even though no one ever called him by his name, he still remembered it. He doubted anyone else did though.

He was called only by his title.

The Dream Weaver.

No one truly understood what it meant to be a Dream Weaver. Not even the Mages of the Inner Circle knew exactly what it meant to hold that sacred and ancient position. There was only ever one Dream Weaver at a time. Currently, Roald Vilas held the title of Dream Weaver. He knew, though, that his time as the Dream Weaver was coming to an end.

He had seen it in his most recent weaving.

It had been something that he had known would be coming for a while. That did not make it any easier to see.

But he was close to three hundred years old, and he knew that he was finally nearing the end of his life. He knew that it was time to pass on the mantle to the next Dream Weaver as Bahala Maranal had, once upon a time, placed the mantle firmly around Roald's neck.

While it was not easy to see that the end was coming, it did come as something of a relief. He was tired. He was especially tired of people coming to him for prophecy. People did not understand that his form of prophecy was limited. He could only see what the future held while he was dreaming. That was the core of a Dream Weaver. But people simply assumed that he could do some form of magic in order to tell them their future.

No matter how many times he told them that it was not the case, they still believed what they wanted to believe.

He looked forward to no longer having to deal with all the little problems people brought him on a regular basis. Soon, he would be off on his last journey before his walk with the gods of magic. He was content in the knowledge that he had earned his walk. He knew that this last journey would finally bring him full circle and the mantle would be passed to another, younger man.

But he had one last task left to do before he passed on the mantle.

The dream he had woken up from this morning had left him disturbed. It was true that he did not always understand the dreams he wove as part of his duties as the Dream Weaver. This one was clearer than almost all of the other dreams he'd woven in his close to three hundred years.

And it terrified him.

In his dream, he had seen the army of Thraal stretched out before him. Whole companies of undead, grouped into different types, slowly gathered together in the land surrounding the city of Tornith. He saw wraiths and spectres, zombies and skeletons and even a few ghouls.

But by far the scariest was the vampire lord in command of the army. The most disconcerting part was that Roald had felt that the vampire lord was staring right at him in his dreams. The vampire lord's eyes had been a deep dark red. Roald knew that he would see those eyes every night that he went to sleep for the rest of his life.

There had been, as there always was, words to go with the weaving. As soon as he woke, he had written those words down with a shaking hand. He tried hard not to focus on what he was writing for fear of seeing those terrible eyes once more.

When he finished writing down the prophecy, he began to pack. For the first time in many years, Torval, the god of magic that Roald served, came to him after a weaving. The god had told him that he needed to share this weaving with the Blademaster, Alana Steeldrake. The god had also said that during this final journey as the Dream Weaver, he would meet the man who would replace him.

Roald remembered the Blademaster. He had sent her off on her journey to Ravendale long before she had known who and what she was. He had known though. And he had given her what aid he could.

And now he would aid the Blademaster one last time.

It did not take him long to pack for his journey. He did not need much, just some clothes and his bedroll. It was not so long a journey to Ravendale and he would travel by the main roads. He would stay at inns when he could at night, but it would take over a week to arrive in the capitol city of the Southern Dales. It did not matter. He knew the Blademaster would be there when he arrived, no matter how long it took.

He simply hoped he arrived in time to help her before the owner of those terrible red eyes arrived to start the war that was coming.

Preview of The Age of Darkness

About the Author

Rick Bentsen released his first novel in 2001. It was a simple science fiction story that was somewhat well received. Although it never sold very well, the people that read his first novel enjoyed it immensely. From that first moment, Rick was hooked.

Rick has long loved science fiction and fantasy books and movies and that love has turned into a writing passion. He has recently added a mystery/thriller series to his normal science fiction and fantasy series as projects to complete.

Rick lives in southeastern Massachusetts which he believes is the most beautiful place in the world. Fall in New England, he finds to be the most inspirational time of the year with all the colors.

Rick can be reached through his facebook page (www.facebook.com/RickBentsenAuthor) or through his webpage at rickbentsen.com

www.ingramcontent.com/pod-product-compliance
Lightning Source LLC
Chambersburg PA
CBHW031058030726
47496CB00002BA/279